THE

EVERYTHING®

FAIRY TALES
BOOK

A magical collection
of all-time favorites
to delight the whole family

Amy Peters

Adams Media Corporation
Avon, Massachusetts

For Peter and Chet, for listening to so many
fairy tales. For Max, for not only listening
but also for helping to shape this book.
And to my parents, for so much.

An Everything® Series Book.
Everything® and everything.com® are registered trademarks of F+W Publications, Inc.

Published by Adams Media, an F+W Publications Company
57 Littlefield Street, Avon MA 02322 U.S.A.
www.adamsmedia.com

ISBN: 1-58062-546-0
Printed in the United States of America.

J I H G F E D C B

Library of Congress Cataloging-in-Publication Data
Peters, Amy.
The everything fairy tales book / Amy Peters.
p.   cm.
Summary: A collection of 100 classic fairy tales.
ISBN 1-58062-546-0
1. Fairy tales. [1. Fairy tales. 2. Folklore.] I. Title.
PZ8.P4427 Ev 2001
398.2--dc21   2001041275

This publication is designed to provide accurate and authoritative information with regard to the subject matter covered. It is sold with the understanding that the publisher is not engaged in rendering legal,
accounting, or other professional advice. If legal advice or other expert assistance is required, the services of a competent professional person should be sought.
—From a *Declaration of Principles* jointly adopted by a Committee of the
American Bar Association and a Committee of Publishers and Associations

Majority of interior illustrations by Barry Littmann. Contributions for other interior art
by Susan Gaber, Kathie Kelleher and Michelle Dorenkamp.
This book is available at quantity discounts for bulk purchases.
For information, call 1-800-872-5627.

Visit the entire Everything® series at everything.com

Introduction

Suspend disbelief as you enter the fairy tale's fantastical world. This is a land where truculent trolls, wily wizards, warted witches, and perfectly splendid princesses reign. It's a region where fortune arrives in unpredictable ways and evil is gratifyingly defeated.

Amazing things are the routine in this exotic locale: A slimy frog becomes a handsome prince, a beautiful maiden soars on the back of the North Wind, an itinerant group of animals decides to form a band, and a rebellious pancake runs away from home. Darning needles and kettles come spontaneously to life, and a man the size of a thumb is swallowed by a fish and lives to tell about it.

This is a world where animals are sometimes craftier than their human masters. With amazing ease, Puss in Boots successfully plots to transform his impoverished master into lord of the land and husband to a princess!

A lesson or two is also learned along the fairy tales' meandering path. "The Ugly Duckling" offers a gentle reminder to avoid teasing. Knowing your own mind and being true to your ideals is a theme of "What Other People Think." A naughty boy in "Mr. Miacca" is very nearly eaten by a fearsome giant, convincing the lad to end his mischievous ways. An enchanted fish teaches the dangers of excessive greed in "The Fisherman and His Wife." In "The Flying Trunk," when a treasure-filled suitcase comes crashing down, a young boy finds his fate unhappily sealed.

Enter this land with an open mind. Think of the enchantment-working piper who tells Tattercoats to take good fortune when it comes. Or, consider Dick Whittington, pauper and optimist, whose good faith brings about even greater good fortune than the golden streets of which he so often dreamed.

* *Note to readers:* Throughout the book you will find words in **bold** type. These words have definitions in the glossary at the end of the book.

Table of Contents

The Everything® Fairy Tales Book

Beauty and the Beast

In "Beauty and the Beast," a nasty witch casts a spell on a handsome prince and turns him into the wretched Beast. This is a form of enchantment; magic is used to transform something into something else. Enchantment is a common theme in fairy tales. Sometimes handsome princes are turned into warty frogs, beautiful maidens are made ugly, or people or animals are transformed into objects.

Can you think of any fairy tales in which a form of enchantment occurs? How is the enchantment broken?

Once upon a time there was a merchant who had three daughters. They lived in a nice house and had many servants. The two eldest daughters were named Marigold and Dressalinda. They weren't particularly nice and they loved to spend money. But Beauty, the youngest, preferred to stay at home with her old father.

One day, great misfortune befell the merchant, who had made his money in shipping. He found that he was no longer the richest man in the city. Now he was a very poor man. He was left with only a little house in the country where he went to live with his three daughters.

Marigold and Dressalinda were very angry at becoming so poor, but Beauty's only thought was to cheer on and encourage her old father. The two eldest sisters did nothing but sulk and complain, while Beauty swept the floors and washed the dishes. In this way a whole year passed. Then one day a letter came for the father. He relayed the good news to them. "My dear children," he said, "at last our luck has turned. This letter says that one of the ships supposedly lost at sea has come safely home to port. If that is so, we need no longer live in poverty. I will go claim my ship. And now tell me, girls, what shall I bring you when I come back?"

"A bag of gold and silver," said Marigold, filled with greed.

"I want fancy new clothes," said Dressalinda.

"And what shall I bring for you, Beauty?" asked the father.

"Oh, I don't know. I think I would like a rose," said Beauty.

The merchant looked at his daughter. "But Beauty, you can have anything. Are you sure that's all you want?"

"Well, we don't have any roses around here, and I do miss the gardens of our old place."

Full of hope, the merchant went to the city. But when he got there, he found that he'd been tricked. No ship of his had come into harbor. With a sad heart, he began the journey home again. He was tired and miserable. He was almost home when he saw a light in the forest. He decided to make his way toward the light. He expected to find a cottage, but as he drew near the light he saw a beautiful castle! He knocked at the gates, but no one answered. So he went in on his own.

There was a big fire in the hall, and when the merchant had warmed up, he looked to see if anyone was home. Behind the first door he opened was a snug room with supper set for one. By this time, he was so hungry that he sat and ate a giant meal.

Once again the merchant started to look for the people who lived in the castle. He opened another door, but there he saw only a bed. He was so tired that he tumbled into the bed and went right to sleep.

When he woke up in the morning, the old man had something else to be happy about. By the bed were clothes with his name stitched on the pockets. He put them on and went down to the garden. It was full of lush roses: red and

white and pink and yellow. As the merchant looked at them, he remembered Beauty's wish.

So he picked the biggest, brightest red rose within his reach.

As the stalk snapped in his fingers, he started back in terror, for he had heard an angry roar. The next minute a dreadful beast sprang upon him. It was taller than any man and uglier than any animal, but, most dreadful of all, it spoke to him with a man's voice. "Ungrateful wretch!" said the beast. "Have I not fed you, lodged you, and clothed you? And you repay my hospitality by stealing the only thing I care for, my roses!"

"Please forgive me!" cried the man.

"No," said the beast, "you must die!" The poor merchant fell upon his knees and tried to think of something to say to soften the heart of the cruel beast. At last he said, "Sir, I only took this rose because when I offered my youngest daughter anything in the world, she wished for a rose."

"Tell me about your daughter," said the beast.

"She is the dearest and kindest child in the world," said the old merchant. "Oh, what will my children do without me?"

"You should have thought of that before you stole the rose," said the beast. "However, if one of your daughters loves you well enough to suffer instead of you, she may. Go back and tell them what has happened to you. But in three months' time, either you or one of your daughters must return, or I will come for all of you."

Believing the beast must have magical powers, the merchant agreed. He thought that this would at least allow him three more months with his daughters.

Then the beast said, "You will not go empty-handed."

So the merchant followed him back into the palace. There, on the floor of the hall, lay a great and beautiful chest of wrought silver.

With a heavy heart, the merchant went away. But as he went through the palace gate, the beast called to him that he had forgotten Beauty's rose.

When the merchant arrived home, Beauty ran to meet him at the door of their cottage. He placed the rose in her hand.

"Take it, my child," he said, "and cherish it, for it has cost your poor father his life." And with that he sat down and told his daughters the whole story.

"No," said Beauty, "it is my life that shall be sacrificed. When the three months are over, I shall go to the beast. He may kill me if he will, but he will never hurt my father."

At the end of the three months, Beauty set out for the beast's palace. Her father went with her, to show her the way. As before, he saw the lights shining through the wood. He knocked and rang in vain at the great gate. Again the door was open, so he led Beauty in and they warmed themselves at the fire in the big hall. Once more he found the little room with the supper that made them hungry just to look at it. Only this time the table was laid for two. The next moment the beast came into the room. Beauty screamed and clung to her father.

"Don't be frightened," said the beast gently. "Tell me, do you come here of your own free will?"

"Yes," said Beauty, trembling.

Quivering, the merchant spoke up, "I . . . I can't let this happen. If anyone is to be punished, it should be me."

The beast did not even look at the merchant. "Go now," he said, "I will give your daughter time to change her mind. If she does so, you will be sent for."

Left alone when her father returned home to her sisters, Beauty tried not to feel frightened. She ran here and there through the palace, and found it more beautiful than anything she had ever imagined.

The most beautiful set of rooms had the words "Beauty's Rooms" written over the doors. Inside, Beauty found books and music, canary-birds and Persian cats, and everything that could be thought of to make the time pass pleasantly.

That night, when Beauty sat down to supper, the beast came in.

"May I have supp⟨...⟩" said he.

"If you like," said ⟨...⟩

So the beast sat d⟨...⟩d, he said: "I am very ugly, Beauty. ⟨...⟩ I love you. Will you marry me?"

"No, Beast," said ⟨...⟩nt away. Every night the same thing ⟨...⟩ then asked her if she would marry h⟨...⟩

One day, she sav⟨...⟩. That night she said to the beast, "⟨...⟩ou let me go home to see my fat⟨...⟩d. Do let me go and cheer him up, ⟨...⟩

"Very well," said the beast kindly, "but don't stay away ⟨...⟩ore than a week. If you do, I shall die of grief, because I love you so dearly. Put on this ruby ring and you will be transported to your father's house."

So in the morning, when she awoke, Beauty found herself at her father's house. The old man was beside himself with joy to see her. But her sisters did

(handwritten) "Go now," he said, "I will be sent for "your daughter" them to change her mind.

not welcome her, and when they heard how kind the beast was to her, they envied her for living in a beautiful palace.

"I wish we had gone," said Marigold. "Beauty always gets the best of everything."

"Tell us all about your grand palace," said Dressalinda.

Thinking it would amuse them to hear, Beauty told them everything, and their envy increased day by day.

At last Dressalinda said to Marigold, "She has promised to return in a week. If we could only make her forget the day, the beast might be angry and kill her. Then there would be a chance for us."

So on the day before Beauty ought to have gone back, her sisters put some poppy juice in a cup of wine, which they gave her. This made her so sleepy that she slept for two whole days and nights. At the end of that time her sleep grew troubled. She dreamed that she saw the beast lying dead among his roses. She woke up so frightened that she immediately put on the ruby ring and found herself back at the beast's palace. She looked for the beast but could not find him.

Then she ran through the gardens, calling his name again and again. Still there was silence.

Then she remembered her dream and ran to the rose garden. There lay the poor beast without any sign of life in him.

Beauty flung herself on her knees beside him. "Oh, dear Beast," she cried, "are you really dead? Then I, too, will die, for I cannot live without you."

Immediately the beast opened his eyes, sighed, and said, "Beauty, will you marry me?"

And Beauty, beside herself with joy when she found that he was still alive, answered, "Yes, yes, dear Beast, for I love you dearly."

At these words the rough fur dropped to the ground, and in place of the beast, there stood a handsome Prince, dressed as if for a wedding. He knelt at Beauty's feet and clasped her hands.

"Dear Beauty," he said, "nothing but your love could have disenchanted me. A witch turned me into a beast and condemned me to remain one until some fair and good maiden should love me well enough to marry me, in spite of my ugliness. Now, dear one, the enchantment is broken. Let us go back to my palace." There, the Prince whispered to one of his attendants, who went out and in a very little time came back with Beauty's father and sisters.

The sisters were cursed and changed into statues. They were set out to stand at the right and left of the palace gates until their hearts softened and they felt sorry for their unkindness to their sister. But Beauty, happily married to her Prince, went secretly to the statues every day and wept over them.

Her tears softened their stony hearts. The sisters were changed into flesh and blood again, and were good and kind for the rest of their lives.

The merchant remained ill for a long time. But the good care he received in the palace, as well as the joy of having all his daughters well and happy again, allowed him to recover and regain prosperity.

And Beauty and the Beast, who was no longer a beast but a handsome Prince, lived happily ever after in a beautiful land where dreams come true.

The End

Bluebeard

Once upon a time, there lived a very powerful and rich man, the owner of estates, farms, and a magnificent castle. He was called Bluebeard. It was a nickname given to him because he had a long black beard that glimmered blue. He was very handsome and considered throughout the land to be quite charming, but he also made people feel a bit nervous.

Bluebeard often went away to wage war; when he did, he left his wife in charge of the castle.

He had had many wives, all young, pretty, and of royal blood. As bad luck would have it, though, they all died, one after the other. So Bluebeard found himself in the position of getting married again and again.

"Sire," someone would ask now and again, "what did your wives die of?"

"Oh, my friend," Bluebeard would answer, "one died of smallpox, one of a hidden sickness, another of a high fever, and still another of a terrible infection. It's been most unfortunate. They're all buried in the castle chapel."

Nobody found anything strange about that. Nor did the sweet and beautiful young girl whom Bluebeard took next as a wife. She went to the castle with her sister Anna, who said, "Aren't you lucky marrying a lord like Bluebeard?"

"He really is very nice, and when you're up quite close, his beard doesn't look as blue as they say!" said the bride, and the two sisters giggled.

A month later, Bluebeard had the carriage brought to the front of his castle. He said to his wife, "Darling, I must leave you for a few weeks. But keep cheerful during that time. Invite whomever you like and look after the castle. Here," he added, handing his bride a bunch of keys, "you'll need these—the keys to the safe, the armory, and the library. Oh, and this one, which opens all the room doors. Now, this little key here"—he pointed to a key that was much smaller than the others—"opens the little room at the end of the great ground floor corridor. You may go wherever you want, open any door you like, but not this one! Is that quite clear?" repeated Bluebeard. "Nobody at all is allowed to enter that little room.

"Don't worry," said Bluebeard's wife as she took the keys, "I'll do as you say."

After a big hug, Bluebeard got into his carriage and went on his way.

The days passed. The young girl invited her friends to the castle and showed them all the rooms except the one at the end of the corridor. "Why shouldn't I see inside the little room? Why? Why is it forbidden?" she asked herself. Well, she thought about it so much that she was bursting with curiosity. One day she just had to open the door and walk into the little room.

There, she found something too horrible to imagine. It was a list of Bluebeard's wives and the poisons he had used to kill them all! Terror-stricken, the girl ran out of the room, but the bunch of keys slipped from her grasp. She picked them up without a glance and hurried to her room, her heart th_____ _____ _____ her chest.

So that is what h__ _____ _____ wives!

Th_____ _____ is when she no_____ _____ the little room—

"I mu_____ _____ back!" she said to _____ _____

wouldn't wa_____ _____ e

rinsed—all w_____

That very e_____

wife—as you ca_____ t ask

his wife for the keys, but he said, "You look a little upset, darling. Has anything nasty happened?"

"Oh, no! No!"

"Are you sorry I came back so soon?"

"Oh, no! I'm delighted!" But that night, the bride didn't sleep a wink.

The next day, Bluebeard said, "Darling, give me back the keys," and his wife hurriedly did so. Bluebeard remarked, "There's one missing, the key to the little room!"

"Is there?" said the young girl shaking. "I must have left it in my room!"

"All right, go and get it." As she put the key in his hand, Bluebeard turned white and, in a deep hoarse voice, demanded, "Why is this key stained with ink?"

"I don't know," stammered his wife.

"You know very well!" he retorted. "You went into the little room, didn't you? Now you must die!"

"Oh no! I pray you!"

"You must die!" he repeated. Just then, there was a knock at the door, and Anna, the wife's sister, entered the castle.

"Good morning," she said, "you seem rather pale."

"Not at all, we're quite well," replied Bluebeard.

His wife whispered in his ear, "Please, please give me ten minutes to live!"

Bluebeard replied, "Not more than ten!"

The girl ran to her sister Anna, who had gone up to one of the towers and asked her, "Anna, do you see our brothers coming? They promised they would come and see me today!"

But Anna replied, "No, I don't see anyone. What's wrong? You look upset."

"Anna, please," said the shaken girl, "look again! Are you sure you can't see someone?"

"No," said her sister, "only one or two peasants."

Just then the voice of Bluebeard boomed up to them. "Wife, your time is up! Come here!"

"I'm coming!" she called, but then said to her sister, "Oh Anna, aren't our brothers coming?"

"No," replied Anna.

Again Bluebeard shouted, "Come down at once! Or I'll come up!"

Trembling like a leaf, his wife went downstairs. Bluebeard was clutching a glass filled with a bubbling potion.

"Sister, I can see two horsemen coming!" called out Anna from the tower at that very moment. Bluebeard made a horrible face. "Then they too will die!"

His wife begged, "Please, please don't kill me. I'll never tell anyone what I saw! I'll never say a word!"

"Yes, you'll never say a word for eternity!" snarled Bluebeard, raising the glass of poison to her lips.

The poor girl screamed, "Have pity on me!"

But he fiercely replied, "No! You must die!" Just as he was about to force her to drink the poison, two young men burst into the room: a **dragoon** and a **musketeer**, the wife's brothers. Drawing their swords, they leaped toward Bluebeard. He tried to flee up the stairs but was caught and killed. And that was the end of the sad story. The young widow, some time later, married a good and honest young man, who helped her to forget her terrible adventure.

The End

Cap o' Rushes

O nce upon a time there was a very rich gentleman who had three daughters. One day, he thought he'd find out how much they loved him. So he said to the first, "How much do you love me, my dear?"

"Why," she said, "as much as I love life itself."

"That's good," he said.

Then he said to the second, "How much do you love me, my dear?"

"Why," she said, "better than all of the world."

Finally, he said to the third, "How much do you love me, my dear?"

"Why, I love you as fresh meat loves salt," she said.

This answer infuriated him.

"You don't love me at all," he said, "you can't live in this house anymore."

So she went away a great distance until she came to a **fen**. There she gathered some **rushes** and made them into a cloak with a hood to cover her from head to foot and to hide her fancy clothes. Then she continued on until she came to a grand house.

"Do you want a maid?" she asked.

"No," the servants answered.

"I don't have anywhere to go," she said, "and I don't need any money. I'll do any sort of work."

"Okay," they said, "You can wash all of the dishes." So she stayed and washed the pots and scraped the saucepans and did all of the dirty work. Because she gave no name, they called her Cap o' Rushes.

One day there was to be a great dance nearby, and the servants went. They invited her too, but Cap o' Rushes said she was too tired to go.

But when everyone else had gone, she took off her cloak, cleaned herself up, and went to the dance. And no one was as beautifully dressed as she.

Well, who should be at the dance but her master's son. He fell in love with her the minute he set eyes on her. He wouldn't dance with anyone else.

But before the dance was done, Cap o' Rushes crept off home and put her cloak back on. When the other maids came back, she pretended to be asleep.

The next morning they said to her, "You missed something grand!"

"What was that?" she asked.

"The most beautiful lady you'll ever see, dressed in the fanciest clothes. The young master, he never took his eyes off her."

"Well, I should have liked to have seen her," said Cap o' Rushes.

"There's to be another dance this evening, and perhaps she'll be there."

But Cap o' Rushes said she was too tired to go with them to the dance. Once they had gone, though, she took off he cloak once again and cleaned herself, and away she went to the dance.

The master's son had been hoping to see her. He danced with no one else and never took his eyes off her. But, before the dance was over, she crept away. When the maids came back, she pretended to be asleep.

The next day they said to her again, "Well, Cap o' Rushes, you should have been there to see the lady. The young master never took his eyes off her."

"Well," she said, "I should liked to have seen her."

They said, "There's a dance again this evening. You must go with us, for she's sure to be there."

That evening, Cap o' Rushes said she was too tired to go. But when they had gone, she took off her cloak, cleaned herself, and away she went to the dance.

The master's son was so happy when he saw her. When she wouldn't tell him her name, or where she came from, he gave her a ring and told her if he didn't see her again he would die.

Before the dance was over, she slipped off. When the maids came home, she pretended to be asleep with her cap o' rushes on.

The next day they said to her, "There, Cap o' Rushes, you didn't come last night, and now you won't see the lady, for there's no more dances."

"That's too bad," she said.

The master's son tried every way to find out where the lady had gone, but he had no luck. Finally, he took ill to his bed because he was so lovesick.

"Make some porridge for the young master," the maids said to the cook. "He's dying for the love of the lady."

The cook had started making the porridge when Cap o' Rushes came in.

"What are you doing?" she asked.

"I'm going to make some porridge for the young master," said the cook, "for he's dying for love of the lady."

"Let me make it," said Cap o' Rushes.

The cook wouldn't agree at first, but at last she said yes. And Cap o' Rushes made the porridge. When it had finished cooking, she slipped the ring into it before the cook took it upstairs.

The young man ate the porridge and then saw the ring at the bottom of the bowl.

"Who made this porridge?" he asked the cook.

"I did," said the cook, lying because she was frightened.

"No, you didn't," he said. "Tell me who made it!"

"Well, then, it was Cap o' Rushes," the cook said.

"Send her here," he said.

When Cap o' Rushes came, he asked, "Did you make my porridge?"

"Yes, I did," she said.

"Where did you get this ring?" he asked.

"From the person who gave it to me," she said. And she took off her cap o' rushes, and there she was in her beautiful clothes.

Well, the master's son quickly got well, and they were to be married right away. It was to be a very grand wedding. Cap o' Rushes's father was asked. But she had never told anybody who she was.

Before the wedding, she went to the cook, and said, "I want you to dress every dish without a bit of salt."

"That'll be rather nasty," said the cook.

"That doesn't matter," she replied.

The wedding day came and they were married. After the ceremony, all of the guests sat down to eat. When they tried the meat, it was so tasteless they couldn't eat it. Cap o' Rushes's father tried first one dish, then another, and then burst out crying.

"What is the matter?" asked the master's son.

"I had a daughter and when I asked her how much she loved me, she said, 'As much as fresh meat loves salt.' I kicked her out of the house, for I thought she didn't love me. Now I see she loved me best of all. She may be dead for all I know."

"No, Father, here she is!" said Cap o' Rushes. And she went up to him, put her arms around him, and gave him a giant bear hug.

And they were all happy forever after.

⬱ The End ⬱

Cinderella

Once upon a time, there was a beautiful girl named Cinderella, who lived with her two stepsisters and stepmother. The stepmother didn't like Cinderella and frequently nagged and scolded her. She made Cinderella do all of the housework.

She had to do all the laundry, all the dishes, and all the cleaning and scrubbing and mending and washing. Despite all this hard work, and the ragged dress she was forced to wear, Cinderella remained kind and optimistic.

One day, it was announced that the king had decided to give a ball in honor of his son, the prince. Invitations were sent out to all the young, unmarried girls in the kingdom. Cinderella and her two stepsisters were invited.

Immediately, the stepmother began purchasing fancy gowns for her daughters, hoping the prince would fall in love with one of them.

Cinderella, of course, was put to work altering the gowns, taking up the hems, and letting out the waists (for her stepsisters were a bit plump).

"Oh, Cinderella," teased the older stepsister, "wouldn't you like to come to the ball?"

Cinderella turned away so her stepsisters wouldn't see the tears in her eyes.

Both stepsisters looked at each other and laughed merrily at the thought of their dirty servant stepsister standing in rags at the ball.

At last the stepsisters were ready, and their carriage pulled up before the front door. Cinderella waved and watched the carriage roll down the street until it was completely out of sight. Then the poor girl burst into tears.

"Why are you crying, child?" said a voice.

Cinderella looked down and saw a tiny, sparkling woman no larger than a teacup standing on the table. "Who are you?" the teary-eyed girl asked.

"I am your Fairy Godmother," said the little woman. "Why are you so sad?"

But Cinderella was too sad to respond.

"You wish you could go to the ball?" The Fairy Godmother finally asked.

"Yes," wept Cinderella. "But I am too poor and ugly, everyone would laugh."

"Nonsense," laughed the fairy. "You are beautiful and kind and have all you need. I'll just give you a little help."

"Okay," Cinderella said.

"First, we'll need a pumpkin," said the little fairy.

Cinderella brought a pumpkin in from the garden, and the Fairy Godmother gently touched it with her wand. Instantly the pumpkin was transformed into a jeweled coach.

Next, her wand transformed mice into prancing horses to draw the carriage. Some frogs became footmen, and two rats became the coachman and the coach driver.

"Now," said the Fairy Godmother, "you have your carriage. We must see to your gown." She touched Cinderella with her wand. Instantly the ragged dress became a stunning white gown of silk, with beads and pearls and diamonds glittering everywhere. On her feet were a pair of glass slippers, the most beautiful shoes Cinderella had ever seen.

"Now, go to the ball," said the Fairy Godmother. "But be sure to leave before midnight. At the last stroke of midnight, the coach will be a pumpkin again, the horses will become mice, the coachmen rats, and the footmen will be frogs. And," she added, "your gown will turn back into rags."

When Cinderella arrived to the ball, the prince hurried to greet her. He gave her his hand and led her into the great hall.

When the two made their entrance, the crowd fell silent. So beautiful a pair was the prince and the strange girl that no one could say a word.

Then, Cinderella and the prince began to waltz.

"What a fine dancer she is," said the stepmother, not recognizing the young girl.

"Her dress is better than mine," sulked the older stepsister.

"Her shoes are nicer than mine," hissed the younger one.

"Quiet, you two," snarled the stepmother.

The hours passed like minutes. Cinderella danced and talked with the prince. Then the clock sounded the hour of twelve. Terrified that she might be discovered, she had time only to kiss the prince softly on the cheek. She rushed down the steps, hopped into her coach, and was gone.

Cinderella ran away so quickly that she didn't even realize one of her slippers had fallen off. It was picked up by the prince who had turned to follow the girl whose name he hadn't even learned.

Just as they were out of sight of the palace, the coach and horses and coachmen and footmen changed back into a pumpkin and rats and mice and frogs.

Next day, a proclamation was issued that the prince himself would be visiting every house in the town to find the owner of the missing glass slipper.

The prince tried the slipper on all the other princesses and duchesses in the court, but none of their feet could fit into it. He then began going to the houses of everyone in the kingdom.

The two stepsisters knew that he would arrive soon. They fluttered and twittered about until the stepmother shouted for them to calm down.

The doorbell rang. "Open the door for the prince."

"Welcome, Your Highness," giggled the first stepsister.

The prince frowned, but he asked the two girls to remove their shoes.

The stepsisters tried to make the shoe fit. They shoved and pried and pushed and squeezed and shoved again, but the slipper would not fit.

At last, Cinderella peeked around the corner. "May I try?" she asked meekly.

"You?" scoffed the stepmother.

"That's just the cleaning girl," said the older stepsister.

"Let her try," said the prince.

Cinderella sat down in the chair, and the prince lifted the slipper to her foot. It fit beautifully.

"Are you my Princess?" the prince asked.

"I am," Cinderella said happily.

"She can't be!" cried the stepmother.

"Impossible!" shouted the two stepsisters.

From her pocket, Cinderella pulled the other glass slipper and put it on.

The prince took Cinderella's hand and led her off to the palace, where they were married in splendor and lived happily ever after.

The stepsisters and stepmother still live together in a rather unkempt home.

⇒ The End ⇐

The Donkey

Once upon a time there lived a king and a queen who were very rich and had everything they wanted, except for one thing—they had no children. The queen wept day and night, unable to think about anything else.

One day, though, their wish was granted and they had a child. This was an unusual child, though, for it did not look like a human but like a little donkey.

When the mother saw her baby, she began to cry bitterly. She said she would far rather have had no child at all than have a donkey. She wanted to throw it into the water so the fish could eat it. But the king said, "No, God has sent him, and he shall be my son and heir. After my death, he shall sit on the royal throne and wear my crown."

So, the donkey was spared. As he grew, his ears grew high and straight. He was a cheerful sort, often jumping about and playing. He especially liked music. He went to a famous musician and said, "Teach me your art so I may play the **lute** as well as you do."

"Oh," answered the musician, "that would be very hard for you because your fingers are not quite suited to it. They are far too big. I am afraid the strings would not last."

But the donkey wouldn't take no for an answer. He was determined to play the lute. And since he was willing to work hard and practice every day, he learned to play as well as the master himself.

One day the young donkey was out walking and came to a well. He looked into it and in the mirror-clear water saw his reflection. He was so upset that he went out into the wide world, taking with him only one faithful companion.

They traveled up and down, and at last they came to a kingdom where an old king reigned. The king had an incredibly beautiful daughter.

The donkey knocked at the gate. When the gate was not opened, he sat down, took out his lute, and played it in the most delightful manner with his two front feet. The gatekeeper opened his eyes, gasped, and ran to the king, saying, "Outside by the gate sits a young donkey that plays the lute as well as an experienced master."

"Then let the musician come to me," said the king. But when the donkey came in, everyone began to laugh at the lute-player. Later the donkey was asked to sit down and eat with the servants, but he said, "I am no common stable-donkey. I am a noble one."

Then the servants said, "If that is what you are, seat yourself with the soldiers."

"No," said he, "I will sit by the king."

The king smiled and said good-humoredly, "It shall be as you like. How does my daughter please you?"

The donkey turned his head toward her and said, "I like her above measure. I have never yet seen anyone so beautiful."

"Well, then, you shall sit next to her too," said the king.

"That is exactly what I wish," said the donkey and placed himself by her side. He ate and drank and used good manners. When the donkey had stayed a long time, he thought, "What good does all this do me? I shall still have to go home again." He let his head hang sadly and went to the king and told him he was going home.

But the king had grown fond of him. He said, "Why are you sad? I will give you what you want. Do you want gold?"

"No," said the donkey.

"Do you want jewels and fancy clothes?"

"No."

"Do you wish for half my kingdom."

"No."

"Then," said the king, "would you like to marry my daughter?"

"Yes," said the donkey, "I would like that."

So a splendid wedding was held. In the evening, before the bride and bridegroom were led into their bedroom, the king ordered a servant to hide himself in the chamber and report back on how the donkey behaved toward his daughter.

When the newlyweds were finally inside their room, the bridegroom bolted the door, looked around, and—as he believed that they were quite alone—suddenly threw off his donkey's skin. He stood before his bride in the form of a handsome royal youth.

"Now," he said, "you see who I am and that I am not unworthy of you."

Then the bride was glad and kissed him, and loved him.

In the morning, he put on his donkey's skin again. Soon he saw the old king.

"Oh," cried the king, "so the little donkey is already up. But surely you are sad," he said to his daughter, "that you don't have a proper man for your husband."

"Oh, no, dear Father, I love him as if he were the most handsome man in the world."

The king was surprised until the servant who had concealed himself came and revealed everything to him.

The king said, "That cannot be true."

"Then watch yourself the next night, and you will see it with your own eyes. If you were to take his skin away and throw it into the fire, he would be forced to show his true form."

"Your advice is good," said the king. That night the king stole into their room. When he got to the bed, he saw by the light of the moon a noble-looking youth lying there, and the skin stretched out on the ground. So the king took the skin away. He had a great fire started outside and he threw the skin into it, remaining by the fire until the skin had burned to ash. But since the king was anxious to know how the young man would behave when he found out, he stayed awake the whole night and watched.

When the youth woke up and went to put on his skin, he could not find it anywhere. He was alarmed and decided to escape. But when he got outside, there stood the king, who said, "My son, where are you running to? Stay here. You are such a handsome man; you shall not go away from me. I will now give you half my kingdom, and after my death you shall have the whole of it."

And so the young man stayed, and they all lived in splendor and happiness.

⌒ *The End* ⌒

The Flea

O nce upon a time a flea bit the king of High-Hill. The flea used such incredible acrobatic tricks to accomplish this feat that the king couldn't bear to kill him.

So he put the flea into a bottle and fed it every day. At the end of seven months, this remarkable flea had grown bigger than a sheep. The king then had the flea's skin removed and issued a statement that whoever could identify the skin could marry the princess.

As soon as this decree was made, people came from all over the countryside to try their luck. One said that it belonged to an ape, another to a lynx, a third to a crocodile. The crowds guessed and guessed, but not one person got it right.

Eventually, though, an ogre, who was the ugliest being in the world, came to try his luck at this guessing contest. No sooner had he turned the skin around and smelled it than he instantly guessed the truth, saying, "This skin belongs to the king of fleas."

Now the king saw that the ogre had guessed correctly, and so he ordered his daughter Petunia to be called. Petunia was so beautiful that you would never tire of looking at her. The king said to her, "My daughter, you know who I am. I cannot go back on my promise whether it is to a king or a beggar. Who would ever have imagined that the ogre would guess correctly! Have patience then and do not argue with me. My heart tells me that you will be happy, for sometimes rich treasures are found inside a rough earthen jar."

When Petunia heard this, her face turned pale and she burst into tears. She said to her father, "What crime have I committed that I should be punished like this! How have I ever behaved badly toward you that I should be given up to this monster?"

Petunia was going to say more when the king exclaimed, "Please, do not be angry. Sometimes appearances deceive."

Poor Petunia, seeing she had no choice in the matter, took the hand of the ogre, who dragged her off, without any servants, to his house in the forest, a rather dismal and gloomy place.

Petunia felt deep despair.

For dinner she had nothing but peas; dessert consisted of parched beans. When the ogre saw that she was still hungry, he said, "I have been invited to a wild boar hunt and will bring you home a couple of boars. We'll make a grand feast with our relations and celebrate the wedding." So saying he went into the forest.

Now as Petunia stood weeping at the window, an old woman passed by. Famished, she begged for some food.

"Oh, my good woman," said Petunia, " I am in the power of the ogre who brings me home nothing but peas and dry beans. I have a miserable life and yet I am the daughter of a king and have been brought up in luxury."

And so saying she began to cry.

The old woman's heart softened at this sight, and she said to Petunia, "Don't worry, my pretty girl. Do not spoil your beauty with crying, for you have met with luck. I can help you. Listen, now. I have seven sons who, you see, are giants: Mase, Nardo, Cola, Micco, Petrullo, Ascaddeo, and Ceccone. They all have special talents. For Mase, every time he lays his ear to the ground, he hears all that is passing within thirty miles. Every time Nardo washes his hands, he makes a great sea of soapsuds. Every time Cola throws a bit of iron on the ground, he makes a field of sharp razors. Whenever Micco flings down a little stick, a tangled forest springs up. If Petrullo lets fall a drop of water, it makes a terrible river. When Ascaddeo wishes a strong tower to spring up, he has only to throw a stone. And Ceccone shoots so straight with the crossbow that he can hit a hen's eye a mile off. Now with the help of my sons, who are all courteous and friendly, I will free you from the ogre."

"No time better than now," replied Petunia.

"It cannot be this evening," replied the old woman, "for I live a long way off. But I promise you that tomorrow morning my sons and I will come and help you out of your trouble."

Then, the old woman departed. Petunia went to rest with a light heart and slept soundly all night.

At morning's first light the woman and her seven children appeared. They gathered Petunia in their arms and started to carry her away. But they had not gone even half a mile when Mase put his ear to the ground and cried, "Oh, no! I hear the ogre chasing us. He wants Petunia back!"

No sooner did Nardo hear this than he washed his hands and made a sea of soapsuds. When the ogre saw all the suds, he ran home and fetched a sack of sand. He threw the sand about, using it for traction on the slippery ground. This time, Cola flung a piece of iron on the ground and instantly a field of sharp razors sprang up. When the ogre saw the path, he ran home to put on his iron suit, which covered him from head to foot. Then he returned and crossed over the razors.

But Micco was ready with his little stick. In an instant he caused a terrible wood to rise up, so thick that it was hard to get through. When the ogre came to this dense forest, he grabbed a knife and began to cut down the trees. With four or five strokes, he had laid the whole forest on the ground.

Then, Petrullo took water from a little fountain, sprinkled it on the ground, and in a twinkling of an eye a large river rose. When the ogre saw this new obstacle, he jumped in and swam across the river with his clothes piled upon his head.

"Never fear," said Ascaddeo, "I will soon settle this ugly ragamuffin." He flung a pebble onto the ground and instantly a tower rose up in which they all hid. When the ogre saw that they had gotten into so safe a place, he ran home, got a ladder, and carried it back on his shoulder to the tower.

The ogre planted his ladder on the ground and began to climb. But Ceccone, taking aim at him, shot out one of his eyes, and laid him at full length on the ground, like a pear dropped from a tree. Then Ceccone climbed out of the tower and cut off the ogre's head. With great joy, they took the head to the king, who was overjoyed to see his daughter again.

Soon after, Petunia was married to a handsome prince. And the seven sons and their mother were given huge bags of gold for their role in saving the beautiful Petunia.

The End

The Frog Prince

Breaking enchantments is not an easy business. In "The Frog Prince," a beautiful princess must be persuaded to kiss a wet, slimy frog. Would you be able to kiss a frog or fall in love with the beast? Or would the Frog Prince be destined to live his life hopping from lily pad to lily pad?

Once upon a time, there was a princess who loved to play with her golden ball. She couldn't wait to throw the ball high into the air and then catch it. Every day she would play for hours in the garden with her ball. She thought of little other than her golden ball.

One day, she decided to see how high she could throw the ball. She threw it up high and caught it easily. "That's too easy," she thought, so she threw it even higher and still it was too easy to catch. Finally, she gave the ball a great heave and threw it so high that she lost sight of it. When it came down, she didn't catch it, and the ball rolled away and landed, *ker-splashhh,* in a nearby pond.

She stood at the edge of the pond, but could not see her ball anywhere.

"Excuse me, Princess," said a voice, "I can get your ball for you."

The princess looked around to see who was speaking. All she could see was a very slimy and warty frog.

"Did you say something to me?" the princess asked the frog, for these were magical times and frogs and other animals were known to speak occasionally.

"Yes," croaked the frog. "I said that I could get your ball for you."

"I'm not used to talking with warty frogs," said the princess arrogantly.

"Well, then," said the frog indignantly, "you shall never see your ball again." And he turned to hop away.

"Wait, wait!" cried the princess. "I'm sorry. Will you please get my ball for me?"

"On one condition," said the frog. "When I retrieve the ball, you will give me one small kiss."

The princess felt that she had little choice since she desperately wanted her golden ball back. So she grudgingly agreed to this condition.

The frog paddled down into the pond and in the wink of an eye came back with the ball.

"Here it is!" he said, dropping the ball at the princess's feet.

"Thank you, good Frog," she said, and she began tossing the ball into the air.

"Wait," said the frog. "Aren't you forgetting your promise?"

"Oh," said the princess. "You can't really expect me to kiss you, can you? After all, I am royalty and you are warty!" With that, she ran away, returning to the palace.

That evening at dinner, a servant came into the dining room.

"There is a frog here to see you, Your Majesty."

"A what?" said the king.

"A what?" said the princess.

"A frog," said the servant. "He says he has business with the princess. Something about a broken promise."

"Send him away immediately!" said the princess.

"Bring him in," said the king.

A few minutes later, in hopped the frog.

"Do you know this frog?" said the king.

"I rescued your daughter's golden ball," said the frog. "But she has broken her promise to me."

"Is that true?" asked the king.

"He wanted me to kiss him," said the princess. "I cannot stand the thought of touching my lips to his green mouth!"

"No daughter of mine will break her promise," said the king. "Do as you must."

"No, sire," said the frog. "She must do it voluntarily."

"Never!" shouted the princess.

This frog was a persistent fellow, though, so for many weeks, he hopped to the palace every morning and sat with the princess. They ate and played together. At the end of six months, as they were going up to bed, the princess turned to the frog and without really thinking said, "Good night, Frog," and gave him a little kiss on the top of his head.

In an instant, the frog vanished, and in his place was a handsome man.

"Who are you?" said the princess, stepping back. "What have you done with my frog?" For by now, the princess loved the little frog, warts and all.

"I am your frog," said the man. "I am also a prince. I was enchanted by a wicked fairy and turned into a frog. Only the kiss of a beautiful princess could break the enchantment."

"Why didn't you tell me before?" said the princess.

"Because," said the prince, "you had to do it of your own free will."

The two were soon married, and the princess grew to love the prince just as much as she had loved the frog. The prince and princess lived happily together and had many children who loved to play with the golden ball and hear the story of how their parents met.

$\approx$ *The End* $\approx$

The Little Pear Girl

Once upon a time, there lived a peasant who worked hard to make a living by farming the land. Every year his pear tree produced four bountiful baskets of fruit, which had to be given to the king. He was a greedy ruler who grew rich by taking from his subjects.

One year, part of the pear harvest went bad, and the peasant was able to pick only three and a half baskets of fruit. The poor man was beside himself with fear, for the king refused to take less than four baskets. The peasant knew he would be punished. All he could do was put his youngest daughter into one of the baskets and cover her with a layer of pears, so that the basket looked full.

The king's servants took away the four baskets without noticing the trick. Soon the little girl found herself all alone in the pantry, under the pears. One day, the cook went into the pantry and discovered her. Nobody could understand where she had come from. Not knowing what to do with her, Cook decided she should become a maid in the castle. She was given the name Violetta because her eyes were the color of violets.

Violetta was a pretty girl, sweet and generous. One day, as she was watering the flowers in the royal gardens, she met the king's son, a boy of her own age, and the two became friends. The other maids, jealous of Violetta's beauty, did everything they could to get her into trouble. They started spreading nasty rumors about her.

One day, the king sent for her and said severely, "I'm told you boast of being able to steal the witches' treasure trove. Is that true?"

Violetta said no, but the king refused to believe her and drove her out of his kingdom. "You may return only when you have laid hands on the treasure," he said.

All of Violetta's close friends, including the prince, were sorry to hear of the king's decision, but they could do nothing to stop her going. The girl wandered through the forest and, when she finally came to a pear tree, she climbed into its branches and fell asleep. She was awakened at dawn by an old woman calling her, "What are you doing up there, all by yourself?"

Violetta told the old woman her tale, and the old woman offered to help her. She gave Violetta a broom, some round loaves of good bread, a little oil, and some good advice. Again, the girl set off on her journey.

Soon she reached a clearing with a large wood stove where she saw three women tearing out their hair and using it to sweep the ashes from the stove. Violetta offered them her broom and, in return, the women pointed out the way to the witches' palace.

As she headed toward the palace, two hungry mastiffs blocked her path. Violetta threw them the loaves. The dogs ate the bread and let her pass. Then she came to the bank of a flooding river. Remembering the old woman's advice, Violetta sang a lullaby to the river to calm it. The minute her song wafted into the air, the water stopped flowing. She crossed the river and at last reached the witches' palace.

The door was unlocked, but Violetta could not push it open for the hinges were rusted. So she rubbed a little oil on them and the door swung open. The little girl walked through the empty halls until she came to a splendid room in which sat a magnificent **coffer** full of jewels. Holding the coffer under her arm, Violetta made for the door. But the coffer was enchanted and it cried out, "Door! Don't let her out! You don't know what she's about!" However, the door opened, for Violetta had oiled its hinges.

Down at the river, the coffer cried out again. This time it said, "Water! Drown her! Please, don't deter." But the river did not stop the little girl from crossing. The two mastiffs did not attack, and the three strange women did not burn her in their stove, for each was repaying the girl's courtesy.

Back at the king's palace again, the prince ran happily to meet Violetta, telling her, "When my father asks you what you want as a reward, ask him for the basket of pears in the pantry!" And this Violetta did. Pleased at paying such a modest price, the king instantly ordered the humble basket to be brought forth.

But nobody ever imagined for a minute that underneath the pears lay the handsome prince. The young man came out of his hiding place, professed his love for Violetta, and said he wanted to marry her. The king gave his consent. They all agreed that when Violetta became old enough, she and the Prince would marry. Happy with this arrangement, Violetta brought her family to the palace, and they all began a new and happy life together.

⁕ The End ⁕

Molly Whuppie and the Two-Faced Giant

When you picture a big, fierce giant, you may find it odd to hear he carries a purse. This isn't like the purses we have today. At the time "Molly Whuppie and the Two-faced Giant" was written, a purse was designed as a pouch to hold gold and coins. No doubt, this particular giant was very worried about someone stealing his purse filled with gold, so he slept with it under his pillow. This, though, wasn't a secure enough place to keep the clever Molly from stealing it away.

Once upon a time there was a poor man and his wife. They were so poor, in fact, that they were unable to feed all of their children. So the parents decided to take the three youngest children, all girls, and leave them in the forest.

Now the two eldest were just ordinary girls, but the youngest, whose name was Molly Whuppie, was brave. She told her sisters not to worry, but to try and find some house where they might spend the night. They set off through the forest but couldn't see any houses. It began to grow dark and all three of the sisters started to feel hungry. At last in the distance they saw a great big light. When they came closer, they saw that it came from a large window in a huge house.

"It must be a giant's house," said the two elder girls, trembling with fright.

"I don't care if giants do live there. I'm hungry," said Molly Whuppie and she knocked at the huge door. The giant's wife opened the door, but she shook her head when Molly Whuppie asked for food and a night's lodging.

"You wouldn't thank me for it," she said, "for my husband is a giant. When he comes home, he will certainly kill you."

"But if you give us supper right away," said Molly craftily, "we'll finish it before he comes home."

Now, the giant's wife was not a mean person, and her three daughters, who were the same ages as Molly and her sisters, wanted these strangers to stay. So she let the girls in and gave them each a bowl of bread and milk. But they had hardly begun to gobble it up before the door burst open, and a fearful giant walked in saying: "Fee-fi-fo-fum, I smell the smell of some earthly one."

"Don't put yourself about, my dear," said the giant's wife trying to make the best of it. "See for yourself. They are only three poor little girls like our girls. They were cold and hungry, so I gave them some supper. They have promised to go away as soon as they have finished. Please let them be."

Now this giant was not at all a straightforward giant. He was a two-faced giant. So he only said, "Umph!" and remarked that as they had come, they had better stay all night since they could easily sleep with his three daughters. After he had had his supper, he made himself quite pleasant and plaited chains of straw for the little strangers to wear round their necks, to match the gold chains his daughters wore. Then he wished them all pleasant dreams and sent them to bed.

But instead of going to sleep like the others, Molly Whuppie stayed awake. She took off her and her sisters' straw chain necklaces, put them around the necks of the giant's daughters, and placed their gold chains around her own and her sisters' necks.

In the very middle of the night when it was pitch-dark, the giant came in, felt for the straw chain necklaces, and then dragged those girls out of their beds and put them in his rather nasty, wet dungeon.

Molly Whuppie, who had not yet gone to sleep, immediately woke up her sisters, and they all fled the giant's home. Soon they came to a moat, which was spanned by a drawbridge that hung by a single strand of hair. Molly's sisters were scared to cross it, but Molly skipped happily and quickly across and came upon a king's castle. Now it so happened that the very giant whom Molly had tricked was the terror of the whole countryside, and it was to keep him away that the Bridge of One Hair had been made. The sentry listened to Molly Whuppie's tale and then took her to the king, saying, "My lord! Here is a girl who has tricked the giant!"

When the king had heard the story, he said, "You are a clever girl, Molly Whuppie. Now, if you could steal the giant's sword, I will let your eldest sister marry my eldest son."

Molly Whuppie thought this would be a very good match, so she decided to try and steal the sword.

That evening, all alone, she ran across the Bridge of One Hair and kept running until she came to the giant's house. She slipped unnoticed into the house, crept up to the giant's room, and tiptoed behind the bed. By and by the giant came home, ate a huge supper, and stomped up the stairs to his bed. Molly kept very still and held her breath. Soon the giant fell asleep and began to snore. Then Molly crept out and grabbed the sword. Unfortunately, her movements woke the giant, and up he jumped and ran after Molly. She ran as she had never run before, carrying the sword over her shoulder. They both ran until they came to the Bridge of One Hair. Molly fled over it, but the giant couldn't cross. So he stopped and yelled angrily after her, "You'll be sorry, Molly Whuppie!"

Molly gave the sword to the king. As he had promised, his eldest son married her eldest sister.

After the marriage festivities were over, the king said again to Molly Whuppie, "You're a clever girl, Molly. If you could manage to steal the giant's purse, I will marry my second son to your second sister. Be careful, though, because the giant sleeps with the purse under his pillow!"

Molly thought this would be a good match, so she agreed to try.

That evening she ran over the Bridge of One Hair and ran until she came to the giant's house. She slipped into the house unnoticed, stole up to the giant's room, and crept in below the giant's bed. The giant came home, ate a hearty supper, stomped upstairs, and soon fell asleep. Then Molly Whuppie slipped from under the bed and grabbed the purse. Her movements woke up the giant, and he ran after her until she reached the Bridge of One Hair. Molly sped across it while the giant shook his fist at her, and cried, "You'll be sorry!"

So she took the purse to the king, and he ordered a splendid marriage feast for his second son and her second sister. But after the wedding was over, the king said to her, "Molly! You are very clever. If you steal the giant's ring from his finger, I will give you my dearest, youngest, best-looking son for yourself."

Now Molly thought the king's son was the nicest young prince she had ever seen, so she said she would try. That evening, all alone, she sped across the Bridge of One Hair and ran, until she came to the giant's house. She slipped inside, stole upstairs, and crept under the bed in no time. The giant came in, ate a rather enormous dinner, and stomped up to bed. He began to snore, louder than he had ever snored before.

As you might remember, though, he was a two-faced giant; so perhaps he snored louder on purpose. For no sooner had Molly Whuppie begun to tug at his ring than the giant sat up with a loud roar! He held her tightly between his finger and thumb and said, "Molly Whuppie, you are a clever girl! Now, if I had done as much harm to you as you have done to me, what would you do to me?"

Molly thought for a moment and she said, "I'd put you in a sack, and I'd put the cat inside with you, and I'd put the dog inside with you. Then I'd put a needle and thread and a pair of shears inside with you, and I'd hang you up on a nail. Next, I'd go to the wood and cut the thickest stick I could get, and come home and take you down and bang you with the stick."

"Right you are!" cried the giant gleefully, "and that's just what I'll do to you!" So he got a sack and put Molly into it with the dog and the cat and the needle and thread and the shears. Then he hung her on a nail in the wall and went out to the woods to choose a stick.

What is that clever Molly up to?

Now the giant's wife was sitting in the next room, and when she heard the commotion she went in to see what was up.

"Whatever is the matter?" she asked.

"Nothing," answered Molly Whuppie from inside the sack, laughing like anything! "If you saw what we see you'd laugh too."

And no matter how the giant's wife begged to know what she saw, there never was any answer but "Ho, ho! Ha, ha!"

At last the giant's wife begged Molly to let her see, so Molly took the shears, cut a hole in the sack, jumped out, helped the giant's wife in, and sewed up the hole! For of course she had taken the needle and thread out with her.

Just at that very moment, the giant burst in. Molly had barely time to hide behind the door before he rushed at the sack, tore it down, and began to batter it with a huge tree he had cut in the wood.

"Stop! Stop!" cried his wife. "It's me! It's me!"

But he couldn't hear because, you see, the dog and the cat had tumbled on top of each other, and such a growling and spitting, and yelling and caterwauling

you've never heard! The giant went on with his big stick until he caught sight of Molly Whuppie escaping with the ring he had left on the table.

He threw down the tree and ran after her. You've never seen such a race. They ran, and they ran, and they ran, and they ran, until they came to the Bridge of One Hair. And then, balancing herself with the ring like a hoop, Molly Whuppie sped over the bridge light as a feather. But the giant had to stand on the other side, and shake his fist at her, and cry louder than ever, "You'll be sorry, Molly!"

Molly laughed, for she and the handsome young prince were to be married. And indeed they were, and lived happily ever after. The two-faced giant was never heard from again.

⇐ The End ⇒

The Prince and the Fakir

O nce upon a time there was a king who had no children. One day, this king lay down in the middle of an intersection of a road. Everyone who passed had to step over him.

Soon, a **fakir** came along and said to the king, "Man, why are you lying here?"

He replied, "Fakir, a thousand men have come and passed by. You pass on too."

But the fakir said, "Who are you?"

The king said, "I am the king, Fakir. I am a rich man, but I am sad that I have no children. So I have come here, to try and find answers as men pass over me."

The fakir said, "Oh, King, if you have children, what will you give me?"

"Anything you want, Fakir," answered the king.

The fakir said, "If you have two sons, I want one of them."

Then he took out two candies, handed them to the king, and said, "King, take these two special candies and give them to your wives. Give them to the wives you love best."

Then the fakir said, "One day, I will return. Of the two sons who will be born to you, one is mine and one is yours. Agreed?"

The king said, "I agree."

Then the fakir went on his way, and the king went home and gave one candy to each of his two favorite wives. After some time two sons were born to the king.

One day the fakir appeared and asked to see the king.

When the king heard this news, he quickly hid his sons in the basement and brought out two of his servants' sons to present to the fakir. While the fakir was waiting for the king, the king's sons were sitting in the cellar eating.

Just then a hungry ant carried away a grain of rice from the boys' food to take to her children. Another stronger ant came up and attacked her in order to get the grain of rice. The first ant said, "Oh ant, why do you drag this away from me? I have long been lame in my feet, and I have got just one grain. I am carrying it to my children. The king's sons are sitting in the cellar eating their food. Go and fetch a grain from them. Why should you take mine from me?"

Hearing this, the second ant let go. He did not rob the first ant but went off to where the king's sons were eating their food.

On hearing this exchange between the ants, the fakir said, "King, these are not your sons. Go and bring to me those children who are eating their food in the cellar."

So the king went and brought up his own sons. The fakir chose the elder son and set off with him on his journey.

When they got to the fakir's home, he told the king's son to go gather firewood. So the boy went out to gather the wood and when he had collected some, he brought it in. Then the fakir looked at the king's son while he put a huge kettle on the fire, and said, "Come around here, my pupil." But the king's son said, "Master first, and pupil after." The fakir told him to come once, he told him twice, he told him three times. And each time the king's son answered, "Master first, and pupil after."

Then the fakir made a dash at the king's son, thinking to catch him and throw him into the cauldron. There were about a hundred gallons of oil in this cauldron, and the fire was burning beneath it. But the king's son caught the fakir, lifted him up, gave him a jerk, and threw him into the cauldron. The fakir was quickly killed in the boiling oil.

Then the king's son saw a key that belonged to the fakir. He took this key and opened the door of the fakir's barn. Many men were locked up in there, as well as two horses, two hounds, and two tigers. So the king's son freed all the men who were in prison. He took the two horses, the two tigers, and the two hounds and set out for another country where he lived on his own for several years.

Now a young man, he one day set out to take a walk. As he went along the road, he saw a bald man tending his herd of calves. The bald man called out to him, "Fellow, can you fight at all?"

The king's son replied, "When I was little I could fight a bit. Now, if anyone wants to fight, I am not so unmanly as to turn my back."

The bald man said, "If I throw you, you shall be my slave. If you throw me, I will be your slave." So they got ready and began to fight, and the king's son threw him.

The king's son said, "I will leave my beasts here: my tigers and dogs and horses. They will all stay here while I go to the city. And you, too, must stay here with my belongings."

So he started off to the city and arrived at a pool. He saw that it was a pleasant pool and thought he would stop and bathe there.

The king's daughter, who was sitting on the roof of the palace, saw from a distance his royal marks. She said, "This man is a prince. When I marry, I will marry him and no other." She didn't tell her father, but told him she was ready to be betrothed.

"Good," said her father. Then he issued a proclamation: "Let all men come to the palace today because my daughter will take a husband."

All the men of the land assembled, and the traveling prince also came.

The king's daughter came out and sat on the balcony, and cast her glance around all those assembled. She noticed that the prince was sitting in the assembly in fakir's attire.

The princess said to her handmaiden, "Take this dish of henna, go to that traveler dressed like a fakir, and sprinkle scent on him from the dish."

The handmaiden obeyed the princess's order, went to him, and sprinkled the scent over him.

Then the people said, "The servant has made a mistake."

But the servant replied, "The servant has made no mistake. It is her mistress who has made the mistake."

At this the king married his daughter to the fakir, who was really no fakir, but a prince. But the king became very sad in his heart, because when so many important men were sitting there, his daughter had chosen the fakir.

One day the traveler prince said, "Let all the king's sons-in-law come out with me today to hunt."

They all set out for the hunt. The newly married prince went to his tigers and hounds and told them to kill and bring in a great number of gazelles and deer. Instantly they did as he asked. Taking the dead animals with him, the prince came to the pool settled on as a meeting place. The other princes had also assembled there, but they had brought in no game, and the new prince had brought in a remarkable amount. Then they returned home and went to the king, their father-in-law, to present their game.

Now the new prince told the king that he was a prince. The king, his father-in-law, was greatly delighted and took him by the hand and embraced him. They all lived very happily in the kingdom for a very long time.

The End

The Princess and the Mouse

Once upon a time in the desert there lived a princess named Safia. One day, a wicked magician disguised as an old woman approached Safia.

"Princess," he croaked, "let me be your washerwoman and clean your sheets."

"Certainly," said Princess Safia, who wanted to help the old woman. "Come to my rooms and I will give you my sheets to wash."

So the disguised magician followed the princess. In the blink of an eye, he stuffed her into a laundry bag and ran away as fast as he could. Using an evil spell, he made her as small as a doll and put her away in a cupboard.

The next day, the magician found the palace in an uproar.

"Princess Safia has vanished" said the **grand vizier**.

The wicked magician smiled at his success.

The next day, the queen was weeping in her garden when the magician entered, disguised as a washerwoman. He put her into a laundry bag and turned her into a doll no bigger than his thumb.

The next day he captured the king in the same fashion, turned him into a doll, and put him in a cupboard with his wife, the queen.

The grand vizier pleaded with the magician, "Please tell us what to do!"

"Until your king, queen, and princess return, let me be your ruler," said the magician. The people agreed. So the wicked magician began to rule, feeling confident that the royal family was locked away forever in the cupboard.

But one day a mouse nibbled its way into the cupboard where Princess Safia was hidden.

"Mouse," whispered the tiny princess, "eat a hole in this cupboard and let me out. My father is the king, and he'll reward you."

"Haven't you heard? The king and queen have disappeared," said the mouse. "The magician is now the ruler of all the land."

"I can't believe it," cried the princess. "Can the wicked magician have captured them too?"

Together, they searched the cabinet and found the king and queen stuffed into the top shelf. But they were as stiff as wood, because the magician had cast a different spell upon them.

"Princess," said the mouse, "tonight when the moon rises, come with me to the wise woman who lives in a hollow tree. She will be able to help you."

So, when the moon rose, they hurried to the hollow tree and climbed in.

"To save your family," said the wise woman, giving the princess a magic grass seed, "you must find an orange-colored horse by the crossroads. Give him this magic grass seed to eat, and whisper into his ear, 'Take me, Orange Horse, to where the sacred pear tree grows, so that I may pick the pear from its topmost branch.'"

"And then will I grow back to my regular size?" asked the princess.

"Not until the wicked magician is dead," said the wise woman. "Ride to the Well of the Green Ogre. Drop the pear into the well. The magician's soul is in the pear, and if it is devoured by the ogre, the magician will die."

"What will happen then?" the princess asked.

"All the creatures turned into other shapes by the magician will return to their original forms."

The princess thanked the wise woman and ran until she reached the crossroads where there stood an orange horse.

"Take me, Orange Horse," said Safia, "to the tree where the sacred pears grow, so I can pick the topmost pear from its branches."

The horse put down his head. Safia fed him the magic grass seed and then climbed on. The horse galloped away.

They arrived in a beautiful orchard with a single pear tree. She climbed into the branches and picked the pear from the topmost branch.

"Now, dear horse, take me to the Well of the Green Ogre," she whispered in the horse's right ear. The horse galloped off and soon they reached the well.

Inside the well, Safia saw an ogre's head, as big as a wagon wheel. She took the pear and dropped it right into the Green Ogre's slimy, smelly mouth, and he instantly chewed the pear into bits.

Safia then found herself growing back to her own size. That meant the wicked magician was dead!

Safia hurried back to the palace, where she found the king and queen, who were their normal size again.

Safia went to the hollow tree to thank the wise woman. But the tree was gone! Instead, she saw a tall handsome young man dressed in regal clothing.

"Dear Princess," he said, "the wise woman is gone."

"How do you know this?" demanded the princess.

"I was the mouse, another victim of the magician's enchantment."

"Come with me to my father so that he can thank you," said Safia.

Together they went, and the young man knelt before the king.

"Please stay here and marry my daughter," said the king.

So they were married in a wedding feast attended by thousands, and they lived and ruled happily ever after.

⪧ The End ⪦

The Princess and the Pea

Once upon a time in a faraway kingdom there was a prince who wanted to marry a princess.

Now, this particular prince was quite finicky. He wasn't willing to marry just any princess. He wanted to find a princess who was beautiful, kind, witty, charming, and, most important of all, sensitive.

"Sensitive," wailed the king. "How will you possibly know if your princess is sensitive until many years have passed? You don't have time for this, Son."

For it was true, the prince would soon be considered rather too old to be searching for a wife. And, in the meantime, his mother and father, the king and queen, were getting older and really wanted to retire to a smaller palace in a warmer climate.

The prince tried to reassure his father, however. He said he had devised a perfect plan for testing the princess's sensitivity, especially to very small things.

So, the prince continued his frustrating search. He traveled to every part of the world by boat, on horseback, and on camel, crisscrossing the desert, climbing mountains, and crossing valleys, searching for the princess of his dreams. He looked in every country, great and small, but nowhere could he find what he wanted.

Sure, there were plenty of princesses available to a prince of his stature, but it was difficult to find out whether they were real, royal ones, with all of the qualifications this particular prince sought. And so it went. There was always something about the princesses he interviewed that was not as it should be. So he returned from his exhaustive search, sad and discouraged, wondering how he would ever find a real princess.

His parents were just about ready to give up and pass the kingdom on to his younger brother. One evening, as the gloomy prince was pondering his dilemma, a terrible storm blew in. There was deafening thunder and brilliant lightning, along with torrential rains and hail the size of goose eggs.

"Oh, my," fretted the king, who was a bit afraid of thunder (although none of his royal subjects knew this!), "I do hope this storm passes through quickly. I don't believe I've seen such a fierce rain in many years. I'm afraid it may flood our moat and endanger our pet dragon, Penelope, who lives there."

The rain continued to pour down in torrents. Then in the midst of this gale, a loud knock was heard at the castle gate. When the old king opened the gate, he found a bedraggled but beautiful maiden standing there.

"Hello, sire," began the maiden, who was drenched beyond belief. "I am a princess from a neighboring kingdom. I am afraid that I've been caught out in this storm and my horse has run off. I'm not able to return home until the storm ends. Could I please pass some time here?"

The king was a bit skeptical about this maiden's royal claims. How could she be a princess? She looked completely miserable. The water ran down from her golden hair and not-so-royal clothes into the toes of her shoes and out again at the heels.

"How can I be so sure that you're a princess and not an impostor, wanting to steal something from my palace?" asked the king.

"You'll simply have to look in your heart and decide for yourself if I am a real princess or not," answered the maiden with a soggy smile.

Well, the king wasn't any too certain that this maiden was a princess, but nevertheless he found her charming—and he wasn't, after all, an ogre. The poor girl was soaking wet, so he invited her in to dry off and warm up by one of the huge fireplaces.

Once inside, the king introduced the maiden to the queen and the prince. The prince, being a bit of a skeptic himself, took one look at the maiden and decided she most certainly could not be a princess. After all, she was drenched and bedraggled. No princess he'd ever interviewed during his travels had appeared like this.

Although the queen was a bit doubtful as well, she and the king insisted the prince administer his sensitivity test. After all, this girl might be the real thing. She was charming and beautiful. And, the king and queen really wanted to see this situation resolved, so they could move to their retirement palace in the south.

So, it was agreed. The prince would test the maiden on her princess qualifications. He went to meet with one of the servants to follow through on his plan.

"Kind servant," said the prince. "We have a guest spending the night in the palace. When you prepare the bed in her bedchamber, please do the following: Remove all of the bedding and the mattress from her bed. Then, place this on the bottom." With these words, the prince handed the servant a tiny, squishy green pea. All peas, of course, are small, but this one was particularly tiny.

"Then," continued the prince, "replace the mattress along with nineteen others, placing them on top of this pea."

"I will do this, Sire," answered the puzzled servant, not quite sure what the prince was up to.

"No, there is still more," said the prince. "After replacing the mattress, then take twenty eiderdown comforters and place them all on top of the mattresses. That should do it!"

The prince then took his leave and returned to the main room where the maiden waited with the king and queen.

"Your bed is being prepared, dear maiden," said the prince. "Let me take you to your chamber."

And so, he led her to the rather unusual bed. The princess glanced at the exceedingly tall bed and wondered how she would climb to the top of the twenty mattresses and twenty comforters.

"Could I have a ladder, prince?" she asked.

"Of course. Servant, please bring one," answered the prince.

The ladder arrived promptly and the maiden climbed it with a good-natured smile. Once at the top, she clambered onto the bed, pulled the twenty covers up to her chin, and planned to fall right to sleep. It had been a rather tiring day, after all.

Unfortunately though, sleep was not to come to the maiden. Try as she might, she simply couldn't get comfortable. She tried sleeping first on one side and then on the other. Then she turned to sleep on her stomach. When she didn't find that comfortable, she switched and tried sleeping on her back. "Maybe I'm too warm," she thought, and she climbed on top of the comforters.

"Maybe I'm lonely," she thought. So she climbed down the ladder, took her favorite stuffed bear out of her coat pocket, and climbed back up the ladder, tucking herself into the towering bed.

Yet, sleep still wouldn't come. The maiden was quite vexed.

When she appeared in the morning at the breakfast table, she had circles under her eyes and felt a bit cross about her lack of sleep.

"Oh, how did you sleep?" asked the prince, sure that his pea could not have caused her any problems.

"Oh, very badly!" she groaned. "I don't want to sound ungrateful, but I have scarcely closed my eyes all night. I tried everything I could think of to fall asleep but I had no luck. Heaven only knows what was in that bed, but I was lying on something incredibly hard and bothersome. Now, I am black and blue all over my body. Oh! It was completely horrible!"

With these words from the princess—for now they knew she was not just a maiden but a true princess—a great cheer went up from the prince, the king, and the queen (for the prince had told them of his plan).

"Hip, hip, hooray!" shouted the king. "You are the sensitive princess our son has been looking for these many, many years. Now, you and the prince can marry, and the queen and I can retire to sunnier climates!"

They knew without a doubt that she was a real princess because she had felt the tiny, soft pea right through the twenty mattresses and the twenty eiderdown comforters. Nobody but a real princess could be as sensitive as that, they all agreed.

So the prince and the princess were married in an incredibly grand celebration. The palace kitchen prepared a huge wedding feast, consisting of many dishes prepared with peas: split-pea soup, creamed peas, stir-fried snow peas, and even sweet pea ice cream.

And, if you'd like to learn more about this family and the pea that brought them together, you may go to the museum where it was placed after the wedding ceremony. I'm told it may still be seen there, if no one has stolen it.

The End

Rapunzel

Once upon a time, a man and a woman lived in a snug home near a beautiful walled garden. They were quite happy, except for one thing: They had no children. Finally, after years of waiting, the wife became pregnant.

Oddly enough, the woman found that she craved something called rampion, a green for making salads. Rampion is also called Rapunzel. Her husband spied some inside the walls of the garden next door. Although he'd never met the person who tended the garden, he thought he'd try his luck at getting some for his hungry wife.

That night, by the light of the moon, he climbed over the stone wall into the beautiful garden and picked a small basketful of the rampion. He rushed back over the wall and gave the leaves to his wife who ate them happily.

The next night she craved more, so he was forced to make another trip over the wall into the neighbor's garden. This time though, he was caught in the act—by an old, warty fairy.

"How dare you steal into my garden and take my rampion?" she hissed.

"Oh, I'm sorry," he said. "But I felt I had to. My wife is pregnant and craving your delicious rampion. You're quite a gardener!"

"I think she'll have a daughter," said the fairy. "I was planning to kill you, but I will spare you on one condition."

"You name it," said the man.

"Your wife shall have as much rampion as she likes, and you shall live," said the fairy, "but when your daughter is twelve years old, you will give her to me. Then, you are never to see her again."

The man agreed, because he was afraid the fairy would kill him otherwise. When he told his wife, she cried, but she agreed that her husband really had no choice.

When the child was born, the hideous fairy appeared and gave her the name Rapunzel. Then she vanished, only to reappear, as promised, on the girl's twelfth birthday.

"I have come for you, Rapunzel," said the fairy.

The girl agreed to go because she did not want her father to die.

The fairy shut Rapunzel up in a stone tower in the middle of a forest. There was no door to this tower, and no stairs. There was only one window high at the top, far too high for any ladder to reach.

When the fairy wanted to go up, she stood at the bottom and cried in her hoarse voice, "Rapunzel, Rapunzel, let down your golden hair."

Rapunzel, who had spectacularly long hair, would drop her luxurious locks down to the fairy standing far below. Then the woman would climb up the hair.

After a few years, a prince riding through the forest happened to hear a beautiful voice singing. He hurried toward the sound and saw the tower. In the window far above, he saw a beautiful girl, singing sweetly to herself.

The prince wanted to climb the tower, but he saw right away that it wasn't possible. There was no door or stairs. He rode home, but every day he came back to the tower and listened to the girl's sweet song and waited for a glimpse of her face in the window.

One day while he was waiting, he saw the fairy arrive and croak, "Rapunzel, Rapunzel, let down your golden hair."

As he watched the wicked woman climb the hair, he came up with a plan to reach the beautiful maiden. The next day when it grew dark, he went to the tower and croaked like the old fairy, "Rapunzel, Rapunzel, let down your golden hair."

Down came the beautiful golden hair, and up he climbed.

As you can imagine, the prince's appearance was a bit of a shock for Rapunzel. The prince reassured her, though, and told her that he had heard her singing for many months and that he had fallen in love with her through her splendid songs. Rapunzel fell in love with him as well. The prince asked her to marry him, and she happily said yes.

"But how will you escape from this prison?" the prince asked.

"Bring a length of silk thread with you every time you visit," Rapunzel said. "I will weave a thread ladder, and when it is ready I will come with you."

So, every evening, the prince returned with a fine silk thread, and as they talked she wove the ladder of silk. Finally, the ladder was finished. It had not been easy hiding it from the old fairy, for she was quite suspicious and questioned Rapunzel harshly about strange human smells in the tower. Rapunzel, however, was able to convince her that nothing was amiss.

One night, by the glowing light of the moon, the prince came to rescue Rapunzel. She hung the delicate ladder from the windowsill and climbed down carefully into the arms of her waiting prince charming! They were married shortly after at the prince's royal residence and lived there very happily.

As for the ugly fairy, to this day she can't understand how Rapunzel escaped. And she's quite vexed about it!

≈ *The End* ≈

The Ruby Prince

Once upon a time a beggar in faraway **Persia** had a bit of good luck for a change. After a fierce flood, the fast flowing river near the capital city shrank back to its old bed, leaving mud and slime behind on the banks. In the dirt, the beggar saw a sparkling red stone. He picked it up and hurried off to visit one of his friends who worked in the kitchens at the royal palace.

"How many dinners would you give me for this shining stone?" he asked the man hopefully and hungrily.

"But this is a ruby!" exclaimed the cook. "You must take it to the **shah** at once!"

So next day, the beggar took the stone to the shah, who asked him: "Where did you find this?"

"Lying in the mud on the bank of the river, Sire!" he said.

"Oh!" thought the shah. "Now why did the great river leave such a sparkling treasure to you? I'll give you a bag of gold for the stone. Will that do?"

The beggar could scarcely believe his ears. "Sire, this is the most wonderful day of my life," he said, barely able to speak. "My deepest thanks!"

Before the shah locked the big stone in his treasure box, he called Fatima, his daughter, and said: "This is the biggest ruby I've ever seen. I'll give it to you for your eighteenth birthday!" Fatima admired the gem in her hand and happily threw her arms round her father's neck.

"It's marvelous! Thank you so much. I know it will bring me good luck!"

Some months later, on Fatima's birthday, the shah went to get the ruby from his box of treasures. But when he lifted the lid of the box, he jumped back in surprise, because out stepped a handsome young man, who smilingly said, "The ruby you want no longer exists! I've taken its place. I'm the Ruby Prince. Please don't ask me how this miracle took place. It's a secret I can never tell!"

When the shah got over his shock, he went wild with rage. "I lose a precious gem, find a prince, and I'm not allowed to ask why?" he roared.

"I'm sorry, Sire," replied the prince, "but nothing and nobody will make me tell how I got here."

Furious at these words, the shah instantly decided to punish the young man. "Since you've taken the place of my ruby," he thundered, "you are now my servant."

"Of course, Sire," replied the young man.

"Good!" exclaimed the shah. "Then take my golden sword. I'll reward you with the hand of my daughter, Fatima, if you succeed in killing the dragon in Death Valley that's stopping the caravans from passing through the forest."

As it happens, many a brave young man had lost his life trying to kill the terrible dragon. And the shah was quite sure that the Ruby Prince would also die trying.

Taking the shah's sword, the Ruby Prince set off for Death Valley. When he reached the edge of a frighteningly dark forest, he yelled for the dragon to come out. But the only reply was the echo of his own voice. He sat down and was about to fall asleep when the sound of snapping branches brought him to his feet. A frightful hissing grew louder and louder, and the earth seemed to shake. The terrible dragon was on its way. When it reached the prince, the huge, horrible beast roared. Unlike all the other warriors who had gone before him, the prince was brave and did not run away. He took a step forward and struck first one heavy blow at the dragon's throat, then another, until at last the monster lay dead at his feet.

When he returned to the palace carrying the dragon's head, the Ruby Prince was called a hero. And so Fatima and the Ruby Prince were married and lived happily together. However, as time passed, Fatima became more and more

curious about her husband's past. "I know nothing about you," she complained. "At least tell me who you really are and where you once lived!"

But every time the Ruby Prince heard such remarks, he became pale and said, "I cannot tell you. You shouldn't ask, or you'll run the risk of losing me forever!"

But Fatima was tormented by the desire to know. One day, as they sat by the river that flowed through the shah's gardens, Fatima pleaded with him to reveal his secret.

White-faced, the young man replied, "I cannot!"

But Fatima only begged more: "Oh, please! Please tell me!"

"You know I can't . . ." The Ruby Prince hesitated, gazing at his beloved wife and gently stroking her hair. Then he made his decision. "I don't want to see you suffer like this. If you really must know, then I'll tell you that I'm—"

At the very second he was about to reveal his secret, a huge wave swept him into the river and dragged him under the water. The horrified princess rushed vainly along the bank, crying loudly for her husband. But he had vanished. Fatima called the guards and even the shah ran up to comfort her. But the princess became very depressed, for she knew that her foolish questioning had been the cause of her husband's death.

One day, her favorite handmaiden hurried up to her. "Your Highness!" she exclaimed. "I saw the most amazing thing last night. An array of tiny lights appeared on the river, then a thousand little genies draped the riverbank with flowers. Such a handsome young man then began to dance in honor of an old man who seemed to be a shah. Beside the shah stood a young man with a ruby on his forehead. I thought he was—"

Fatima's heart leaped: Could the young man with the ruby be her husband? That night, the princess and her handmaiden went into the garden and hid behind a tree close to the water's edge. On the stroke of midnight, tiny lights began to twinkle on the river. And then a stately old man with a white beard, dressed in a golden robe and holding a **scepter**, rose from the water. Fatima recognized her husband as the young man beside the throne.

Covering her face with her veil, she left her hiding place and gracefully began to dance. Wild applause greeted her at the end. Then a voice came from the throne, "For such a divine dance, make a wish and it will be granted!"

Fatima tore the veil from her face and cried, "Give me back my husband!" The old king rose to his feet. "The King of the Waters of Persia gave his word. Take back your husband, the Ruby Prince. But do not forget how you lost him and be wiser in future!"

Then the waters opened once more and closed over the king and his court, leaving Fatima and the Ruby Prince on the bank, reunited and happy at last. And Fatima *was* a bit wiser from then on.

⁓ *The End* ⁓

Rumpelstiltskin

Once upon a time there lived a **miller** who had a beautiful daughter. One day the miller had to visit the king's castle. While he was there, he happened to meet the king face to face. The king stopped and spoke to the miller. Hoping to impress the king, the miller boldly told him that he had a daughter who could spin straw into gold.

"Oh," said the king, "that is indeed a wonderful gift. Tomorrow you must bring your daughter to my castle, so she may spin some gold for me."

Then the miller was sorry he had lied, but he had to do as the king ordered.

This particular king loved gold more than anything else, so he was very pleased at the prospect of turning straw into gold. He led the poor girl into one of the giant castle rooms. There, in the middle of the room, stood a spinning wheel, and near it was a great heap of straw.

The king turned to the miller's daughter, and said, "There is your spinning wheel, and here is the straw. If you do not spin all of it into gold by morning, your head shall be cut off." Then the king left the room and locked the door.

Tears flowed down the poor girl's face, for she had no idea how to spin straw into gold. While she was crying, the door flew open and a little old man stepped into the room. He had bowlegs and a long red nose and wore a tall, peaked cap. Bowing low to the girl, he said, "Good evening, my dear young lady. Why are you crying?"

"Oh," said the girl, "the king has ordered me to spin all this straw into gold, and I do not know how."

Then the little man said, "What will you give me if I will spin it for you?"

"This string of gold beads from my neck," said the girl.

The little man took the beads and, sitting down, began to spin. As the young girl watched, she could scarcely believe her eyes. The coarse straw was turning into glittering gold threads. The little man kept working until the entire pile of straw was transformed into gold.

The next morning the king unlocked the door. He was delighted to see the pile of gold, but seeing it made him want even more. He led the girl to a still larger room, which was also full of straw. Turning to the trembling girl, he said, "There is your spinning wheel, and here is the straw. If you do not spin all of it into gold by morning, your head shall be cut off."

The maiden's eyes filled with tears at the sight of the huge heap of straw. Again, she began to cry. All at once the door opened and in jumped the little old bowlegged man. He took off his pointed cap and said to the miller's daughter, "What will you give me if I help you again, and spin this straw into gold?"

"This ruby ring from my finger," said the maiden.

The little man took the ring and began to spin. In the morning the straw had all been turned into the finest gold.

When the king opened the door, how his eyes glistened at the sight of the gold! Yet, as before, it made him desire even more. Taking the poor girl by the hand, he led her to an incredibly large room. This room was so full of straw that there was hardly space for her to sit at the spinning wheel.

Turning to the girl, the king said, "There is your spinning

wheel, and here is the straw. If you do not spin all of it into gold by morning, your head shall be cut off. But if you do spin the gold, I will marry you and make you my queen."

Hardly had the door closed behind the king when the little old man came hopping and skipping into the room. Taking off his pointed cap, he said to the girl, "What will you give me if I will again spin this straw for you?"

"Oh!" said the maiden, "I have nothing more to give."

"Then you must make me a promise," said the little man. "You must promise to give me your first child, after you become queen."

The girl saw no other way to save her life, so she made the promise. Then the little man sat down and spun all the straw into gold. When the king opened the door the next morning, he saw the maiden sitting beside a large heap of shining gold. The king kept his promise and married the girl.

About a year later the queen had a lovely child, but she had forgotten all about her promise. One day the little old man came hopping into the queen's room and said, "Now give me what you have promised."

The queen was frightened and began to cry, and the little man felt sorry for her.

"I will give you three days," he said, "and if, in that time, you can guess my name, you shall keep the child."

The queen lay awake that night, thinking of all the names she had ever heard. In the morning men were sent to every part of the kingdom to find strange names.

The next day the little man came again. The queen began to call off to him all the unusual names she had found—Caspar, Melchior, and many, many others.

As she read through her list, the little man shook his head and said, "No, that is not my name."

Then the queen had her men go from house to house throughout the town. They took down the name of every man, woman, and child.

When the little man came again, the queen had another long list of names. "Is your name Cowribs, or Sheepshanks, or Bandylegs?" she asked.

He answered to each one, "No, that is not my name."

On the third day the queen's men began to come back from all parts of the kingdom. One of the men said, "As I was going by some deep woods, I came upon a little house, in front of which a little man was dancing around a fire. He wore a pointed cap and had a long nose and bowed legs. As he went hopping and jumping about, first on one leg and then on the other, he sang:"

My baking and sewing I will do straight away,
For the queen's son tomorrow I will take away,
No wise man can show the queen where to begin,
For my name, oh it is true, is Rumpelstiltskin.

On hearing this, the queen wept with joy. She knew that at last she had found the name. At sunset the little fellow came skipping up to the queen.

"Now," he said, "this is your last chance. Tell me my name."

The queen, still pretending not to be sure, decided to have a little fun first. She asked, "Is your name Peter?"

"No."

"Harry?"

"No."

"Then your name is Rumpelstiltskin."

"The fairies have told you!" shouted the little man. He became so angry that, in his rage, he stamped his foot right into the ground. This made him angrier still, and taking hold of his left foot with both hands, he pulled so hard that he tore himself in half.

⌐ The End ⌐

The Sea-Hare

Although the name "sea-hare" may conjure up an image of some sort of aquatic bunny, the truth is a little slimier than that! A sea-hare is a sluglike creature with a protruding pair of front tentacles. It's no wonder that the princess in "The Sea-Hare" is alarmed and throws the creature to the ground when she discovers it in her hair!

Once upon a time, there was a princess who lived in a castle turret with twelve windows that looked out in all directions. From her windows, she could inspect the entire kingdom.

With her twelve windows and her extremely keen eyesight, she was able to see absolutely every person and thing in the land. Nothing at all could be kept secret from her.

She tended to be a bit difficult, so she proclaimed that she would only marry a man who was able to conceal himself from her. Many men had tried, but she had spotted them all. Once she spotted one of these potential suitors, he was hauled off to the dungeon. So far, ninety-seven men had been locked up in this dank place below the castle.

The princess really didn't want to marry, so she was pleased at the failure of these men. Since no one had tried to conceal himself for some time, she thought happily that she would never have to marry and settle down.

Then three brothers appeared before her and announced that they would like to try their luck. The eldest believed he would be quite safe if he crept into a deep quarry. But the princess saw him from the first window, made him come out, and had him hauled to the dungeon. The second crept into a distant corner of the palace, but she quickly spotted him and his fate was also sealed. Then the youngest came to her. He begged the princess to give him a day for consideration and also to be so kind as to overlook it if she should happen to discover him twice. But if he failed a third time, he would take his place in the dungeon.

He was so handsome, and begged so earnestly, the princess agreed.

The next day, he thought for a long time about how he should hide himself, but he couldn't come up with any good ideas. So he seized his gun and went out hunting. He saw a raven, took good aim at him, and was just going to shoot, when the bird cried, "Don't shoot! I will reward you."

He put his gun down, went on, and came to a lake where he surprised a large fish that had come up to the surface of the water. When he aimed at it, the fish cried, "Don't shoot, and I will reward you."

He allowed it to dive down again, went on, and met a fox that was lame. He fired and missed, and the fox cried, "You had much better come here and draw the thorn out of my foot for me."

He did this, but when he wanted to kill the fox, the animal said, "Stop, and I will reward you."

The youth let him go and then returned home. Next day he was to hide himself, but no matter how he puzzled over it, he did not know where to go. He went into the forest to the raven and said, "I let you live on, so now tell me where I am to hide myself so that the king's daughter will not see me."

The raven hung his head and thought it over for a long time. At length he croaked, "I have it!" He fetched an egg out of his nest, cut it into two parts, and shut the youth inside. Then the raven made the egg whole again and sat on it. When the king's daughter went to the first window, she could not discover him, nor could she see him from the other windows. She began to feel uneasy, but from the eleventh she finally saw him. She ordered the egg be brought to her and broken, and the youth was forced to come out.

She said, "For once you are excused, but if you don't do better than this, you are lost."

The next day he went to the lake, called the fish, and said, "I let you live, now tell me where to hide myself so that the king's daughter won't see me."

The fish thought for a while, and at last cried, "I have it! I will shut you up in my stomach."

It swallowed him and went down to the bottom of the lake. The king's daughter looked through her windows, and even from the eleventh did not see him. She was alarmed, but at length from the twelfth window, she saw him. She ordered the fish to be caught and killed, and then the youth appeared. It is easy to imagine the state of mind he was in.

She said, "Twice you are forgiven, but you have only one more chance!"

On the last day, he went with a heavy heart into the country, and met the fox. "You know how to find all kinds of hiding places," he said. "I let you live, now advise me where I can hide myself so that the king's daughter won't discover me."

"That's a hard task," answered the fox, looking very thoughtful. At length, though, he cried, "I have it," and took him to a spring. This was a magic spring and when the fox dipped himself in it, he came out as a merchant and dealer in animals. The youth had to dip himself into the water too and was changed into a small sea-hare.

The merchant went into the town and showed the pretty little animal. Many people gathered to see it. At length the king's daughter came and since she liked it very much, she bought it for a lot of money.

Before he gave it over to her, the merchant said to it, "When the king's daughter goes to the window, creep quickly under the braids of her hair."

When the time arrived to search for the youth, the princess went to one window after another in turn, from the first to the eleventh, and did not see him. When she did not see him from the twelfth either, she was full of anxiety and anger. She shut the window with such violence that the glass in every window slivered into a thousand pieces, and the whole castle shook. She went back and felt the sea-hare beneath the braids of her hair. Then she seized it and threw it on the ground, exclaiming, "Away with you, get out of my sight!"

It ran to the merchant, and both of them hurried to the spring. In they plunged and were transformed back into their true forms. The youth thanked the fox and went straight to the palace.

The princess was expecting him and they were soon married. He never told her where he had concealed himself for the third time, and who had helped him. She believed that he had done everything on his own and so she had great respect for him.

⇜ The End ⇝

Sleeping Beauty

*O*nce upon a time, a baby girl was born into a royal family. To celebrate her arrival, all the fairies in the land were invited to be godmothers. After the baptism, a banquet was planned. Seven places of honor were set with golden dishes and diamond goblets.

At the royal banquet, each of the seven fairy godmothers gave their gifts and advice to the tiny baby. There was great jubilation in the palace until, suddenly, an old, wizened fairy angrily appeared.

"Why is there no place for me?" the old fairy demanded.

No place had been set for the fairy because it was known that she was not a good fairy. Enraged at being spurned, she pulled out her magic wand and cackled, "I'll give her a gift she'll never forget. When she turns sixteen, the princess will cut her finger on a spindle, and she will die!" She then vanished in a flash of lightning.

The king and queen wept, but the seventh fairy urged them not to despair. "Your Majesties, I can't completely undo this curse, but I can make it milder. Instead of dying, when the princess cuts her finger, she and the entire kingdom will fall asleep, and slumber for 100 years. All will be awakened by the kiss of a prince."

This brought some comfort to the king and queen. In hopes of thwarting the curse altogether, however, they banned all spindles from the kingdom.

The evil fairy's magic was very powerful, though. On the princess's sixteenth birthday, she

was exploring the highest, most isolated turret of the castle, where she found an old woman smiling and spinning golden thread.

"What is that?" the princess asked. She had never seen a spinning wheel.

"A spindle," said the old woman. "Would you like to see it?"

The princess reached her hand out and cut her finger on the spindle. She immediately fell asleep.

At that same instant, everyone in the castle fell into a deep sleep: the king and queen, all the servants, and even the animals in the stables.

A hundred years passed, and the old castle was overgrown by a big forest.

One day, a prince was lost in this dark forest. He was just about to give up all hope of finding his way when he saw the glint of stone in the distance. As he got closer, he was amazed to see the wall of a castle. It was quite magnificent, despite the vines creeping up along its walls and the huge lawn that was choked with weeds.

He made his way inside and marveled at the inhabitants of the castle, who were all asleep. Guards slept standing at their posts, seamstresses sat sleeping on their stools, cooks stood sleeping in midstir, and a sleeping musician sat poised to play the piano. It was a very odd sight, thought the prince.

As he walked through the castle, he came to the very room where the beautiful princess slept. There he saw the most beautiful girl he had ever seen. The prince leaned forward and kissed the sleeping girl on her forehead.

Just then, the princess's eyes opened, and she looked at the prince as if she'd known him forever.

"Is that you, my prince?" she whispered. "I've waited so long."

Then, the prince told her that he had loved her from the first moment he'd laid eyes on her. One by one the servants awoke, and they prepared a great wedding feast.

The prince and princess were married that very afternoon and loved each other forever after.

The End

Snow-White and Rose-Red

Once upon a time a poor widow lived in a little cottage that had a colorful garden in front of it. In the garden grew two rose trees. One had white roses and the other had red. The widow had two children, who were just like the two rose trees. One was called Snow-White and the other Rose-Red, and they were wonderful children.

The two children loved each other and always walked about hand in hand. When Snow-White said, "We will never leave each other," Rose-Red always answered, "No, never."

Snow-White and Rose-Red kept their mother's cottage perfectly clean. In summer Rose-Red looked after the house. Every morning before her mother awoke, she placed a bunch of flowers by the bed. In winter Snow-White lit the fire and put on the kettle. In the evening when the snowflakes fell, their mother would say, "Snow-White, go and close the shutters." They would sit around the fire, while the mother put on her reading glasses and read aloud from a book. It was cozy and snug.

One evening, they heard a knock on the door. Rose-Red answered the door and found a bear standing there. The bear began to speak, "Don't be afraid. I won't hurt you. I am half frozen, and only wish to warm myself a little."

"My poor bear," said the mother, "lie down by the fire, just don't burn your fur." The bear asked the children to help dry his fur. They fetched a towel and rubbed him until he was dry. Then the beast stretched himself in front of the fire and growled quite happily and comfortably.

After that, the bear was their friend. He came to visit every night to lie in front of their fire.

When spring came, the bear said to Snow-White, "Now I must go away. I'll be gone the whole summer."

"Where are you going to, dear Bear?" asked Snow-White.

"I must go to the woods and protect my treasure from the wicked dwarfs. In winter, when the earth is frozen hard, they stay underground because they can't work their way through. Now when the sun has thawed and warmed the ground, they break through and come up above to steal what they can."

Snow-White was sad over their friend's departure. When she opened the door for him, the bear caught a piece of his fur in the door-knocker. Snow-White thought she caught sight of glittering gold beneath it, but she couldn't be certain.

A short time after this the mother sent the children into the wood to gather mushrooms. They came to a big tree that lay on the ground. The girls noticed something jumping up and down on the trunk, but they couldn't tell what it was. When they got closer, they saw it was a dwarf with a wizened face and a beard a yard long. The end of the beard was jammed into a cleft of the tree, and the little man sprang about trying to get his beard loose.

He glared at the girls and screamed, "What are you standing there for? Can't you come and help me?"

"What were you doing, little man?" asked Rose-Red.

"You stupid silly girl!" replied the dwarf, "I wanted to split the tree in order to get little chips of wood for our kitchen fire. I had driven in the wedge, and all was going well, but the cursed wood closed up so rapidly that I had no time to take my beautiful white beard out, so here I am, stuck!"

The children tugged and tugged, but they couldn't get the beard out. It was tightly wedged in.

"Don't get impatient," said Snow-White, taking scissors out of her pocket and cutting off the end of his beard. As soon as the dwarf was free, he seized a bag full of gold that had been hidden among the roots of the tree and scampered off.

Another day, Snow-White and Rose-Red went fishing. As they approached the stream, they saw their old friend the dwarf again, being dragged into the water by a fish. The little man had been sitting on the bank fishing, when the wind had entangled his beard in the line. Just then a big fish bit and the little dwarf had no strength to pull it out. The girls tried to untangle his beard but had no luck. Finally, Snow-White had to use her scissors again.

The dwarf was angry to have his beard cut once more. He waved his fists at the girls, grabbed a sack of pearls that lay among the **rushes**, and, without saying another word, dragged it away and disappeared behind a stone.

The next day the girls went to town to buy sewing supplies. While walking they saw a big bird hovering in slowly descending circles until at last it settled on a rock not far from them. Immediately they heard a sharp, piercing cry. They ran to the rock and saw that the eagle had pounced on their old friend the dwarf and was about to carry him off.

The good children wrestled the little dwarf away from the eagle.

The dwarf was still nasty to them though. "Couldn't you have treated me more carefully? You have torn my thin little coat to shreds."

The girls were accustomed to his ways by now and went on to town. On their way home, they were again passing the heath and surprised the dwarf pouring out his precious stones in an open space. They stopped to say hello. The dwarf was just opening his mouth to say something rude when they all heard a sudden growl, and a black bear trotted out of the woods. The dwarf jumped up in fright and cried, "Dear Mr. Bear, spare me! I'll give you all my treasure. Look at those beautiful precious stones lying there. Spare my life. There, eat these two wicked girls, they will be a tender and tasty meal for you!" But the bear, paying no attention to his words, killed the dwarf with one blow from his giant paw.

The girls had run away, but the bear called after them: "Snow-White and Rose-Red, don't be afraid. Wait, I'll come with you." Then they recognized his voice and stopped. When the bear was quite close to them, his skin fell off and revealed a beautiful man dressed in dazzling gold.

"I am a king's son," he said, "I had been cursed by that horrid little dwarf, who had stolen my treasure, to roam about the woods as a wild bear till his death should set me free."

Snow-White married him and Rose-Red married his brother, and they shared the vast treasure the dwarf had collected. The old mother came to live with them, bringing the two rose trees with her. Every year they produced the most magnificent red and white roses.

The End

Tattercoats

In a grand palace by the sea lived a very rich old lord. His wife and child had died, leaving him with only one little granddaughter. He had never seen this granddaughter. He hated her because his favorite daughter had died giving birth to her. When the nurse had brought him the baby, he swore that he would never look at her, as long as he lived.

So he sat, looking at the sea and crying for his dead daughter. His white hair and beard grew down over his shoulders and twined round his chair.

Meanwhile, his granddaughter grew up with no one to care for her. She wore torn petticoats from the ragbag. The other servants would heckle her, calling her "Tattercoats," and point to her bare feet and shoulders, until she ran away crying.

So she grew up spending her days out-of-doors, her only companion a lame goose herder. One day people told each other that the king was traveling through the land, and he was to give a great ball for all the lords and ladies of the country in the town nearby. The prince, his only son, was to choose a wife from among the maidens attending the ball.

One of the royal ball invitations was brought to the palace by the sea. The servants carried it up to the old lord, who still sat by his window, wrapped in his long white hair and weeping. But when he heard the king's command, he dried his eyes. He told his servants to bring scissors to cut him loose, for his hair had made him a prisoner and he could not move. And then he sent them for fancy clothes and jewels, which he put on. He mounted his white horse and set off for the ball.

Meanwhile Tattercoats sat by the kitchen door crying because she could not go to see the grand event and all of the regal lords and ladies. Eventually, the girl ran to her friend the goose herder and told him how unhappy she was because she could not go to the king's ball.

The goose herder listened to her story and then he told her to cheer up. He said they should go together into the town to see the king and all of the fancy party people. When she looked sadly down at her rags and bare feet, he played a note or two upon his pipe. He was an accomplished pipe player, and the tune was so merry that she forgot all about her tears and her troubles. They took each other's hand and set out for the ball.

Before they had gone very far, a handsome young man on horseback stopped to ask Tattercoats and the goose herder the way to the castle where the king was staying. When he found that they too were going there, he got off his horse and walked beside them along the road.

"You seem happy," he said, "and will make good company."

"Good company, indeed," said the goose herder, and he played a new tune that was not a dance.

It was a curious tune, and it made the strange young man stare and stare and stare at Tattercoats until he couldn't see her rags. All he could see was her beautiful face.

Then he said, "You are the most beautiful maiden in the world. Will you marry me?"

The goose herder smiled to himself, and played more sweetly than ever.

But Tattercoats laughed. "Not me," she said, "I am too poor and wretched to marry you."

But the more she refused him, the sweeter the pipe played and the deeper the young man fell in love. At last he begged her to come that night at twelve to the king's ball. He told her to come just as she was, with the goose herder and his geese, in her torn petticoat and bare feet, and see if he wouldn't dance with her before the king. If she did this, he said, she would be his bride.

At first Tattercoats said she would not, but the goose herder said, "Take fortune when it comes, little one."

The night came, and the hall in the castle was filled with light and music, and the lords and ladies were dancing before the king. Just as the clock struck twelve, Tattercoats and the goose herder entered, followed by his flock of noisy geese. They walked straight into the ballroom, while on either side the ladies whispered, the lords laughed, and the king seated at the far end stared in amazement.

But as they came in front of the throne Tattercoats's handsome lover rose from beside the king, and came to meet her. Taking her by the hand, he kissed her three times before them all. Then he turned to the king.

"Father!" he said—for it was the prince himself—"I have made my choice, and here is my bride, the loveliest girl in all the land and the sweetest as well!"

Before he had finished speaking, the goose herder had put his pipe to his lips and played a few notes that sounded like a bird singing far off in the sky. As he played, Tattercoats's rags were changed to shining robes sewn with glittering jewels and a golden crown lay upon her shining hair.

"Indeed," said the king, "The prince has chosen for his wife the loveliest girl in all the land!"

The goose herder was never seen again, and no one knew what became of him. The old lord went home once more to his palace by the sea, for he could not stay at the court when he had sworn never to look at his granddaughter's face.

So there he sits by his window, still weeping.

And Tattercoats and the prince lived happily every after.

⌒ *The End* ⌒

The Three Spinners

There was once a girl who was lazy and refused to do her spinning. No matter what her mother said, the girl would not do her work. At last the mother was so angry with her daughter that she yelled loudly at her. This made the girl cry. Now at this very moment the queen drove by. When she heard the weeping, she stopped her carriage, went into the house, and asked the mother why she was yelling at her daughter.

The woman was ashamed to reveal the laziness of her daughter and said, "I cannot get her to stop her spinning. She insists on spinning forever and ever, and I am poor and cannot buy the **flax**."

"Oh," answered the queen, "there is nothing I like better than to hear the sound of spinning. Let me have your daughter with me in the palace. I have lots of flax, and there she can spin as much as she likes."

The mother was very satisfied with this arrangement, and so the queen took the girl with her. When they arrived at the palace, the queen led the girl to three rooms that were filled from floor to ceiling with the finest flax.

"Now spin me this flax," said the queen, "and when you have done it, you shall have my eldest son for a husband. I don't mind that you're poor. I like the fact that you're such a hard worker."

The girl was terrified, for she could not have spun the flax even if she had lived until she was five hundred years old and had worked on it day in and day out. When left alone, she began to cry. She wasn't able to spin at all. On the third day, the queen came. When she saw that nothing had been spun, she was surprised, but the girl excused herself by saying that she had not been able to begin because she missed her mother.

The queen was satisfied with this excuse, but she said that now it was time to get to work. When the girl was alone again, she did not know what to do. In her distress, she went to the window. Then she saw three women coming toward her. The first had a broad, flat foot, the second had such a great lower lip that it hung down over her chin, and the third had a wide thumb. They stopped before the window, looked up, and asked the girl what was wrong. She told them and the women offered to help. They said, "We will help if you will invite us to your wedding, not be ashamed of us, and call us your aunts, and likewise place us at your table. Then we will spin the flax for you in short order."

"With all my heart, I promise to these conditions," she replied. Then she let in the three strange women and cleared a place in the first room, where they seated themselves and began their spinning. The one drew the thread and **trod** the wheel, the other wet the thread, and the third twisted it and struck the table with her finger. As often as she struck the table, a **skein** of thread fell to the ground that was spun in the finest manner possible.

The girl concealed the three spinners from the queen whenever she came to inspect the great quantity of spun thread. When the first room was empty, she went to the second, and at last to the third, and that too was quickly cleared. Then the three women got ready to leave and said to the girl, "Do not forget what you have promised us—it will make your fortune."

When the maiden showed the queen the empty rooms and the great heap of yarn, the queen gave orders for the wedding. And the bridegroom rejoiced that he was to have such a clever and industrious wife.

"I have three aunts," said the girl. "They have been very kind to me, and I want to invite them to the wedding and let them sit with us at the table."

The queen and the bridegroom agreed. When the wedding feast began, the three women entered in strange apparel, and the bride said, "Welcome, dear Aunts."

"Oh," said the bridegroom, "how do you come by these odious friends?"

He went to the one with the broad, flat foot, and said, "How do you come by such a broad foot?"

"By treading," she answered.

Then the bridegroom went to the second, and said, "How do you come by your large lip?"

"By licking," she answered.

Then he asked the third, "How do you come by your broad thumb?"

"By twisting the thread," she answered.

At this, the queen's son was alarmed and said, "Neither now nor ever shall my beautiful bride touch a spinning wheel!"

And so, the lucky girl never had to spin again.

The End

The Weeping Princess

Once upon a time there lived a greedy emperor who forced his subjects to pay heavy taxes. Every person, rich or poor, was highly taxed.

At last, the nobles of the land decided to protest. When the emperor heard about this, he was afraid of a rebellion so he sent out this proclamation: "The nobleman who can make my daughter, Sunny, smile again—for she's mourning the loss of her fiancé—will never pay taxes again."

Upon hearing the proclamation, most of the noble princes decided there was no need to complain about the high taxes, for each was quite sure he would succeed in cheering up the princess. So off they all went to get ready to try to make Sunny smile. A long line of noble knights came from far and wide to try to console the weeping princess. The crowds cheered them as they passed, but when they returned with bowed heads, the same crowds booed at their failure.

The days went by and the list of defeated knights grew. From all over the provinces came bold young men brimming with confidence. But the minute the princess set eyes on them, she just wept and wept. The emperor was delighted, for each failure meant another taxpayer. The common folk were content with this turn of events since it meant that the rich did not always get what they wanted.

The only unhappy person among them was Sunny, who went on weeping. One day, a Mongol prince seemed to be on the point of winning a smile. He thrummed his **balalaika** for hours, playing first a sad tune, then a more cheerful one, until he finished by playing a merry jig. The princess sat for ages staring at him, and onlookers thought she was about to smile.

Instead to everyone's dismay, she burst into floods of tears. A Kurdish chief, famed for his charm and easy wit, tried to earn a smile from Sunny. But the princess's dark eyes filled with tears. Noblemen came from as far away as **Persia**, but none had any luck with the weeping princess.

The only person who had not yet appeared was Omar, the chief of the tiniest, most distant province. He was an intelligent young man. Finally, one evening, he reached the palace. When the tired and dusty traveler explained to the stableboys why he had come, they laughed. But they had orders to obey, so they told him to enter. "It's late," they said, "you cannot see the princess until tomorrow."

The emperor's other daughters, however, were soon told of the new arrival. "He's the most handsome of them all!" exclaimed one of the servants. So Marika, the emperor's youngest and prettiest daughter, with her sisters, peeked through a window at the sleeping Omar.

Next morning, the emperor ordered the newcomer to be led before Sunny. The court crowded around to watch. Unlike all the other suitors, Omar did nothing at all to amuse the princess. He stared at Sunny without saying a word. And she stared back, with an empty look on her face. The two young people stared silently at each other. Then Omar went back to the emperor and said: "Sire! Give me your **scepter** and I will solve Sunny's problem."

Surprised at such an odd request, the emperor followed Omar into Sunny's room. The other princesses clustered round, smiling and admiring this handsome fellow. With a deep bow to Sunny, Omar straightened up and dealt her a blow on the head with the scepter. Screams filled the air and the emperor threw up his arms in anger. His daughters fled. The guards drew their swords.

Then the whole room stopped, hushed, in amazement. For, out of Sunny's head, which had been broken off by the blow, rolled loose springs and metal fragments. The princess who never smiled was a doll—a perfect, mechanical doll. Nobody had ever been aware of it except Omar.

Marika, after witnessing this scene and realizing what had happened, began laughing uncontrollably. The emperor glared at her. "Be quiet," he ordered.

Then the emperor began to see the funny side of it as well. For the crafty emperor had been making use of the doll as a way of guaranteeing himself a steady flow of taxes. And now, a man more cunning than himself had exposed his scheme. The emperor had a sudden thought, a way he could get rid of the cheeky Marika and gain a smart son-in-law.

"You should be put to death for this," he said, "but I'm going to spare your life, if you marry my youngest daughter. Of course, you won't need to pay taxes!"

Smiling at a happy Marika, Omar nodded silently. But in the depths of his mind he was thinking, "One day, I'll be sitting on your throne." And he was, just a few years later.

≈ *The End* ≈

The Tale of Scheherazade

"The Tale of Scheherazade" is commonly called a "frame tale" because it is a story with many more stories within it. It's a device that keeps the reader wanting more and, as you'll see in this case, the king wanting more too!

Once upon a time in a land far away, there was a king who had been so brutally betrayed by his wife that he made a promise to himself. Each night King Shahryar required his **grand vizier** to bring him a new bride, each night he was married, and each morning, he ordered the bride's head cut off.

This horror continued for many years until one day, the vizier's eldest daughter, Scheherazade, came to her father to ask for a rather unusual favor.

"Oh, Father," she cried, "how long will you allow this killing to go on? I think I can stop the killing. I have a favor to ask. Will you grant it to me?"

"Please, my Daughter," said her father. "I can't deny you anything that is fair. What is your favor, dear?"

Scheherazade was a very smart woman. She had read every book in the royal library. She knew the stories of kings and the works of the poets. Not only was she well-read, but also she was well-mannered, able to tell a good story, and kind-hearted.

"I would like you," Scheherazade paused, "to give me in marriage to King Shahryar. I have a plan to keep myself and the other women from being killed."

"No!" cried the vizier. "I have worked for years to keep you away from him."

"You must make me his wife," Scheherazade said. "It's the only way."

The vizier cried and begged his daughter to rethink her plan, but in the end it was of no use. At last he agreed to her wish.

The evening of the wedding, Scheherazade spoke in confidence to her sister, Dunyazad. "Pay attention to what I am going to tell you. After the wedding, I will ask the king to send for you so that we may spend my last few hours together. You must not be sleepy. Ask me to tell you a story. I will tell you a story that will save our kingdom."

Dunyazad bowed her head and agreed to this plan.

That evening King Shahryar was married to Scheherazade. When the ceremonies were complete and they were in the royal bedroom, Scheherazade dropped to her knees and began to weep.

"Oh, great and powerful King," Scheherazade said. "I have a younger sister, and I would like to say good-bye to her before I die."

The king agreed and sent for Dunyazad. The young girl sat at the foot of the bed.

"Oh, Sister," Dunyazad said, "tell me a delightful story to while away the last few hours of our waking life."

"That would please me," Scheherazade said. "If our wise king will permit me, then I will begin."

"Tell on," said the king, who for once was having trouble sleeping.

Scheherazade rejoiced, for this was part of her plan. And on this, the first night of the Thousand and One Nights, she began to tell her stories.

⮞ *The End* ⮜

The Tale of the Merchant and the Genie

So, Scheherazade began her story: Once upon a time there was a wealthy merchant who traveled on horseback across the country. One day, as he made his way across the land, he sat down under a tree to get some relief from the midday sun. He made his lunch of some dry bread and a scant handful of dry dates. When he had finished his meal, he threw away the date pits. This was his usual routine.

Now, he stood refreshed and ready to get back on his horse. Suddenly, he found his way blocked by a **genie**!

This genie was of a remarkable height and wearing a frightening scowl. He had drawn a sword and said, "You must die since you have killed my son!"

"I did not kill your son," the merchant insisted.

"Yes, you did. When you ate your dates and threw away the pits," replied the genie, "one of the stones struck my son through the heart as he was walking by, and he died immediately."

"Oh no!" cried the merchant. "It was an accident. I had no idea your son was walking by."

"Nevertheless, your ill-thrown pit killed him. You must die," stormed the genie.

"If I must die," begged the merchant, "please let me travel back to my home and say good-bye to my children and wife."

The genie agreed. He told the merchant that he had a week to say his good-byes. And with that, the genie vanished.

The merchant returned home and bid his wife and children good-bye. On the last day of his life, he went to the great **mosque** and prayed. Afterward, he sat outside the mosque and began to weep.

Just then, two **sheiks** came across the tearful merchant. One sheik traveled with a gazelle and the other with two large dogs. "What has happened?" the sheiks asked. "Why do you weep?"

The merchant told them his tale. The two sheiks offered to stay with him so he would not have to face his death alone. The merchant agreed, and the two sheiks sat down with the gazelle and two dogs beside them.

Seemingly out of nowhere, the genie appeared, his sword drawn, ready to kill the merchant.

"Wait, wait!" shouted the first sheik. "If I tell you the story of myself and this gazelle, and you like it, will you give me half of this merchant's blood?"

"Why not?" said the genie. "I agree to this plan."

⌒ The End ⌒

The Tale of the First Sheik

*A*nd so, the first sheik began: Once upon a time, oh Genie, this gazelle was my wife. She also happened to be a magician. We had been married for nearly thirty years, but we had no children. As was allowed then, I married another woman and soon had a baby boy. My first wife was very jealous of the young boy and his mother.

When the boy was fifteen years old, I had to go on a trip. While I was gone, my wicked wife used her magic to change my son into a calf and his mother into a cow.

When I returned, she told me, "Your second wife is dead, and your son ran away because he doesn't like you. I don't know where he went."

For a year I grieved and ate practically nothing. Then, as an important feast approached, I ordered my herdsman to bring me a fat cow to butcher.

He brought me the one that had been my second wife. I rolled up my sleeves and took the knife to kill it, but the cow began to weep. I had never seen a cow cry, and I said to my herdsman, "I can't kill this cow. Please, bring me another."

He said to me, "This is the best there is. I will kill her for you."

So he killed the poor cow. But instead of finding meat inside her skin, there was nothing but bones.

"Bring me a calf then," I ordered. The herdsman brought to me the calf that was my son. The calf also began to cry.

"Do I need to kill this one, too?" said the herdsman.

"No," I cried, "I will do it myself." I took the knife in my hand and held it to the throat of the calf.

Just then Scheherazade noticed the light of dawn creeping in through the window, and stopped talking.

"What a wonderful story!" Dunyazad said. "Can you tell me the end?"

"If the king wills me to live another day," the brave girl replied, "I will finish the tale."

The king, who was held spellbound by the tale, agreed. "You may live until I have heard the rest of your story."

That morning, the vizier went to the bedroom, prepared to kill his beloved daughter. He was astonished when the king did not give him the order but went about the business of the day.

When the second night finally fell, Dunyazad said to her sister, Scheherazade, "Please, finish the story of the merchant and the genie."

"If the king will let me," said Scheherazade.

"Begin," said the king.

So, she began: Just as the merchant was about to kill the calf, he saw it weeping and he couldn't bring himself to use the knife.

"Keep this calf among my cattle," he told his herdsman.

All of this, the sheik told the genie, who listened in wonder.

"Oh, Genie," the sheik said, "While all this occurred, my wicked wife watched and laughed at her revenge. She turned to me and ordered me to kill the calf, but I would not. Instead I sent it away with my herdsman."

The next day the herdsman returned. "Oh, my master," he said. "I have good news for you. My daughter learned magic in her childhood from an old woman. Yesterday, when I brought that calf home, she took one look at it and said, 'This calf is the son of our master, who has been bewitched by his wicked stepmother. The first fat cow that was killed was the boy's poor mother.'"

"Is this true? Bring her to me now! Bring the calf as well."

The herdsman brought his daughter and the calf, and all stood before me.

"Oh, please," I begged, "will you release my son? I will give you everything I own."

The good girl smiled and answered, "I don't want your riches, but I have two conditions. First, I would like to marry your son. Second, I would like to bewitch the witch who bewitched him."

The sheik immediately agreed.

The herdsman's daughter took a cup and filled it with a magic potion she kept in a vial. Then she chanted words the sheik could not understand. Instantly, the calf shivered and became a man!

"Then, Genie," said the sheik, "I married the girl to my son. She ordered my wicked wife brought before us. Then she transformed my wife into this gazelle, who travels with me even unto this day. You see her standing here."

"And that is the end of my story."

The genie turned to the first sheik and said, "I like your tale. I gladly give you half of this merchant's blood!"

The genie stood and held his sword high.

"Wait, oh Genie," said the second sheik. "If I tell you an even better tale, about these two dogs, and about what happened to me because of my brothers, will you grant me the other half of this man's blood?"

"If your story is even better," replied the genie.

⌒ The End ⌒

The Tale of the Second Sheik

And so the second sheik began: These two dogs are my brothers. When our father died, he left each of us a small fortune in gold. I opened a shop with my money and sold fine embroidered silks, brocades, and linens. My two brothers decided to use their money to travel around the world and buy and sell spices.

After my brothers had been gone about a year, a beggar appeared in my shop. It took me some time to recognize that this bedraggled fellow was my brother. I took him back to my home, where he bathed. I gave him some of my fine clothes and a portion of the gold I had earned from my shop. He took this money and opened a shop of his own near mine.

Not long after that, another beggar appeared at my shop. And, as had happened before, it took me some time to recognize this filthy creature as my second brother. When I realized that indeed it was my brother, I took him to my home, bathed him, and gave him some decent clothing and gold I had earned from my shop. He, too, took the gold and opened a shop of his own near mine.

All went well for some time, but my brothers became consumed by **wanderlust** and asked me to join them on a journey around the globe. For some time, I resisted their entreaties, but finally I agreed. First, though, I asked that we all share what we had earned from our shops to finance our travels.

My brothers had not saved a single gold piece! They had spent their money on parties and fun. I, on the other hand, had saved six thousand pieces. It was agreed that we would take three thousand of the gold pieces on our travels and bury the other three thousand in our town. Then, when we returned from our travels, we would have some gold with which to reopen our shops.

So, we set sail and traveled around the globe. We bought and sold and traded, earning back ten gold pieces for every one that we invested.

Then, one day, we came upon a maiden in tattered clothes standing on the beach.

When she saw me, she kissed my hand and asked me if I could help her.

"Yes, of course," I answered and offered her some gold pieces.

She responded by saying, "Marry me, then. I will be a wonderful wife."

My heart warmed when I heard these words, and we agreed to be married. We found room for her on the ship and once again set sail. My brothers, though, became jealous of the time I was spending with my new wife and the gold I was accumulating through my savvy business dealings and trades. So, they plotted to throw my new wife and me overboard. After we were dead, they would take all of our gold.

One night, the brothers crept into our cabin and threw us off the ship. At that instant, my wife turned into an Ifritah, a wonderfully powerful spirit. She picked me up from the sea, rescuing me, and carried me to an island.

"Now you know that I am a genie," she said, "but you did not know that when we were married. You were kind to me, so I have saved your life. However, your wicked brothers have made me angry and now I must go and kill them."

I thanked her for saving my life but begged her not to kill my brothers. She would not relent. First, though, she picked me up and flew me back to the roof of my own house. I dug up the gold and reopened my shop.

One evening, I came home and found these two dogs tied up at the door to my house. They nuzzled me and whined and acted as if they wanted to speak to me.

Before I knew what had happened, my wife told me, "These two dogs are your brothers. I would have killed them, but my sister said I should be more forgiving. So instead, my sister has turned them into two dogs. They will remain dogs for ten years."

"That is why," concluded the sheik, "I am here, searching for my wife's sister, so that she may remove the curse that has turned my two brothers into dogs. That is my tale."

Then, the genie turned to the second sheik and said, "Your tale is even stranger than the first. I happily give you the other half of this merchant's blood."

At that, the merchant tearfully embraced the two sheiks and thanked them for saving his life.

So, Scheherazade continued to spin tales for one thousand and one nights. As she was telling her fanciful stories, the years passed and the king and Scheherazade had three sons together. By then, the king realized what a wonderful woman Scheherazade was and he no longer wanted to kill her. The two ruled wisely and happily. And the vizier was very relieved to know his beloved daughter was safe and content.

⁌ The End ⁌

The Bremen Town Musicians

There once was a man who had a donkey, which he had used to carry corn sacks to the mill for many years. The donkey was becoming weak from old age and unable to do his work. His master began to consider what to do with the donkey. Sensing that his master was becoming angry with him, the donkey ran away and set out on the road to Bremen. "There," he thought, "I can surely be a town musician."

When he had walked some distance, he found a hound lying on the side of the road, panting.

"Why are you gasping so, big fellow?" asked the donkey.

"Oh," replied the hound breathlessly, "as I am old and growing weak and can no longer hunt, my master wanted to kill me. So I ran away, but now how am I to earn a living?"

"I tell you what," said the donkey, "I am going to Bremen and shall be a town musician there. Go with me and become a musician, too. I will play the **lute**, and you shall beat the **kettledrum**."

The hound agreed, and on they went. Before long they came upon a cat sitting on the path, with a dismal face.

"Now then, old shaver, what has gone wrong with you?" asked the donkey.

"Who can be merry when his life is in danger?" asked the cat in reply. "Because I am now getting old, and my teeth are worn to stumps, and I prefer to sit by the fire and relax rather than chase after mice, my mistress wanted to drown me. So I ran away, but now I don't know where to go."

"Go with us to Bremen. You can be a town musician too," said the donkey.

The cat thought this sounded like a good plan so he went with them.

After this the three runaways came to a farmyard, where a rooster was sitting on a fence, crowing with all his might.

"Why is your crow so loud?" asked the donkey.

"Because," moaned the rooster, "guests are coming Sunday, so the wife has told the cook that she intends to put me in the soup tomorrow. This evening I am to have my head cut off. Now I am crowing at the top of my lungs while I still can."

"Oh," said the donkey, "you had better come away with us. We are going to Bremen. You have a good voice, and if we make music together, it will sound wonderful."

The rooster agreed to this plan, and all four went on together. They could not reach the city of Bremen in one day, however, and as night fell they came to a forest where they planned to sleep. The donkey and the hound laid themselves down under a large tree, and the cat and the rooster settled themselves in the branches.

The rooster flew right to the top, where he was most safe. Before he went to sleep, he looked round on all four sides and thought he saw in the distance a little flame burning. So he called out to his companions that there must be a house not far off, for he saw a light.

"If so," said the donkey, "we had better get up and go on to that house for it's not very comfortable sleeping here in the woods."

So they all made their way to the place where the light was and soon saw it shine brighter and grow larger, until they came to a brightly lit robbers' house. The donkey, as the biggest, went to the window and looked in.

"What do you see?" asked the rooster.

"I see a table covered with good things to eat and drink, and robbers sitting at it enjoying themselves," answered the donkey. "If only we were there."

The table inside looked so tempting that the animals decided to drive away the robbers. After some time, they thought of a way. The donkey was to place himself with his front feet upon the window ledge, the hound was to jump on the donkey's back, and the cat was to climb upon the dog. Finally, the rooster was to fly up and perch upon the head of the cat.

When this was accomplished, they began to perform their music. The donkey brayed, the hound barked, the cat meowed, and the rooster crowed. Then they burst through the window into the room, shattering the glass.

At this horrible din, the robbers sprang up, thinking that a ghost had come in. They fled in a great fright out into the forest.

The four companions now sat down at the table, very happy with what was left, and ate as if it were going to be their only meal for a month. When they finished, the four musicians put out the light, and each found a suitable place to sleep.

The donkey lay down upon some straw in the yard, the hound behind the door, the cat upon the hearth near the warm ashes, and the rooster perched upon a beam of the roof. And being tired from their long walk, they soon went to sleep.

When it was past midnight, the robbers saw from a distance that the light was no longer burning in their house, and all appeared quiet. The leader said, "We were silly to have been frightened by those animals." He then ordered one of the robbers to examine the house. This unfortunate messenger, finding all still, went into the kitchen to light a candle. He mistook the glowing eyes of the cat for live coals and held a match up to them, hoping to light the coals. The cat flew in his face, spitting and scratching. The robber was terrified and ran to the back door, but the dog, lying there, sprang up and bit his leg. And as he ran across the yard, the donkey gave him a sharp kick with its back foot. The rooster, too, had been awakened by the noise, and he cried down from the beam, "Cock-a-doodle-doo."

The robber ran back as fast as he could to his leader.

"Oh," he said, "there is a horrible witch sitting in the house. She spit on me and scratched my face with her long claws. And by the door stood a man with a knife. He stabbed me in the leg. And in the yard a black monster beat me with a wooden club. And up on the roof sits the judge who said, 'Put the robber in jail.' So I ran away as fast as I could."

After this terrible fright, the robbers never again dared enter the house. But it suited the four musicians of Bremen so well that they did not care to leave it ever again.

The End

The Conference of the Mice

O nce upon a time there was a large tabby cat. She was brown with dark stripes and had impressively large paws. Although the cat looked rather fierce due to her large size, she wasn't a very satisfactory mouser. At least, her human owners didn't find her to be so. This was rather frustrating to the humans, because they'd hoped the tabby would help free their home from all the mice that raced relentlessly through it.

The cat's owners devised a plan to improve the tabby's mousing prowess. They decided to send her to stay on a distant farm to gain experience and expertise in the field of mousing from the rural cats.

The frisky farm cats took the urban cat into their confidence and shared all of their best mousing techniques and secrets. After a few days, the city cat was ready to try her paw at capturing a few mice. Well, the training had worked. The mice ran scared as this feline spread terror among the multitudes of rodents that lived in the farm's cellar, pantry, and barns.

None of the mice dared go outside for fear of falling into the cat's clutches. With their numbers quickly diminishing, the mouse colony decided to hold a conference in order to figure out a way of stopping themselves from becoming extinct.

They waited until the city cat was away for the day. The tabby's human folks had come to visit and took her for a walk in the fields. Taking advantage of this rare absence, anxious and agitated mice of all ages streamed into the conference room and arranged themselves in a large circle. Although terrorized by the tabby, these mice were confident that they could resolve the matter. They went around the mouse circle, each little creature putting forward a suggestion.

As it turned out, though, none of the ideas were really practical.

"Let's build a giant trap," one mouse suggested enthusiastically. The rest of the mice weren't so excited and the idea was unanimously vetoed.

Then another jumped up, tail swishing, and said, "What about poisoning her?" At first cheers filled the room, but then the group realized that none of them knew of a poison that would kill a cat.

This went on for some time. Mouse after mouse offered suggestions, ideas, and possible plans. None held any promise. They were just about to give up hope, when one of the smallest mice, wiser than the rest, scrambled to the top of the lantern that shone out over the meeting room. Waving and shaking a sparkling bell, he called for silence. "I believe I have a solution. We'll simply tie this jangling bell to the cat's tail. By doing so, we will always know where she is! Then, we'll always have time to escape. Even the slower and weaker mice will hear her coming and be able to scamper off and hide!"

First, there was an awed silence at the mouse's wise words. Then, a round of hearty applause met the mouse's idea. Finally, all of the assembled mice came over to the mouse and congratulated him on his original and clever idea.

"Why," said one, "We will tie it on so tightly that it will never come off, no matter how hard the tabby tries to shake it off!"

Another mouse added, "She'll never be able to sneak quietly up on us again! Why, the other day, she suddenly loomed up right in front of me! Just imagine how frightened I felt. Now, none of us will ever have to experience that horrible fright again."

After the clamor died down a bit, the wise mouse rang the bell again and asked for silence from the group.

"We have an important decision to make," he announced. "We must now decide who is going to tie the bell on the cat's tail."

This pronouncement was greeted with silence. Not a murmur could be heard. Finally, though, the silence was broken as first one mouse then another began to exclaim.

"I certainly couldn't do it. I'm just not suited for such a task."

"Not me. I really don't know enough about a tabby's tail to tie a bell on correctly. I'd worry that it would come off if I were sent to do this job."

"Normally, I'd do it willingly, but I haven't been feeling so well. I think it might be wise to send another mouse to do it."

Some mice were more honest and simply expressed fear at the thought of approaching the huge cat.

"Not me! No way! I won't go near that horrible tabby!"

So much for the idea of the wise mouse; it fizzled. It turned out that none of the mice were brave enough to come forward to put the bell-on-the-tail plan into action. So it was that the feline returned from her walk in the fields, and the conference of the mice ended without any decision being made.

The tabby's owners were pleased with her improved mousing prowess but decided—much to the chagrin of the farm mice—to leave her in the country a bit longer to hone her skills.

The End

The Country Mouse
and the City Mouse

Once upon a time there was a city mouse that, having tired of the hustle and bustle of his neighborhood, took a trip to the country. Once there, he met a country mouse.

They spent the day together and became friends. The country mouse took his new friend into the lush meadows and vegetable gardens. The city mouse sampled all of the vegetables and found them to be very good. Never having seen the beauties of the country, the city mouse was thrilled. But the country mouse's plain food wasn't nearly as fine as his own usual meals of fine cheeses and hams found in the home where he lived.

To thank his friend for the lovely outing, he invited the country mouse to visit him in town. And when the country mouse saw the pantry at his friend's house—full of hams, cheese, oil, flour, honey, jam, and stacks of other delicious goodies—he stood speechless.

After he got over his surprise, he said, "I've never seen anything like it! Are all those wonderful things for eating?"

"Of course!" came the reply. "You're my guest. Dig in!"

So, the pair began to feast. The country mouse tried not to stuff himself, taking small samples of everything, as he wanted to taste each item before finding his tummy full.

"You're the luckiest mouse I've ever met!" said the country mouse. The city mouse was listening with delight to his friend's praise, when suddenly the sound of heavy footsteps interrupted their feast.

"Run for it!" whispered the town mouse to his friend. They were just in time; for within an inch of them was the ungainly foot of the lady of the house. Luckily, the lady went away, and the two mice returned to enjoy their feast.

"It's all right! Come on!" reassured the town mouse. "Don't worry, she's gone. Now let's have some honey! It's delicious! Have you ever tasted it?"

"Yes, once, a long time ago," the country mouse lied, trying to sound casual. But when he tasted it, he couldn't contain his enthusiasm: "Wow! It's scrumptious! By the king of mice, I've never eaten anything so remarkable in my life!"

Suddenly there came the sound of footsteps, this time thumping heavily. The two mice fled. The man of the house had come to get some bottles; and when he saw the spilt honey, he groaned, "Those rotten mice again! I thought I'd gotten rid of them. I'll send the cat!"

And trembling with fear, the mice hid. This time it was not only the sudden visit that had given them a fright; it was the man's terrifying words. The mice were so scared that they held their breath, making absolutely no sound. Then,

since all remained quiet, they began to feel braver and gathered enough courage to venture out. "We can come out now! There's nobody here!" the town mouse whispered.

Suddenly, the pantry door creaked, and the two luckless mice froze in fear. Out of the dim light glowed a pair of horrid, ghostly yellow eyes. But this was no ghost. It was a large cat. The country mouse and the town mouse tiptoed silently back to their hiding place. They wished their pounding hearts would stop beating, for fear the cat would hear the noise they made. But, as luck would have it, the cat discovered a juicy sausage. Forgetting why his master had sent him into the pantry, he stopped to eat it. No longer hungry after that, the cat decided that he might as well leave mouse hunting for another day.

Off he padded to have a nap. Now, as soon as the country mouse realized that all danger was past, he did not lose a second. He hastily shook hands with his friend, saying, "Thanks so much for everything! But I must rush off now! I can't stand all these shocks! I'd far rather sit down to a meal of a few crumbs in peace, than face a fancy feast, surrounded by danger."

⌒ The End ⌒

East of the Sun
and West of the Moon

*"East of the Sun and West of the Moon" is a Scandinavian fairy tale.
Many of the Scandinavian countries have fierce winters. The polar bear
in this tale is probably a symbol of this cold, windy season.*

Once upon a time there was a poor husband and wife who had many children. They were all beautiful, but the most beautiful of all was their youngest daughter.

One day the man heard a knock on the door so he went to answer it. When he opened the door, he found a great white bear.

"Will you give me your youngest daughter?" asked the white bear. "If you will, I'll make you rich."

The father asked his daughter, who at first said no. Eventually, though, when he told her many times how nice it would be to have wealth, she agreed to go with the bear.

So the white bear came to fetch her and he asked, "Are you afraid?"

"No," she said.

Off they went through the air, for the white bear could fly, until they came to a great mountain. The white bear knocked on it, and a door opened. They were inside a castle where there were many brilliantly lit rooms that shone with gold and jewels. The white bear gave the girl a silver bell. He told her that when she needed anything, she should ring it and what she desired would appear. She was sleepy after her journey and thought she would like to go to bed. She rang the bell, and instantly a bed appeared before her.

When she had tucked herself in and put out the light, a man came in and lay down beside her. It was the white bear. He could shed the form of the bear during the night. She never saw him, however, for he always came after she had turned out her light and went away before daylight appeared.

So all went well for a time, but then she began to be very sad because she missed her family. She told the bear why she was sad. He agreed that she could go visit her family if she promised never to talk with her mother alone.

Next day, the white bear took her to visit her family. Now, though, they lived in a grand home. As the white bear had promised, they had great wealth.

Her family was delighted to see her and they cried with joy. Everyone was grateful to her for all she had done for them.

One afternoon, her mother wanted to talk with her alone in her bedroom. But she remembered what the white bear had said and wouldn't go. But somehow or other her mother at last persuaded her, and she spilled the beans. She told how every night a man came and lay down beside her when the lights were all out. She also told how she never saw him, because he always went away before it grew light in the morning, and how she was sad because she missed her family.

Her mother listened. She then gave her a candle, so the girl could light it at night and see who crept into her bed. The girl took the candle and hid it in her pocket, and when evening came the white bear came to get her.

When they reached the white bear's home, she went right to bed. As it had happened before, a man came and lay down beside her. Late at night, when she could hear that he was sleeping, she got up and lit her candle. She saw the handsomest prince she had ever seen and fell in love with him. She leaned over to kiss him and accidentally dropped three spots of candle wax on his nightshirt.

This caused the white bear to wake up.

"What have you done?" he asked. "You have brought misery on both of us. If you had waited for just one year I would have been free. My stepmother bewitched me so that I am a white bear by day and a man by night. Now all is at an end between us. I must now go to her. She lives in a castle that lies east of the sun and west of the moon. There lives a princess with a nose that is monstrously long. Because you spied me with your candle, the enchantment won't be broken. Now I must marry the long-nosed princess."

She cried, but there was nothing she could do. The white bear had to go.

"Where is this castle? I will find you," she sobbed.

"You will never find it," he said. "It lies east of the sun and west of the moon, and you'd never find your way there."

When she awoke in the morning, both the prince and the castle were gone. She was lying on a small green patch in the midst of a dark, thick wood. By her side lay the same bundle of rotten rags that she had brought with her from her own home.

She set out on her way to find the prince. She walked until she came to a great mountain. Next to the mountain sat an old woman. In her hand she held a golden apple. The girl asked her if she knew the way to the castle that lay east of the sun and west of the moon.

"I really don't know how to get to the castle, but I'll lend you my horse. You can ride on it to an old woman who is a neighbor of mine. Perhaps she can tell you about him. When you get there, send the horse back to me, but you may take the golden apple with you."

So the girl rode for a long, long way. At last she came to the mountain, where an old woman was sitting outside with a gold **carding comb**. The girl asked her if she knew the way to the castle that lay east of the sun and west of the moon.

"I know nothing about it, but that it is east of the sun and west of the moon, and that you will be a long time in getting to it, if ever you get there at all. But you may borrow my horse and ride to an old woman who lives near me. Perhaps she may know where the castle is. When you get to her, send the horse back to me. You may keep the gold carding-comb, though."

So the girl rode a long way. After a time she came to a great mountain, where an old woman was sitting, spinning at a golden spinning wheel. This woman couldn't help the girl either, but she offered her the use of her horse.

"Ride to the East Wind, and ask him," the old woman said. "When you get to the East Wind, send my horse back to me. You can keep my gold spinning wheel, though."

The girl had to ride for a great many days before she got there. But at last she did arrive, and then she asked the East Wind if he could tell her the way to the prince. "Well," said the East Wind, "I have heard of the prince and of his castle, but I do not know the way to it, for I have never blown so far. If you like, I will go with you to my brother, the West Wind. He may know, for he is much stronger than I am. You may sit on my back, and then I can carry you there."

So she seated herself on his back and off they went! When they got there, the East Wind went in and said that the girl he had brought was looking for the prince at the castle that lay east of the sun and west of the moon.

"I don't know where the castle is," said the West Wind. "I've never blown that far. If you like I will go with you to the South Wind, for he is much stronger than either of us. He has roamed so far and wide that perhaps he can tell you what you want to know."

So they all journeyed to the South Wind. And they asked him if he knew the way to the castle that lay east of the sun and west of the moon, for she was the girl who ought to marry the prince who lived there.

"Well," he said, "I have wandered about a great deal in my time, and in all kinds of places, but I have never blown so far as that. If you like, however, I will go with you to my brother, the North Wind. He is the oldest and strongest. You may sit upon my back, and then I will carry you there."

Off they went to the North Wind's dwelling.

"What do you want?" he roared, and they froze as they heard his booming voice. Said the South Wind, "It is your brother, and this is she who should have married the prince who lives in the castle that lies east of the sun and west of the moon. And now she wishes to ask you if you have ever been there, and can tell her the way, for she would like to find him again."

"Yes," said the North Wind, "I know where it is. I once blew an aspen leaf there, but I was so tired that for many days afterward I was not able to blow at all. I will take you on my back, and try to see if I can blow you there."

"Okay," she said. "Let's go!"

"Very well then," said the North Wind.

They set out in the morning, and the North Wind blew and blew until he finally threw the girl onto the shore, immediately under the windows of a castle that lay east of the sun and west of the moon.

Next morning she sat down beneath the walls of the castle to play with the golden apple. The first person she saw was the maiden with the long nose, who was to marry the prince. "How much do you want for that golden apple of yours, girl?" she said.

"It can't be bought with money," answered the girl.

"If it cannot be bought with money, what will buy it?" asked the princess.

"Well, if I may go to the prince who is here, you shall have it," said the girl who had come with the North Wind.

"You may do that," said the princess. So the princess got the golden apple, but when the girl went up to the prince's apartment that night he was asleep, for the princess had put a spell on him. The poor girl called to him and shook him, but she could not wake him.

In the morning, in came the princess with the long nose and drove her out again. In the daytime she sat down once more beneath the windows of the castle and began to card with her golden carding comb. And all happened as it had happened before. The princess asked her what she wanted for it, and she replied that it was not for sale for money.

If, though, she could go to the prince and be with him during the night, the princess could have the carding comb. the princess agreed, but when the girl went up to the prince's room, he was again asleep. No matter what she did, the prince continued to sleep. When daylight came, the princess with the long nose came too, and once more drove her away.

Next day, the girl seated herself under the castle windows to spin with her golden spinning wheel, and the princess with the long nose wanted to have that also. They agreed to the same bargain.

This time, though, the prince was awake, because he didn't take the magic potion the long-nosed princess had given him.

"You have come just in time," said the prince when he saw the girl, "for I was to be married tomorrow. I will not have the long-nosed princess, but you alone can save me. I will say that I want to see what my bride can do, and I will ask her to wash the shirt that has the wax on it. She won't be able to do it because she is not really human. She is a **troll**."

The next day, the prince said, "I must see what my bride can do. I have a fine shirt that I want to wear as my wedding shirt, but three drops of wax have gotten on it, which I want to have washed off. I have vowed to marry only the woman who is able to do it. If she cannot do that, she is not worth having."

The princess with the long nose began to wash the shirt as well as she could, but the more she washed and rubbed, the larger the spots grew.

"Oh! You can't wash at all," said the old troll-hag, who was her mother. "Give it to me." But she had not had the shirt very long in her hands before it looked worse still. The more she washed it and rubbed it, the larger and blacker grew the spots.

So the other trolls had to come and wash, but the more they did, the blacker and uglier grew the shirt. Finally the shirt was as black as if it had been used to scrub a chimney.

"Oh," cried the prince, "not one of you is good for anything at all! There is a beggar-girl sitting outside the window. I'll bet that she can wash better than any of you! Come in, you girl there!" he cried. So she came in. "Can you wash this shirt clean?" he cried.

"Oh! I don't know," she said, "but I will try." And no sooner had she taken the shirt and dipped it in the water than it was white as snow.

"I will marry you," said the prince.

Then the old troll-hag flew into such a rage that she exploded. The princess with the long nose and all the little trolls must have burst too, for they have never been heard of again.

⇒ The End ⇐

The Fisherman and His Wife

Once upon a time a fisherman lived with his wife in a little **hovel** close by the sea. The fisherman used to go out all day fishing.

One day, he pulled a great fish out of the water. The fish said to him, "Please, let me live. I am not really a fish. I am actually an enchanted prince. Let me go."

"Oh!" said the man, "I have never seen a talking fish before. There must be something special about you. Go on your way now." He then put the fish back into the water, and the fish darted away.

When the fisherman got home to his wife, he told her how he had caught a great fish and how it had told him it was an enchanted prince, and that on hearing it speak he had let it go again.

"Did you ask it for anything?" said the wife.

"No," said the man, "what should I have asked for?"

"We live in a very wretched hut. Ask the fish for a little cottage."

The fisherman didn't want to ask the fish for a favor, but his wife insisted so off he went. He stood at the edge of the water, calling the great fish.

The fish came swimming to him and said, "What do you want?"

"My wife wants a little cottage."

"Go home, then," said the fish. "She is in the cottage already."

So the man went home and saw his wife standing at the door of a cottage. It was a lovely cottage with a living room and bedroom and a colorful garden.

Everything was okay for a week or two, and then the fisherman's wife insisted her husband ask the fish for a stone palace.

The fisherman went, but his heart was very heavy. He was content with their cozy cottage and felt greedy asking for more. When he came to the edge of the sea, it looked blue and gloomy, though it was quite calm. He called for the fish.

"Well, what is it now?" asked the fish.

"My wife wants to live in a stone castle."

"Go home then," said the fish. "She is standing at its door already."

So away went the fisherman. When he arrived home, he found his wife standing before a great castle. There were many servants and the rooms were all richly furnished and full of gilt chairs and tables.

The fisherman was quite content but, once again, his wife grew restless.

"I want to be king," she cried. "Go demand this of the fish."

The fisherman's heart was heavy as he trudged to the ocean to ask the fish. Reluctantly, he called for the great fish.

"What must she have now?" said the fish. The ocean look troubled.

"My wife wants to be king."

"Go home," said the fish. "She is king already."

Then the fisherman went home. As he came close to the palace, he saw a troop of soldiers and heard a trumpet fanfare. When he entered he saw his wife sitting on a high throne of gold and diamonds, with a golden crown upon her head. She was, indeed, a king.

Unfortunately, the wife's satisfaction at being king was short-lived.

"I think I should like to be emperor," she announced. "Go demand this from the fish."

The fisherman was obliged to go because the king, his wife, demanded that he do so. He muttered as he went along, "This will come to no good. It is too much to ask."

He soon arrived at the sea, and the water was quite black and murky, and a mighty whirlwind blew above it. But he went to the shore and called for the fish.

"What does she want now?" asked the fish.

"She wants to be emperor."

"Go home," said the fish. "She is emperor already."

So he went home again. As he came near, he saw his wife sitting on a very lofty throne made of solid gold, with a great crown on her head two yards high. On each side of her stood her guards and attendants in a row. Before her stood princes and dukes and earls. The fisherman went up to her and she was, indeed, emperor.

Yet, she became dissatisfied even more quickly this time.

"Husband," she said, "I will be the Pope next!"

So the fisherman went to ask the fish to make his wife the next Pope. When he came to the shore the wind was raging, and the sea was tossed up and down like boiling water. It looked as if a dreadful storm were rising. At this the fisherman was terribly frightened. He trembled, but he went to the shore and called for the great fish.

"What does she want now?" asked the fish.

"My wife wants to be the Pope."

"Go home," said the fish. "She is the Pope already."

Then the fisherman went home and found his wife sitting on a throne that was two miles high. She had three great crowns on her head, and around her stood all the pomp and power of the Church. She was truly the Pope.

Now, though, she wanted even more power.

"Husband, go to the fish and tell him I want to be lord of the sun and moon."

The fisherman was half asleep, but the thought frightened him so much, that he fell out of bed. As ordered, he went to ask the great fish for this favor. As he was going down to the shore, a dreadful storm arose, so that the trees and the rocks shook and the thunder rolled. The fisherman called the great fish.

"What does she want now?" said the fish.

"She wants to be lord of the sun and moon."

"Go home," said the fish, "and see your wife."

The fisherman went to his home and found his wife at the very same wretched hovel where they had spent so many years. And there they live to this very day, a little wiser, perhaps.

The End

The Golden Goose

Once upon a time in a land far away there was a woodcutter called Thaddeus, a dreamy, funny-looking kid with a big heart.

One day, his father sent him to a distant forest to chop down trees. Thaddeus saw that these trees were a kind he had never seen before and that it was hard work trying to hack through their thick trunks. Sweating after all his efforts, he had barely sat down to have a bite to eat, when a strange old man with a white beard popped out from behind a bush and asked him for some food.

Thaddeus was a generous type so he gave the old man some bread and cheese, and together they drank a flask of wine. "Of all the woodcutters that have tried to cut down these trees, you're the first one who has been nice to me," said the old man. "You deserve a reward. If you cut down that tree in the middle of the forest, you'll find that all the others will fall down by themselves. Have a look in its roots where there's a gift for you! You see, I'm the Wizard of the Woods."

Thaddeus did as he was told, and in a flash, his work was done. From under the roots of the tree the Wizard had pointed toward, the woodcutter found a golden goose. Slipping the bird under his arm, Thaddeus set off toward home.

Then, sad to say, Thaddeus lost his way. In the middle of the night, he reached a strange village. An inn was still open, so he went in. "Something to eat for myself and for this golden goose," he ordered the innkeeper's daughter. "That's a bite for me and a bite for you," he said, sharing his food with the goose.

The innkeeper's other two daughters came to stare at the strange sight, and then all three asked, "Why are you so kind to a goose?"

"This is a magic goose," replied Thaddeus, "and worth a lot. I shall stay the night here and I need a safe room, with a lock, for I don't want to be robbed."

However, during the night, one of the sisters was persuaded to steal at least one goose feather. "If it's a magic bird, then one of its feathers will be precious too!"

But the second her hand touched the goose's tail, it stuck fast, and nothing would unstick it. In a low voice, she called her sisters, but when they tried to pull her free, they too stuck fast. They tried everything, but couldn't get unstuck.

A little later, Thaddeus woke, not at all surprised to see the three sisters, who were rather ashamed at being discovered, stuck to the golden goose.

"How can we get free?" they wailed.

But the woodcutter coolly replied, "I have to leave with my goose. Too bad for you if you're stuck to her. You'll just have to come too!"

And when the innkeeper saw the strange little procession go past, he shouted, "What's going on?" and grabbed the last sister by the arm. It was the worst thing he could have done! For he too found himself attached to the tail of the little group.

The same fate awaited a nosy village woman, the plump minister, and the baker who had placed a hand on the minister's shoulder as he rushed past. Last of all came a guard who had tried to stop the procession. People laughed as they went by, and crowds gathered along the sides of the roads.

Close to the village where Thaddeus had spent the night stood the royal palace. Though rich and powerful, the king had a great sorrow:

His only daughter suffered from a strange illness that no doctor had been able to cure. She was always sad and unhappy. The king had once proclaimed that the man who succeeded in making his daughter laugh would be granted her hand in marriage. But so far, nobody had so much as brought a smile to the princess's lips.

As it happened, the princess chose that day to drive through the village square, just as the woodcutter with the goose under his arm solemnly marched by with his line of unwilling followers. When she heard the people chuckle, the princess raised the carriage curtains. The minute she set eyes on the amazing sight, she burst into peals of laughter. Everyone was amazed to hear the princess laugh for the first time. She stepped down from the carriage for a closer look at the golden goose and got stuck to the baker.

Laughing and chattering, the procession headed toward the palace, with the crowds at their heels. When the king saw his daughter, he could hardly believe it. "How amazing!" he said. But in spite of all the merriment, it was a serious situation. How would they all get unstuck from this goose?

Suddenly, a large man with a tall peaked hat and a white beard stepped forward and snapped his fingers three times. Then, Thaddeus and the others became unstuck. The woodcutter was about to thank the Wizard of the Woods, but he had already vanished into thin air.

And that's how the simple woodcutter, Thaddeus, married a princess and lived happily every after.

≈ *The End* ≈

The Greedy Dog

Once upon a time in a tiny village there was a rather greedy dog that would go to great lengths to get good food. This greedy dog was a bulldog, with a flat nose, broad paws, and big, floppy jowls. All of the other village dogs and cats rather dreaded the bulldog's presence because of his dreadful, greedy manner, which intimidated them all.

One day, a small schnauzer had managed to procure a juicy bone from the local butcher. The butcher had given it to the small dog, because the dog often helped watch his shop at night. The schnauzer had retreated to a quiet village alley to gnaw the bone when the big bulldog suddenly loomed over him.

"Give me that bone, little Schnauzer," growled the greedy bulldog.

"No, I won't. You can ask the butcher for your own bone. I earned this one fair and square," insisted the schnauzer.

As you might have guessed, the small schnauzer was no match for this greedy bulldog. Having asked and been denied, the greedy dog simply reached over with his big, drool-filled mouth, and snatched up that bone. Before you could say, "Jack Spratt could eat no fat," that rotten dog had eaten every last bit of the juicy bone and left the schnauzer feeling sad, hungry, and mad.

Soon after, a rather puffy and fancily attired poodle went to visit the village baker. This baker rather admired the poodle's fluffy black shape and the colorful ribbons she always wore tied in bows on her topknot and tail. He also liked her friendly, frisky manner. So, when the poodle asked politely if there might be a few crumbs left over from the day's baking, the baker readily agreed to share a few of these samples with her.

The kindly baker filled a small pink bowl with the crumbs and set it outside the bakery door for the poodle to enjoy. Just then, who should appear but the greedy dog. He seemed to have a sixth sense, knowing when extra special tidbits were about to be served!

"Move aside, silly Poodle," grumbled the bulldog. "I want those crumbs and I want them now."

Well, the poodle certainly did not want to share her crumbs with a dog as greedy as this one and she also didn't take kindly to being called "silly."

"No," she snapped back. "You ask the baker for your own samples. These belong to me!"

Having asked and been denied, the big bulldog shouldered the little poodle aside and with one wet bulldog bite, he finished those sweet crumbs. Licking his chops happily, he sauntered away with his bowlegged gait. The poodle was left with nothing, feeling forlorn and angry.

Not long after that, a peppy corgi visited the town market and asked the fruit vendor for a piece of overripe fruit that was not suitable for selling. This vendor had a soft spot for the red dog and chose a handful of grapes (that really were suitable for selling) to set down in front of the corgi, just outside the market entrance. As she prepared to eat the first juicy grape, who should loom in front of her but that greedy bulldog!

"Put down those grapes," he growled. "They are meant for me. A little dog like you has no need for such morsels. I need the grapes to maintain my grand figure!"

"No," barked the corgi fiercely. Though smaller than the bulldog, she was not intimidated. "I asked the vendor for the grapes. If you'd like some too, go ask for them."

Having asked and been denied, the bulldog leaned over with his big head and ate the bunch of grapes—stems and all—in one crunchy bite.

Then the bulldog wandered off, satisfied with his fruity snack. The corgi, left behind, felt wistful at the memory of the missed grapes and a little angry.

As you can imagine, the village dogs were getting quite upset about this greedy dog. They decided to hold a meeting and decide how to deal with the ever-growing problem.

They met that night by the butcher's shop, hoping to find a stray morsel about. Dogs of every shape and size streamed in from all parts of the village to discuss the situation and to devise a plan to cure the greedy dog of his avarice.

After much plotting and planning, a decision was made and roles were assigned to various dogs. They implemented the plan the very next day.

The greedy dog was sitting by the village fountain, wondering where he would find his next snack, when the schnauzer happened by.

"Hey, Bulldog," barked the schnauzer. "I have a tip for you, if you're interested in having a fat, juicy steak. The butcher is not in the shop right now. He's home having lunch with his wife. The shop door is open, and sitting on the counter is a steak as big as your head! If you hurry, you can run into the shop and make off with the steak before the butcher returns."

The bulldog thanked the dog, although he was a bit mystified as to why this dog, who didn't like him, should give him such a valuable tip. "Oh, well," thought the bulldog. "No need to think about it too long or I'll be too late to get the steak!"

So, he trotted off from the fountain to the butcher's shop and greedily snatched up that steak. Just as the schnauzer had predicted, the butcher was out of the shop and the door had been left open.

The bulldog was just setting out for the woods to eat it (for he didn't want the butcher to catch him with it), when the corgi wandered by with another tip.

"Hey, Bulldog," said the corgi, "listen up! I know where you can get another steak just as thick and juicy as the one you're holding in your mouth. You'd better hurry, though, and not eat that one yet or you won't be in time to get another one."

Although the bulldog really wanted to eat the juicy steak that instant, he also wanted another steak just as fine, so he agreed to listen to the corgi's plan.

"Go over by that stream, just over the hill. When you get there, look into the water and there you'll see a dog holding a steak, thick and perfect just as the one in your mouth."

Hardly able to believe his good fortune, the bulldog loped over the hill to the edge of the babbling stream.

And, as the corgi had told him, there truly was another dog holding a thick steak.

"Oh my," thought the bulldog. "I must have that steak, too!"

Well, as you may have guessed this greedy bulldog was none too clever. He didn't realize that he was looking at a reflection of himself in the water. What he thought he saw was another dog, holding a large steak in its mouth.

Being a greedy and rather silly dog, he quickly jumped into the rushing stream to snatch the other dog's meat. Of course, the reflection vanished at that instant and he could see no sign of dog or steak.

Only then did he realize that when he had barked to frighten the other dog into dropping his steak, he had dropped his stolen meat.

Unluckily for him, the stream's current was swift and the steak had been carried away in the churning water. The bulldog was determined to find the steak so he jumped headfirst into the stream, sniffing and snorting, hoping to find a trace of the lost meat. He paddled in the stream for a very long time before finally giving up, and sadly returned to the stream's bank.

So, this greedy dog went from having one juicy steak to having none at all. And as the other village dogs had hoped, this episode did indeed teach the greedy dog a thing or two.

From that day forward, he worked hard to be kinder to the other dogs and better about sharing. Although these traits didn't come naturally to the big dog, he tried his best, and that turned out to be good enough!

 The End

Henny-penny

Once upon a time a rather gullible little chicken named Henny-penny was picking up corn in the farmyard when—whack!—something hit her on the head.

"Good grief," said Henny-penny. "I think the sky is going to fall. I must go and tell the king."

So off she went and along the way she met Cocky-locky. "Where are you going, Henny-penny?" asked Cocky-locky.

"I'm going to tell the king the sky's falling," said Henny-penny.

"May I come with you?" asked Cocky-locky.

"Certainly," said Henny-penny. So Henny-penny and Cocky-locky went to tell the king the sky is falling.

They went along for quite some time till they met Ducky-daddles. "Where are you going, Henny-penny and Cocky-locky?" asked Ducky-daddles.

"We're going to tell the king the sky's falling," said Henny-penny and Cocky-locky.

"May I come with you?" asked Ducky-daddles.

"Certainly," said Henny-penny and Cocky-locky. So Henny-penny, Cocky-locky, and Ducky-daddles went to tell the king the sky is falling.

They went along for what seemed a long, long time till they met Goosey-poosey.

"Where are you going to, Henny-penny, Cocky-locky, and Ducky-daddles?" asked Goosey-poosey.

"Oh! We're going to tell the king the sky's falling," said Henny-penny and Cocky-locky and Ducky-daddles.

"May I come with you?" asked Goosey-poosey.

"Certainly," said Henny-penny, Cocky-locky, and Ducky-daddles. So Henny-penny, Cocky-locky, Ducky-daddles, and Goosey-poosey went to tell the king the sky is falling.

So they went along, and they went along, till they met Turkey-lurkey.

"Where are you going, Henny-penny, Cocky-locky, Ducky-daddles, and Goosey-poosey?" asked Turkey-lurkey.

"Oh! We're going to tell the king the sky's falling," said Henny-penny, Cocky-locky, Ducky-daddles, and Goosey-poosey.

"May I come with you, Henny-penny, Cocky-locky, Ducky-daddles, and Goosey-poosey?" asked Turkey-lurkey.

"Oh, certainly, Turkey-lurkey," said Henny-penny, Cocky-locky, Ducky-daddles, and Goosey-poosey. So Henny-penny, Cocky-locky, Ducky-daddles, Goosey-poosey, and Turkey-lurkey all went to tell the king the sky is falling.

They went along a great distance till they met Foxy-woxy.

Foxy-woxy said to Henny-penny, Cocky-locky, Ducky-daddles, Goosey-poosey, and Turkey-lurkey, "Where are you going, Henny-penny, Cocky-locky, Ducky-daddles, Goosey-poosey, and Turkey-lurkey?"

And Henny-penny, Cocky-locky, Ducky-daddles, Goosey-poosey, and Turkey-lurkey said to Foxy-woxy, "We're going to tell the king the sky's falling."

"Oh! But this is not the way to the king," said Foxy-woxy. "I know the proper way. Shall I show you?"

"Certainly, Foxy-woxy," said Henny-penny, Cocky-locky, Ducky-daddles, Goosey-poosey, and Turkey-lurkey.

So they went along, and they went along, and they went along, till they came to a narrow, dark hole. Now this was the door of Foxy-woxy's cave.

But Foxy-woxy said to Henny-penny, Cocky-locky, Ducky-daddles, Goosey-poosey, and Turkey-lurkey, "This is a shortcut to the king's palace. You'll soon get there if you follow me. I will go first and you come after, Henny-penny, Cocky-locky, Ducky-daddles, Goosey-poosey, and Turkey-lurkey."

"Why, of course, certainly. Why not?" said Henny-penny, Cocky-locky, Ducky-daddles, Goosey-poosey, and Turkey-lurkey.

So Foxy-woxy went into his cave. He didn't go very far but turned round to wait for Henny-penny, Cocky-locky, Ducky-daddles, Goosey-poosey, and Turkey-lurkey. First Turkey-lurkey went through the dark hole into the cave. He hadn't gone far when Foxy-woxy snapped off Turkey-lurkey's head and threw his body over his left shoulder. Then Goosey-poosey went in and off went her head and Goosey-poosey was thrown beside Turkey-lurkey. Then Ducky-daddles waddled down and Foxy-woxy snapped, and Ducky-daddles's head was off and Ducky-daddles was thrown alongside Goosey-poosey. Then Cocky-locky strutted down into the cave, and he hadn't gone far when snap went Foxy-woxy, and Cocky-locky crowed, and Foxy-woxy snapped again, and Cocky-locky was thrown alongside Ducky-daddles.

But when Henny-penny heard Cocky-locky cry out, she turned and ran home, so she never told the king the sky was falling.

⌇ The End ⌇

The Lion and the Mosquito

Once upon a time there lived a tiny and particularly pesky mosquito. Although, of course, all mosquitoes are noted for being nuisances, this one was even worse than the others. Every day, he chose a different animal to bother. One day, he decided to torment a bird in the jungle. He whizzed relentlessly around the colorful, feathered fellow.

"Who is bothering me?" squawked the bird. He could hear the whirring but was unable to see the mosquito since the pesky creature was buzzing around so quickly.

"It's me, a little mosquito. Small but mighty, I say!"

The mosquito continued whirring and whizzing and being a nuisance. Finally, he bit the poor feathered creature and flew off laughing at his own bothersome behavior.

The next day, the mosquito decided to pick on a particularly graceful gazelle.

"BUZZZZZZZZZZZ!" went the mosquito.

The gazelle tried to lope away but had no luck. The pesky mosquito continued to buzz after him.

"Who is this bothering me?" asked the troubled gazelle.

"It is none other than a tiny mosquito. Surely, you thought a creature as small as I am could never bother you, but you were wrong!" said the mosquito, as he continued to buzz and whir around the beleaguered gazelle.

Finally, the mosquito made one final passing buzz at the gazelle, bit him on the nose, and flew away quickly, smiling because he'd been such a bother.

The next day, pleased with his success, the mosquito decided to taunt an even larger target: a hippopotamus. So, off he went whirring and buzzing over muddy ponds where hippos were wading. Finally, he eyed his target: an impressively large, rather fierce-looking hippo.

"*ZOOOM,*" buzzed the mosquito by the hippo's ear. "*BUZZZZZ.*"

The hippo, though, was really a gentle sort and wondered mildly what could possibly be bothering him. Not one to stir up trouble, the hippo tried to ignore the constant buzzing and whizzing, but finally he'd had enough.

"Who is that bothering me?" he called out.

In answer, that rude mosquito buzzed yet again.

Well, this was almost more than the gentle hippo could stand.

"*WHO IS THAT?*" he bellowed.

"Why, it is just a small mosquito," answered the pesky creature. "I couldn't be bothering a hulky fellow like you, could I?"

"As a matter of fact, you are," answered the hippo, "and I'd appreciate it if you'd just leave me alone."

"I'll leave you alone after I bite you on the snout!" And that's just what the mosquito did. He then flew off, gleeful at his success.

The mosquito then decided that there was really only one animal left in the jungle to conquer: the king of them all, the lion.

So, as before, the bothersome pest started to buzz around the jungle, looking for a lion to annoy. He spotted several before he found the perfect target: a particularly grand-looking lion with a massive mane and an impressive roar.

Down buzzed the mosquito, whirring around the lion's face.

Finally, the lion, who had been sleeping, grumbled, "Go away! Who is bothering me, anyway?"

"Well, well, King of the Jungle," laughed the mosquito. "It is just a lowly mosquito. Surely I am not bothering you!"

"Yes, you are. Now go away before I do something to you," roared the lion.

The mosquito, though, paid no attention to the lion's words and continued to buzz around the lion's great head.

Finally, the lion grew tired of this insect. He used his giant, powerful paw to smack his own cheek in an attempt to drive the pesky insect away.

"I mean it," roared the lion, his cheek smarting from the blow he'd given himself. "You leave me alone *NOW!*"

"Why should I?" demanded the pesky mosquito. "You're king of the jungle, not of the air! I'll fly wherever I want and land wherever I please. So there." And with this, he boldly tickled the lion's ear.

This made the lion very angry and in the hope of crushing the tiny insect, the lion pawed at his own ears, but the mosquito was quick and sly and he slipped away from the dazed and irritated lion.

"Finally, it's gone," thought the lion. "I don't feel it any more, thank goodness. Either it is squashed or it has gone away."

But the lion spoke too soon, for at that very moment, the irritating *buzz, buzz, buzz* began again, and the mosquito flew brazenly right into the lion's nose. Now, wild with rage, the lion leaped to his hind legs and started to throw punches at his own nose. But the pesky insect, safe inside the lion's nose, refused to budge.

This went on for some time until the lion had a swollen nose and watery eyes. The mosquito buzzed around a bit in the lion's nose, causing the king of the jungle to give a terrific sneeze, blowing the mosquito right out. Angry at being dislodged so abruptly, the mosquito returned to the attack: *BUZZ . . . BUZZZ!* It whizzed around the lion's head yet again.

Although the lion was large and tough, he could not get rid of this tiny troublemaker. The more he thought about this, the angrier he became. The lion roared fiercely.

At the sound of his terrible, frightening voice, all of the forest creatures fled quickly in fear. But the mosquito paid no attention to the exhausted lion. Instead, the mosquito said triumphantly, "There you are, King of the Jungle! Beaten by a lowly, tiny mosquito like me!"

And highly delighted with his victory, off he buzzed for a victory flight.

"So," gloated the mosquito as he buzzed high above the lush jungle, "I am mightier than all of the jungle animals. I even beat the king of the jungle!"

But, while the mosquito was so busy gloating, he did not notice a spider web hanging close by, and became stuck in it. Once stuck, the pesky insect began turning and twisting, trying to escape from the trap set by a large spider.

"Oh," he thought, "how could this happen to me? I've just beaten the king of the jungle and now I am captured by one of the jungle's smallest creatures, a simple spider!"

To be fair, the spider didn't think much of the mosquito either and was rather unimpressed to find it stuck in his web.

"Yuck!" said the spider in disgust, as he ate it up. "Another tiny mosquito. Not much to get excited about, but better than nothing, I guess. I was hoping for something better and a little more filling."

And, so, the gloating of the mosquito turned out to be a bit premature. For he may have beaten the lion, but that really didn't get him very far, did it?

⌒ *The End* ⌒

The Little Golden Bird

The monks in "The Little Golden Bird" are followers of Buddhism, which originated in India 2,500 years ago. It follows the teachings of Buddha, who lived from 563 to 483 B.C. Monks are men who live apart from the world for religious reasons.

Once upon a time several Buddhist monks lived in a great temple. The temple was a quiet place that stood in the middle of a magnificent garden. The monks carefully and lovingly tended the garden, and it was filled with splendid flowers and rare plants. There were flowers blooming in every shade of the rainbow, and the monks tended them with such care that, it was said, their blossoms were more beautiful than those of similar flowers elsewhere. People traveled from distant lands to see these beautiful gardens.

The monks spent their days contentedly praying and meditating. This is how life had been at the temple for hundreds of years. Surrounded by the incredible beauty of their gardens, the monks never thought about life outside of the temple walls. They felt truly and completely content with their cloistered lives.

One day, though, something happened to change their life in this peaceful, thoughtful corner of the world.

That day, they heard a knock at the temple door. One of the monks went to answer the knock and found a young
monk standing there.

"Hello," said the temple monk. "May I help you with something?"

"I have been traveling and am looking for a place to spend the night and perhaps partake in a bit of food. Would I be able to stay here?"

"But, of course," said the temple monk, for they were kind and generous and willing to share whatever they had.

And so, the traveling monk came into the temple and sat down to share their evening meal.

"How many of you have traveled outside the walls of the temple?" he asked.

At first there was silence, and then the monks admitted that none of them had traveled outside the temple since they'd arrived there many, many years earlier.

"Well," continued the traveling monk, "you'd be amazed at what is happening in the world outside the temple walls. It's hard to describe, but I'll try."

And so, the traveling monk began to tell them of life in the outside world. He went on for some time, long after the monks had finished their evening meal, and even long after the time that most of them would have retired to their chambers.

He regaled them with stories of his travels—tales of bustling and brightly lit cities, of theater and of musical performances, of traveling fairs and exotic foods. He told them about parties and grand gatherings. He told them about the amazing people he had met on his travels, people who had occupations so varied the monks could hardly believe that such jobs existed. On and on, the traveling monk went, spinning his tales to a silent, spellbound audience.

Finally, when it was closer to day than to night, the monks retired to their chambers, their heads filled with amazing visions of the world outside the temple walls.

And when they awoke in the morning, they found that the traveling monk had already departed. The stories he had told, however, remained in their minds. He'd planted a dangerous seed in their minds, and the monks were no longer quite so content or at ease in their cloistered world.

They began to argue.

First, they disagreed about who was to tend to the garden.

"It is not my turn to do the weeding," said one of the monks to another. For he was no longer so interested in the splendid gardens since he had heard about the outside world.

Then, they disagreed about who should prepare their simple meals. Nobody wanted to put together these basic dishes since they'd heard about the exotic foods available outside the temple walls.

Far from feeling content, the monks began to feel as if they were trapped in some sort of prison.

Now that the monks heard about this different, outside world, they no longer wanted to remain in what had, until then, seemed a paradise. Now, their temple life had turned into a lonely, isolated existence.

Finally, one group decided to leave the temple. Not long after, another group packed their meager belongings and set out to explore the outside world. Then another group left, and yet another.

Soon, weeds overtook the garden. Grass started to sprout up between the stones of the sidewalk and very few monks remained in the temple, leaving it almost deserted. There were only five monks left, trying without success to maintain the gardens and building.

Finally, these last five monks, torn between their love for the sacred spot they tended so well and their wish to see the new world they'd heard about, sadly and reluctantly got ready to leave.

As they prepared to close the temple gate behind them, a beautiful golden bird flew overhead. The bird was dangling five long white strings, which fluttered over their heads. Although later they couldn't explain why, each monk felt himself drawn to clasp one of the strings.

Once they'd grasped the strings, the golden bird took the group of monks to the land of their dreams, the place the traveling monk had described so vividly.

The golden bird took the monks to cities and villages, to the tops of mountains and deep into the valleys. The bird took them into homes and through the streets. And what did the monks see?

They found that the land of their dreams wasn't quite as they'd imagined. Instead of happiness and contentment, they saw the outside world as it really was. Yes, there were bright spots, but there was also plenty of hate, misery, and violence. On their tour with the golden bird, they saw a world without scruples, where, they feared, peace was never to be found.

It was a long journey, and when the golden bird brought them back to the temple garden, they were quite exhausted by all that they'd seen. They knew now, though, that they would never leave their temple again.

Three times the bird circled overhead before it vanished into the sky. And the monks knew then that Buddha had come to help them find the pathway to true happiness.

⌒ *The End* ⌒

The Magic Tinderbox

In the hundreds of years since this fairy tale was written, the meaning of the word tinderbox has changed. In the time of the soldier in "The Magic Tinderbox," the word tinderbox referred to a metal box that was used to hold flint. Flint is a material that produces sparks when struck by a piece of metal and was used for starting fires. Today, the word tinderbox refers to any highly flammable object or building. Maybe you've heard someone say something like, "That deserted building is a tinderbox." This means that it would burn easily.

Once upon a time a brave soldier was returning from war. His only possession was his sword. As he walked through a forest on his way home, he ran into a witch, who said to him: "Hello, good soldier, would you like to earn a bag of money?"

"Money? Yes, I'd do anything for money."

"Great!" said the witch. "It won't be hard! All you have to do is go down that hollow tree till you reach a cave. There, you'll find three doors. When you open the first door, you'll see a big dog with eyes like plates, guarding a large chest of copper coins. Behind the second door is a treasure of silver coins, guarded by a dog with eyes the size of **millstones**. When you open the third door, you'll come upon another dog, with eyes the size of a castle tower, beside a treasure of gold. Now, if you lay this old apron of mine before these dogs, they'll crouch on it and won't hurt you. You'll be able to carry away all the coins you want. What do you think of that?"

The soldier asked, "What do you want in return?"

"Just bring me back an old tinderbox my grandfather left down there, long ago."

So the young soldier tied a rope around his waist and he lowered himself into the hollow tree. To his surprise, he found the three doorways and the three dogs, just as the witch had said. Soon he was back, his pockets bulging with coins, but before he handed the tinderbox to the old witch, he asked her, "What do you want it for?"

The witch threw herself at the soldier, screaming, "Give it to me!"

When the witch attacked him, the soldier exclaimed, "So this is the thanks I get! I'll show you!" He undid the rope from around his waist and tied up the old woman. Then off he went. When he reached the town, he said to himself, "Now I can eat at as many restaurants as I like!" After years of getting by on little pay, with his sudden wealth the soldier felt almost like a prince. He bought a new pair of boots and he went to the best tailor in town, ordering up lots of fancy new clothes.

The soldier was quick to spend his newfound wealth, and the money soon ran out. When the innkeeper discovered that the soldier could no longer pay his bill, he kicked him out. So the poor soldier ended up in an attic of a deserted building.

One evening, he realized he had never used the old witch's tinderbox. So he rubbed it, and as it sparked, the dog with the eyes like saucers suddenly appeared. "Tell me your wish," it said.

"Bring me loads of money!" said the soldier. A second later, the dog was back with a bag of coins. Every time he rubbed the tinderbox, the dog brought him more money. Then when he rubbed it quickly twice in a row, the dog with eyes like millstones stood before him, carrying silver coins. And when the soldier rubbed the tinderbox three times in a row, the third dog came carrying gold.

Rich once again, the soldier chose the best hotel in town and went back to living the high life. One day, the soldier was told that the king would not allow anyone to meet his gorgeous daughter, for he believed in a saying that the Princess's **fate** was to marry a simple soldier.

That evening, the soldier rubbed the tinderbox. "Bring me the princess," was his new wish. Immediately the dog returned with the beautiful princess, fast asleep. The soldier kissed her. Next morning, the girl told her parents that she had had a dream that she was kissed by a soldier. The queen became suspicious, and ordered one of the ladies-in-waiting to guard her daughter every minute. The dog was seen when it came the next evening and the alarm sounded. The king's guards followed the dog, and the soldier was arrested and put in the dungeon.

When the king asked the prisoner to appear before him and present his case, the soldier brought the tinderbox. He rubbed it and the three dogs appeared. Amazed at this, the king agreed that the soldier and his daughter should marry. They lived happily every after, occasionally using the tinderbox to charm the people of the kingdom.

The End

The Magpie's Nest

*O*nce upon a time—a very long time ago—birds all made nests that looked just the same. This really wasn't very effective, because different birds had different housing needs. Big birds needed sturdier nests that wouldn't collapse under their weight. Delicate birds needed softer nests that would soothe their bodies. Birds living in regions without twigs, such as desert dwellers, needed a type of nest that could be made without sticks and branches. Birds living in the rain forest needed nests that would withstand the heavy rain that came during the rainy season.

The birds were all very unhappy about this state of affairs.

"I don't know," squawked the robin. "It's not very good for all of us, if we're not able to learn how to build better nests."

"I agree," chirped a chickadee, "but what are we to do about it?"

The birds chirped and chattered for some time, trying to come up with a solution to their nest-building dilemma.

Finally, a wise old blue jay spoke, "I have heard of a bird that is wise in the ways of building nests. It is the **magpie**. Perhaps we could convince this knowledgeable feathered friend to teach us to build better nests."

So the call was put out to the magpie. First one bird told another, and then another, and then yet another, until the news had been broadcast to the entire bird kingdom. So it came to be that the magpie heard she was needed.

The magpie was not surprised to find she was being called to help teach the other birds. After all, she thought,

"I am known throughout the bird world to be the cleverest of all at building sturdy nests. These birds could most certainly learn a thing or two from me."

She called a conference of all of the birds, and soon, one after another, birds of every shape and description flew down into the field that had been designated by the magpie as the meeting place. There were small birds and large, colorful and drab. All were excited to learn how to build a better nest.

The magpie called the birds to gather around her, and then she began to teach them the art of nest building.

The first bird to ask for instruction was a thrush. This thrush wasn't much to look at, with his plain plumage, but he had an extremely beautiful song, which he sang to the magpie.

"Oh, please, dear Magpie," he sang, "teach me how to build a beautiful nest!"

"But, of course, little Thrush," answered the magpie.

The magpie began by taking some mud. Deftly using her little clawed feet, she made a sort of round cake with it.

"That," said the magpie, "is all there is to building a sturdy thrush nest with materials that are readily available to you!"

"Oh, that's how it's done. Thank you so much," said the thrush and away he flew. And to this day, that is how thrushes build their nests.

Next, a blackbird spoke up from the back of the bird conference. "Oh, hello there, dear Magpie. I really haven't had success with building a nest for my family. Can you be of some assistance?"

"Absolutely," answered the magpie.

And, with that, the clever magpie took a variety of twigs and arranged them with a bit of mud, which served to sort of glue them together.

"There you have it, dear Blackbird," said the magpie. "Now, you can build a home for your family."

"Now I know all about it and my family will be very pleased, too. Thank you," said the blackbird, and off he flew. And that is how the blackbirds make their nests to this very day.

Next the hoot of an owl was heard. Now, owls are usually only heard from at night, but this poor creature was so desperate to make a good nest that he'd ventured out during the day.

"Hoot, dear Magpie," said the owl. "I would be so grateful if you could teach me the trick of building a good owl's nest."

"But of course, Owl," said magpie.

Then the magpie began to show the owl, taking the nest of the blackbird and putting yet another layer of mud over the twigs.

"There you have it, Owl. That's all there is to it," said the magpie cheerfully.

"Oh, I should have thought of that," said the wise, old owl, a bit annoyed with himself since he was, after all, reputed to be so wise. "Thank you for your kindness," and away the owl flew. And owls have never made better nests since that day.

Next to chirp out from the bird crowd was a rather common-looking sparrow.

"Hello, Magpie," he said a bit shyly. "Do you suppose you might have the time to help me learn to build a good sparrow nest?"

"Absolutely," said the magpie. "You don't need to be shy!"

And the magpie began to show the sparrow, taking the owl's nest and adding some additional twigs, which he twisted around the outside.

"There you have it, shy creature," said the magpie. "Here is an ideal sparrow's nest."

"Perfect! Thank you so much, Magpie," said the sparrow, and off he went. This was, in fact, a rather messy nest and sparrows make rather sloppy nests to this day.

Next to ask for help was a starling, a dark-colored bird with a short tail and a sharp beak.

"I've never been able to build a nest that held up to the elements," he complained. "Could you teach me to build a better nest."

"I know all about starlings' nests," said the magpie, puffing her chest out proudly, for she really was quite clever about nest building.

The magpie began showing the starling by taking some feathers and animal fur and lining the nest very thoroughly with these soft materials.

"There you have it, dear Starling," said the magpie. "Sturdy *and* comfortable!"

"That's great. My family will love it. Thank you," cried the starling, and off he flew; and to this day starlings have very comfortable, plush—and sturdy—nests.

So, on and on the lessons went for most of the day. Every bird, after his lesson with the magpie, took away some knowledge about how to build nests, but none of them stayed to the end of the conference to hear all of the nest-building information.

Meanwhile, the seemingly tireless magpie went on working and working and teaching and teaching without looking up until the only bird that remained was the turtledove, a bird known for his unique cooing. It was no surprise, then, that this particular turtledove had not paid any attention to the day's lessons.

Instead, while the magpie worked and taught, the turtledove just kept on crying, "Take two, Tally, take two-o-o-o."

The magpie had been too absorbed in work to pay any attention to the cooing, but at last she heard this cry just as she was putting one twig across a nest.

"No," said the magpie," "One twig is enough, Turtledove."

But the turtledove wasn't really listening to the magpie. He kept saying, "Take two, Tally, take two-o-o-o."

Finally, the magpie got angry and said, "I told you. One twig is enough!"

Still the turtledove persisted and cried: "Take two, Tally, take two-o-o-o." The turtledove really meant nothing by his cry. It was just the song he often sang, but the magpie thought the turtledove was trying to tell her how to build nests. And the magpie didn't like this, because after all, she was the nest-building expert, not the turtledove.

"Take two, Tally, take two-o-o-o. Take two, Tally, take two-o-o-o." The turtledove continued with his song.

At last, the frustrated magpie looked up and saw nobody near her but the silly turtledove. Angered that the turtledove was being bossy, the magpie flew away and refused to tell the birds how to build nests ever again.

So, the lessons learned that day still dictate how birds build their nests today. And that is why different birds build their nests differently.

The End

The Metal Pig

In the Italian city of Florence stands a pig made of brass and curiously formed. The bright color has been changed by age to dark green; but clear, fresh water pours from the snout, which shimmers as if it had been polished. So indeed it has, for hundreds of poor people and children seize it in their hands as they place their mouths close to the mouth of the animal to drink.

It was a late winter evening. In the garden of the grand duke's palace, a little ragged boy had been sitting the whole day. He was hungry and thirsty, yet no one gave him anything. When it became dark, the porter turned him out. He stood a long time and then walked away toward the metal pig, clasped it with his arms, and then put his mouth to the shining snout and drank deep drafts of the fresh water. Close by were a few salad leaves and a crust of bread, which were to be his supper. No one was in the street, so he boldly seated himself on the pig's back and fell asleep.

It was midnight when the metal pig raised himself gently, and the boy heard him say quite distinctly, "Hold tight, little boy, for I am going to run." Away he started for a most fantastic ride. He took the boy through the city of Florence, by wondrous buildings and through magnificent museums filled with breathtaking artwork.

When the ride ended, the little boy said, "Thank you, thank you, you beautiful animal," caressing the metal pig as it ran down the steps.

"Thanks to you, too," replied the metal pig. "I have helped you and you have helped me, for it is only when I have an innocent child on my back that I receive the power to run. Don't get down yet or I will lose that power."

"I will stay with you, my dear pig," said the little boy. So then they went on at a rapid pace through the streets of Florence until they came to the square before the church of *Santa Croce*. The doors flew open, and light streamed from the altar through the church into the deserted square.

The boy stretched his hands toward the light, and at the same moment the metal pig started again so rapidly that he was obliged to cling tightly to him. The wind whistled in his ears. He heard the church door creak on its hinges as it closed, and it seemed to him as if he had lost his senses—then a cold shudder passed over him—and he awoke.

It was morning. The metal pig stood in its old place on the *Porta Rosa,* and the boy found he had slipped nearly off its back. Fear came upon him as he thought of his mother. She had sent him out the day before to get some money, and he had not done so. Now he was hungry and thirsty. Once more he clasped the neck of his metal pig, kissed its nose, and nodded farewell to it. Then he wandered away into one of the narrowest streets, where there was scarcely room for a loaded donkey to pass. A great ironbound door stood ajar. He passed through it and climbed up a brick staircase with dirty walls. A woman with an unpleasant face saw him and asked, "What have you brought home?"

"Don't be angry," he pleaded. "I have nothing at all."

"Certainly you must have some money," she said. The boy began to cry, and then she struck him with her foot till he cried out louder.

"Will you be quiet?" and she swung the pot that she held in her hand, while the boy rushed back out into the city. The poor child ran until he was quite out of breath. At last he stopped at a church and went in. He crept into a corner behind the marble monuments and went to sleep. Toward evening he was awakened by a pull at his sleeve. He started up, and an old man stood before him.

"Are you ill? Where do you live? Have you been here all day?" asked the old man. After hearing the boy's answers, the old man took him home to a small house close by, in a back street. They entered a glove maker's shop, where a woman sat sewing busily. These good people gave the child food and drink and said he should stay with them all night. And the next day the old man, who was called Giuseppe, would go and speak to his mother.

Indeed, Giuseppe went out the next morning. The poor child was not glad to see him go, for he knew that the old man had gone to his mother, and that, perhaps, he would have to go back. He wept at the thought. And what news did Giuseppe bring back? At first the boy could not hear, for he talked a great deal to his wife, and she nodded and stroked the boy's cheek.

Then she said, "He is a good boy, he shall stay with us." So the boy stayed with them and the woman herself taught him to sew. He ate well and slept well and became quite happy. But he began to tease their little poodle dog Bellissima, as the dog was called. This made the woman angry, and she scolded him.

That night he lay awake, thinking of the metal pig. Indeed, it was always in his thoughts. The next morning, their neighbor, an artist, passed by, carrying a box of paints and a large roll of canvas.

"Help the gentleman carry his box of paints," said the woman to the boy. He obeyed instantly, taking the box and following the painter. They walked on until they reached an art gallery he had visited that night during his ride on the metal pig. He remembered all the statues and pictures.

"You may go home now," said the painter, while the boy stood watching him as he set up his easel.

"May I see you paint?" asked the boy. "May I see you put the picture on this white canvas?"

"I am not going to paint yet," replied the artist. Then he brought out a piece of chalk. His hand moved quickly. "Why don't you go?"

Then the boy wandered home silently and seated himself on the table, and learned to sew gloves. All day long his thoughts were in the picture gallery, so he pricked his fingers and was slow at his sewing. But he did not tease Bellissima. When evening came, and the house door stood open, he slipped out. It was a bright, beautiful, starlit evening, but rather cold. Away he went through the already deserted streets and soon came to the metal pig. He stooped down and kissed its shining nose, and then seated himself on its back.

"You happy creature," he said, "how I have longed for you! We must take a ride tonight."

But the metal pig lay motionless, while the fresh stream gushed forth from its mouth. The little boy still sat astride its back, when he felt something pulling at his clothes. He looked down, and there was Bellissima, barking as if she would have said, "Here I am too. Why are you sitting there?"

He kissed the metal pig once more and then took Bellissima in his arms. The poor little thing trembled so with cold that the boy ran homeward as fast as he could.

"What are you running away with there?" asked two policemen he met. "Where have you stolen that pretty dog?" they asked, and they took her away from him.

"Oh, I have not stolen her. Do give it to me back again," cried the boy.

"If you have not stolen the dog, you may tell them at home that they can pick up the dog at the police station." Then they told him where the station was and went away with Bellissima.

He knew he was in dreadful trouble. The boy did not know whether he should jump into the Arno River, or go home and confess everything. They would certainly be angry, he thought.

He decided to go home and confess to sneaking out of the house that night.

The door was locked, and he could not reach the knocker. No one was in the street; so he took up a stone and threw it at the door.

"Who is there?" asked somebody inside.

"It is me," he said. "Bellissima is gone."

There was a great panic. Madame was so fond of Bellissima.

"Bellissima at the police station!" she cried. "You bad boy! Why did you let her out?"

Giuseppe went off at once, while his wife lamented and the boy wept. Several of the neighbors came in, including the painter. He took the boy between his knees and questioned him. In broken sentences, he soon heard the whole story, and also about the metal pig, and the wonderful ride to the art gallery. The painter consoled the little fellow and tried to soften the lady's anger, but she would not be pacified until her husband returned with Bellissima.

Then there was great happiness, and the painter hugged the boy and gave him a number of pictures. Oh, what beautiful pictures these were, including one of the metal pig. Oh, nothing could be more delightful. With just a few strokes, it appeared on the paper. Oh, if only he could draw and paint, thought the little boy!

The first spare moment during the next day, the boy got a pencil. On the back of one of the other drawings, he attempted to copy the drawing of the metal pig, and he succeeded. Certainly it was rather crooked, rather up and down, one leg thick, and another thin, a little rough. Still it was like the copy, and he was over-joyed at his work. The next day he tried again. He drew a second pig by the side of the first, and this looked much better. The third attempt was so good, that everybody would know what it was meant to represent.

One day Bellissima came walking before him. "Stand still," he said, "and I will draw you beautifully."

But Bellissima would not stand still, so he tied her up, just long enough to draw her. Unfortunately, at that moment the woman walked in.

"You naughty boy!" she cried.

She pushed the boy from her and told him never to enter the house again.

In the year 1834 there was an exhibition in the Academy of Arts at Florence. Two pictures, placed side by side, attracted a large number of spectators. The smaller of the two represented a little boy sitting at a table, drawing. Before him was a little white poodle, curiously shaven. The animal would not stand still, so it had been fastened with a string to its head and tail, to keep it in one position. The truthfulness and life in this picture interested everyone. The painter was said to be a young Florentine, who had been found in the streets, when a child, by an old glove maker, who had brought him up. The boy had taught himself to draw and was now a famous artist. The glove maker's boy had become a great painter, as the picture proved. But the larger picture by its side was a still greater proof of his talent. It represented a handsome boy, clothed in rags, lying asleep, and leaning against the metal pig in the street of the *Porta Rosa.* All the spectators knew the spot well. The child's arms were round the neck of the pig, and he was in a deep sleep. It was a beautiful picture. A large golden frame surrounded it, and on one corner of the frame a laurel wreath had been hung. But a black band, twined unseen among the green leaves, hung down from it because within the past few days the young artist had died.

⤜ The End ⤛

The Monkey-Crab War

*O*nce upon a time a kind crab was walking along sideways when she found a delicious rice ball. She picked it up with her large pincer to take home to her family. A monkey perched high on top of a persimmon tree spotted the crab. He wanted her rice ball, even though he was full from the meal of persimmons he'd just finished.

"Hello!" the monkey called, "Do you want to trade your rice ball for a persimmon?"

"Okay," the crab replied.

Well, this is almost too easy, thought the monkey. So, he said, "I'm almost out of persimmons. Will you take a persimmon seed instead?"

"Sure," the crab replied.

The monkey slid down the tree and picked off a persimmon seed that was stuck in his fur. He dropped it in front of the crab, stuffed her rice ball greedily in his mouth, and then ran to sit on a rock to sun himself.

"Thank you, Saru-don," the crab called to him. She took the seed back to her hole and planted it. Every day the crab tended the seed and before long a sprout popped up, and it quickly grew.

Some time later, when the sprout had become a tree and was covered with blossoms, a bee pollinated them. When the blossoms fell, they left behind the start of fruit that grew into shiny green balls, and by late fall many of them had become delicious orange persimmons.

The crab realized she had a problem—the fruit was far beyond the reach of her pincers. She was too short! Just then, the monkey came by.

"Saru-don, Saru-don," the crab called. "Do you remember the seed you traded for a rice ball? It's grown now, and the fruit is ripe. Will you help me pick some?"

The monkey scampered up the tree, and stuffed a juicy orange persimmon in his mouth. "Almost ready," he called down, and stuffed in two more. "These aren't too bad," he said as he moved up to the next branch, "delicious, in fact."

As the monkey continued to eat one persimmon after another, the crab called up to him, "Saru-don, please save me one!"

"Don't nag so much," the monkey growled. He plucked a hard, green persimmon and threw it down so hard that it cracked the poor crab's shell.

The bee found the crab at the foot of the persimmon tree. He helped her back to her home and then flew off to find the rice-flour **mortar**.

"Usu-don, Usu-don! The monkey has injured the crab!" the bee said.

The mortar, cut from a tree stump years before, rolled out of the kitchen. They hurried back to the crab's home, but on the way they met the chestnut.

"Kuri-don, Kuri-don!" the mortar said. "The monkey has injured the crab!"

When the three friends arrived, the crab told them the whole story. The mortar advised her not to worry, and the friends devised a plan.

"This monkey is a real threat, Usu-don," the chestnut said. "Someone has to do something."

"There is no one to do it but us, Kuri-don," the mortar replied.

The bee flew off a little before dawn, leaving the others to watch over the crab. He returned late in the morning and reported that the monkey was out taking a walk

and swinging through trees. The three left the crab in the care of her three sons and hurried to the monkey's home.

"I'll wait here in the back of the fire pit," the chestnut said. "Perhaps you could wait in the water barrel, Hachi-don."

The bee flew into the water barrel, and the mortar went up into the eaves.

Finally, late in the afternoon, the monkey returned. He puffed on the coals in the fire pit until they began to glow. The chestnut found himself growing hotter and hotter as he thought about the monkey's rude manner. Finally he burst with rage and flew out of the fire pit, striking the monkey in the eye with tremendous force and great heat.

In agony, the monkey leaped to the water barrel. Once he removed the lid, the bee stung his nose. The monkey rushed to the door to escape. Just then, the heavy mortar dropped from the eaves and pinned the monkey to the dirt floor. They remained there while the chestnut explained how angry everyone was about the monkey's wild deeds.

In the end, the monkey went with the others back to the crab's home. They stopped by the persimmon tree, and the monkey, accompanied by the bee, climbed up and selected four shiny, ripe, orange persimmons.

Once inside the crab's home, the monkey pushed the fruit forward and apologized. "Kani-san, I'm sorry for being so rude and nasty to you. I won't do it again."

The monkey was true to his word. After that, the monkey visited the crab often. He helped to pick persimmons, and he helped protect the crab and her family from other rude characters, such as he himself had once been!

⇐ The End ⇒

The Nightingale

Once upon a time in China there was a great emperor. His palace was the most beautiful in the world, and was surrounded by a garden with the most beautiful flowers. They had pretty silver bells tied to them, which tinkled so that everyone who passed could not help noticing them. Nearby, there was a forest that was home to a **nightingale** that sang so beautifully even the fishermen, who had so much to do, would stop to listen.

Travelers from every country in the world came to the city of the emperor, which they admired very much. When the visitors heard the nightingale, they all declared it to be the most wondrous of all.

The emperor had never heard of this nightingale. When he heard travelers speak of it, he said, "What is this? I know nothing of any nightingale. Is there such a bird in my empire?"

The emperor demanded that the nightingale be brought to him.

But where was the nightingale to be found? All of his lords-in-waiting looked high and low for the famous bird but were unable to find it. At last, a poor little girl in the kitchen said, "Oh, yes, I know the nightingale quite well; indeed, she can sing. She lives down by the seashore."

"Please lead us to the nightingale," said a lord-in-waiting. So she did.

"My excellent little nightingale," said the lord-in-waiting, "I have the great pleasure of inviting you to a court festival this evening, where the emperor can hear your charming song."

"My song sounds best in the green wood," said the bird. But still she came willingly when she heard the emperor's wish.

At the festival, the nightingale sang so sweetly that tears came into the emperor's eyes and rolled down his cheeks. Her song touched everyone's heart.

The nightingale's visit was so successful that she was now to remain at court, to have her own cage, with liberty to go out twice a day and once during the night. Twelve servants were appointed to attend her on these occasions. Each servant held her by a silk cord fastened to her leg. There was certainly not much pleasure for the nightingale in this kind of flying.

One day the emperor received a large packet on which was written, "The Nightingale." Inside was an artificial nightingale made to look like the living bird and covered with diamonds, rubies, and sapphires. As soon as the artificial bird was wound up, it could sing like the real one and could move its tail, which sparkled with silver and gold, up and down. It was a gift from the emperor of Japan.

This new bird was as successful as the real bird, and it was even prettier to look at. It sang without ever getting tired. The people would gladly have heard it again, but the emperor said the living nightingale should sing something. But where was she? No one noticed when she flew out of the open window, back to the forest.

The emperor missed the real nightingale, but the music-master praised the artificial bird. He said it was even better than a real nightingale, not only because of its beauty but also because of its musical power.

"With a real nightingale we can never tell what is going to be sung, but with this bird everything is settled. It can be opened and explained, so that people can understand how the waltzes are formed, and why one note follows upon another," said the music-master.

So, the real nightingale was banished from the empire, and the artificial bird placed on a silk cushion close to the emperor's bed. A year passed, and the emperor, the court, and all the people knew every little turn in the artificial bird's song. For that same reason, it pleased them better. They could sing with the bird, which they often did.

One evening, when the artificial bird was singing and the emperor lay in bed, something inside the bird popped. Then a spring cracked and the music stopped.

The emperor immediately sprang out of bed and called for his doctor. But what could he do? Then they sent for a watchmaker. After a great deal of talking and examination, the bird was sort of fixed. But the watchmaker said that it must be used very carefully because the bird's mechanism was getting old and it would be impossible to put in a new one without injuring the music. The bird could only be played once a year.

Five years passed, and a real sadness came upon the land. The emperor was ill and not expected to live much longer. Cold and pale, he stayed in his royal bed. One day, the emperor awoke with a strange weight on his chest. He opened his eyes and saw Death sitting there. He had put on the emperor's golden crown, and held in one hand his sword of state, and in the other his beautiful banner. All around the bed and peeping through the long velvet curtains, were a number of strange heads—some very ugly, and others lovely and gentle-looking. These were the emperor's good and bad deeds that now stared him in the face.

Death continued to stare at the emperor with his cold, hollow eyes, and the room was fearfully still. Suddenly there came through the open window the sound of sweet music. Outside, on the branch of a tree, sat the living nightingale. She had heard of the emperor's illness and had come to sing to him of hope and trust. And as she sang, the shadows grew paler and the blood in the emperor's veins flowed more rapidly, giving life to his weak limbs. Even Death himself listened, and said, "Go on, little nightingale, go on."

"Then will you give me the beautiful golden sword and that rich banner? And will you give me the emperor's crown?" said the bird.

Death gave up each of these treasures for a song, and the nightingale continued her singing. Soon, Death floated out through the window in the form of a cold, white mist.

"Thanks, you heavenly little bird. I know you well. I banished you from my kingdom once. Yet you have charmed away the evil faces from my bed, and banished Death from my heart. How can I reward you?"

"You have already rewarded me," said the nightingale. "I shall never forget that I drew tears from your eyes the first time I sang to you. These are the jewels that rejoice a singer's heart. But now sleep, and grow strong and well again. I will sing to you again."

And as she sung, the emperor fell into a sweet sleep. When he awoke, he was strengthened and restored.

"You must always remain with me," said the emperor. "You shall sing only when it pleases you; and I will break the artificial bird into a thousand pieces."

"No, don't do that," replied the nightingale. "The bird did very well as long as it could. Keep it here. I cannot live in the palace, but let me come when I like. I will sit on a bough outside your window, in the evening, and sing to you." Then the nightingale flew away.

The servants now came in to look after the emperor. To their tremendous joy and astonishment, there he stood, healthy, saying a happy good morning.

 *The End*

The Old Woman and Her Pig

Fairy tales with repeating phrases, such as "The Old Woman and Her Pig," are particularly fun to read out loud. Have fun with it; experiment. Modulate the old woman's voice so that each time she speaks, she sounds a bit more frustrated. Or, each time the old woman speaks, read a bit more quickly.

Once upon a time an old woman was sweeping her house, and she found a little crooked sixpence.

"What," she pondered, "shall I do with this little sixpence? I will go to market, and buy a little pig." So she bought a little pig. But as she was coming home, she came to a **stile**, and the piggy would not go over the stile.

So, she went a little farther, and she met a dog. So she said to him, "Dog! Dog! Bite pig; pig won't go over the stile; and I won't get home 'till midnight." But the dog wouldn't.

She went a little farther, and she met a stick. So she said, "Stick! Stick! Beat dog; dog won't bite pig; pig won't get over the stile; and I won't get home 'till midnight." But the stick wouldn't.

She kept going, and she saw a fire. So she said, "Fire! Fire! Burn stick; stick won't beat dog; dog won't bite pig; pig won't get over the stile; and I won't get home 'till midnight." But the fire wouldn't.

She went on, and she ran into some water. So she said, "Water! Water! Quench fire; fire won't burn stick; stick won't beat dog; dog won't bite pig; pig won't get over the stile; and I won't get home 'till midnight." But the water wouldn't.

The woman went still farther, and she met an ox. So she said, "Ox! Ox! Drink water; water won't quench fire; fire won't burn stick; stick won't beat dog; dog won't bite pig; pig won't get over the stile; and I won't get home 'till midnight." But the ox wouldn't.

She went a little farther, and she met a butcher. So she said, "Butcher! Butcher! Kill ox; ox won't drink water; water won't quench fire; fire won't burn stick; stick won't beat dog; dog won't bite pig; pig won't get over the stile; and I won't get home 'till midnight." But the butcher wouldn't.

She went on some more, and she found a rope. So she said, "Rope! Rope! Hang butcher; butcher won't kill ox; ox won't drink water; water won't quench fire; fire won't burn stick; stick won't beat dog; dog won't bite pig; pig won't get over the stile; and I won't get home 'till midnight." But the rope wouldn't.

So, she went a little farther, and she met a rat. So she said, "Rat! Rat! Gnaw rope; rope won't hang butcher; butcher won't kill ox; ox won't drink water; water won't quench fire; fire won't burn stick; stick won't beat dog; dog won't bite pig; pig won't get over the stile; and I won't get home 'till midnight." But the rat wouldn't.

She went a little farther, and she met a cat. So she said, "Cat! Cat! Kill rat; rat won't gnaw rope; rope won't hang butcher; butcher won't kill ox; ox won't drink water; water won't quench fire; fire won't burn stick; stick won't beat dog; dog won't bite pig; pig won't get over the stile; and I won't get home 'till midnight."

But the cat said to her, "If you will go to that cow over there and get me a saucer of milk, I will kill the rat." So away went the old woman to the cow.

But the cow said to her, "If you will go to that haystack and get me a handful of hay, I'll give you the milk." So away went the old woman to the haystack, and she brought the hay to the cow. As soon as the cow had eaten the hay, she gave the old woman the milk.

As soon as the cat had lapped up the milk, the cat began to kill the rat; the rat began to gnaw the rope; the rope began to hang the butcher; the butcher began to kill the ox; the ox began to drink the water; the water began to quench the fire; the fire began to burn the stick; the stick began to beat the dog; the dog began to bite the pig; the little pig squealed and jumped over the stile; and so the old woman got home before midnight. It was a good thing, too, for she was ready for her dinner!

⤳ The End ⤳

Puss in Boots

Once upon a time a **miller** died, leaving the mill to his eldest son, a donkey to his second son, and nothing but a cat to his youngest son. Now, some would say this wasn't right. But this is what happened, because that was the miller's nature.

The eldest son kept the mill. The second son took the donkey and set off in search of his fortune, while the third, finding the whole situation quite unfair, sat down on a stone and sighed, "A cat! What am I going to do with a lousy cat?"

The cat, though, heard his words and said, "Don't worry. Do you think I am worth less than a half-ruined mill or a mangy donkey? Give me a cloak, a hat with a feather in it, a bag, and a pair of boots, and you will see what I can do."

The young man gave the cat what he asked for, and with his new equipment in hand, the cat was off. He swiftly caught a plump wild rabbit, popped it into his bag, knocked at the castle gate, went before the king and, removing his hat with a sweeping bow, said: "Sire, the famous Marquis of Carabas (for this is what he called his master) sends you this fine plump rabbit as a gift."

"Oh," said the king, "thank you very much."

"Until next time," replied the cat as he went on his way. And the next day, back he came with some partridges tucked away in his bag. "Another gift from the brave Marquis of Carabas," he announced.

The queen remarked, "This Marquis of Carabas is indeed a very courteous gentleman."

In the days that followed, Puss in Boots regularly visited the castle, carrying rabbits, hares, partridges, and skylarks, presenting them all to the king in the name of the Marquis of Carabas. People at the palace began to gossip about this noble gentleman. "He must be a great hunter," someone remarked. "He must be very loyal to the king," said someone else. And yet another, "But who is he? I've never heard of him."

The queen was very interested in the generous man who sent this abundance of presents. "Is your master young and handsome?" she asked the cat.

"Oh yes. And very rich, too," answered Puss in Boots. "In fact, he would be very honored if you and the king called to see him in his castle."

When the cat returned home and told his master that the king and queen were going to visit him, the master was horrified. "Whatever shall we do?" he cried. "As soon as they see me, they will know how poor I am."

"Leave everything to me," replied Puss in Boots. "I have a plan."

For several days, the clever creature continued presenting gifts to the king and queen. One day he discovered that they were taking the princess on a carriage ride that very afternoon. The cat hurried home in great excitement. "Master, come along," he cried. "It is time to carry out my plan. You must go for a swim in the river."

"But I can't swim," fretted the young man.

"That's all right," replied Puss in Boots. "Just trust me."

So they went to the river. When the king's carriage appeared the cat pushed his master into the water.

"Help!" cried the cat. "The Marquis of Carabas is drowning."

The king heard his cries and sent his escorts to the rescue. They arrived just in time to save the poor bedraggled man, who really was drowning. The king, the queen, and the princess tended to him and ordered new clothes to be brought for the Marquis of Carabas. In these new clothes from the royal wardrobe, the master looked extremely handsome.

"Wouldn't you like to marry such a handsome man?" the queen asked her daughter.

"Oh, yes," replied the princess.

However, the crafty cat overheard one of the ministers remark that they must find out how rich he was.

"He is very rich indeed," said Puss in Boots. "He owns the castle and all this land. Come and see for yourself. I will meet you at the castle."

And with that, the cat scurried off in the direction of the castle, shouting at the peasants working in the fields, "If anyone asks you who your master is, answer: the Marquis of Carabas. Otherwise you will all be sorry." And so, frightened by what the cat might do to them if they didn't follow his orders, the peasants told the King, when his carriage swept past, that their master was the Marquis of Carabas.

In the meantime, Puss in Boots had arrived at the castle, the home of a huge, cruel ogre. Before knocking at the gate, the cat said to himself, "I must be very careful, or I'll never get out of here alive."

When the door opened, Puss in Boots removed his feather hat, exclaiming, "My Lord Ogre, my respects!"

"What do you want, Cat?" asked the ogre rudely.

"Sire, I've heard you possess great powers. That, for instance, you can change into anything you like."

"That's perfectly true," said the ogre, "and what of it?"

"Well," said the cat, "I was talking to certain friends of mine who said that you can't turn into a tiny little creature, like, for instance, a mouse."

"Oh, so that's what they say, is it?" exclaimed the ogre, puffing up his chest indignantly.

The cat nodded, "Well, Lord Ogre, that's my opinion too, because those who can transform into big things never can manage to squeeze themselves into little ones."

"Oh, yes? Well, just watch this!" retorted the ogre, turning into a mouse. In a flash, the cat leaped on the mouse and ate it whole. Then he dashed to the castle gate, and just in time, for the king's carriage had arrived.

With a bow, Puss in Boots said, "Sire, welcome to the castle of the Marquis of Carabas!" The king and queen, the princess, and the miller's son who, dressed in his princely clothes, really did look like a marquis, got out of the carriage. The king said, "My dear Marquis, you're a fine, handsome, young man. You have a great deal of land and a magnificent castle. Tell me, are you married?"

"No," the young man answered, "but I would like to find a wife." He looked at the princess as he spoke. She in turn smiled at him.

Soon, they married and lived happily together in the castle. And from time to time, the cat would wink and whisper, "You see, Master, I am worth a lot more than a mangy donkey or half-ruined mill, aren't I?"

The End

The Queen Bee

Once upon a time, two princes went out in the world to seek their fortunes. Unfortunately, they were rather lazy, and, having made some rather foolish choices while out in the world, they were too embarrassed to return to the palace.

Then their young brother, who was a dwarf, went out to look for his brothers. When he found them, they only laughed at him. Who did this simpleton think he was, seeking his fortune?

They decided, however, to travel together. After some time, they came to an anthill. The two elder brothers would have pulled it down to frighten the poor insects, but the little dwarf said, "Leave the poor things alone."

So on they went until they came to a lake where many ducks were swimming. The two brothers wanted to catch two and roast them for dinner. But the dwarf said, "Let the poor things enjoy themselves. Don't kill them."

And so, on they went. Next, they came to a bees' nest in a hollow tree; there was so much honey that it ran down the trunk. The two brothers wanted to light a fire under the tree and kill the bees and get at the honey. But the dwarf held them back, and said, "Leave the pretty insects alone."

They continued on and finally came to a castle. As they passed by the stables, they saw fine horses standing there, but all were of marble. And there was nobody about. Then they went through all the castle rooms, until they came to a door with three locks. In the middle of the door there was a **wicket**, so that they could look into the next room. There they saw a little old man sitting at a table. They called to him a couple times, but he did not hear. When they called a third time, though, he got up and came over to them.

He said nothing, but took hold of them and led them to a beautiful table covered with all sorts of good things to eat and drink. When they had finished their meal, he showed each of them to a bedroom.

The next morning he came to the eldest and took him to a marble table, where there were three **tablets**, telling how to break the enchantment affecting the castle. The first tablet said: "In the wood, under the moss, lie the thousand pearls belonging to the king's daughter; they must all be found. If one is missing at sunset, he who seeks them will be turned into marble."

The eldest brother set out and looked for the pearls the whole day, but the evening came. He had not found the first hundred, so he was turned into stone.

The next day the second brother tried to find the pearls, but he had no luck and so, too, was turned into stone.

Then came the little dwarf's turn. He looked in the moss, but it was so hard to find the pearls and the job was so tedious! He sat down upon a stone and cried. And as he sat there, the king of the ants (whose life he had saved) came to help him, with five thousand ants. It was not long before they had found all the pearls and laid them in a heap by his feet.

The second tablet said: "The key to the princess's bedroom must be fished up out of the lake."

As the dwarf came to the edge of the lake, he saw the two ducks whose lives he had saved swimming about. They dove and soon brought up the key from the bottom.

The third task was the hardest: to select the youngest and the best of the king's three daughters. They were all beautiful, and all exactly alike. But he was told that the eldest had eaten a piece of sugar, the next some sweet syrup, and the youngest a spoonful of honey. He was to guess which one had eaten the honey.

Then, just in time, came the queen of the bees, who had been saved by the little dwarf from the fire, and she tried the lips of all three. Finally, she sat upon the lips of the one who had eaten the honey, and so the dwarf knew which was the youngest. Thus the spell was broken, and all who had been turned into stone awoke and took their proper form.

And the dwarf married the youngest and sweetest of the princesses, and was king after her father's death many years later. His two brothers married the other two sisters, and they all lived happily together.

⪻ The End ⪼

The Red Dragon

Once upon a time many thousands of years ago animals were not the same as they are now. It was a rather strange time in history because, you see, it was hard to distinguish one animal from another.

"Look at that magnificent striped cat," one person might exclaim to another, only to be told by a rather indignant animal, "Why, you silly human. I am no cat. I am a rhinoceros!" For you see, these were very magical times, and not only did the animals all look the same, but they all had the ability to talk to humans.

This situation led to very confusing conversations.

"Do you know the gazelle that lives by the edge of the great lake?" asked one woman of another as they walked through the village market.

"I know of no gazelle," responded the other woman. "I do know of a hippo that likes to wade along the banks of the great lake, though."

As it turns out, they were both speaking of the same animal, but it was just so difficult to identify it. For although, in general, a hippo weighed a bit more than a gazelle, in every other way they were indistinguishable. Almost all of the animals were more or less the same height. And all had four legs, of similar size and style.

And, yes, there were very slight signs indicating which animal was which. For instance, it was true that the elephant *did* weigh a whisker more than the nimble hyena. But to the unpracticed human eye, it was really impossible to say which animal was which.

You should know that there were just a few in the animal kingdom that did look distinct. These included the lion, who, as we know it today, already had his luxurious mane and tremendous roar; the tiger, who had his distinctive black stripes; and the butterfly with his lovely coloring and delicate wings.

This is how life went on in the animal kingdom for a long, long time. Although at times it was frustrating, all were accustomed to the animals looking quite similar.

One day, though, this all abruptly changed.

This occurred as all the animals were relaxing in a field.

"Do you know," asked the gazelle, "that a woman at the market thought I was a hippo? Isn't that amazing?"

"Oh, it is not so surprising," said a jaguar, who looked very much like the gazelle. "Humans aren't as clever as they think they are."

As they rested and chatted about their lives, a red dragon suddenly swooped down upon them. This red dragon was out of breath and clearly very upset about something. "Oh, no!" the dragon cried out. "We're in danger, everyone! Listen to me! I have evidence that the world is about to come to an end!"

At first, his announcement was met with stunned silence by the assembled animals, but then they all began to chatter, mutter, squeak, and squawk at once.

"How do you know?" cried the gazelle.

"Who told you this?" roared the hippo.

"What makes you think this will happen?" snorted the rhino.

The dragon replied, "I read it in the stars. There really isn't time for discussion. We must escape right away!"

"But where can we go?" the animals asked in unison.

"I am afraid that there is only one place to go. And it won't be easy getting there. We must all go to another world," he replied. "But I can take you there. I can fly, and I'll take you to a faraway planet that is safer than this one. Now, hurry!"

The animals looked at one another. Did this red dragon know what he was talking about?

They whispered to one another.

"Should we go?" asked the hippo.

"I don't know," responded the gazelle, "but I don't know that we have any choice. If what he says is true, we are in great danger here. So, perhaps, we'll just have to be brave and climb onto his massive back."

So, frightened as they all were, all the animals clambered, one by one, onto the red dragon's scaly, ridged back.

A few of the animals, though, chose not to go. For instance, the lion turned away with a bored look and said, "I'm not scared of anything. What could possibly endanger a fierce creature like me? So, I'll just stay here on Earth."

Most of the others, however, were getting terribly anxious about the impending world's end and were fighting to get on the dragon's back.

"Don't push. You're hurting me," shouted the angry crocodile.

"Hey, move that paw! You just hit me on the back," another animal cried.

Maybe you've seen a similar scene. Have you ever been to a popular movie and seen people pushing and shoving to get in? Or, maybe, you've seen people pushing and shoving and being generally rude, trying to move unfairly to the front of the line. This type of animal behavior still exists today!

At last, though, all of the animals were aboard the dragon's scaly back. It wasn't too comfortable there. For one thing, the scales were quite prickly and hard. And it was very crowded. The red dragon was gigantic, but there were hundreds of animals crowded onto his back and there wasn't any room to spare. There wasn't room for a tail to swish or a paw to move.

Finally, the red dragon cried, "Ready? Off we go," and he started to run for takeoff. He had misjudged the weight of the animals on his back, though, so the first and the second runs weren't fast enough. The red dragon wasn't one to give up, though, so on the third attempt he finally got off the ground, flapping his wings as vigorously as he ever had in his whole life and waving his huge, lumpy tail.

Right away, complaints came from his animal passengers.

"Not so fast!" shouted one of the animals.

Then another voice yelled: "Faster, faster, faster, or we will end up crashing back onto the ground!"

The dragon replied, "Please, please! I'm doing the best I can. Why don't all of you please keep quiet?" The dragon needed to concentrate on his flying and the incessant chatter was bothering him. He worried that he would indeed crash if the animals continued to yell at him.

Unfortunately, because they were all so frightened, the animals did everything but keep still. And so, inevitably it seems, after a while the poor red dragon, now very tired, simply could not flap his wings any longer, and he crashed. Fortunately, he crashed onto a lush green meadow that offered a relatively soft landing pad to his animal load. All the animals shrieked with terror but none of them lost their lives.

There were other effects, though, from the forced landing. For instance, the snake lost his legs and slithered away through the grass. The rhino bumped his head as he tumbled off of the dragon and grew a horn. The elephant took a particularly spectacular tumble from the dragon's back. As a result, all of the elephant's teeth fell out, except for two that became very long. As you probably know, today's elephants still have these two very long teeth, called tusks.

The giraffe, which had been seated near the dragon's head, fell a particularly long way and sprained his neck. This resulted in the neck growing to an astonishing length. The hippo, given to being rather dramatic in worrisome situations, rolled about and groaned so much he became nearly round. Finally, he rolled right into a pond and didn't come out. He found his round shape rather peculiar and was too ashamed to be seen.

After their traumatic ride on the scaly back of the red dragon, all of the animals looked different and became what they are today. Now, as you know, it's very easy to tell the difference between a rhino and a cat. Or a hippo and a gazelle.

When the bored lion saw them, what he said was, "Oh, how funny you look." He was glad he hadn't climbed aboard the back of the red dragon.

⌒ The End ⌐

The Seven Ravens

Two of the most famous people to ever write fairy tales are the brothers Jacob and Wilhelm Grimm. These brothers wrote "The Seven Ravens" in the early 1800s. They were born in Germany in the 1780s, where they remained their entire lives. Both brothers loved books so much that they became librarians. Jacob was a librarian to Jerome Bonaparte, king of Westphalia, a German province. Wilhelm worked in an elector's library. Between 1812 and 1822 they wrote and published three books we know as Brothers Grimm's Fairy Tales. Perhaps you and a friend could work together as the brothers did and write a fairy tale of your own.

Once upon a time, there was a man who had seven sons, but no daughters. He and his wife both wished for the birth of a girl, and at long last, their wish came true.

The whole family was jubilant. The day came to baptize the tiny girl and the father sent his seven sons down to the river to get water for the baptism. In a hurry to return to their family, the boys accidentally dropped the pitcher into the water. Although they looked and looked, they couldn't retrieve it. They knew their father would grow frustrated at their delay, and they were right.

The father had become very impatient and cried out, "I wish those boys were all turned into ravens."

That instant, he heard the flapping of wings over his head and saw seven coal-black ravens fly past in the sky. The father was horrified that his careless curse had come true, but he had no idea how to reverse it.

Now, they had only their daughter, who grew to be happy and beautiful. Her parents didn't tell her that because of her, they had lost their seven boys.

But one day, the girl overheard a woman say, "Oh, yes, she's a beautiful child, but it was because of her that her seven brothers were lost."

Then she went to her parents and asked them to explain this to her.

"It wasn't your fault, " her father said sadly. And he told her about his careless curse. The young girl still felt that she was at fault and she grew very sad, worrying about her brothers living as ravens.

Finally, she decided to set out to find and rescue her brothers. She took an old golden ring that her mother had given her and a loaf of good bread to eat. She walked and walked until she came to the end of the world. Then she walked toward the sun, but it was too hot and threatened to burn her. Then she walked toward the oceans, but they were too deep and threatened to drown her. So she ran toward the moon, but it was too cold and threatened to freeze her. At last she went to the stars, and they were very generous and fed her a delicious chicken dinner.

Then, they gave her a small chicken bone and said, "You'll need a bone to open the glass mountain where your brothers are." The little girl put the bone in her pocket and went in search of the glass mountain. When she came to it, the gates were locked. She searched her pocket for the bone, but it had fallen out.

The girl was brave, as well as beautiful and strong. She knew she needed a bone to open the gate so she cut off her little finger and put it in the door. The new bone opened the gates to the glass mountain, and she went in.

Inside, she met a gnome who said, "Little girl, what are you looking for?"

"I am looking for my seven brothers," said the girl, "the seven ravens."

"The ravens are my masters," said the gnome. "They are not at home. If you wait, they'll be here soon because it is nearly time for their dinner."

The gnome led her into a dining room where there were seven gold plates and seven crystal glasses. The girl drank a sip from each glass and took a bite from the food on each plate. Then into the last glass she dropped her mother's ring, and hid behind a door.

Suddenly there was a flapping of wings and a rushing of air, and the sounds of cawing ravens.

The seven ravens flew into the room and looked at their plates and glasses.

"Someone has been drinking from my glass," they said, one after another. "Someone has been eating from my plate. It was a human being." Still, the ravens were hungry, so they ate and drank.

At last the seventh raven drank until his glass was empty. Then he almost choked on the ring.

He took it from his beak and knew at once it was his mother's.

"Is our sister here?" said the ravens. "It's so far from home. Perhaps she has broken the spell. Perhaps we can be humans again."

"If we could just see her," said the seventh raven.

Just then the girl, who had been hiding behind a door, stepped forward.

The moment her brothers saw her, the careless curse was broken. They all became humans again. Then, in merry company, they returned to their parents' home.

☞ The End ☜

The Bear's Tail

Once upon a time there was a fisherman who earned a living selling fish from a cart. One cold winter day, while the fisherman was crossing the woods, a wily fox smelled the fish and began following the cart at a close distance. The fisherman kept his fish in long wicker baskets, and the sight of the fish made the fox's mouth water. Oh, she was hungry for some fish!

The fox, however, was reluctant to jump on the cart to steal a fish because the fisherman had a long whip that he cracked from time to time to spur on the horse. He didn't want that whip used on him! But the smell of fresh fish was so enticing that the fox overcame her fear of the whip, leaped on the cart, and with a quick movement of her paw, dropped a wicker basket on the snow.

The fisherman did not notice anything and continued his journey. The fox was very happy. She opened the basket and got ready to enjoy her meal. She was just about to taste the first bite of fresh fish when a huge bear appeared.

"Where did you get all that tasty trout?" the big bear asked, looking terribly hungry.

"I've been fishing," the fox lied.

"Fishing? How? The lake is frozen over," the bear said, incredulous. "How did you manage to fish?"

The fox knew that unless she could get rid of the bear with some kind of excuse, she would have to share her fish. Finally, she said, "I fished with my tail."

"With your tail?" said the bear, even more astonished.

"Sure, with my tail. I made a hole in the ice, and I dropped my tail in the water. When I felt a bite, I pulled it out, and a fish was stuck on my tail," the fox told the bear.

The bear, a gullible type, touched his tail and his mouth began watering. He said: "Thanks for the tip. I'm going fishing, too." And the bear lumbered away.

The lake was not too far away, but the ice was very thick and the bear had a hard time making a hole in it. Finally, his long, sharp claws got the job done. As time went by and evening approached, it got colder and colder. The bear shivered, but he kept sitting by the hole with his tail in the water. No fish had bitten yet. The bear was very cold, and the water of the lake began freezing around his tail. It was then that the bear felt something like a bite on the end of his frozen tail. Oh! Success at last, he thought.

The bear pulled with all his strength, heard something tear, and at the same time felt a very sharp pain. He turned around to find out what kind of fish he had caught and realized that his tail, trapped in the ice, had been torn off. Ever since then, bears have had a little stump instead of a long and thick tail.

⇜ *The End* ⇝

The Three Billy Goats Gruff

"The Three Billy Goats Gruff" is an excellent fairy tale to read aloud because there are so many interesting voices. Make your voice tiny and meek when reading the words of the smallest goat. Make your voice LOUD and FIERCE when reading the words of the biggest Billy Goat Gruff.

Once upon a time there were three **billy goats** that lived in a small village. These three billy goats had rather a nice life. They lived on a farm where they had occasional chores to do, but other than these little odd jobs, they were free to play games and graze, their favorite occupation of all. All of these billy goats were named "Gruff."

One day, their owner sent them down the road and up to the hillside to graze and fatten up. So, following their owner's orders, they set off down the road toward the hill where they were to graze. They were eager to get there because this rolling hill had particularly sweet grass growing on it.

On the way up the hill there was a small bridge they had to cross. Now, under the bridge, as everyone in the village knew, lived a great ugly **troll**, with eyes as big as saucers and a nose as long as a baseball bat. He was an awful-looking creature!

When the three goats arrived at the bridge, they decided that the youngest should cross first.

"Trip, trap! Trip, trap!" went the goat, lightly tripping over the bridge.

"Who's that tripping over my bridge?" roared the troll.

"Oh, it's only me," said the tiniest Billy Goat Gruff, who was a bit afraid of that roaring creature, "and I'm going up to the hill to graze on some grass."

"Oh, no you're not, because I'm coming out to gobble you up," said the ill-behaved troll.

"Oh, no! Please don't take me. I'm too little." said the billy goat in a wee, quivering voice. "Wait a bit until the second Billy Goat Gruff comes, he's much bigger, probably tastier, too."

"Well, be off with you, then," said the troll, who, come to think of it, was feeling quite hungry and thought that bigger probably would be better in choosing a goat meal.

Soon came the second Billy Goat Gruff, setting out to cross the bridge.

"Trip, trap! Trip, trap! Trip, trap! " went the goat on the bridge, not nearly as light on his feet as the first Billy Goat Gruff.

"Who is that tripping over my bridge?" roared the troll.

"Oh, it's only the second Billy Goat Gruff, and I'm going up to the hill to eat some grass. The grass on that hill is particularly tasty," said the billy goat, a bit troubled by the gruesome voice from under the bridge.

"Oh, no you don't—I'm coming out from under the bridge to gobble you up," said the troll, who by now really was getting quite hungry and crabby.

"Please, don't take me, wait a little while until the oldest Billy Goat Gruff comes, he's much bigger. He'll be the best meal of all. Tasty and substantial," said the second Billy Goat Gruff.

"Okay! Get away then," said the troll, already drooling at the thought of a really large and delicious goat. Just as he was thinking about this prospect, up came the biggest Billy Goat Gruff.

"TRIP, TRAP! TRIP, TRAP! TRIP, TRAP!" went the bridge, for the billy goat was so heavy that the bridge, which wasn't very sturdy anyway, practically buckled under him.

"WHO'S THAT TRAMPING OVER MY BRIDGE?" roared the troll, very hungry and very crabby by now.

"It is the big Billy Goat Gruff and I am going to graze on the hill across the bridge," roared the billy goat, who had an ugly, hoarse voice of his own, to match the troll's.

"You think so, do you? Well, think again! I'm coming out from under my bridge to gobble you up," roared the troll.

"Well, come along then! I've got two spears and I'll use them to poke your eyeballs out. And I've got two curling stones, and I'll crush you to bits," answered the third Billy Goat Gruff, who was not at all scared.

Well, true to his word, the troll ran out from under the bridge, ready to eat the biggest Billy Goat Gruff. But this big goat flew at the troll, and poked his eyes out with his horns. Then he crushed him to bits, and tossed him back under the bridge. After that, he calmly went up the hillside where he joined the other two Billy Goats Gruff and told them what had happened. On that hillside, the billy goats got so fat they were hardly able to walk home again.

≈ *The End* ≈

The Tiger, the Brahman, and the Jackal

Be creative in the type of voices you use. Perhaps the Brahman has a sad voice, the jackal a high-pitched confused voice, and the tiger a loud, threatening tone. By varying the voices, it makes the tale even more fun to hear. Use different voices for all of the different fairy tales in this book.

Once upon a time, a tiger was caught in a trap. He tried to escape, but he couldn't.

It happened that a **Brahman** came by.

"Let me out of this cage, please!" cried the tiger.

"Oh no, my friend," replied the Brahman calmly, "you would probably eat me if I did."

"Not at all," promised the tiger. "If you release me, I'll be your servant for life!"

Now when the tiger sobbed some more, the Brahman's heart softened, and at last he agreed to open the door of the cage.

Out popped the tiger, and, seizing the poor man, it cried, "You're a fool. Now I'm going to eat you!"

The Brahman begged for his life. Finally, the tiger agreed to ask the first three things they met for their opinion on the matter.

First, the Brahman asked a tree what it thought of the matter, but the tree replied coldly, "What have you to complain about? Don't I give shade and shelter to every one who passes by, and don't they in return tear down my branches to feed their cattle? The tiger should eat you!"

Then the Brahman saw a buffalo, and he asked the buffalo his opinion on the matter. "You are a fool to expect me to help you! Look at me! Humans only treat me well when I produce milk. Eat him, tiger!"

The Brahman then asked the road. "My dear sir," said the road, "how foolish you are. Here I am, useful to everybody; yet all, rich and poor, trample on me as they go past, giving me nothing in return."

So the Brahman thought his **fate** was to be dinner for the tiger. Just then, he met a jackal, which called out, "Why, what's the matter, Mr. Brahman? You look as miserable as a dog without a bone!"

The Brahman told him what had happened.

"How very confusing!" said the jackal, when the recital had ended. "Would you mind telling me over again, for I'm confused."

The Brahman told it all over again, but the jackal shook his head in a distracted sort of way, and still could not understand.

"It's very odd," he said, "it all seems to go in one ear and out the other. I will go to the place where it happened, and perhaps I shall understand."

So they returned to the cage, where the tiger was waiting for the Brahman, and sharpening his teeth and claws. "You've been away a long time!" he growled. "Now, I'm ready to eat you for dinner."

"Please," the Brahman pleaded, "let's hear what the jackal has to say."

The tiger consented, and the Brahman began the whole story over again, not missing a single detail.

"Oh, my poor brain," cried the jackal, wringing its paws. "Let me see. How did it all begin? You were in the cage, and the tiger came walking by—"

"Silly," interrupted the tiger, "*I* was in the cage."

"Of course! " cried the jackal, "the tiger was in the Brahman, and the cage came walking by—no, that's not it, either! Well, don't mind me, begin your dinner, for I shall never understand!"

"Yes, you shall!" returned the tiger, in a rage at the jackal's stupidity. "I'll make you understand! Look here—I am the tiger."

"Yes, I got that part."

"And that is the Brahman."

"Okay then . . ."

"And that is the cage."

"Right."

"And I was in the cage—do you understand now?"

"Yes . . ."

"Well?" cried the tiger impatiently.

"Please, how did you get in?"

"Why in the usual way, of course!"

"Oh, dear me, but what is the usual way?"

At this the tiger lost patience, and, jumping into the cage, cried, "This way! Now do you understand how it was?"

"Perfectly!" grinned the sly jackal, as he quickly shut the door. "And if you will permit me to say so, I think that's where you'll stay!"

⮞ *The End* ⮜

The Ugly Duckling

Once upon a time a mother duck was waddling by the lake, when she found a strange-looking egg.

"This is odd," said Mother Duck, "I must have misplaced one of my eggs." So, using her wide, able bill, she pushed the egg back to her nest, where she sat on it and its five brother and sister eggs, keeping them warm until they hatched.

One day the eggs hatched, and out popped six little ducklings. All the ducklings were cute and cuddly, except for one. The duckling that popped out of the odd-looking egg was the ugliest duckling Mother Duck had ever seen.

"What a strange-looking fellow you are," said Mother Duck. "But you're still one of my babies, and I love you no matter what."

The Ugly Duckling loved his Mother Duck and all his little brother and sister ducklings, and they loved him as well.

But the other ducks on the pond weren't so nice.

"What an ugly duckling," said one.

"He really isn't very pretty," said another.

Whenever the family was on the pond, the other ducks would laugh or call the Ugly Duckling names.

Finally, the Ugly Duckling could stand it no longer, so he swam away to a marshy corner of the pond and hid. This was a very inhospitable place for ducks, so he was all alone. He felt very lonely and missed his mother and brothers and sisters, but it was still better to live alone than to be teased so relentlessly. From his hiding place he could see almost the whole pond, which at times made him feel lonelier.

Summer passed and fall came. The Ugly Duckling noticed some new birds swimming on the pond. They were much larger than ducks and had long white necks and beautiful thin beaks.

"They are so beautiful," thought the Ugly Duckling. "But I am so ugly, I can't let them see me." So the Ugly Duckling stayed hidden in the **rushes**.

One day, the Ugly Duckling heard a voice say, "Look at that beautiful bird."

He turned around and was surprised to see one of the beautiful white birds talking to him.

"Are you making fun of me?" asked the Ugly Duckling.

"Oh no," said the white bird. "You're very handsome."

The Ugly Duckling didn't understand. The bird seemed to be telling the truth.

"What are you?" the Ugly Duckling asked.

"I am a swan. Just like you."

"Me? A swan?" said the Ugly Duckling. "That can't be, I'm just an ugly duckling."

"No, you're not," said the swan. "Come here."

The Ugly Duckling followed the swan into the middle of the pond and looked down into the water at his reflection. The swan was right—the Ugly Duckling had grown into a beautiful swan!

⁓ The End ⁓

The Blinded Giant

O nce upon a time, there lived a fierce giant at a mill in Yorkshire. He had no friends, except for his dog, Hamlet. The giant's ears were abnormally large, and his hands were the size of wagon wheels. His head itself was the size of a wagon, and he had a wart the size of a loaf of bread at the end of his bulbous nose. To make matters worse for this rather hideous fellow, he had only one eye, placed like a bull's-eye in the middle of his broad forehead. Along with being ugly, he had a rather nasty diet. What was his preferred meal? One hundred giant loaves of bread that he made from the bones of people he ground in his mill.

As you can imagine, grinding the bones for all of this bread was a rather Herculean task. In fact, the giant thought long and hard (his head was large, but his brain was not!) about how to find an assistant to help him with the bone grinding and bread making. He was so completely feared and loathed that he thought it unlikely anyone would volunteer for this odious job. So, he decided to find a capable youth and steal him away.

He spent some time wandering through the local countryside, looking for the right assistant. He wanted a hard worker who wouldn't complain and wouldn't run away from him. After weeks of searching, he found his desired prey—a boy named Jack. He'd watched Jack help his mother and father without ever uttering a complaint. The giant liked Jack's polite demeanor, so he scooped him up and took the boy back to the mill.

Of course, Jack thought he was destined to be bone meal for the next batch of bread. But instead, the giant roared, "Fee, fi, fo, find. I want you to help me grind!"

And, so it went. Jack was so relieved at not being made into the giant's next meal that he agreed to stay on and work as a servant. It was hard and torturous work, running the mill all day; but Jack stayed and did as he was told, fearing for his life if he did otherwise.

Jack served the fierce giant for seven long years. In all of that time, the mean giant never gave Jack so much as one day off. Jack had no bed—just a pile of straw on a cold stone floor—and very little to eat. Finally, Jack was fed up. He couldn't bear it for one more minute. The county fair was coming and Jack begged to go. Everybody in the land went to the fair to see the traveling musicians, to meet their friends, and eat exotic foods. The giant, though, showed no mercy.

"No, no," roared the giant. "You will never leave this mill. You are to work for me forever!"

"I've been grinding and grinding for seven years," said Jack, "and I haven't had one day off. I haven't had one good night's rest, because the floor is so hard and so cold. I get barely enough food to live, and I've had enough! I'm taking a day off to go to the fair. I don't care what you have to say about it!"

"Don't talk to me like that," yelled the giant. "You absolutely will not be allowed to go to the fair."

Feeling defeated, as if he might never set foot outside the giant's mill, Jack went back to his grinding, weeping quietly. The day dragged on and became hotter and hotter. It was the middle of summer, and the sun was high and strong and burning bright in the sky. The giant ate his usual lunch of bread and then decided to take a nap.

He put his giant, one-eyed head on a burlap sack stuffed with straw and dozed off almost instantly. He was napping right next to the huge table where he'd had his midday meal. There, he had laid down the last great loaf of bone bread. But he still held a giant-size knife in his hand. As he napped and his snores shook the stones of the mill, his gnarled fingers relaxed their grip on the knife, and it started to slip out of his hand.

Jack had been watching all of this while he worked at his grinding. He knew that while the giant was sleeping, he had a chance to escape, so he flew into action. Jack sprinted like the wind across the mill floor and seized the knife from the giant's relaxed hand. Then, holding the huge weapon with both hands, he drove the blade into the giant's single eye. The giant awoke with a terrible howl of agony, and then lurched up and moved to block the mill's door.

"Oh, no!" thought Jack. "How will I escape now? Surely, with the giant blocking the door, I am going to be made into his next loaf of bread!"

But Jack didn't lose his wits. He quickly came up with a plan to outsmart the ugly, warted giant. He grabbed the giant knife again and then captured the giant's dog. Then, he skinned it and threw the dog's hide over his back.

"Woof, woof," said Jack, imitating as best he could the voice of the dog.

"Go get him, Hamlet," said the giant, fooled by Jack's voice. "Get this horrible, ungrateful wretch who has blinded my only eye."

"Woof, woof," said Jack again. Then, he ran between the giant's legs on all fours, barking till he got to the door. He unlatched it and ran away as fast as he could from the giant's mill.

He returned to his home in the village, and his mother and father cried with joy to have their son back. The villagers celebrated his return and applauded him for blinding the giant who had terrorized their country for so many years.

⁘ *The End* ⁘

The Book of Spells

O nce upon a time an ogre lived in the middle of a deep, dark forest. He was big, extremely cruel, and heartless. Given all of these rather nasty traits, it may be surprising to learn that he liked his house very clean and tidy. So one day he said to himself, "I'm always out hunting, foraging, and tormenting the peasants. I need somebody to clean my house, scrub the floors, wash plates, and do the laundry every week."

So, out he went and crouched down beside one of the cottages near the edge of the woods that belonged to a family of poor peasants. When he saw their children come out, a boy and a girl, he stretched out his big, warty hand, grabbed them, and carried them away. "You'll be my servants," he said, "and I will give you your food. But if you try to run away, you will be my food!"

Terrified, the two children agreed, and they lived in the ogre's house for a long time. After some time they noticed that every evening the ogre pulled out a large book, which he would read carefully. It was named, the children noticed, *The Book of Spells!* The two children, who were quick thinkers, read the book when the ogre was out causing trouble, and they too learned the magic spells.

After studying *The Book of Spells* for some time, the boy said, "Sister, I think I know enough now! Come on, let's run away!"

"Are you sure you know how to cast spells?" asked the girl anxiously.

"Of course!" he said. "Let's go, before the ogre comes back!"

So the pair ran out of the house into the forest.

Suddenly, the girl cried out, "I can hear somebody running! The ogre's following us!"

The ogre was determined to catch the pair, and with his long legs, it wouldn't take long to nab them. So the boy cast the first of the spells. He turned himself into a pond and his sister into a minnow!

A moment later, the ogre rushed up, saw what had taken place and growled: "If only I had a fishing line! I'd catch and eat that little minnow. I'll run and fetch one!" and off he went.

The two children turned back into their normal selves and started to run again. But the ogre was soon right behind them. He was just about to lay hands on them, when the boy cast the second spell. He turned himself into a **shrine** and his sister into an angel painted on the wall.

The ogre would have loved to kick the shrine to bits, but he thought of a better idea. He shouted, "I'll burn you down instead!" and ran to gather some firewood.

Before he could return, the children were off again. They ran and ran, 'till they were almost exhausted. Just as the ogre was about to grab them, the boy, working a third spell, turned himself and his sister into grains of corn that mingled with thousands and thousands of other grains on the **threshing floor**.

The ogre exclaimed, "You think you can beat me with my own spells, but I'm far more cunning than you!" and he turned into a **cockerel** that hurriedly began to peck all the grains. A second before being pecked, the boy turned into a fox, pounced on the cockerel, and gobbled him up!

Now that the ogre was gone, the relieved boy and girl were able to return home to their very worried parents.

 The End

The Brave Tin Soldier

*Hans Christian Andersen was born in Denmark in 1805. He didn't
have an easy childhood. He was the son of a poor shoemaker and
worked at a young age in a factory. Soon, though, he found he had a
talent for poetry. He wrote several books of poetry as well as novels,
travel books, and plays. He is best remembered, though, as the author
of some of our most-loved fairy tales, including "The Brave Tin
Soldier" and "The Ugly Duckling."*

Once upon a time there was a little tin soldier made from an old spoon.
He was one of twenty-five soldiers made from the same tin spoon.
They all stood straight and wore decorated uniforms of red and blue.
They were all exactly alike, except for one who had only one leg. He had been
the last one made and there had not been enough tin to finish him.

The little boy who was given the twenty-five soldiers loved his one-legged
tin soldier best of all. On the table where the boy played with his tin soldiers
was a small black puzzle box, and a beautiful white-paper ballerina who held a
red rose made of tinsel and glitter in her hands. Her dress was made from a
fine silk handkerchief.

As soon as the tin soldier glimpsed her across the table, he fell in love.
"She stands as straight and true as a soldier. I would give anything in the world
to be with her."

Just then, a little mischief-making goblin, who lived in the black puzzle box,
popped out and said, "Tin Soldier, stop wishing for things you cannot have."

The tin soldier ignored the goblin. He was fascinated by the ballerina, who stood high on one tiptoe, with her other leg stretched out. They both stood on one leg, so they had that in common, the tin soldier thought to himself.

The goblin was jealous of the attention that the tin soldier was giving to the ballerina, so he pushed the tin soldier off the table and out the window!

The little tin soldier fell to the ground, where he was found by two little boys.

"Look, there's a tin soldier!" said one boy.

"Let's put him in a boat," said the other boy.

So they built a small boat and set the tin soldier afloat. Down the tiny stream he floated, standing straight and still.

At the entrance to the sewer stood a rat.

"Halt! Who goes there?" demanded the rat.

The tin soldier said nothing and floated past the ranting rat into the dark sewer where he swirled around in the darkness and floated out into the great river.

It wasn't long before a fish in the river saw the glint from the soldier's red coat and snapped him up in one bite. A moment later, the fish found itself caught in a net and hauled ashore.

"This is all the goblin's fault," thought the tin soldier. "If only the ballerina were here with me, I wouldn't mind being caught in this fish's belly."

Just then, there was a poke of a knife, and the fish's belly was slit open wide.

"Why look!" said the boy's mother, "Here is the lost tin soldier!" The fish had been caught and taken to market, and sold to the family of the very boy who owned the tin soldier.

The mother cleaned the soldier and put him back on the table where all of his brothers welcomed him home with quiet salutes.

The tin soldier was pleased to be back at last in full sight of the ballerina whom he loved.

Perhaps it was the goblin's curse, or perhaps it was just a mistake, but at that moment the boy ran into the room in a rage. He was angry because he had been unable to find his favorite toy, a special set of colorful marbles.

He picked up the tin soldier, which was the first thing he saw, and threw him into the fireplace.

The tin soldier felt the heat of the flames melting first his hat and then his gun. His legs were turning as red as his coat, and soon he knew he would be melted and gone.

Suddenly, though, the door to the room flew open, and a gust of wind caught the little ballerina. She flew into the air, and landed in the fire right next to the tin soldier. For a moment they stood beside each other, engulfed in bright flames.

In the next instant the ballerina caught on fire, and was gone. The tin soldier melted down into a little tin lump.

The next morning, there was nothing left of the little tin soldier but a tiny tin lump, shaped like a heart. Of the little dancer, nothing was left but her tinsel-and-glitter rose.

The End

The Elves and the Shoemaker

Once upon a time a poor shoemaker lived with his wife in a cozy home. Although he had once done very well at his cobbling trade, he now struggled to make ends meet. As a young man, he had been known for his speed and accuracy and flair for fashion, producing fine footwear that was much sought after. Now, because of his failing vision, he was unable to do repairs and make shoes as quickly as he once had. He worried that his customers would leave him for a younger, more able shoemaker.

One night he went to bed feeling particularly teary about his situation, unable to finish a simple repair job he had started that morning. He felt fretful, because he had promised his customer to have the repair job completed first thing in the morning.

In the morning, though, he was met with a happy surprise. As he made his way out of bed and walked slowly toward his workbench, he found that the repair job had been finished—and finished very well, with neat, even stitches.

This puzzled him, for he couldn't imagine who had done this for him. Although these were magical times, the shoemaker had had few encounters with fairies or elves, so he could hardly believe that they were the ones helping him out. But who else could have done such a perfect job on the repair?

After puzzling over it all day, he once again prepared to tuck into his snug bed. First, though, he set out all the tools and materials necessary to make a new pair of shoes for a wealthy and demanding customer. "Tomorrow morning, when it is sunny and bright and I'm able to see more clearly, I will begin working on them," he thought. "Or perhaps whoever completed that repair last night, will return tonight and help me again. I would be very grateful if they did."

And sure enough, instead of the fine leather that he had left out on the workbench the night before, the shoemaker was very surprised and very pleased and relieved to find a beautiful pair of brand new shoes, perfectly crafted. The cobbler admired the craftsmanship and felt he couldn't have done a better job on them himself.

Later on in the day, the customer came by the shop to see how his new shoes were coming along. When he found a very nice pair of shoes already made, he was very pleased and happy and paid the shoemaker twice the price they had originally agreed on.

These occurrences left the shoemaker feeling very confused and wondering what had happened at his workbench during the night hours. That evening, before he tucked into his bed, the cobbler left out some more leather and the tools for making a pair of shoes. And, once again, the next morning he found another shiny and perfect pair of new shoes. If anything, these shoes were even more finely crafted then those the cobbler himself made. "Who was making these shoes?" the confused cobbler wondered aloud.

Later that day, the customer who had ordered the shoes stopped to check on the cobbler's progress. She was surprised and delighted to see the finished shoes. These shoes, too, were sold at a higher price than was originally agreed on.

Although mystified by the nightly occurrences, the shoemaker was also relieved to have the magical help. So, now as a matter of course, the shoemaker left out leather and tools for his mysterious helpers every night. And every morning like clockwork, he found a new pair of perfectly crafted shoes.

It really seemed too good to be true. Pretty soon, the overjoyed shoemaker was able to save a lot of money. This reassured him, for he knew that the money would come in handy when his mysterious helpers disappeared.

The shoemaker had not shared the news of his mysterious nighttime helpers with his wife. She became suspicious when she saw all of the gold the shoemaker had collected from his enthusiastic customers. She asked the shoemaker for an explanation.

"Well, my dear, it really is most strange," began the cobbler, and he told his wife all about the nocturnal mysteries, beginning with the first surprise repair job.

After he finished telling his tale, his baffled wife made a proposal: "Let's wait until nightfall. Then, we will only pretend to be sleeping in our beds. Instead, we will stay awake, peek around the corner at your workbench, and find out what has been happening during the nights around here!"

The shoemaker agreed that this was a sound plan. And so, that night, they tucked in as usual and pretended to sleep. Then, around midnight, they saw two tiny elves silently sneak into the shoemaker's shop and hop up onto his workbench. The quick and skilled elves worked together to create a beautiful new pair of shoes in a flash. Although they were working hard and moving around quickly, it was winter—and a particularly wretched one—and the elves, dressed in ragged, tattered clothes, shivered while they worked.

"Poor fellows! They must be very cold," the shoemaker's wife whispered sympathetically to her husband. "I know! Tomorrow I will make them two heavy wool jackets, made just to fit their little elf figures. That way they will be warmer, and maybe instead of one pair of shoes, they will make two!"

The next day, the shoemaker's wife laid out red wool and carefully cut out two little elf jackets. She sat by the fire all day and stitched on little sleeves and collars. It was very fine work, requiring lots of tiny, tiny stitches because the jackets were only a few inches tall from collar to hem. The cobbler's wife worked happily, though, as she thought about how pleased the elves would be to find the small, warm jackets on the workbench that night. With perfect timing, just as the sun set, she finished her work, showing the red jackets to her husband, who thought the little coats were very fine.

That night, along with the leather and tools, the cobbler laid out the two warm, red jackets. Then, at midnight, next to the leather, the two elves found the two elegant red jackets with sparkling gold buttons. They put on the jackets and were very pleased and happy. They danced a little jig, singing: "Tweedle dee, tweedle dum! What beautiful jackets! We'll never be cold again!"

After their dance was finished, one of the happy elves said, "Let's get to work now and make a pair of shoes."

But the other answered, "Work? What for? With two jackets like these, we are very rich. We will never have to work again."

And so it went that the two elves left the shop, never to be heard from again.

It made the shoemaker and his wife sad to see them go because their help had been invaluable to the ailing cobbler. However, with the money saved during the elves' stay at the cobbler's home, the shoemaker and his wife were able to live comfortably and happily for the rest of their lives.

≈ *The End* ≈

The Enchanted Knife

O nce upon a time there lived a young man who vowed to marry a woman with royal blood. One day, he gathered his courage and traveled to the palace to ask the emperor if he could marry his daughter.

Considering himself a fair and just ruler, the emperor said, "Very well, if you can do the following things, you may marry her. In eight days you must tame three wild horses. The first must be pure white, the second bright red with a black head, and the third coal-black with white head and feet. And, as a present to the empress and me, you must bring back as much gold as the three horses can carry."

The young man listened with dismay, wondering how he could ever tame these horses and find so much gold. He thanked the emperor politely and went on his way. Luckily for him, the emperor's daughter had overheard everything her father had said, and peeping through the curtains, she thought the young man was more handsome than anyone she had ever seen. She hurried back to her room and wrote him a letter, which she gave to her trusty servant to deliver. She begged the young man to come to her room early the next day and not to begin without her advice.

That night, when her father was sleeping, she crept into his bedroom and took an enchanted knife from the chest where he kept his treasures. Then she hid it carefully before she went to bed.

The sun had barely risen in the morning when the princess's assistant brought the young man to her room in the palace. Neither spoke, but they stood holding hands, realizing how much they loved each other.

Then, the maiden gave him the enchanted knife and said, "Take my horse and ride straight toward the sunset until you come to a hill with three peaks.

When you get there, you will find a field with horses grazing. Pick out the three my father described to you. If they are shy, hold the knife up to the sun, so that its rays light the whole meadow. Then the horses won't be afraid of you. When you have them safely, look until you see a cypress tree whose roots are brass, branches are silver, and leaves are golden. Cut away its roots with your knife, and you will come to countless bags of gold. Load the horses with all they can carry and return to my father."

The young man set out with the knife. He found the field without any difficulty. He held up the knife so the rays of the sun hit it and lit up the field with bright light. As the princess had foretold, the horses were no longer shy, and the young man chose the three that the emperor had described. Then, he found the cypress tree. He dug deeper and deeper until far down, below the roots of brass, his knife struck the buried gold. He lifted the gold from the ground and laid the bags on the horses' backs until they could carry no more. Then, he led them to the emperor.

The emperor agreed that the young man could marry his daughter. They had a grand wedding and lived happily together. And the emperor wondered but never guessed how it was that the young man had outsmarted him.

The End

The Happy Prince

Once upon a time, high above a city on a tall column stood the statue of the Happy Prince. He was gilded all over and had two bright sapphire eyes. His sword hilt was decorated with a sparkling ruby.

He was very much admired indeed. "He is as beautiful as a weathervane," remarked one of the town council members who wished to gain a reputation for having artistic tastes.

"Why can't you be like the Happy Prince?" asked a sensible mother of her little boy who was crying for a toy he couldn't have. "The Happy Prince never dreams of crying for anything."

One night there flew over the city a little bird, a swallow. His friends had all flown to Egypt for the winter, but he had stayed behind. He saw the statue on the tall column and decided to rest there for the night. So he landed there just between the feet of the Happy Prince.

Just as he was putting his head under his wing to sleep, a large drop of water fell on him. "How strange!" he cried, "there is not a single cloud in the sky."

Then another drop fell.

"What is the use of a statue if it cannot keep the rain off?" he said. "I must look for a good chimney," and he decided to fly away. But before he had opened his wings, a third drop fell, and he looked up, and saw that the eyes of the Happy Prince were filled with tears. His face was so beautiful in the moonlight that the little swallow was filled with pity.

"Who are you?" he asked.

"I am the Happy Prince."

"Why are you crying?" asked the swallow.

"When I was alive and had a human heart," answered the statue, "I did not know what tears were, because I lived in the palace of Sans-Souci, where sorrow is not allowed. I was called the Happy Prince, and happy indeed I was, if you think pleasure is happiness. Now that I am dead, they have set me up here so high that I can see all the ugliness and misery of my city. And though my heart is made of lead I can't help but cry.

"Far away," continued the statue, "there is a poor house. One of the windows is open, and through it I can see a woman seated at a table. Her face is thin and worn, and she has coarse, red hands, all pricked by the needle, for she is a seamstress. In a bed in the corner of the room, her little boy is lying ill. He has a fever and is asking for oranges. His mother has nothing to give him but river water, so he is crying. Swallow, will you not bring her the ruby out of my sword-hilt since I can't move?"

"My friends are waiting for me in Egypt," said the swallow.

"Swallow," said the prince, "the boy is so thirsty, and the mother so sad."

"I don't think I like boys," answered the swallow. "Last summer, when I was staying on the river, there were two rude boys, the **miller's** sons, who were always throwing stones at me."

But the Happy Prince looked so sad that the little swallow was sorry. "It is very cold here," he said, "but I will stay with you for one night, and be your messenger."

"Thank you, little swallow," said the prince.

So the swallow picked out the great ruby from the prince's sword and flew away with it in his beak. At last he came to the poor house and looked in. The boy was tossing feverishly on his bed, and the mother had fallen asleep. In he hopped and laid the great ruby on the table beside the woman's thimble. Then he flew gently round the bed, fanning the boy's forehead with his wings.

"How cool I feel," murmured the boy, "I must be getting better."

Then the swallow flew back to the Happy Prince and told him what he had done. "It is strange," he remarked, "but I feel quite warm now, even though it's so cold."

"That is because you have done a good deed," said the prince.

"Tonight I go to Egypt," said the swallow, and he was happy at the thought. When the moon rose he flew back to the Happy Prince. "I am getting ready to go to Egypt," he told the prince.

"Swallow," asked the prince, "will you please stay one more night?"

"My friends are waiting for me in Egypt," answered the swallow.

"Swallow," said the prince, "far away across the city I see a young man in an attic. He is leaning over a desk covered with papers. He is trying to finish a play, but he is too cold to write any more. There is no fire in the grate."

"I will stay one more night," said the swallow, who really had a good heart. "Shall I take him another ruby?"

"Unfortunately, I have no rubies now," said the prince. "My eyes are all that I have left. They are made of rare sapphires. Pluck out one of them and take it to him. He will sell it to the jeweler, and buy food and firewood, and finish his play."

"Dear Prince," said the Swallow, "I can't do that," and he began to cry.

"Swallow," said the prince, "do as I ask of you."

So the swallow plucked out the prince's eye and flew away to the student's attic. It was easy enough to get in, as there was a hole in the roof. Through this he darted and came into the room. The young man had his head buried in his hands, so he did not hear the flutter of the bird's wings, and when he looked up he found the beautiful sapphire.

"This must be from some great admirer. Now I can finish my play," he said, and he looked quite happy.

The next evening, the swallow came to bid the prince good-bye.

"Swallow," said the prince, "please stay one more night."

"Dear Prince," said the swallow, "I must leave you. But I will never forget you, and next spring I will bring you back two beautiful jewels in place of those you have given away. The ruby shall be redder than a red rose, and the sapphire shall be as blue as the great sea."

"In the square below," said the Happy Prince, "there stands a little match-girl. She has let her matches fall in the gutter, and they are all spoiled. Her father will beat her if she does not bring home some money, and she is crying. She has no shoes or stockings, and her little head is bare. Pluck out my other eye, and give it to her, and her father will not beat her."

"I will stay with you one night longer," said the swallow, "but I cannot pluck out your eye. You would be blind then."

"Swallow," said the Prince, "do as I ask."

So he plucked out the prince's other eye and darted down with it. He swooped past the match-girl, and slipped the jewel into the palm of her hand. "What a lovely bit of glass," cried the little girl, and she ran home, laughing.

Then the swallow came back to the prince. "You are blind now," he said, "so I will stay with you always."

"No, little swallow," said the poor Prince, "you must go away to Egypt."

"No, I will stay with you always," said the swallow, and he slept at the prince's feet.

All the next day he sat on the prince's shoulder and told him stories of what he had seen in strange lands.

"Dear little swallow," said the prince, "you tell me of marvelous things, but more important than anything is the sadness of men and women. Fly over my city, little swallow, and tell me what you see there."

So the swallow flew over the great city and saw the rich making merry in their beautiful houses, while the beggars were sitting at the gates.

Then he flew back and told the prince what he had seen.

"I am covered with fine gold," said the prince, "you must take it off, piece by piece, and give it to my poor."

The swallow picked off the gold, till the Happy Prince looked quite dull and gray. He brought leaf after leaf of the fine gold to the poor. The children's faces grew rosier, and they laughed and played games in the street.

Then the snow came, and after the snow came the frost. The streets looked as if they were made of silver, they were so bright and glistening.

The poor little swallow grew colder and colder, but he would not leave the prince; he loved him so much. He picked up crumbs outside the baker's door and tried to keep himself warm by flapping his wings.

But at last he knew that he was going to die. He had just enough strength to fly up to the prince's shoulder once more.

"Goodbye, dear Prince!" he murmured.

"I am glad that you are going to Egypt at last, little swallow," said the prince, "you have stayed too long here."

"It is not to Egypt that I am going," said the swallow. "I am dying."

And he kissed the Happy Prince on the lips and fell down dead at his feet.

At that moment a curious crack sounded inside the statue, as if something had broken. The fact is that the leaden heart had snapped right in two. It certainly was a dreadfully hard frost.

Early the next morning the mayor was walking in the square below with the town council members. As they passed the column he looked up at the statue: "How shabby the Happy Prince looks!" he said.

"The ruby has fallen out of his sword, his eyes are gone, and he isn't golden anymore," said the mayor. "In fact, he is little better than a beggar!"

"And, to make things worse, there is actually a dead bird at his feet!" continued the mayor.

So they pulled down the statue of the Happy Prince.

"As he is no longer beautiful, he is no longer useful," said the art professor at the university.

The mayor held a meeting of the corporation to decide what was to be done with the metal. "We must have another statue, of course," he said, "and it shall be a statue of myself."

"Of myself!" cried each of the town council members and they quarreled. In fact, they are quarreling still.

The statue was dismantled and sent to be melted down, but the prince's broken lead heart would not melt. It was tossed into the garbage, where it landed next to the poor dead swallow.

⁀ The End ⁀

How Sun, Moon, and Wind Went out to Dinner

O nce upon a time, three creatures named Sun, Moon, and Wind went out to dinner with their Uncle Thunder and Aunt Lightning. The three creatures were very excited about spending the evening with their uncle and aunt and had been thinking about little else all day.

Sun and Wind spent the day arguing about who would have a better time at the dinner.

"Aunt and Uncle like me better than you, so I'll get to sit by them," exclaimed Sun. "They love my bright rays."

"That's not true," countered Wind. "They like my breezy manner and will definitely want to be right next to me at the dinner table."

Then, they bickered about who would have better food.

"Certainly, the best and tastiest delights will be given to me, the bright light of the sky," said Sun.

"On, no! I'll be honored with the choicest items on the menu," countered Wind once again.

And so it went on like this all day. Meanwhile, gentle Moon kept to herself, humming and looking forward to an evening with her beloved relatives. She also helped her mother around the house, doing errands and helping to clean and cook.

Finally, Thunder and Lightning came for Sun, Moon, and Wind. Their mother, who was a distant but bright star in the sky, was not going with them. Instead, she waited alone for Sun, Wind, and Moon's return. She looked forward to hearing about their adventures.

Thunder and Lightning took the children on their backs and traveled far to the North. When they arrived, Sun, Moon, and Wind were astonished to see a massive granite table set with the most amazing array of food they could imagine. The utensils were made of gold and encrusted with sparkling jewels. The goblets were of shimmering crystal. Their chairs were massive brass thrones with **damask** cushions.

As Sun and Wind hurried to take their places next to their aunt and uncle, Thunder said, "We would like the gentle Moon to sit between us, so she can cast her gentle beams of light on our feast while we enjoy it."

Moon happily complied while her siblings grumpily seated themselves, one by Thunder and one by Lightning. Why, they wondered, had Moon been honored with the seat between their aunt and uncle?

After saying a few words of thanks for the feast, Aunt and Uncle invited Sun, Wind, and Moon to partake and enjoy the abundant offerings. Both Sun and Wind dug in greedily, hurrying to eat as much as possible and as quickly as possible. They were eating so quickly that they didn't even notice the magnificent flavor of the stardust bread or the unbelievable sweetness of the hummingbird nectar.

Moon, though, sat quietly and thoughtfully, enjoying the array and turning often to thank Thunder and Lightning for their kindness and generosity.

Eventually, Sun and Wind were stuffed and became impatient to return home.

"Let's go," whined Sun. "I'm tired and want to settle into bed."

"Me too," groaned Wind, "and I think I have a bit of a stomachache!"

Aunt and Uncle implored them to be patient, so Moon could finish her meal. But Sun and Wind put up such a fuss that at last Thunder and Lightning agreed to take the three siblings back to their mother's home.

Sun and Wind clambered aboard without so much as a thank you to their kind hosts. Moon, though, took her time, wanting to look one more time at the magnificent table and to take a portion of every dish back home to her mother.

"Hurry, hurry," said Sun.

And so, with a plate loaded with food in her delicate hand, Moon climbed onto Lightning and the five of them sped back to the mother's home.

When they got home, their mother, who had kept watch for them all night long with her little bright eye, was very happy to see them, for she had missed her children.

"Did you enjoy yourself, dear children?" she asked.

"It was okay," said Sun, ungraciously.

"Just okay?" said the mother.

"Yes, that's right," said Sun.

"What about you, Wind? What did you think of the feast?" mother asked.

"It wasn't that exciting," said Wind.

"And, what about you, Moon? How did you find the feast?" mother asked.

"It was incredible, Mother. I wish you could have been there," and Moon went on to describe their dinner out to her mother. She finished by saying, "Since you couldn't be there, I brought back something for you." And from behind her back, Moon brought forth the plate full of fanciful treats.

"Oh, that is so lovely, Moon," the mother said. "What did you bring me, Sun?"

Then Sun, who was the oldest and should have been wiser for her years, said petulantly, "I have brought nothing home for you. I went out to enjoy myself with my friends and family. I didn't go to the feast to bring home dinner to you!"

"What did you bring me, Wind?" asked the mother.

Wind said, "I didn't bring anything home for you, Mother. You could hardly expect me to bring a collection of good things for you, when I only went out for my own fun. I just wanted to make sure that I had a good time!"

Sun and Wind's behavior upset their mother, Star, who had tried to teach them to be kind creatures. So, Star turned to Sun and said, "Because you went out to amuse yourself with your friends, and feasted and enjoyed yourself without any thought of your mother at home, you shall be punished. From now on your rays will be hot and scorching, and they will burn all that they touch. And because of this, people will hate you, complain about your intense rays, and cover their heads when you appear."

And that is why the Sun is so hot to this day.

Then she turned to Wind and said, "You also forgot your mother in the middle of your selfish fun! This will be your punishment: You shall always blow in the hot, dry weather and shall parch and shrivel all living things. And men shall avoid you from now on."

And that is why the Wind in the hot weather is to this day so disagreeable.

But to the kind and gentle Moon, she said, "Daughter, because you remembered your mother and shared your abundance with her, from now on, you shall be cool and calm and bright. All people will admire your beauty and serenity."

And that is why the Moon's light is so soft and cool and beautiful even to this day.

⪻ *The End* ⪼

Jack and the Beanstalk

Once upon a time, a little boy named Jack lived with his poor mother. One day, Jack's mother said, "Son, we have nothing left but our old cow. Take her into town and sell her so we can buy some food."

So, Jack set out to sell the cow. On his way to town, Jack met a man.

"I'd like to buy your cow," the fellow said. "I don't have gold, but I have some magic beans. They will bring you great fortune."

Jack thought for a moment and then agreed. He gave the man the rope and kissed the cow good-bye. He took the colorful magic beans and went home.

When Jack arrived there, his mother said, "Well, Jack, I see you've sold the cow. How much gold did you get for her?"

"Oh, Mother, I got something even better than gold," Jack said.

"What could be better than gold? Diamonds? Pearls?" she asked.

"Look," Jack said as he spilled the beans on the kitchen table.

"Four beans?" his mother asked incredulously.

"They're magic beans," Jack said. "The man told me so."

"Jack, you are a fool!" his mother cried. "You've been swindled, you silly. These beans are worthless. Hungry or not, they're not even worth cooking."

With that, she picked up the beans and threw them out the window. Then she sent Jack to bed.

The next morning, Jack woke up and looked out his window and saw the most amazing thing: A beanstalk that was thick and strong had grown overnight, reaching high into the sky. Jack looked up the beanstalk and decided to climb it in hopes of finding his fortune.

Jack climbed until at long last he reached the top of the beanstalk, which just poked through a patch of clouds. Jack stuck his head up and was surprised to discover a beautiful field of grass. Way off in the distance, he saw a huge castle.

He jumped off the beanstalk onto the grass and began walking to the castle. It took quite some time to get there, and by then he was very hungry, since he hadn't had a meal for at least a day.

When he reached the castle, he knocked on the massive front door.

"Who's there?" said a woman's booming voice.

"Just a hungry boy," Jack shouted back. He looked everywhere but didn't see anyone, until he looked up and saw a giant woman looking back down at him.

"You're very small for a boy," said the woman, "but I don't suppose you'll eat much. You can come in. But my husband will be home soon, and when he comes, you'll have to hide in the cupboard. If my husband sees you, he'll eat you in one bite!"

The giant's wife picked Jack up and carried him into the kitchen, where she gave him a crumb of brown bread the size of a boulder and a bit of cheese the size of a piano. Jack ate and ate until he was very full.

Suddenly, he heard a distant rumble coming toward the castle.

"My husband!" shouted the giantess. "Run, run, into the cupboard."

Soon a giant burst into the kitchen. He had feet the size of horses, legs as tall as tree trunks, a head the size of a house, and just one eye.

"Fee, fi, fo, fum," roared the giant. "I smell the blood of an Englishman. Be he alive, or be he dead, I'll grind his bones to make my bread."

The giant began sniffing and looking around the kitchen.

Just then, the giantess brought her husband his dinner, and so hungry was the giant that he forgot all about finding Jack.

When the giant had finished eating his dinner, he barked, "Wife, bring my golden goose!"

The giant's wife hurried from the kitchen and was back in a minute with an ordinary-looking goose that looked surprisingly tiny in her hands.

"Goose, lay!" the giant ordered.

The goose sat down and laid a golden egg! The giant picked the egg up, squinted at it, and then put the egg in his pocket. Then he fell asleep at the table.

Jack saw his opportunity. He jumped from the cupboard onto the table and snatched up the goose. Then he ran as fast as he could out of the castle, across the great green field, and began climbing down the beanstalk.

When he returned home, his mother said, "Jack, where have you been?"

"Winning riches," said the young boy. He reached into his shirt and brought out the golden goose, which had fallen asleep while he had climbed down the beanstalk. Then he commanded, "Goose, lay!"

And the goose sat down and laid a golden egg. Jack and his mother hugged each other and jumped for joy.

And from that day on, Jack and his mother lived happily ever after.

⬐ The End ⬐

Johnnycake

A johnnycake is a type of bread from the northern region of England. It's made with oatmeal or wheat flour and cooked on a griddle just like a pancake.

Once upon a time there was an old man and an old woman and a little boy. One morning the old woman made a johnnycake and put it in the oven to bake. "You watch the johnnycake while your father and I go out to work in the garden," she told the little boy.

So the old man and the old woman went out to harvest carrots, and they left the little boy to tend the oven. But he looked away for just a moment. When he did, he heard a loud noise and he looked up and saw the oven door open. Out of the oven jumped the johnnycake, and went rolling along end over end, toward the house's open door. The little boy hurried to shut the door, but the crafty johnnycake was too quick for him and rolled through the door, down the steps, and out into the road before the little boy could catch him.

The little boy ran after him as fast as he could, crying out to his father and mother, who heard the uproar and threw down their carrots and joined in the chase. But Johnnycake outran all three and was soon out of sight.

Eventually Johnnycake came to two well-diggers who looked up from their work and called out, "Where are you going, Johnnycake?"

"I've outrun an old man, an old woman, and a little boy, and I can outrun you too!"

"You can, can you?" they said, and they threw down their tools and chased after Johnnycake. Soon, though, they tired and sat down to rest.

On ran Johnnycake and he soon came to two ditch-diggers.

"Where are you going, Johnnycake?" they asked.

"I've outrun an old man, an old woman, and a little boy, and two well-diggers. I can outrun you too!"

"You think so, do you?" and they started chasing Johnnycake. Soon, they grew too tired to run after Johnnycake and they sat down to rest.

On went the mischievous Johnnycake, who eventually came to a bear. The bear said, "Where are you going, Johnnycake?"

"I've outrun an old man, an old woman, and a little boy, and two well-diggers, and two ditch-diggers, and I can outrun you too!"

"We'll see about that," snarled the bear. He started trotting as fast as he could after Johnnycake. Before long, though, the bear was left so far behind that he gave up the chase and sat down to rest and eat some honey.

On went Johnnycake until he came to a wolf, who asked, "Where are you going, Johnnycake?"

"I've outrun an old man, an old woman, and a little boy, and two well-diggers, and two ditch-diggers, and a bear, and I can outrun you too!"

"You can, can you?" asked the wolf. "We'll see about that." And he set off at a brisk gallop after Johnnycake. Eventually, though, when the wolf saw there was no chance of overtaking Johnnycake, he sat down to rest.

On went Johnnycake until he encountered a fox, who called out in a sharp voice, "Where are you going, Johnnycake?"

"I've outrun an old man, an old woman, and a little boy, and two well-diggers, and two ditch-diggers, and a bear, and a wolf, and I can outrun you too!"

The fox said, "I can't quite hear you, little Johnnycake. Won't you come a little closer?"

Johnnycake stopped his race for the first time and came a little closer. He repeated in a loud voice, "I've outrun an old man, an old woman, and a little boy, and two well-diggers, and two ditch-diggers, and a bear, and a wolf, and I can outrun you too!"

"Can't quite hear you, Johnnycake. Won't you just come a bit closer?" said the fox in a quivering voice.

Johnnycake came up quite close, leaned toward the fox, and yelled, "I've outrun an old man, an old woman, and a little boy, and two well-diggers, and two ditch-diggers, and a bear, and a wolf, and I can outrun you too!"

"You can, can you?" exclaimed the fox, and he snapped up Johnnycake in his sharp teeth before Johnnycake could run another step.

⟨ The End ⟩

The Little Match Girl

*I*t was a terribly cold and nearly dark evening, and the thick flakes of snow were falling fast. It was the last night of the year. In the cold and the darkness, a poor little girl, her head bare, roamed through the streets. The little girl went about with little naked feet, which were blue with the cold.

In an old apron she carried a number of matches and had a bundle of them in her hands. No one had bought any matches from her the whole day. Nobody had given her even a penny.

Shivering with cold and hunger, she crept along. The poor little child was miserable. The snowflakes fell on her long, blond hair, which hung in curls.

Lights were shining from every window, and there was a savory smell of roast goose, for it was New Year's Eve. In a corner, between two houses, she sank down and huddled, trying to warm herself. She had drawn her little feet under her, but she could not keep out the cold. She dared not go home, because she had sold no matches, and could not take home even a penny. Her father would certainly beat her. Besides, it was almost as

cold at home as here. They had only the roof to cover them, and the wind howled through it, even though the largest holes had been stopped up with straw and rags.

Her little hands were almost frozen with the cold. Perhaps a burning match might do some good if she could draw it from the bundle and strike it against the wall, just to warm her fingers. She drew one out and lit it. It gave a warm, bright light, like a little candle, as she held her hand over it. It was really a wonderful light. It seemed to the little girl that she was sitting by a large iron stove with polished brass feet. The fire burned and seemed so warm that the child stretched out her feet as if to warm them. Then, though, the flame of the match went out, the stove vanished, and she had only the remains of the half-burned match in her hand.

She lit another match and it burst into flame, and where its light fell upon the wall, it became transparent and she could see into the room. The table was covered with a snowy white tablecloth, and had a splendid dinner service with a steaming roast goose, stuffed with apples and dried plums. And what was still more wonderful, the goose jumped down from the dish and waddled across the floor to the little girl. Then the match went out. And there remained nothing but the thick, damp, cold wall before her.

She lit another match and found herself sitting under a beautiful Christmas tree. It was larger and more beautifully decorated than the one that she had seen through the glass door at the rich merchant's. Thousands of candles were burning upon the green branches. The little one stretched out her hand toward them, and the match went out.

The Christmas lights rose higher and higher, until they looked to her like the stars in the sky. Then she saw a star fall, leaving behind it a bright streak of fire.

"Someone is dying," thought the little girl, for her old grandmother, the only person who had ever loved her and who was now dead, had told her that when a star falls, a soul was going up to heaven.

She again lit a match, and the light shone round her. In the brightness stood her old, loving grandmother.

"Grandmother," cried the little one, "take me with you. I know you will go away when the match burns out. You will vanish like the warm stove, the roast goose, and the large, glorious Christmas tree."

And she hurried to light the whole bundle of matches, for she wished to keep her grandmother there. And the matches glowed with a light that was brighter than the midday sun, and her grandmother had never appeared so beautiful. She took the little girl in her arms, and they both flew in brightness and joy far above the earth, where there was neither cold nor hunger nor pain.

In the morning there lay the poor little one, with pale cheeks and smiling mouth, leaning against the wall. She had frozen to death on New Year's Eve. The child still sat, holding the matches in her hand, one bundle of which was burned.

"She tried to warm herself," said some. No one could imagine what beautiful things she had seen or the wonderful place she had entered with her grandmother on that last day of the year.

The End

216

The Little Mermaid

Once upon a time, far out in the deepest part of the ocean, a sea king lived in a magnificent underwater castle with walls of coral, windows of amber, and a roof made of iridescent shells.

The sea king had been a widower for many years, and his old mother kept house for him. She was a very wise woman and very good to the little sea princesses who were her granddaughters. They were six beautiful children, but the youngest was the prettiest of them all, with eyes as blue as the sea. Like all the others, she had no feet—her body ended in a fish's tail. She was a strange child, quiet and thoughtful. While her sisters were delighted with the wonderful things that they obtained from shipwrecks, she cared for nothing but the pretty red flowers she grew in the sea garden outside the castle.

She loved to hear about the world above the sea. She made her old grandmother tell her all she knew of the ships and of the towns, the people and the animals.

"When you turn fifteen," the grandmother would tell her, "you will have permission to rise up out of the sea. Then you will see both forests and towns."

In the following year, the oldest of the sisters would be fifteen. But as each was a year younger than the other, the youngest would have to wait five years before her turn came to rise up from the bottom of the ocean. However, each sister promised to tell the others what she saw on her first visit.

As soon as the eldest was fifteen, she was allowed to rise to the surface of the ocean. When she came back, she had hundreds of things to talk about. But the most beautiful, she said, was to lie in the moonlight and to gaze on a large town nearby, where the lights were twinkling like hundreds of stars.

In another year the second sister received permission to rise to the surface of the water. She rose just as the sun was setting, and this, she said, was the most beautiful sight of all.

The third sister's turn followed. She swam up a broad river that emptied into the sea. On the banks she saw green hills covered with beautiful vines, and palaces and castles scattered throughout the forest.

The fourth sister was more timid. She remained in the middle of the sea, but she said it was as beautiful there as near the land.

The fifth sister's birthday came in the winter, so when her turn came, she saw what the others had not seen the first time they went up. The sea looked quite green, and large icebergs were floating about.

When the sisters had permission to rise to the surface for the first time, they were each delighted with the new sights. But now, as grown-ups, they could go when they pleased, and they had become indifferent to it. They wished themselves back again in the water. After a month had passed, they said it was much more beautiful down below and better to be at home.

Their youngest sister, though, thought, "Oh, I wish I were fifteen years old. I know that I shall love the world up there."

At last she reached her fifteenth year. So she said, "Farewell," and rose to the surface as lightly as a bubble. The sea was calm. A large ship lay on the water. There was music and song on board; and, as darkness came on, a hundred colored lanterns were lighted. The little **mermaid** swam close to the cabin window and saw the people inside. Among them was a young prince, the most handsome of all; he was sixteen years old.

It was very late, yet the little mermaid could not take her eyes from the ship or from the beautiful prince.

A dreadful storm was approaching. The waves rose as high as mountains. Eventually, the ship's thick planks gave way, and the ship turned over on her side. Water rushed into the ship.

The little mermaid knew that the crew was in danger. At one moment it was so dark that she could not see a single object, but a flash of lightning revealed the whole scene. She could see everyone who had been on board except the prince. When the ship parted, she had seen him sink into the deep waves; and she was glad, for she thought he would now be with her. Then she remembered that human beings could not live underwater.

She dove into the water to search for him. When she managed to reach the young prince, his eyes were closed and he would have died without the little mermaid's help. She held his head above the water.

In the morning, the prince's eyes remained closed. The mermaid kissed his forehead and wished that he would live. Presently they came in sight of land. She swam with the handsome prince to the beach and there she laid him in the warm sunshine. Then, the little mermaid swam out from the shore and placed herself between some high rocks that rose out of the water. She covered her head and neck with seafoam, so that her little face wasn't visible and watched to see what would become of the poor prince. She did not wait long before she saw a young girl approach him. Then, the mermaid saw that the prince came to life. She dove sorrowfully into the water, happy that the prince had been saved but sad to be away from him. She returned to her father's castle.

Her sisters asked her what she had seen during her first visit to the surface of the water, but she would tell them nothing.

At length she could bear it no longer and told one of her sisters all about it. Then the others heard the secret, and very soon it became known to two mermaids whose close friend happened to know who the prince was.

"Come, little sister," said the other princesses. They entwined their arms and rose up in a long row to the surface of the water, close by the spot where they knew the prince's palace stood. The little mermaid loved to swim near the shore and watch the prince take his daily walks and make jaunts in his little boat.

The little mermaid was able to think of nothing except the handsome prince. Her grandmother told her that humans found mermaid's tails unattractive and, therefore, the prince would have no interest in her. Desperate for advice, the little mermaid decided to consult an underwater sorceress.

When she arrived at the sorceress's home, the sea witch said, "I know what you want. It is very stupid of you, but you shall have your way and you will be sorry. You want to get rid of your fish's tail and have two legs, so that the young prince may fall in love with you. I will prepare a potion for you. You must swim to land tomorrow before sunrise and drink it. Your tail will then disappear and shrink up into legs. Every step you take will feel as if you were treading upon sharp knives. If you can bear this, I'll help you."

"Yes, I can," said the little mermaid.

"But think again," said the witch, "for once your shape has become like a human, you can no longer be a mermaid."

"I will do it," said the little mermaid.

"But I must be paid also," said the witch, "you must give me your beautiful voice."

"But if you take away my voice," said the little mermaid, "what is left for me?"

"Your beautiful form, your graceful walk, and your expressive eyes."

"All right, then," said the little mermaid.

Then the witch began to prepare the magic potion. When it was finished, the mermaid took it and swam to the prince's palace. Then the little mermaid drank the magic potion, and it seemed as if a two-edged sword went through her delicate body. Soon she recovered and felt a sharp pain, but before her stood the handsome young prince. She then became aware that her fish's tail was gone and that she had legs but no clothes. She used her long hair to cover herself.

The prince asked her who she was and where she came from, but she could not speak. Every step she took was, as the witch had said, like treading on the points of needles or sharp knives. She followed the prince to the palace and soon was dressed in robes of silk and was the most beautiful creature in the palace. But, because of her deal with the witch, she could not speak.

The prince said she should remain with him. He had a page's dress made for her, so she could ride with him on horseback. While at the prince's palace, and when all the household were asleep, she would go and sit on the broad marble steps, for it eased her burning feet to bathe them in the cold seawater.

Once during the night her sisters came up arm-in-arm, singing sorrowfully as they floated on the water. She beckoned to them, and then they recognized her and told her how much they missed her.

As the days passed, she loved the prince more and more, and he loved her as he would love a little child, but it never crossed his mind to marry her. Yet, according the laws of the underwater world, unless he married her, she would dissolve into the foam of the sea.

"Do you not love me the best of them all?" the eyes of the little mermaid seemed to say to the prince.

"Yes, you are dear to me," said the prince, "for you have the best heart. You are like a young maiden whom I once saw. I was in a ship that was wrecked and a young maiden found me on the shore and saved my life. She is the only one in the world whom I could love.

"Oh, he doesn't know that I saved his life," thought the little mermaid.

Very soon it was said that the prince must marry, and that the beautiful daughter of a neighboring king would be his wife.

The prince and the little mermaid set sail to meet the woman who was to be his wife. When the princess appeared in front of the palace, her perfect beauty astonished the little mermaid.

"It was you," said the prince, "who saved my life when I was thought to be dead on the beach," and he took his soon-to-be bride into his arms.

The little mermaid kissed his hand and felt as if her heart were already broken. The prince's wedding day would bring death to her, and she would change into sea foam.

The little mermaid, dressed in silk and gold for the wedding ceremony, held up the bride's train, but her ears heard nothing of the festive music. She thought of the night of death that was coming to her, and of all she had lost in the world.

On the same evening the bride and bridegroom went on board the ship. The ship, with swelling sails and a favorable wind, glided away smoothly and lightly over the calm sea. The little mermaid could not help thinking of her first rising out of the sea, when she had seen similar festivities. She knew this was the last evening she would ever see the prince, for whom she had given up everything.

When the party had ended and night fell, she saw her sisters rising out of the flood. They were as pale as herself, but their long beautiful hair waved no more in the wind because it had been cut off.

"We have given our hair to the witch," they said, "so you won't die tonight. She has given us a knife. Before the sun rises you must plunge it into the heart of the prince. When his blood falls upon your feet, they will grow together again and form into a fish's tail, and you will once more be a mermaid."

That night, the little mermaid drew back the curtain of the tent where the prince and his bride were sleeping. She bent down and kissed him. Then she glanced at the sharp knife, and again looked at the prince. She was in his thoughts, and the knife trembled in the hand of the little mermaid. Then she flung it far away from her into the waves. She then threw herself into the sea, and thought her body was dissolving into foam. The sun rose above the waves and the little mermaid did not feel as if she were dying. She saw the bright sun, and all around her floated hundreds of transparent beautiful beings. The little mermaid felt as if she had a body like theirs. She continued to rise higher and higher out of the foam. When the mermaid called out "Where am I going?" she heard this answer: "Among the daughters of the air. You, poor little mermaid, have tried with your whole heart to do the right thing. You have suffered and endured and raised yourself to the spirit world by your good deeds and kind and happy heart."

∾ The End ∾

The Magic Kettle

A fairy tale from Japan.

High up in the mountains of Japan there once lived a good old man. He loved his little house and gardens and was very proud of them. He never tired of admiring the beauty of his home and that of the bountiful plants surrounding it.

One day, he was looking across at the mountain when he heard a rumbling in the room behind him. He turned around, and in the corner he saw a rusty old iron kettle. The old man had no idea how the kettle got there, but he picked it up, looked it over carefully, dusted it off, and carried it to the kitchen.

"This was a lucky find," he thought. "A new kettle costs money, and it's a good thing to have a spare on hand just in case."

He filled the kettle with water, and put it on the fire. No sooner was the water in the kettle getting warm than a strange thing happened. First, the handle of the kettle changed its shape and became a head, and the spout grew into a tail, while out of the body emerged four paws. In a few minutes, the man found himself watching not a boiling kettle but a kind of badger called a "tanuki"!

The creature jumped out of the fire and bounded about the room 'till the old man cried out in alarm that the animal would damage his beautiful house and gardens. He cried to his neighbor for help, and between them they managed to capture the tanuki and shut him safely in a wooden chest. Then, exhausted, they sat on their mats, trying to decide what to do with this bothersome beast. After some discussion, they decided to sell him, so they sent a neighbor child to bring a tradesman called Jimmu. Jimmu came and agreed to buy the kettle.

When Jimmu arrived home, he went right to bed, for he was exhausted from hauling the heavy kettle. In the middle of the night, he heard a loud noise. When he raised himself to look, he saw that the kettle had become a tanuki, which was chasing its own tail! After that, the happy creature began turning somersaults. Jimmu didn't know what to do about this odd situation, so he decided to sleep on it. When he awoke, however, there was no tanuki—just the kettle.

Jimmu decided to build a booth where people could come see the kettle. People came in crowds, and the kettle was passed from hand to hand. They would examine it all over and even look inside. Then Jimmu would take it back and, setting it on the platform, would command it to become a tanuki. In an instant the kettle transformed into the creature and entertained the crowds. Day after day, the booth was so full, it was hardly possible to enter it. Jimmu became a rich man. Yet, he did not feel happy. He was an honest man and felt he owed some of the money to the good old man who had sold him the kettle. So, one day, he filled the kettle with 100 gold pieces and returned to the old man's home. He told about his travels with the kettle and said, "I have brought it back to you, as I have no right to keep it any longer."

The man thanked Jimmu and said that few people would have been so honest. The kettle brought them both luck and everything always went very well for them.

≈ The End ≈

The Peasant and the Water Sprite

This story was adapted from the version written by the Russian author Tolstoy, whose rather impressive full name is Count Lev Nikolayevich Tolstoy. He lived from 1828 to 1910, and is considered one of the world's greatest novelists.

O nce upon a time, there was a very poor man who worked hard trying to make a living chopping trees in the forest. After chopping the trees, he'd sell the wood to villagers who would use it to warm their homes and to make fires to cook their meals.

It was difficult work, but the peasant enjoyed it. He loved the solitude of the forest and the kindness of the forest animals.

Many of the forest creatures had become his friends. When he would pause at midday for his meager lunch of bread and water, a friendly squirrel or deer would often sit near him, keeping him company. The peasant would repay the animal for its kind company with a crust of his bread.

Although he did not always have an easy life, the peasant was a happy man. But then, hard times came to his country.

A terrible drought caused the plants to shrivel and die. The dry spell went on and on. The livestock began to perish because there wasn't enough water for them to drink or grass for them to graze on.

These were sad times. The villagers who had bought wood from the peasant woodsman were unable to do so any longer. They weren't able to sell their crops or the milk from their cows. So, in turn, they didn't have the money to pay the peasant for his wood.

At first, the peasant was able to scrape by, eating root vegetables he'd stored from the previous growing season, foraging in the woods for a scrap of this or that, or occasionally eating one of his remaining bread crusts. Finally, though, his food was virtually all gone, and he didn't know how he would go on.

He continued to go to the forest and work. He had quite a stockpile of cut wood! He still enjoyed seeing his woodland friends, although they, too, were suffering from the dry conditions.

One day, when the peasant was already feeling particularly low, he accidentally dropped his prized ax into the river. He was so unhappy that he sat down on the muddy banks and began to cry. "After all," he thought, "now I really am without any hope. For how can a woodcutter survive without his ax?"

So he sat crying until a nearby water **sprite** heard him. The water sprite, a small and magical sparkling creature who lived in the river, felt sorry for the kindly woodcutter. She had observed him often in the forest and knew him to be a big and kindhearted fellow.

She decided to help him, so she fluttered to the top of the river's surface and brought him a golden ax that sparkled in the sunlight. The peasant was almost blinded by its brilliant finish.

"Is this your ax?" the sprite asked.

"No," said the honest man. "It's not mine."

The water sprite fluttered away and brought him another ax from the bottom of the river. This time it was a glistening silver one. It, too, shone brilliantly.

"That's not my ax, either, " said the man, again answering honestly.

Then the water sprite dove back down to the bottom of the river and brought up yet another ax. This was a rather plain and *very* worn-out ax.

"Now, that one is mine," said the man, happy and relieved to have it back. Now, he could go back to his business of being a woodcutter.

The water sprite, though, wanted to reward the man for his good heart and honest manner. So, she gave the man all three axes.

"But," protested the peasant, "why are you doing this for me?"

"Because," trilled the tiny sprite, "you have shown compassion for the creatures of the forest, and you have an honest spirit. For these things, I am rewarding you."

"Oh, thank you, precious Water Sprite," said the overwhelmed peasant.

The peasant finished his work in the woods, cutting trees with his old ax and patting the forest creatures. Then, as the sun started to set, the peasant went to his humble little home. As he made his way there, he showed his friends the three axes and told them what had happened.

"How can this be?" one of his friends thought to himself. "This really isn't fair that a common woodcutter should have such good fortune. I think I will go to the banks of that very river and try the same thing. After all, it is someone such as I, a shop owner, who should have treasures bestowed upon me by this water sprite."

So, off he went to the banks of the river. Once there, he quickly threw his ax into the water. Then, he perched on the banks of the river and pretended to cry.

The magical water sprite heard him. She was a bit skeptical—she'd never seen this man in the woods, and his crying sounded distinctly false. However, being a kindly sprite she decided to offer him a golden ax from the bottom of the river. She surfaced with it and asked, "Is this your ax?"

The man was overjoyed and shouted dishonestly, "Yes, yes, it's mine. Oh, thank you, Water Sprite."

The water sprite instantly disappeared, back to the bottom of the river with the golden ax.

"Hey, come back," shouted the dishonest man.

But the water sprite did not reappear, and did not give him the golden ax or, for that matter, his own ax, because he had lied to her.

The peasant, in the meantime, continued to live a kind and good life, remaining a friend to the forest animals. He took the golden ax, sold it in a faraway city, and used the money to help out the villagers who still suffered from the drought. He kept the silver ax for himself.

For the rest of his life, the villagers regarded him as a hero. They credited him with saving their lives during the worst dry spell the village had ever known.

In fact, if you visit the village today, there is a statue of the poor peasant, standing on the town green, to honor this simple man who saved his village.

⌒ *The End* ⌒

Pinocchio

Once upon a time a poor carpenter picked up a piece of wood while fixing a table. When he began to chisel it, the wood started to moan. This frightened the carpenter, and he decided to get rid of it at once. So he gave it to his friend, Geppetto, who wanted to make a puppet.

Geppetto, a cobbler, took the wood home, thinking about the name he would give his puppet. "I'll call him Pinocchio," he told himself. "It's a lucky name."

Back at his home, Geppetto started to carve the wood. Suddenly a voice squealed, "Oh! That hurt!"

Geppetto was astonished to find that the wood was alive. Excited, he carved a head, hair, and eyes, which immediately stared right at the cobbler. But the second Geppetto carved out the nose, it began to grow. No matter how often the cobbler cut it down to size, it just grew longer and longer.

When he finished carving the puppet, Geppetto taught him to walk. But the minute Pinocchio stood upright, he opened the door and ran into the street. Luckily, a policeman saw Pinocchio running from the cobbler. He grabbed the runaway and handed him over to his father.

Pinocchio apologized for running away, and Geppetto forgave his son. The cobbler made Pinocchio a suit out of colorful paper, a pair of tree-bark shoes, and a soft felt hat with a big feather. The puppet hugged his father.

"I'd like to go to school," he said, "to become clever and help you when you're old!"

"I'm very grateful," Geppetto replied, "but we haven't enough money to buy you even the first reading book!" Pinocchio looked sad, then Geppetto suddenly stood and went out of the house. Soon he returned carrying a first reading book, a little worn but still perfectly usable.

It was snowing outside. "Where's your coat, Father?" Pinocchio asked.

"I sold it."

"Why did you sell it?"

"It kept me too warm!"

Pinocchio threw his arms round Geppetto's neck and kissed him.

The next day, Pinocchio started toward school, but was distracted when he heard the sound of a brass band. He ended up in a crowded square where people were clustering round a booth.

"What's that?" he asked a boy.

"Can't you read? It's the Great Puppet Show!"

"How much do you pay to go inside?"

"Fourpence."

"Who'll give me fourpence for this book?" Pinocchio cried. A nearby junk seller bought the reading book, and Pinocchio hurried into the booth. Once inside the booth, Pinocchio knew he had made a mistake selling the book Geppetto had bought for him. He decided to return to his home and apologize to Geppetto.

Pinocchio sadly trudged home and told Geppetto that a bully had stolen his book. But as he spoke, something strange happened: His nose started to grow. And as he continued to insist the book had been stolen, his nose grew and grew.

"What is happening?" asked Pinocchio, alarmed.

"You're not telling the truth, Pinocchio," answered Geppetto. "When you lie, your nose grows. If you tell me the truth, your nose will return to its normal size."

So, Pinocchio told Geppetto what had happened to the book and his nose shrunk to its normal size. After scolding the puppet for selling the book, Geppetto forgave him and sent Pinocchio off to school.

But someone else was about to cross his path and lead him astray. This time, it was Carlo, an extremely lazy boy.

"Why don't you come to Toyland with me?" he said. "Nobody ever studies there and you can play all day long!"

"Does such a place really exist?" asked Pinocchio in amazement.

"The wagon comes by this evening to take me there," said Carlo. "Would you like to come?"

Forgetting all his promises to his father, Pinocchio was again heading for trouble. Midnight struck, and the wagon arrived to pick up the two friends, along with some other lads who could hardly wait to reach Toyland.

Twelve pairs of donkeys pulled the wagon, and they were all shod with white leather boots. The boys clambered into the wagon. Pinocchio, the most excited of them all, jumped onto a donkey. Toyland was just as Carlo had described it: The boys all had fun and there was no school.

One day, however, Pinocchio awoke to a rather nasty surprise. When he raised a hand to his head, he found he had sprouted a long pair of hairy ears, in place of the sketchy ears that Geppetto had never got around to finishing. The next day, they had grown longer than ever. Pinocchio pulled on a large cotton cap and went off to search for Carlo. He too was wearing a hat, pulled right down to his nose. With the same thought in their heads, the boys stared at each other. Then snatching off their hats, they began to laugh at the funny sight of the long hairy ears. But as they screamed with laughter, Carlo suddenly went pale and began to stagger. "Pinocchio, help! Help!" But Pinocchio himself was stumbling about, and he burst into tears. For their faces were growing into the shape of a donkey's head, and they felt themselves go down on all fours.

Pinocchio and Carlo were turning into donkeys. When the Toyland wagon driver heard the braying of his new donkeys, he rubbed his hands in glee.

"There are two fine new donkeys to take to market. I'll get at least four gold pieces for them!" Carlo was sold to a farmer. A circus man bought Pinocchio, and he had to learn circus tricks. One day, as he was jumping through the hoop, he stumbled and went lame.

The circus man called the stable boy. "A lame donkey is of no use to me," he said. "Take it to market and get rid of it at any price!" But nobody wanted to buy a useless donkey. Then along came a little man who said, "I'll take it for the skin. It will make a good drum for the village band."

And so, for a few pennies, Pinocchio was purchased. His new owner led him to the edge of the sea, tied a large stone to his neck, and a long rope round his legs, and pushed him into the water. Clutching the end of the rope, the man sat down to wait for Pinocchio to drown. Pinocchio struggled for breath at the bottom of the sea. In a flash, he remembered all the trouble he had given Geppetto and all his broken promises, too, and he called on a fairy to help him.

A fairy heard Pinocchio's call and sent a school of big fish. They ate away all the donkey flesh, leaving the wooden Pinocchio. Just then, as the fish stopped nibbling, Pinocchio felt himself hauled out of the water. The man gasped in astonishment at the living puppet, which appeared in place of the dead donkey. Pinocchio told the man the whole story and dived into the sea. Thankful to be a wooden puppet again, Pinocchio swam happily out to sea and was soon just a dot on the horizon.

But his adventures were far from over. Out of the water behind him loomed a shark with huge teeth! Pinocchio tried to swim away as fast as he could, but the shark glided closer and eventually swallowed him. When Pinocchio came to his senses, he was in darkness. Suddenly, he noticed a pale light and, as he crept toward it, he saw it was a flame in the distance.

"Father! It can't be you!"

"Pinocchio! Son! It really is you."

Weeping for joy, they hugged each other and, between sobs, told their adventures. Geppetto told him how he came to be in the shark's stomach. "I was looking for you everywhere. When I couldn't find you on dry land, I made a boat to search for you on the sea. But the boat capsized in a storm, and then the shark ate me."

"Well, we're still alive!" remarked Pinocchio. "We must get out of here!"

The pair started to climb up the shark's stomach, using a candle to light their way. This shark happened to sleep with its mouth open, so they quietly hurried out while it was napping.

At long last, Pinocchio and Geppetto reached home. Geppetto was so ill from his adventures that he was near death. Pinocchio took care of him until he recovered. He went to work for a nearby farmer to earn money to buy food for his father.

One night, in a wonderful dream, the fairy appeared to reward Pinocchio. When the puppet looked in the mirror next morning, he found he had turned into a real boy. Geppetto hugged him happily.

"Where's the wooden Pinocchio?" the boy asked.

"There!" exclaimed Geppetto, pointing at him. "You've shown you're a real boy with a real kind, giving heart."

The End

Rip Van Winkle

Once upon a time, high in the Catskill Mountains, lived an amiable fellow named Rip Van Winkle. Rip Van Winkle was not an ambitious guy; and in fact some, including his wife, called him lazy.

He was, though, a very popular fellow who, as far as anyone could tell, had just one failing: his uncanny ability to find employment and business anywhere but on his own farm. He could fish all day without a single nibble. The village women asked him to run their errands and to do other odd jobs since their own husbands wouldn't.

Rip Van Winkle was happy and would have believed his life to be quite perfect if it weren't for one particularly pesky thorn in his side: his wife. She kept at him day and night about his chronic idleness.

Rip's only friend at home was his dog, Wolf. As frequently as possible, both Rip and Wolf would sneak out of the house and sit on the bench outside the town's inn, underneath the sign with the picture of His Majesty George the Third. There they would sit and talk with other lazy folk like Derrick Van Bummel, the schoolmaster, or Nicholas Vedder, the landlord of the inn.

One fine autumn day, Rip put his musket on his shoulder, whistled Wolf to his side, and climbed up to one of the highest points of the Catskill Mountains. He hunted squirrel for a bit. Then, panting and fatigued, he threw himself on a green knoll and snoozed in peace.

"Rip Van Winkle!" said a voice. And he woke with a start.

He looked round and saw nothing but a crow. At the same time, though, Wolf bristled up his back and gave a low growl. Then Rip saw a strange, short, square-built man lumbering toward him. He had thick bushy hair and a grizzled beard. Rip followed the short fellow up into the mountains.

As they climbed, Rip heard sounds like distant thunder that seemed to come from a deep ravine. Here, the short man poured a glass of liquid from his keg for Rip, who obliged by taking a small taste. He then fell into a deep sleep.

On waking, he found himself on the green knoll where he had first seen the old man. He rubbed his eyes—it was a bright sunny morning. "Surely," thought Rip, "I have not slept here all night." He recalled the occurrences before he fell asleep—the strange man with a keg of potent liquid, the mountain ravine, and the deep sleep. For now, though, he was worried about what his wife would have to say about his absence!

He looked round for his gun, but in place of the clean, well-oiled musket, he found an old gun lying by him, the barrel coated with rust, the lock falling off, and the stock filled with worm holes. Perhaps that fellow had played a trick on him, poisoning his drink and taking his gun. Wolf, too, had disappeared. Rip whistled and shouted, but with no success.

As he rose to walk, he found him-self stiff in the joints. He again called and whistled for his dog; he was answered only by the cawing of a flock of idle crows. He shook his head, shouldered the rusty musket, and, with a heart full of trouble and worry, turned his steps homeward.

As he approached the village, he met a number of people, but he didn't recognize any of them. This somewhat surprised him, for he had thought him-self acquainted with everyone in the area.

Their clothing, too, seemed different. They all stared at him in surprise. Rip stared back and pulled at his beard, and, to his astonishment, he found his beard had grown over a foot long!

A cluster of children ran at his heels, hooting and hollering after him, and pointing at his long gray beard. He hardly recognized his village. It was larger and more crowded. There were rows of houses that he had never seen before. Strange names were over the doors, strange faces at the windows—everything was strange. What was going on? he wondered.

He found the way to his own house, expecting to hear the shrill voice of Mrs. Van Winkle. He found the house gone to ruin—the roof fallen in, the windows shattered, and the doors off their hinges. A half-starved dog that looked like Wolf was skulking about, but it only snarled at him.

Eventually, a group of villagers gathered around this odd looking man. Rip thought for a moment, and then inquired of them, "Where's Nicholas Vedder?"

"Nicholas Vedder! Why, he's been dead for eighteen years!"

"Where's Brom Dutcher, or Van Bummel, the schoolmaster?"

"They went off to the army at the beginning of the war. Dutcher never came back. Van Bummel became a great general and is now in Congress."

Rip's heart sunk. At last he cried out in despair, "Does nobody here know Rip Van Winkle?"

"Oh, Rip Van Winkle!" exclaimed two or three, "Oh, yes! That's Rip Van Winkle up there, leaning against the tree."

Rip looked up and saw an exact image of himself as he looked the day he went up the mountain: apparently as lazy, and certainly as rough around the edges. The poor fellow was now completely mystified. He doubted his own identity and whether he was himself or another man.

"Who are you? What's your name?" asked the gathered crowd.

"I'm not sure," said the old fellow.

At this critical moment a familiar-looking woman with a baby in her arms came to peek at Rip.

"What is your name, my good woman?" he asked.

"Judith Gardenier."

"And what was your father's name?"

"Oh, poor guy. Rip Van Winkle was his name, but it's been twenty years since he went away from home with his gun and never has been heard of since—his dog came home without him. We don't know what happened to him."

Rip had only one more question to ask: "Where's your mother?"

"Oh, she too died. She died in a fit of rage!"

Finally, Rip said, "I am your father. Young Rip Van Winkle once—old Rip Van Winkle now. Does nobody know poor Rip Van Winkle?"

All stood amazed, until an old woman, tottering out from among the crowd, put her hand to her brow, and peering under it at his face for a moment, exclaimed, "Sure enough! It is Rip Van Winkle—it is him! Welcome home again, old neighbor. Why, where have you been these twenty years?"

Rip's story was soon told. His daughter took him home to live with her. She had a snug house, and a round, happy farmer for a husband, whom Rip remembered as one of the urchins who used to torment him. As for Rip's son and heir, who was lazy like Rip Senior, he attended to just about anything except his business.

For many years, Rip Van Winkle (Senior) could be found hanging out at the new village inn, under the sign of George Washington, recounting the story of his strange travels into the mountains. Often Rip Van Winkle (Junior) would find the time to be there, too!

The End

The Saucy Boy

Once upon a time there was an old poet. He was a very good and wise poet.

One evening, as he was sitting at home, there was a terrible storm raging outside and the rain was pouring down. The old poet, though, sat comfortably by the fire, which was burning, and there were apples roasting.

"There will not be a dry thread left on the poor people who are out in this weather," he said.

"Oh, open the door! I am so cold and wet," called a little child outside. He was crying and knocking at the door, while the rain continued to pour down and the wind rattled all the windows.

"Poor little guy!" said the poet, and got up and opened the door. Before him stood a little boy who was naked, and the water flowed from his long blond hair. He was shivering with cold; if he had not been let in, he would certainly have died in the storm.

"Poor little thing!" said the poet, and took him by the hand. "Come in. I will soon warm you. You shall have some juice and an apple."

He was a handsome boy. His eyes sparkled like two bright stars, and he had lush, curly hair. He looked like a little angel, but he was pale with cold and trembling all over. In his hand he held a splendid bow, but it had been entirely ruined by the rain, and the colors of the pretty arrows had run into one another because of the rain.

The old man sat down by the fire, and taking the little boy on his knee, wrung the water out of his locks and warmed his hands in his own. He then made the boy some hot spiced juice, which quickly revived him. So with glowing cheeks, the boy sprang upon the floor and danced around the old man.

"You are a merry boy," said the poet. "What is your name?"

"My name is Cupid," he answered. "Don't you know me? There is my bow. I shoot with that, you know. Look, the weather is getting fine again—the moon is shining."

"But your bow is ruined from the rain," said the old poet.

"That would be unfortunate," said the little boy, taking it up and looking at it. "Oh, it's quite dry and isn't damaged at all. The string is quite tight. I'll try it." So, drawing it back, he took an arrow, aimed, and shot the good old poet right in the heart. "Do you see now that my bow was not ruined?" he said, and, loudly laughing, ran away. What a naughty boy to shoot the old poet, who had taken him into his warm room, had been so good to him, and had given him the nicest juice and the best apple!

The good old man lay on the floor crying. He was really shot in the heart. "Oh!" he cried, "what a rotten boy this Cupid is! I shall tell all the good children about this, so that they never play with him."

And all good children were on their guard against wicked Cupid, but he tricks them still. When the students come out of class, he walks beside them with a book under his arm and wearing a black coat. They cannot recognize him. And then, if they take him by the arm, believing him to be a student too, he sticks an arrow into their chest. He is always after people. He sits in the large chandelier in the theater and blazes away, so that people think it is only a light fixture; but they soon find out their mistake. He walks about in the castle garden. Yes, once he shot your father and your mother in the heart, too. Just ask them. He is a bad boy, this Cupid, and you must never have anything to do with him, for he is after every one of you!

⌒ The End ⌒

The Snow Maiden

Once upon a time there lived an old man and woman. They lived in a tiny town at the edge of a great forest. They'd had a very happy life, always having plenty to eat, a roof over their heads, and many good friends.

The man had worked as a farmer and loved toiling on the land. The woman had kept house and cooked lovely meals. All in all, they felt they shouldn't complain about what life had given them.

They did, though, have one sorrow. They wished that they had children, but they had never been able to have any. So, here they were, getting on in years and feeling lonely without little ones about.

Then, one lovely winter day the couple saw some neighborhood children playing outside in the newly fallen snow. First, the children took turns on a little red sled, barreling down a small hill. Then, they attached makeshift snowshoes to their feet and they explored the area. Next, they lay down in the snow, waving their arms and legs, and made snow angels.

Although the man and woman enjoyed watching the lively, happy children, it made the disappointment of not having a child of their own stronger than ever. Finally, the old man turned to his wife and said, "I have an idea that might help us feel just a tiny bit better. Let's go outside and build a snowgirl— it will be like the daughter we never had."

So the two worked together to build a snowgirl. They started by carefully forming her hands and feet. Then they turned their attention to her button nose, her small mouth, and her dimpled chin. Their efforts took some time, for they wanted the snowgirl to look just right. Finally, they stood back, satisfied with their work, and smiled at each other happily.

Just seconds after they finished, the snowgirl's lips suddenly turned rose red and her eyes began to open. She smiled warmly at the old couple, not at all surprised to be there, shook the spare flakes of crisp snow off her just-formed body, and emerged from the snowdrift as a pretty young girl!

The old couple were so happy. They couldn't believe their incredible good fortune, and they cried with joy as they hugged their new snow daughter. Then they took her into their hut and named her Snow Maiden.

Amazingly, their little Snow Maiden began to grow quickly, not by the day but rather by the hour. Before long, she became quite beautiful, and the old couple loved her more than they had ever thought possible. For the first time, they felt truly, completely happy.

The Snow Maiden was a lovely, willing child. She always did her chores, never complained, and was very affectionate. She would help her father bring in wood for the fire and help her mother prepare meals. She even learned to knit and crochet and to read a bit. She often told her parents how much she loved them.

Most of all, though, the Snow Maiden loved to spend a lot of time outdoors. She liked the feel of the cool breeze on her fair skin and enjoyed spending time with the small creatures of the forest.

So it went that winter passed, and soon the warm

spring sun started to heat the land and bring about a thaw. The girl became quite depressed. She couldn't understand why she was feeling so sad.

"What's the matter?" the old couple would ask. "Are you not feeling well? Is there anything we can do to help you? We are worried about you."

"No, I'm fine, Mother and Father. Please, do not worry," she would reply, because she didn't want her parents to worry.

But there was no denying that something was wrong. Her parents could see it and so could the woodland creatures. No longer did the girl run and skip and sing when she came with their little treats. Now, she walked slowly and carefully, and the gleam was missing from her eyes.

Soon, the last of the winter's snow melted. Daffodils, crocus, and other flowers began to bloom in the meadows, giving vivid color to the arrival of spring.

When the larks started to sing, the girl became even sadder. And she would hide from the sun at every opportunity. "What is going on?" she wondered.

Just when it seemed winter was finished for the year, a cold day arrived and dark clouds moved through, bringing with them a flurry of hail. The girl rejoiced, looking at the stones of hail as if they were giant, precious pearls. But soon, spring temperatures prevailed, and the hail melted. Then, the Snow Maiden cried as if her heart would break.

Spring continued with the arrival of more birds, and the blossoming of many lovely plants. The Snow Maiden tried to enjoy herself and be good company to her kind parents.

Finally, though, summer arrived. One day a group of friendly girls called out to the Snow Maiden, "Come with us for a nice walk in the woods!"

The Snow Maiden didn't want to go, but her parents urged her on, saying, "Go play with them, dear. You'll have fun." They worried that she was lonely, and they hoped she would enjoy the company of other young girls.

So she went reluctantly with the girls, who began collecting flowers, singing songs, and dancing. The Snow Maiden didn't join in, though, and wasn't having a very good time. She felt anxious and worried.

As the sun started to set and darkness grew, the other girls made a fire from some twigs they had collected. They continued to laugh and sing and tell stories, and the Snow Maiden could see how much fun the girls were having. Finally, she decided to join in. For the first time since winter, a smile formed on her face as she laughed, sang, and danced with the others. "This *is* fun," she thought.

Then, one by one, the other girls began playfully jumping over the small twig fire they had built. The Snow Maiden jumped over when it was her turn, but halfway through her leap, she suddenly melted and turned into a white cloud. She disappeared into the air.

A faint good-bye was heard before the cloud rose up and disappeared into the heavens. The Snow Maiden was gone.

But her sad parents were not to worry, for she would return the following year. And, indeed she did, and every year after. In fact to this day, the Snow Maiden returns every winter to bring joy and love to a lonely family.

⌒ *The End* ⌒

The Snowman

Once upon a time there was a snowman who wanted to learn to run like the human boys who had made him.

"Don't worry," barked the old yard-dog. "The sun will make you run some day. Last winter, I saw him make your predecessor run and his predecessor before him. They all have to go away. It never fails."

"I don't understand you, friend," said the snowman. "Is that thing glowing in the sky supposed to teach me to run? I saw it running itself a little while ago, and now it has come slinking up from the other side."

"You know nothing at all," replied the yard-dog, "but then, you've only just been made. What you see over there is the moon; the one before it was the sun. It will come again tomorrow and, most likely, teach you to run down into the ditch by the well because I think the weather is going to change. I can feel it in my bones."

"I don't understand him," said the snowman to himself, "but I have a feeling that he is talking about something unpleasant. The one who stared so just now, that he calls the sun, is not my friend. I can feel that too."

The dog was right. There was a definite change in the weather. Toward morning, a thick fog covered the whole country, and a brisk wind arose, so that the cold seemed to freeze to the bone. But when the sun rose, the sight was splendid and glittering. Trees and bushes were covered with frost and looked like a forest of dazzling diamonds.

"This is really beautiful," said a young girl, who had come into the garden with a young man. They both stood still near the snowman and contemplated the sparkling, white scene.

"Summer cannot compete with winter's beauty," she exclaimed.

They admired the snowman and then skipped away over the snow.

"Who are these two?" asked the snowman of the yard-dog. "You have been here longer than I have. Do you know them?"

"Of course I know them," replied the yard-dog. "She has patted my back many times, and he has given me a bone of meat. I never bite those two."

"But who are they?" asked the snowman.

"They're sweethearts," he replied. "They will go and live in the same kennel some day, chew at the same bone, and share the same water bowl."

"Are they the same kind of beings as you and I?" asked the snowman.

"Well, they belong to the same master," said the yard-dog. "I can see that people who were born just yesterday know very little. I can see that in you. I have age and experience. I know everyone here in the house, and I know there was once a time when I did not lie out here in the cold, fastened to a chain."

"The cold is delightful," said the snowman, "but tell me about being a puppy."

"I used to lie in a velvet-covered chair, up at the master's house, and sit in the mistress's lap," the dog began. "They used to kiss my nose and wipe my paws with an embroidered handkerchief. I was called 'My Sweet Puppy Love.' But after a while I grew too big for them, and they sent me away to the house-keeper's room. I went to live in the basement. You can look into the room from where you stand, and see where I was master once, for I was master to the housekeeper. It was certainly a smaller room than those upstairs, but I was comfortable. I was not always being taunted by the kids. I received good food, and I had my own cushion with my name, Theodore, stitched on it. There was a stove. I'd lie in front of it."

"Does a stove look beautiful?" asked the snowman. "Is it at all like me?"

"It is just the opposite of you," said the dog. "It's as black as a crow and has a long neck and a brass knob. It eats firewood, so that fire blows out of its mouth."

"And why did you leave her?" asked the snowman, for it seemed to him that the stove must be a female. "How could you give up such a comfortable place?"

"I had to," replied the yard-dog. "They turned me out-of-doors and chained me up here. I had bitten the youngest of my master's sons in the leg, because he kicked away the bone I was gnawing and always teased me."

The snowman was no longer listening. He was looking into the house-keeper's room on the lower level where the stove stood on its four iron legs, looking about the same size as the snowman himself. "What a strange crackling I feel within me," he said. "Shall I ever get in there? I must go in there and lean against her, even if I have to break the window."

"You must never go in there," said the yard-dog, "for if you approach the stove, you'll melt away."

"I might as well go," said the snowman, "for I think I am melting anyway."

During the whole day the snowman stood looking in through the window. As the sun set the room became even more inviting, for from the stove came a gentle glow, not like the sun or the moon. When the door of the stove was opened, the flames darted out of its mouth. The light of the flames fell directly on the snowman's face.

The night was long, but it did not seem so to the snowman. He stood there, enjoying his own reflection and crackling with the cold. In the morning, the windowpanes of the housekeeper's room were covered with ice. They were the most beautiful ice-flowers any snowman could imagine, but they hid the stove. These windowpanes would not thaw, and he could see nothing of the stove. This upset the snowman.

"That is a terrible disease for a snowman," said the yard-dog. "I have suffered from it myself, but I got over it. The weather is going to change."

And the weather did change. It began to get warm and thaw.

One day, the snowman melted to the ground, leaving only the broomstick around which he had been built and a stove scraper.

"Oh, now I understand why he had such a great love for the stove," said the yard-dog. "Why, there's the scraper that is used for cleaning out the stove. The boys used it when they built him and put it inside his body."

Yes, the snowman had had a stove scraper inside his body; that was what made him desire the stove.

And so, winter left, and spring arrived. Nobody thought of the snowman until he came again the following winter.

The End

The Snow Queen

O nce upon a time a magician made a magic mirror. It was a mirror of opposites. If a kind face looked into the mirror, a wicked face looked back. If a loving look was cast at the mirror, a look of hate was reflected.

One day the mirror broke. If a sliver of glass from the mirror entered someone's eye, that person became evil; if another sliver pierced a heart, that heart grew hard and cruel.

Two children, Karl and Gerda, were very close friends. One evening Karl was watching the snow fall when he noticed a white flake slowly turn into a beautiful ice maiden. Karl was startled to hear the ice maiden speak his name. He didn't know he was looking at the Snow Queen.

Spring came and one afternoon, as Karl and Gerda looked at a book, the little boy told her, "I feel a pain in my heart! And something's pricking my eye!"

"Don't worry," said Gerda comfortingly. "I don't see anything!"

But, unfortunately, splinters from the shattered mirror had pierced the little boy. Now he was under an evil spell. Because of this, he snapped at his best friend, "You're so ugly!"

Ripping two roses from her rosebush, he ran off. From that day on, Karl turned into a very nasty boy, and nobody knew what had happened to cause this. Only Gerda still loved him, though all she got in return were insults and angry words.

Winter came again, bringing far more snow than anyone could remember. One day, just after going outdoors to play in the snow, Karl saw the beautiful maiden he had seen before. She was coming toward him wrapped in a luxurious white fur coat. She stood in front of him and told him to tie his sled to her own, which was drawn by a white horse, and they sped away.

Suddenly, the great sled soared into the sky and through the clouds. Stretched out on his own little sled, Karl didn't dare move a muscle for fear of falling into space. At last, they came to a halt on a huge white plain, dotted with lots of sparkling frozen lakes.

"Come into my arms," said the Snow Queen, opening her soft fur coat. "Come and keep warm!"

Karl allowed himself to be hugged by the unknown maiden, and a chill ran up his spine as two icy lips touched his forehead. The Snow Queen kissed him again, and in an instant, the little boy forgot all about Gerda and his past life and fell into a deep sleep.

In the meantime, Gerda was anxiously searching for Karl, but no one had seen him. Finally, she went down to the river. "Great River," she said, "please tell me if you've seen Karl or if you've carried him away! I'll give you these, if you do!" And she threw her shoes into the river.

But the river's swift current paid no attention to her and just swept the shoes back to the bank. Not far away stood an old boat and Gerda climbed into it. As she drifted with the current, she pleaded, "Great River, take me to Karl."

As night fell, she stopped by a riverbank carpeted with all kinds of colorful flowers. After resting, she went into the forest. Although she did not know how she would ever find her friend, a mysterious voice inside her told her to be brave. After wandering for hours, Gerda stopped, tired and hungry. A crow flapped out from a hollow tree. "Caw! Caw! If you're looking for Karl," it said, "I know where he is! I saw him with the Snow Queen on her sled in the sky!"

"And where is her kingdom?" Gerda asked the crow.

"In Lapland, where all is icy cold. That reindeer over there might take you!"

Gerda ran over to the big reindeer, threw her arms around his neck, and, laying her cheek against his soft muzzle, said, "Please help me to find my friend!"

The reindeer's kindly eyes told her that he would, and she climbed onto his back. They traveled 'till they came to the frozen **tundra**, lit by the fiery glow of the **Northern Lights**.

"Karl! Karl! Where are you?" shouted Gerda.

When, at last, she found the little boy, Karl was still in the deep sleep of the wicked spell. Gerda threw her arm around him, and teardrops dripped onto his chest and heart. The tears washed away the slivers of glass, and the evil spell was broken. Karl woke from his long sleep, and when he set eyes on Gerda, he too began to cry. They had found each other again at last, thanks to Gerda's love, and the reindeer carried them home.

From then on, they remained close friends, happily ever after.

The End

The Story of the Greek King and the Physician Douban

O nce upon a time there lived a Greek king. This king was a **leper**, and no doctor had been able to cure him until a very clever physician came to his palace.

This physician spoke many languages and knew a great deal about herbal remedies and medicines. As soon as he was told of the king's illness, he put on his best robe and presented himself to the king.

"Sire," he said, "I know that no physician has been able to cure you. But if you will follow my instructions, I promise to cure you while you play your favorite sport."

The king listened to this proposal and said to the doctor, "If you are clever enough to do this, I promise to make you and your descendants rich forever."

The physician went to his house and made a **polo** club. He hollowed out the handle and put in it the drug he wished to use. Then he made a ball. The next day he took these things to the king.

He told the king that he wished him to play polo. So, the king mounted his horse and went into the place where he played. There the physician approached him with the mallet he had made and said, "Take this, Sire, and strike the ball till you feel your hand and your whole body glow. When your hand warms, the remedy that is in the handle of the club will soak into your body. Then you must return to your palace, bathe, and go to sleep. When you awake tomorrow morning, you will be cured."

The king took the club and urged his horse after the ball, which he had thrown. He struck it, and then it was hit back by the courtiers who were playing with him. When he felt very hot, he stopped playing, went back to the palace, took a bath, and did all that the physician had said. The next day when he woke up, he found, to his astonishment, that he was completely cured!

The physician Douban entered the hall and bowed low to the ground. The king, seeing him, called him and made him sit by his side to honor him.

That evening he gave him a long, regal robe of state to wear and presented him with two thousand gold coins. The physician had done what no other doctor had been able to accomplish: cure the king. For this, the king was forever grateful.

⌖ *The End* ⌖

The Three Wishes

What if you encountered an enchanted elf or some other wish-granting creature or person who offered to make three of your wishes come true? What would you ask for?

Once upon a time a woodcutter lived happily with his wife in a pretty little log cabin in the middle of a dense forest. Each morning he set off merrily to work. When he came home in the evening, a bowl of hot steaming soup or a plate of savory casserole was always waiting for him.

One day, however, he had an odd surprise. He came upon a big fir tree with strange holes on the trunk. It looked a bit different from the other trees. Just as he was about to chop it down, the alarmed face of an elf popped out of a hole.

"Hey, what's all this banging?" asked the elf. "You're not thinking of cutting down this tree, are you? It's my home. I live here!"

The woodcutter dropped his ax in astonishment.

"Well," the elf exclaimed, "Lucky I was in, or I would have found myself homeless."

Although he was surprised by the appearance of the elf, the woodcutter quickly recovered, for after all the elf was quite tiny, while he himself was a big, stocky fellow. He boldly replied, "I'll cut down any tree I like!"

"All right! All right!" broke in the elf. "Let me put it this way: If you don't cut down this tree, I'll grant you three wishes. How does that sound?"

The woodcutter scratched his head. "Three wishes, you say? Yes, okay."

And he began to chop down another tree. As he worked and became sweaty, the woodcutter kept thinking about the magic wishes. "I'll see what my wife thinks."

The woodcutter's wife was busy working in the garden when her husband arrived. Grabbing her round the waist, he twirled her in delight.

"Hooray! Hooray! This is our lucky day!" The woman could not understand why her husband was so pleased with himself. At dinner, though, the woodcutter told his wife of his meeting with the elf. She too began to picture the wonderful things that the elf's three wishes might give them.

The woodcutter's wife took a sip of her wine and, without thinking, said, "I wish I had a string of sausages to go with it." Instantly she bit her tongue, but it was too late. Out of the air appeared the sausages, while the woodcutter shouted with rage.

"Look at what you have! Sausages! What a stupid waste of a wish! You foolish woman! I wish they would stick up your nose!"

Oh, no! No sooner said, than done. For the sausages zipped up and stuck fast to the end of the woman's nose. This time, the woodcutter's wife flew into a rage. "You idiot, what have you done? With all the things we could have wished for."

As his wife complained and blamed him, the poor man burst out laughing. "If only you knew how funny you look with those

sausages on the end of your nose!" Now that really upset the woodcutter's wife. She hadn't thought of her looks. She tried to tug away the sausages, but they would not budge. She pulled again and again, but with no luck.

Feeling sorry for his wife and wondering how he could ever put up with a woman with such an odd nose, the woodcutter said, "I'll try." Grasping the string of sausages, he tugged with all his might. But he simply pulled his wife over on top of him. The pair sat on the floor, gazing sadly at each other. "What shall we do now?" they said, each speaking the same thought.

"There's only one thing we can do," said the woodcutter's wife.

"Yes, I'm afraid so," her husband said, remembering the dreams of riches. Finally, he said, "I wish the sausages would leave my wife's nose." And they did.

Instantly, the couple hugged each other tearfully, saying, "Maybe we'll be poor, but we'll be happy again!"

And, so they were.

⇜ *The End* ⇝

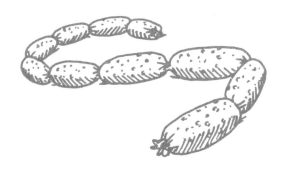

Thumbelina

Once upon a time there was a woman who wanted a child. Since these were magical times, she went to a fairy and asked the little **sprite** if her wish would be granted.

"Oh, yes," said the fairy. "Here is a barleycorn. Put it into a flowerpot, and see what happens."

"Thank you," said the woman. So she went home and planted it, and immediately a large handsome flower grew up. "It is a beautiful flower," said the woman, and she kissed the leaves. When she did so, the flower opened, and within the flower perched a tiny maiden. She was scarcely half as long as a thumb, and the woman gave her the name of Thumbelina because she was so small.

Thumbelina's bed was formed of blue violet-leaves and a walnut shell. One night, while she lay in her pretty bed, a large, slimy toad crept through a broken pane of glass, and leaped right upon the table where Thumbelina lay sleeping under her roseleaf quilt. "What a pretty wife she would make for my son," said the toad, and she took the walnut-shell bed in which little Thumbelina lay asleep and jumped through the window with it.

The toad's son was even uglier than his mother, and when he saw the pretty little maiden in her walnut-shell bed, he could only croak happily.

They placed the bed on a water-lily leaf out in a stream where Thumbelina couldn't escape, while the toad and her son made plans for a very fancy wedding ceremony.

Thumbelina woke the next morning and began to cry when she found where she was. She could see nothing but water on every side and no way of reaching land.

Eventually, the toad swam out with her ugly son to the leaf on which they had placed Thumbelina. "Here is my son, he will be your husband, and you will live happily in the **marsh** by the stream," the toad croaked.

Thumbelina cried because she could not bear to think of living with the old toad and having her ugly son for a husband. The little fishes, who swam about in the water beneath, had seen the toad and heard what she said, so they lifted their heads above the water to look at the little maiden. As soon as they caught sight of her, they saw she was very pretty. It made them very sorry to think that she must go and live with the ugly toads. So they gnawed away at the root of the leaf where Thumbelina was sitting. When they had finished, the leaf floated down the stream.

As Thumbelina sailed, a large beetle flew by. The moment he caught sight of her, he grabbed her and flew with her into a tree. Oh, how frightened little Thumbelina felt when the beetle flew with her to the tree! He seated himself by her side on a large green leaf, gave her some honey to eat, and told her she was very pretty. But all of the other beetles turned up and said, "She has only two legs! How ugly that looks."

The beetle believed the others when they said she was ugly and had nothing more to do with her. He told her she might go where she liked.

During the summer, poor little Thumbelina lived alone in the forest. Summer and autumn passed, then came winter—a long, cold winter. Thumbelina felt so cold. She went looking for shelter and found the door of a field mouse, who had a little den under the corn-stubble. There dwelt the field mouse in warmth and comfort, with a whole roomful of corn. Poor little Thumbelina stood before the door just like a little beggar-girl and asked for help.

"You poor little creature," said the field mouse, who was really a good, kind field mouse, "come into my warm room and dine with me. We shall have a visitor soon. My neighbor pays me a visit once a week. He is rich. If you could only have him for a husband, you would be well provided for indeed. But he is blind, so you must tell him a pretty story."

But Thumbelina did not feel at all interested in this neighbor, for he was a mole. But, the mole, upon hearing Thumbelina's lovely voice, fell in love with her. He said nothing yet, for he was very cautious. Instead, he invited Thumbelina and the field mouse to visit him.

A short time before, the mole had dug a long passage under the earth, which led from the dwelling of the field mouse to his home. He warned them not to be alarmed at the sight of a dead bird in the passage.

When Thumbelina saw the bird—which was a swallow—she felt very sad. She stooped down and stroked aside the soft feathers that covered the head and kissed the closed eyelids.

That night Thumbelina could not sleep. So she got out of bed and wove a large quilt of hay. Then she carried it to the dead bird and spread it over him. She laid her head on the bird's breast, and was alarmed to hear the bird's heart beat. He was not really dead, only numb with the cold, and the warmth had restored him to life. Thumbelina trembled, for the bird was a great deal larger than herself. But she took courage and laid the blanket more thickly over the poor swallow. The next morning she again stole out to see him. He was alive but very weak.

"Thank you, pretty little maiden," said the sick swallow. "I have been so nicely warmed that I shall soon regain my strength and be able to fly about again in the warm sunshine."

The whole winter the swallow remained underground, and Thumbelina nursed him. Neither the mole nor the field mouse knew anything about it, for they did not like swallows. Very soon the springtime came, and the sun warmed the earth. Then the swallow bade farewell to Thumbelina. The swallow asked her if she would go with him—she could sit on his back—but Thumbelina knew it would make the field mouse very sad so she said no.

"Good-bye, then," said the swallow and flew away.

"You are going to be married, Thumbelina," said the field mouse soon after the swallow left. "My neighbor has asked for you."

Thumbelina wept and said she would not marry the disagreeable mole.

"Nonsense," replied the field mouse. "Now don't be stubborn."

So the wedding day was set, and the mole was to fetch Thumbelina away to live with him, deep under the earth. The poor child was very unhappy at the thought of saying farewell to the beautiful sun. The field mouse had given her permission to stand at the door, so she went to look at the sun once more.

"Farewell, bright sun," she cried.

Tweet, tweet, sounded over her head suddenly. She looked up, and there was the swallow flying close by. As soon as he spied Thumbelina, he was delighted. She told him that she didn't want to marry the ugly mole, to live beneath the earth and never see the bright sun again.

"Cold winter is coming," said the swallow, "and I am going to fly away into warmer countries. Will you go with me? Fly now with me, dear little Thumbelina. You saved my life when I lay frozen."

"Yes, I will go with you," she said, and seated herself on the bird's back.

Then the swallow rose in the air and flew over forest and over sea, high above the mountains. At last they came to a blue lake, and by the side of it, shaded by trees of the deepest green, stood a palace of dazzling white marble.

Vines clustered round its lofty pillars, and at the top were many swallows' nests. One was the home of the swallow that carried Thumbelina.

"This is my house," said the swallow, "but it would not do for you to live there. You must choose one of those lovely flowers, and I will put you down upon it."

"That will be delightful," she said.

A large marble pillar lay on the ground broken into pieces. Between them grew the most magnificent white flowers. The swallow flew down with Thumbelina and placed her on one of the broad leaves. But how surprised she was to see in the middle of the flower a tiny little man, as transparent as glass! He had a golden crown on his head and delicate wings at his shoulders, and he was not much larger than Thumbelina herself. He was the angel of the flower. A tiny man and a tiny woman dwelt in every flower. This was the prince of them all.

The little prince was at first quite frightened of the bird, who was like a giant, compared to such a delicate little guy like himself. But when he saw Thumbelina, he was delighted, and thought her the prettiest little maiden he had ever seen. He asked if she would be his wife and queen of all the flowers. Thumbelina happily agreed.

Then all the flowers opened, and out of each came a little lady or a tiny lord. Each of them brought Thumbelina a present. The best gift of all was a pair of beautiful wings, which had belonged to a large white fly. They fastened them to Thumbelina's shoulders, so that she might fly happily from flower to flower and visit her new friends.

And there, Thumbelina lived happily ever after.

⤙ The End ⤚

Tom Thumb

Once upon a time, in the days of King Arthur, there lived a very wise wizard named Merlin. He knew all the fairies, and even the fairy queen was a friend of his.

One day Merlin knocked at the door of a small cottage and asked for some food. He looked so hungry that the farmer and his wife took pity on him. They not only gave him a bowl of milk with some tasty bread, but they said he could spend the night in their home.

Merlin saw that the farmer and his wife were very sad.

"Why are you so sad?" asked Merlin.

"Oh!" said the woman, "we are unhappy because we have no children. I would be the happiest woman in the world if I had a son. Why, even if he were no bigger than my husband's thumb, we would love him dearly."

"That would be a very unique kind of child," said Merlin, "but I hope your wish comes true."

Then Merlin went on his way to visit the queen of the fairies. When he came to her castle, he told the fairy the wish of the farmer's wife. The queen of the fairies said, "The good woman shall have her wish. I will give her a son the size of her husband's thumb."

Soon after this the farmer's wife had a son—exactly the size of his father's thumb.

People came from far and wide to see the famous tiny boy. One day the fairy queen and some other fairies came to see him. The queen kissed the little boy and named him Tom Thumb.

Tom never grew any larger than a man's thumb, but he got into quite a bit of mischief. One day his mother was mixing a cake. Tom leaned over the edge of the bowl to see and fell in, headfirst. His mother did not see him fall, and she kept stirring. Tom kicked and kicked inside the batter, and it moved and tossed about.

His mother was afraid. "There must be gremlins in it," she said.

She went to the window to throw the batter out. Just then a poor beggar was passing by.

"Here is some batter you may have, if you like," said Tom's mother.

The beggar thanked her and took it. He had not gone very far, when Tom got his head out of the batter and shouted, "Take me out! Take me out!" The poor beggar was so frightened that he dropped the batter and ran off.

Tom crawled out of the batter and ran home where his mother scrubbed him thoroughly and put him to bed.

Another time, Tom's mother took him with her when she went to milk the cow. So she wouldn't lose him, she tied him to a piece of hay. When Tom's mother was not looking, the cow took the wisp of hay into her mouth. She began to chew and chew.

Tom began to jump and shout. He frightened the cow, so she opened her great mouth and Tom jumped out. Then Tom's mother took him in her apron and ran with him to the house, but, fortunately, he was not hurt.

One day Tom was in the field helping his father.

"Let me drive the horse home," said Tom.

"You drive the horse?" said the father. "How could you hold the reins?"

"I could stand in the horse's ear and tell him which way to go," said Tom. So his father put him in the horse's ear, and he got them home safely.

"Mother! Mother!" cried Tom. But when Tom's mother came out, she could see no one. She began to be afraid.

"Where are you, Tom?" she cried.

"Here I am in the horse's ear. Please take me down," said Tom. His mother lifted him gently down, kissed him, and gave him a plump blueberry for supper.

Tom's father made him a whip out of a straw. Tom tried to drive the cows, but he fell into a deep ditch. There a great bird saw him and thought he was a mouse. The bird seized Tom in her claws and carried him toward her nest.

As they were passing over the sea, Tom got away and fell into the water, where a great fish swallowed him. Soon after this, the fish was caught, and it was such a big one that it was sent at once to King Arthur.

When the cook cut open the fish, out jumped Tom Thumb. Tom was brought before the king and he told his story.

The king grew very fond of Tom and took Tom with him wherever he went. If it began to rain, Tom would creep into the king's pocket. In the hot sun, he also found shade in the king's pockets.

The king had a new suit made for Tom and gave him a needle for a sword. A mouse was trained for Tom to ride. The king and queen never tired of seeing him ride his little mouse-horse and bravely wave his sword.

One day, as they were going hunting, a cat jumped out and caught Tom's mouse. Tom drew his needle-sword and tried to drive the cat away. The king ran to help poor Tom, and the cat ran away. Tom was scratched and bitten badly, but he did not die.

Soon he was well again, and fought many brave battles and did many brave deeds to please the king. And, several times a year, the king took Tom to see his parents, for he always loved his dear mother and father.

The End

The Witch in the Tower

Once upon a time the citizens of the Japanese city of Kyoto were terribly afraid because a fierce witch had taken possession of the tower over the city gate.

For years, people in the city of Kyoto had been free to come and go as they chose. But then, this fierce witch appeared. When the good citizens of Kyoto awoke in the morning and looked out their windows, they saw that the tower over the city gate had been blackened with smoke. Coming from the tower was a spine-tingling, hair-raising cackle.

The citizens feared that the Witch of the Dark World had come to their beautiful city. All the citizens of Kyoto had heard of her evil ways and appearances in faraway lands and cities, but none had ever believed she would appear in their fair city.

Soon, though, it was made clear to the Kyoto citizens that it was indeed the Witch of the Dark World. That first morning, as the people of Kyoto cautiously gathered on the streets to investigate the strange presence in the city gate tower, the evil witch cackled and spoke.

"Citizens of Kyoto," she said in her hideous voice, "I am now in control of your city. Nobody may come or go unless I allow it. And, if I find that any of you is plotting against me, it will be the end of that person. So, I warn you against any treason!"

And so, a new way of life began for the citizens of Kyoto. The witch opened and closed the city's gate when she felt like it. If in the mood, she was capable of locking the gate in the face of travelers bringing food and merchandise. One group of travelers carried vast stores of exotic fruits and vegetables to share with the people of Kyoto. Jealous that she would not be given any, she refused to open the gates for the generous travelers.

Another time, the witch threw the gates wide open to a vicious tribe that savagely scoured the village for anything of value.

The citizens of Kyoto were saddened and frightened, but they felt there was little that they could do to defeat this powerful and evil creature. It wasn't that some citizens of Kyoto didn't try to destroy her, though.

Many, many brave samurai, the strongest and the best fighters in the land, had boldly faced up to the devious and powerful witch, but the minute she set eyes on any one of them, she hurled herself out of the tower at lightning speed, hair flying wildly in the wind. Then, screeching furiously and brandishing a fiery sword, she would attack them, one by one, until she left them lying dead in the dust by the city gates. Most of the citizens of Kyoto felt that there was no hope for their beloved city, and many people began to think of leaving it—if, that is, the wicked witch would let them.

As they discussed their plans to flee, they also spoke sadly of the warrior who would have saved them. "All of our brave samurai are dead, killed by the witch's fiery sword. If only our beloved Watanabi were still here, the bravest, most courageous of them all! But all that remains of him is his sword, and there is no one left who is able to use it."

However, that wasn't quite true. The sword was not all that remained of the valiant Watanabi. There was also his son, a young boy who lived in Kyoto. As he began to hear what the citizens of the city were saying about his father, he wondered, "My father died fighting and now is gone, but we still have his powerful sword. I shall take it and face the witch. Win or die, I shall fight as a tribute to my father and in hopes of saving the people of the city."

So the young boy bravely armed himself with his father's sword—which was almost too heavy for him to carry—and went off to the tower where the witch lived. Immediately, the witch saw him arrive and she grinned wickedly, but she did not make a move. She decided not to bother even using her fiery sword on that scrawny kid. Instead, she would wither him with a glance. So, she paid little attention to Watanabi's son as he quietly crept into the tower, climbed the hundreds of stairs, and entered the witch's room.

When, however, the witch heard the door close, she turned round and laid her wild burning gaze on the boy. But she'd neglected to think through her entire plan. She had not anticipated the splendor of Watanabi's sword. As the boy held up the hero's sword, it blinded her.

"This is Watanabi's sword!" shouted the young boy bravely, and before the witch could defend herself, he struck a blow and killed her.

In his father's memory and in honor of his sword, the boy had freed the city of Kyoto forever. He is still remembered today as one of the city's true heroes.

⋙ The End ⋘

The Broken Pot

Once upon a time in distant India there lived a **Brahman**, whose name was Svabhavakripana, which means "a born **miser**." This man was truly stingy and miserly. He was unwilling to spend even a single rupee. When forced to spend money on food, drink, or shelter, he became very cross indeed and would yell at anyone who was near.

In fact, he was rather famous—or infamous—throughout the land for some of his most monstrously miserly misdeeds. Indeed, he was unwilling to part with even a single crumb or grain of rice from his bare and miserly pantry.

Consider this: One day, a hungry ant approached the miser as he sat in his home. It had been a particularly dry year, and there was very little for the members of the insect world to eat. This particular ant had a rather large family to feed and had been searching anxiously for a stray seed or bit of grass to carry on his back and take to his hungry family in their anthill. Try as he might—and he tried mightily—he was unable to find anything.

So, in desperation, he approached the miser. Even the lowly ant had heard tales of this stingy fellow, but he was exhausted and near the miser's home. So he went to the man and said, "Please, kind sir. Could you find it in your heart to spare a single grain of rice to share with my ant family?"

At this, the miser guffawed and continued laughing until the ant thought the man would split in half.

"Do you know nothing, lowly, common Ant?" roared the miser. "I have nothing to spare. Not a single grain of rice or a crumb of noodle. No, you must find food elsewhere. Do not come here ever again!"

At this the ant crept off, crying softly. As luck or good fortune would have it, though, the miser had accidentally dropped a grain of rice earlier in the day.

He'd dropped it by his front door when he'd rinsed the evening's rice before cooking it. As the ant walked through the miser's door, he saw the grain, plucked it up (all the while looking over his tiny ant shoulder to make sure the miser was not taking note), placed it on top of his back, and marched off happily to present it to his family.

So, as you can see, this was indeed a very selfish, miserly, thoughtless fellow.

Along with being a miser, this Brahman was a rather lazy fellow. He'd do anything to avoid working. His preferred method of providing for his needs was to beg for money and sustenance. He was well known in his village for begging. To keep him from becoming an even angrier nuisance, local folks would occasionally indulge him and give him a rupee or two, or a bit of food. This usually succeeded in calming his temper, at least temporarily.

Recently, he had collected a very large quantity of rice by begging. One of the villagers gave it to him in hopes that it would keep the miser off the streets and away from the town's children for some time. He was especially fierce to the young ones, who dreaded his presence. The miser would yell at the children for cheering while playing ball or for making noise while playing tag. This miser really was an insufferable fellow!

So, the miser took the rice home and made a very nice meal with it. He ate and ate and ate, gloating at the day's bounty. Then when his stomach was quite round and full and he felt completely satisfied, he took the rice and filled a pot with what was left over.

He hung the heavy pot rather precariously on a peg on the wall. Although he was a bit worried that the peg might pull out of the wall with the weight of the pot, he decided, after some examination, that all was well and he would not move the pot. Remember, this miser was a lazy man, and he was worn out from his day of begging. So, he placed his sleeping mat underneath the pot and tucked himself in. From this position, the miser thought, he could keep an eye on his prized rice throughout the night.

And so he did, looking intently at it all through the night. As he stared at the heavy pot, he started to think, "Oh my, that pot is indeed filled to the very top with rice. Lucky me, lucky me! Now, if there is a famine and there is not enough food in the land, I will certainly make at least a hundred rupees by selling it. Probably more! With such a windfall, I will buy two or three goats. Then, they will have young ones every six months or so. And, at that rate, before I know it, I will have a whole large herd of goats. Then, I'll sell the herd of goats for lots and lots of rupees! And then, I will buy cows, lots of cows! As soon as they have calves, I will sell the calves. Then, with the money I make from selling the calves, I will buy some buffaloes. Then, when the buffaloes have babies, I will sell them to buy mares. Yes, horses, that would be good. When the mares have foaled, I will have plenty of horses. Then, when I sell the foals I will have gold, lots of gold. More than I could have ever imagined! With that gold I will get a grand house with four stories,

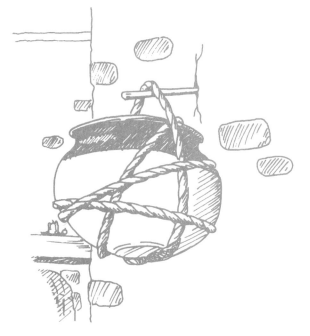

maybe more. It will be built of the best materials and furnished with wonderful furniture and fabrics.

"And then a Brahman will come to my house and will give me his beautiful daughter. She will be the most beautiful woman anyone has ever beheld. And she will be given to me with a large **dowry**. We will live together happily and then we will have a son. What will I call him? I think I will call him Somasarman. And when he is old enough, I will sit with an interesting book at the back of the stable, and while I am reading, the happy boy will see me, jump eagerly from his mother's lap, and run toward me to be danced and bounced on my knee. But then, he will come too near the horse's hoof. Full of anger, I will call to my wife, 'Take the baby; take him! Hurry!' But distracted by her housework, she will not hear me. Then I will get up and give the wall a kick because of my frustration that my wife is not listening to me."

As he was thinking about this, he gave the wall by his sleeping mat a hard, sudden kick. The kick dislodged the heavy pot from its precarious position on the peg; it tumbled to the floor, shattering into many pieces. The rice fell everywhere, including on the miser, making him look as if he'd been caught in a snowstorm, covered with white rice from head to toe.

Under the layer of white, though, the miser was quite red with anger. But, after all, it was his fault that he had foolishly planned a future based on a pot of rice obtained by begging.

⇒ The End ⇐

Dopey Dennis

Once upon a time there was a little boy called Dennis. Everyone called him Dopey, though.

Dennis lived with his mother. One day his mother said to him, "I'll be away for an hour or two, Son. The hen is sitting on her eggs. Make sure nobody goes near her. Keep the house tidy. Don't touch the jar in the cupboard—it's full of poison."

"Okay, Mom," the little boy said, and when his mother had gone, he went into the yard to watch the hen. Tired of sitting, the hen got up to stretch her legs before going back to the eggs. Dennis picked up a stick and yelled: "You nasty creature, get right back on those eggs!" But the hen, annoyed, only said, "*Cluck!*" and so Dennis hit her with his stick. He didn't really mean to do her any harm, but the blow killed the poor hen.

"Oh!" gasped the lad. "Who's going to sit on the eggs now? Well, I had better do something about that!" So he sat on the eggs and broke them all!

He knew his mother would be angry. To help make amends, the boy decided to make lunch. He picked up the hen, plucked its feathers, and put it on the spit to roast.

"A roast calls for wine!" he said to himself. He took a jug and went down to the cellar where he started to draw sparkling red wine. At that moment, there was a dreadful noise in the kitchen. Dennis ran upstairs forgetting to turn off the tap on the barrel. Up he ran and saw the cat with the roast hen in its jaws and the spit overturned.

"Hey thief!" shouted the lad. "Put my hen down!" He picked up a rolling pin and started to chase the cat from room to room. The pair of them knocked against the cupboards; overturned tables, chairs, and stools; and smashed vases, pots, plates, and glasses. Finally, the cat dropped the hen and ran away.

Dennis got the roast, put it on the table, and said, "Now, I'll get the wine." He went back to the cellar, which was flooded. He didn't dare go in, for he was wearing new shoes: There were nearly six inches of wine all over the floor.

Then, Dennis had an idea. He picked up one of the bags lying on a table, opened it and started to scatter all the flour it contained. "Great! The flour will absorb the wine and I can walk about the cellar without wetting my feet," he said. In the end, the floor was covered with a wine-colored, sticky paste, and as he walked on it, it stuck to his shoes. Dennis went to get the jug he had filled and carried it in great delight back to the table, leaving red footprints everywhere. Then, he thought of all the mess he had made, and he began to fear his mother would be angry.

"Never mind," he said, "I'll drink the poison and die." So he went to the cupboard and picked up the jar. He thought the poison would be a black liquid, but the jar contained a beige cream. Just as he was about to take his first spoonful, he realized how silly he was. Nobody should ever eat poison, not even Dopey Dennis. Instead, he decided to hide from his mother.

Soon, his mother returned. When she saw the overturned furniture, the broken plates, and the red footprints, she was afraid Dennis had been injured. She suddenly noticed a pair of legs sticking out of the oven. "I'm not surprised you are hiding from me, Dennis, after causing all this mess," she said, for she realized by now the mess was of Dennis's making.

"While I am cleaning up, take this roll of cloth to the market and try and sell it for a good price."

When he got to market, Dennis began to shout, "Cloth! Who'll buy this lovely cloth?" Several women came over and asked him, "What kind of cloth is it? Is it soft? Is it durable? Is it expensive? How long is it? How much does it cost?"

Dennis exclaimed, "You talk too much, and I don't sell things to **magpies**," and off he went. He passed by a statue and mistook it for a fine gentleman, so he asked it, "Sir, would you like to buy this fine cloth? Yes or no? If you don't say anything, that means you do. Look here! Do you like it? Yes? Good! Then take it," and he left the cloth beside the statue and went home. "Mother!" he cried. "I've sold the cloth to a very dapper gentleman!"

The woman asked: "How much did he give you for it?"

"Oh! I forgot to ask him for the money! Don't worry, I'll go and ask him for it." He ran back to the statue but the cloth was gone. Dennis said to the statue, "I see you've taken the cloth home already. Fine, now give me the money!"

Of course, the statue was unable to reply. Dennis repeated his request, and then losing his temper, he picked up a stick and began to beat the statue. He hit it so hard its head broke off. Out poured a handful of gold coins, which had been hidden there. Dennis picked up the coins, put the head back in position, and went home.

"Look!" he called. And his mother stared in astonishment.

"Who gave you such so much money for the cloth?" his mother asked him.

"A very dignified-looking gentleman. He didn't speak. And do you know where he kept his money? In his head!"

At this, Dennis's mother exclaimed, "Dennis, listen! You killed the hen, broke the eggs, flooded the cellar with wine, wasted five bags of flour, and smashed plates, bottles, vases, and glasses. If you think you're going to tell me lies as well, you're badly mistaken! Get out of here!"

And grabbing the broom, she chased him out of the house.

But the boy sat on the doorstep and did not budge. His exasperated mother picked up the first thing that she could grab and hurled it at Dennis. It was a big basket of dried fruit. Dennis shouted, "Mother! Quick! It's raining dried fruit!"

His mother slumped into a chair and said sadly, "What can I do with a boy like him?"

Then, Dennis went about telling people he had a lot of gold coins, so the magistrates sent for him.

"Where did you find those coins?" they asked him.

"A gentleman gave them to me in payment for a roll of cloth," Dennis replied.

"What gentleman?" said the magistrates sternly.

"The gentleman who is always standing at the corner of Ridge Road and Fifth Street," replied the boy.

"But that's a statue!" gasped the magistrates.

"He didn't say what his name was, but maybe it is Mr. Statue. He kept his money in his head."

The magistrates looked at each other in astonishment. Then the chief magistrate asked, "Tell us, Dennis, when did you do this piece of business?"

"It was the day it rained dried fruit!" the boy replied.

Again the magistrates exchanged looks. Now certain that Dennis really was dopey, they said, "You can go home, lad. You're free!"

And so Dennis went home and lived there happily with his mother. A bit dopey, yes, but he never did anybody any real harm. And even though he could be dopey, his mother loved him dearly.

⁓ The End ⁓

The Emperor's New Clothes

Once upon a time there lived a rather vain emperor whose only care in life was to dress in fancy clothes. He spent hours every day looking through his vast wardrobe, changing his royal garments almost every hour and showing them off to the people in his kingdom. In fact, it was difficult for him to think about anything other than what to wear next.

Word of the emperor's vain habits soon spread throughout the land. As the news traveled, two schemers who had heard of the emperor's desire for the latest clothing fashions decided to take advantage of the situation. They introduced themselves at the gates of the palace with a grand plan in mind.

"We are two very good tailors. After many years of research, we have invented an extraordinary method to weave a cloth so light and fine that it looks invisible. As a matter of fact, it is invisible to anyone too stupid and incompetent to appreciate its quality."

The chief of the guards heard the schemers' strange story and sent for the court **chamberlain**. The chamberlain notified the prime minister, who ran to the emperor and disclosed the incredible news.

The emperor's curiosity and his desire for up-to-the-minute fashions got the better of him, and he decided to see the two men.

"Besides being so light and fine, Your Highness, this cloth will be woven in colors and designs created especially for you."

The emperor gave the two men a large bag of gold coins in exchange for their promise to begin working on the fabric immediately. "Just tell us what you need to get started and we'll give it to you," he told them.

The two scoundrels asked for a loom, silk, and gold thread. Then they pretended to begin working. The emperor thought he had spent his money quite well, for he would gain in two ways. In addition to getting a new extraordinary suit, he would discover which of his subjects were ignorant and incompetent. A few days later, he called in the old and wise prime minister, who was considered by everyone to be a man with common sense.

"Go and see how the work is proceeding," the emperor told him, "and come back to let me know."

The two scoundrels welcomed the prime minister. "We're almost finished, but we need a lot more gold thread. Here, Excellency! Admire the colors, feel the softness!"

The old man bent over the loom and tried to see the fabric that was not there. He felt cold sweat on his forehead. "I can't see anything," he thought. "If I see nothing, the emperor will think I am incompetent." If he admitted that he didn't see anything, he would be discharged from his office. "What a marvelous fabric," he said. "I'll certainly tell the emperor."

The two scoundrels rubbed their hands gleefully. Finally, the emperor received the announcement that the two tailors had come to take all the measurements needed to make his new suit.

"Come in," the emperor ordered. Even as they bowed, the two scoundrels pretended to be holding an enormous bolt of fabric.

"Here it is, Your Highness, the result of our labor," the scoundrels said. "We have worked night and day, but at last the most beautiful fabric in the world is ready for you. Look at the colors and feel how fine it is."

Of course, the emperor did not see any colors and could not feel any cloth between his fingers. He panicked; he felt like fainting. But luckily the throne was right behind him, so he sat down. But when he realized that no one would know that he did not see the fabric, he felt better. Nobody would find out he was stupid and incompetent. Now the emperor didn't know that everybody else around him thought and did the very same thing.

The scheme continued just as the two scoundrels had hoped. Once they had taken the measurements, the two began cutting the air with scissors while sewing with their needles an invisible cloth.

"Your Highness, you'll have to take off your clothes to try on your new ones." The two scoundrels draped the new clothes on him and then held up a mirror.

The emperor was embarrassed, but since none of the bystanders seemed to notice that he had nothing on, he felt relieved. "Yes, this is a beautiful suit, and it looks very good on me," the emperor said, trying to look comfortable. "You've done a fine job."

"Your Majesty," the prime minister said, "we have a request for you. The people have found out about this extraordinary fabric, and they are anxious to see you in your new suit."

The emperor was doubtful about showing himself naked to the people, but then he abandoned his fears. After all, only the ignorant and the incompetent wouldn't be able to see his new suit.

"All right," he said. "I will grant the people the delight of seeing my new clothes."

He summoned his carriage and the ceremonial parade was formed. A group of dignitaries walked at the very front of the procession and anxiously scrutinized the faces of the people in the street.

All the people had gathered in the main square, pushing and shoving to get a better look at the famous new clothes. Applause welcomed the regal parade. Everyone wanted to know how stupid or incompetent his or her neighbor was. But as the emperor passed, strange murmurs rose from the crowd that were loud enough for everyone to hear: "Look at the emperor's new clothes. They're beautiful!" "What a marvelous train!" "And look at the magnificent colors! The colors of that beautiful fabric! I have never seen anything like it in my life."

The people all tried to conceal their disappointment at not being able to see the clothes. But since no one was willing to admit his or her own stupidity and incompetence, they all behaved as the two scoundrels had predicted.

A child, however, who had no important job and could only see things as his eyes showed them to him, went up to the carriage. "The emperor is naked," he said.

"Fool!" his father said. "Don't talk nonsense!" He grabbed his child and took him away.

But the boy's remark, which had been heard by the others, was repeated over and over until everyone cried: "The boy is right! The emperor is naked! It's true!"

The emperor realized that the people were right, but he certainly could not admit it. He though it wiser to continue the procession under the illusion that anyone who couldn't see his clothes was either stupid or incompetent. And he stood stiffly on his carriage, while behind him a page held his imaginary royal cloak.

⇐ The End ⇒

The Fish and the Ring

Once upon a time there lived a rich and powerful **baron** who was also a great magician. One of his magical gifts was his ability to see into the future.

This great lord had a little son. When he was four years old, the baron used his powers to see what would become of his son. He was quite distressed about what he saw: His precious child was to marry a common maiden, a woman with no noble blood at all!

So the baron set to work using his magical powers to discover if this maiden was already born, and if so, where she lived. He found out that she had just been born in a very poor house, and the poor parents were already burdened with five children. The baron called for his horse and galloped to the man's house, where he found him sitting at his doorstep, looking very sad.

"What is the matter, my friend?" asked the baron.

The poor man replied, "May it please Your Honor, we've just been blessed with a child, but we have five already. We don't know where we'll get the food to feed another child."

"Maybe I can help you," said the baron. "Don't be downhearted. I am looking for a little girl to be a friend to my son. I'll give you ten crowns for her."

This cheered the sad man up right away. Not only was he getting money, but his daughter was getting a good home, or so he thought.

The baron wrapped the baby in his cloak and rode away. But when he got to the river, he flung the little thing into the turbulent stream and said to himself as he galloped back to his castle, "There goes **fate**!"

But the little girl didn't drown. The stream was very swift, and her clothes kept her afloat until she caught in a net just opposite a fisherman.

The fisherman and his wife had no children, and they had been longing for a baby. So when the good man saw the little lass he was overcome with joy and took her home to his wife, who received her with open arms. And there she grew up, the apple of their eyes, into the most beautiful maiden ever seen.

Fifteen years later, the baron and his friends went hunting along the banks of the river and stopped to get a drink of water at the fisherman's hut. And who should bring the water out but the fisherman's daughter.

Now the young men of the party noticed her beauty. One of them said to the baron, "She should marry well. Read us her fate since you are so good at seeing into the future."

Then the baron, barely looking at her, said carelessly, "I could guess her fate! She's just a poor girl meant to marry a peasant. But to please you, I will read her future in the stars. Tell me, girl, what day you were born?"

"That I cannot tell, sir," replied the girl, "for I was picked up in the river about fifteen years ago."

Then the baron grew pale, for he guessed at once that she was the little lass he had flung into the stream and that fate had been stronger than he was. But he kept silent and said nothing at the time. Afterward, however, he thought of a plan, so he rode back and gave the girl a letter.

"See you!" he said. "I will make your fortune. Take this letter to my brother, who needs a good girl, and you will be settled for life."

The fisherman and his wife were growing old and needed help getting by, so the girl said she would go with the letter to try and find her fortune.

Meanwhile, the baron rode back to his castle, saying to himself once more, "There goes fate!" Or so he hoped!

This is what the letter said: *"Dear Brother, take the bearer of this letter and put her to death immediately."* But once again he was mistaken. On the way to the town where his brother lived, the girl had to stop to spend the night in a little inn. That very night a gang of thieves broke into the inn and, not content with carrying off all that the innkeeper possessed, they searched the pockets of the guests. They found the letter that the girl carried. And when they read it, they agreed that it was a mean trick and a shame. So their captain sat down and taking pen and paper wrote instead: *"Dear Brother, take the bearer of this letter and marry her to my son without delay."*

Then, after putting the note into an envelope and sealing it, they gave it to the girl and told her to go on her way. When she arrived at the brother's castle, he read the baron's note. Although he was rather surprised at the contents of the note, he gave orders for a wedding feast to be prepared. The baron's son, who was staying with his uncle, saw the girl's great beauty and was pleased to marry her.

When the news was brought to the baron, he was furious. So he rode quickly to his brother's castle and pretended to be quite pleased about the recent marriage. One day, when no one was near, he asked the young bride to come for a walk with him. When they were close to some cliffs, he seized hold of her and tried to throw her over the edge. But she begged for her life.

"It is not my fault," she said. "I have done nothing. It is fate. If you will spare my life, I promise that I will fight against fate also. I will never see you or your son again until you desire it. That will be safer for you, since the sea may save me, as the river did."

The baron agreed to this. So he took off his gold ring from his finger and flung it over the cliffs into the sea and said, "Never dare show me your face again unless you can show me that very ring."

The girl wandered and wandered, until she came to a nobleman's castle. They needed a girl to help in the kitchen, so she began to work there. One day as she was cleaning a big fish, she looked out of the kitchen window and saw the baron and his young son, her husband, arriving for dinner. At first, she thought that to keep her promise she must run away. But she remembered they would not see her in the kitchen, so she went on cleaning the big fish.

Suddenly, she saw something shiny inside the fish, and there, sure enough, was the baron's ring! She was glad enough to see it and slipped it onto her thumb. But she went on with her work, dressing the fish as nicely as she could and serving it up as pretty as could be.

The guests liked it so well that they asked the host who cooked it. And he called to his servants, "Send up the cook who prepared that fine fish."

When the girl heard she was wanted, she made herself ready. With the gold ring on her thumb, she went boldly into the dining room. All the guests were struck dumb by her beauty. The young husband started up gladly; but the baron, recognizing her, jumped up angrily and looked as if he would kill her. Without a word, the girl held up her hand and the gold ring glittered on it.

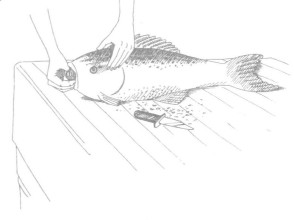

Then the baron understood that fate had been too strong for him. So he took her by the hand, and, placing her beside him, turned to the guests and said, "This is my son's wife. Let us drink a toast in her honor."

And after dinner he took her and his son home to his castle where they lived happily ever after in the life fate had planned for them.

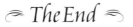

↬ The End ↫

The Flying Trunk

Once upon a time, many years ago in Copenhagen, Denmark, there lived a very rich merchant. This man was quite content and believed in working hard and enjoying his life. He did, though, have one regret: His only child had grown up to be rather slothful.

The child's name was Erik. The lad was extremely handsome, personable, and smart; but to the merchant's never-ending frustration, he was also very lazy.

His father tried coaxing and cajoling the boy to be productive. He made threats on the one hand and bribes with the next, hoping to induce the lad to end his lazy ways. It was of no avail, though.

Instead of studying or working, the boy liked to spend his days running around. He kept himself busy, amusing himself playing tricks on his friends and frittering away his father's money on things he didn't need.

When Erik was a young man, the wealthy merchant died. Having no other children, he left all of his vast fortune to Erik. This rich reward just led to increased laziness, and Erik spent the merchant's immense fortune quickly, entertaining friends and buying silly, worthless things.

One day, Erik realized he'd spent all of the money, and he was rather alarmed. He went to some friends for advice, but they weren't so friendly now that he had no money or gifts to offer them. He thought about looking for work, but this prospect was truly appalling to a lazy bloke like Erik.

There was, though, one item left from his father's estate: a magic trunk. The trunk was nothing special to look at, but it had very magical properties. The minute anyone stepped inside, it rose into the air, taking the occupant to the place of his dreams.

It seemed to Erik, who had decided he had no intention of ever working for a living, that his only choice in the matter was to hop into the magic trunk and see where **fate** would take him. He decided that facing the unknown was superior to going to work. So he clambered into the trunk, sat down, and went soaring into the skies to seek his fortune. For almost a year, he flew around the world in the magic trunk. He flew across glittering seas and over dense forests, arid deserts, and lush jungles.

At last, though, he tired of his journey and decided to find a place to land the magic trunk. He found himself above a large city in the East and ordered the trunk to land on the grand marble terrace of a wonderful palace.

The trunk complied and smoothly touched down. Then, Erik hastily stepped out of the trunk. There in front of him stood an incredibly beautiful girl, staring at Erik in amazement.

"I'm Tamara, the **sultan's** daughter," she said. "Who are you?"

Although physically lazy, Erik was a quick thinker. He replied, "I'm the god of your people, and I want to marry you." He felt sure she would believe him because who, other than a god, would arrive in a flying trunk?

His plan worked. Fascinated by the handsome stranger and certain that he really was a god from the skies, she happily agreed to his proposal. She immediately called for her family to come meet this mysterious sky god.

The sultan was a believing fellow like his daughter and warmly welcomed the devious youth, as did the rest of the sultan's family.

All of the sultan's servants began to make elaborate plans for a grand wedding ceremony. They worked day and night for a month, preparing for the wedding celebration.

This gave Erik time to come up with a plan for making off with much of the sultan's wealth. As the staff and family planned the ceremony and wedding feast, Erik surveyed the palace and compiled a list of its valuables.

The night before the ceremony, as all of the palace inhabitants slept, Erik crept about with a large burlap sack, packing up rubies, emeralds, diamonds, gold, fine silks, and anything else of value he could stuff into his bulging sack. Then, the naughty, thoughtless lad stuffed the trunk full of the stolen loot and commanded it to fly away from the palace toward his home.

This is where Erik's plan failed, though. As nimble as his brain was, he couldn't devise a scheme to overcome his own greed. The magical flying trunk, weighed down by its valuable, stolen cargo, crashed abruptly into a churning, angry sea off the Danish coast, just miles from Erik's home. Erik managed to swim ashore and get home.

Once there, he sang sad songs at street corners for a living, hoping passers-by would toss him a coin or two. His clothes became tattered and he had no shoes. He often went without enough to eat. But the lazy boy still couldn't accept the thought of getting a job. So he continued with his wistful songs, while in a city in the East, on the grand marble terrace of a magnificent palace, a young girl sadly glanced at the sky from time to time, hoping that the god, who had suddenly disappeared, would come back again.

⌒ The End ⌒

The Game of Chess

Historians believe chess originated in Persia around A.D. 600. The game's popularity spread to Spain in the early eighth century and by the eleventh century was probably being played throughout Europe as far north as Scandinavia.

Once upon a time there was a king in **Persia** who had a beautiful wife and a handsome son called Gav. Life was very happy until one day when he went hunting, the king fell from his horse and was killed.

The dead ruler's brother was named the new king. His name was May. He fell in love with the widowed queen and married her, and they soon had a son named Talend.

Some time later, the new king died and only the queen and her two sons remained. They were brothers, of course, but with different fathers. The question was soon raised: "Which brother will become king of Persia?"

"It will be Gav," was one reply, "because he is the oldest."

But others said, "It will be Talend, because he is the son of our last king."

The queen said nothing at all. However, sooner or later, she would have to come to a decision, and she didn't want to disappoint either boy. As long as the two boys were small, it didn't matter. But when they grew up and began to ask when one or the other was going to be crowned king, the problems began.

The queen simply couldn't make up her mind. When the ministers asked her to make a decision, she would reply, "Yes, I will do it tomorrow."

Years went by. Gav and Talend grew up to be young men, and became rivals. As children they were always together; as youths, they saw little of each other. Each had his own group of friends. In that way, two opposing sides were formed: one supported Talend, the other supported Gav.

The ministers were very worried and insisted that the queen choose the king. But she couldn't bring herself to do it, for fear of disappointing one of her dearly loved sons.

As the years passed, the kingdom drifted toward civil war. The two princes did not see eye to eye. Neither one wanted to give up the throne; neither one wanted to step down. Some of the provinces sided with Talend, others with Gav. Certain battalions in the army swore allegiance to Talend, others to Gav. The two young men met, but only to stare at each other coldly and to promise war instead of peace, and war was fast approaching.

Two opposing armies were built. Gav's army began to march against Talend's. All Persia held its breath, awaiting the conflict that was to decide its fate. The battle was fought with equal forces. Both armies had the same number of foot soldiers, standard-bearers, and elephants. Elephants were very important in Persia because they carried on their backs wicker turrets from which archers fired arrows at the enemy.

Neither of the brothers wanted the other to die. In spite of everything, the brothers felt the pull of their family ties. Indeed, each had given an order that if the soldiers found they were about to kill the enemy leader, they were to stop and warn him by shouting, "Watch out, King!"

The conflict lasted for a long time, until Gav's troops were overcome and Talend found himself with only a few soldiers to defend him. Then, a little later, quite alone, Talend found himself surrounded on all sides by Gav's turreted elephants, slowly advancing on him. No arrows were fired on the prince; he turned this way and that, searching for a way to escape. But his heart failed at that moment, and he fell to the ground dead. High in the palace tower, the queen had watched the battle with deep sadness in her heart, knowing that she was at that moment losing one of her sons.

When she saw that the dust had settled on the distant plain and the cries of battle had faded, the queen came down from the tower and rushed through the palace to meet those returning from the field. She stopped in her tracks. Her son Gav, his clothes in tatters and splashed with blood, staggered sadly toward her. "Talend?" stammered the queen.

Gav shook his head, "Oh, Mother," he said, "my brother Talend is dead."

"Dead! Did you kill him?"

"No, Mother!" exclaimed Gav. "I would never have done such a thing."

"But you ordered his death!" exclaimed the queen.

The young man then knelt before her and, taking the hem of her dress in his hand, said, "Mother, I swear nobody was responsible for my brother's death. He died, but not violently."

"I shall never believe that is the truth," wept the queen.

But Gav said, "I shall prove that it is."

He then thought of a way to show his mother how the battle had been fought. First of all, he asked a carpenter to make him a board, as flat as the plain. Then to mark the positions and maneuvers of the two armies, the board was divided into white and black squares. A wood carver made him a miniature army of foot soldiers, a king, standard-bearers, knights, and towers, to take the place of the elephants and their turrets.

When everything was ready, Gav called the queen and, moving one piece at a time, acted out the various stages of battle. "You see, Mother, my foot soldiers advanced like this, so Talend maneuvered his like that. Each time my brother was about to be killed, I had the men cry out, 'Watch out, King!' so that he could reach safety," said Gav.

"In the end, though, my Talend was no longer safe," murmured the queen.

Gav sadly replied, "That's true. He was surrounded. But I would never have had him killed, Mother. It was his heart that gave out. My brother realized he had lost, and so he died."

The queen then said, "I understand, Son, and I forgive you. I believe you'll be a good king for our country. But I wonder why, in a battle between two kings, one must win and the other lose."

The poor queen kept asking herself the same question for a very long time. She would sit all day long beside the little battlefield moving the pieces—foot soldiers, standard-bearers, and towers—always trying to save the king. In the end, she understood that, in make-believe as in real life, when there is a fight to the last, one of the opponents must fall, just as her son Talend had fallen.

One day, they found the poor queen dead on what was, by then, known as the chessboard. That is how chess came to be. Today, it is a peaceful contest that recalls a real-life battle. In the modern world it is fun, but then it caused a poor mother great sadness.

The End

The Girl Who Trod on a Loaf

Once upon a time there was a girl who **trod** on a loaf to avoid getting dirt on her shoes. As I'm sure you've heard, the misfortunes that befell her are well known.

Her name was Inge. She was a poor child, but proud and arrogant, with a rotten, cruel disposition. As a tiny child, she delighted in catching flies and tearing off their wings to make creeping things of them. And, sad to report, as the years passed, she grew worse instead of better. Unfortunately, she was very pretty, which caused people to excuse her behavior, when she should have been punished.

Inge was taken to the house of some rich neighbors. They treated her as their own child and dressed her in such fancy clothes and showered her with so many gifts that that her arrogance grew.

After a year, Inge set out to visit her parents; but when she reached the village, she saw her mother working as a laborer, picking up stones. Inge turned back. How could she, in her fine clothes, be the daughter of a common laborer?

Six months passed, and her mistress said, "You ought to go home again and visit your parents, Inge. I will give you a large loaf of bread to take to them. They will be so happy to see you."

So Inge put on her best clothes and her new shoes and set out, stepping very carefully so as not to dirty her shoes. When she came to some small pools of water, and a great deal of mud, she threw the loaf into the mud and trod upon it, so she might pass without wetting her

feet. But as she stood with one foot on the loaf and the other lifted up to step forward, the loaf began to sink under her. She sank lower and lower, until she disappeared altogether. Finally, only a few bubbles on the surface of the muddy pool remained to show where she had gone.

But where did Inge go? She sank into the ground and went down to the **Marsh** Woman. Nothing is known of the Marsh Woman, except that when a mist arises from the meadows, it is because she is brewing beneath them. Inge sunk down to the Marsh Woman's brewery, a place no one can endure for long. A heap of mud could be considered a palace compared with the Marsh Woman's **brewery**. As Inge fell, she became cold and stiff as marble. Her foot was still firmly fastened to the loaf.

An evil spirit soon took possession of Inge and carried her to a still worse place, where she saw crowds of unhappy people. Inge's punishment was to stand there as a statue, with her foot fastened to the loaf. She could move her eyes about and see all the misery around her, but she could not turn her head. When she saw the people looking at her, she thought they were admiring her pretty face and fine clothes, for she was still vain and proud. But she had forgotten how dirty her clothes had become while in the Marsh Woman's brewery. They were covered with mud. Worse than all was the terrible hunger that tormented her, and she could not stoop to break off a piece of the loaf on which she stood. No; her back was too stiff, and her whole body like a pillar of stone. And then creeping over her face and eyes were flies without wings. She winked and blinked, but they could not fly away, for their wings had been pulled off.

To add to her torture, Inge could hear what others were saying about her. They knew the sin she had committed in treading on the loaf because a young boy had seen her as she crossed the marsh and disappeared.

When her mother wept and exclaimed, "Oh, Inge! What sadness you have caused me," Inge would say, "Oh, I wish I had never been born. My mother's tears are useless now."

And then the words of the kind people who had adopted her came to her ears: "Inge was a vain and arrogant girl."

A song was made about "the girl who trod on a loaf to keep her shoes from getting dirty." It was sung everywhere. Inge heard the song and she became full of bitterness.

But one day Inge heard a child, while listening to the tale of Inge, burst into tears and exclaim, "But will she never come up again?"

She heard the reply, "No, she will never come up again."

"But if she were to say she was sorry, and ask pardon, and promise never to do so again?" asked the little one.

"Yes, then she might come; but she will not beg pardon," was the answer.

"Oh, I wish she would!" said the child.

A long, bitter time passed before Inge heard her name again and saw what seemed like two bright stars shining above her. Many years had passed since the little girl had lamented and wept about "poor Inge." That child was now an old woman and God was taking her to heaven. In heaven, as she had done when a little child on Earth, she wept and prayed for poor Inge. Her tears freed Inge from her torment. Inge changed from stone to a little bird and she soared, with the speed of lightning, to the world above the marsh. Soon, the little bird discovered the beauty of everything around it.

Christmas drew near, and a peasant who lived close by an old wall stuck up a pole with some ears of corn fastened to the top for the birds to feast. On

Christmas morning, the sun arose and shone upon the ears of corn, which were quickly surrounded by a number of twittering birds. Then, from a hole in the wall, gushed forth in song the thoughts of the bird about to perform her first good deed on Earth.

The winter was very hard. The ponds were covered with ice, and there was very little food. The bird found here and there, in the ruts of the roads, a grain of corn and some crumbs. Of these she ate only a few. She shared the rest with the hungry birds around her. During the course of the winter, the bird collected many crumbs and gave them to other birds. Finally, the weight of the crumbs equaled the weight of the loaf on which Inge had trod to keep her shoes clean. And when the last bread crumb had been found and given away, the gray wings of the bird became white, and she spread them out for flight.

"Look, there is a seagull!" cried the children, when they saw the white bird, as it dived into the sea and rose again into the clear sunlight, glittering white. But no one could tell where it went, although some were sure it flew straight to the sun.

◈ The End ◈

Hansel and Gretel

Once upon a time there were a little boy and a little girl who lived deep in the forest with their father, a poor woodcutter, and their cruel stepmother. The little girl was called Gretel, and the boy was named Hansel.

One year, a severe winter settled upon the land and seemed to go on and on without mercy. So it came that the family found itself without enough food to eat. The wicked stepmother told the father that he must take the two children into the forest and leave them behind.

"How can I do that to my poor children?" cried the woodcutter.

"You must!" argued the stepmother. "If you do not, we all will starve."

Hansel and Gretel were not asleep. When they overheard this conversation, Gretel began to cry.

"Don't worry," Hansel said, "I will find a way to keep us from harm."

The moon shone brightly that night, and Hansel crept downstairs and went outside to collect a pocketful of pebbles that shone brilliantly like the moon.

When morning came, the cruel and wicked stepmother woke the children and gave them each a piece of dry, hard toast for dinner. Then, their father took them into the forest. There, he explained to them that they must remain in the dark woods because there was not enough food at home to feed them. He kissed them and cried as he said good-bye.

As soon as he was gone, Hansel told Gretel about his plan. He had dropped pebbles from out of his pocket, as they walked into the woods with their father. When the moon rose that night, Hansel took his little sister by the hand and they carefully followed the pebbles, which shone like moonbeams. Just as the sun was rising, they arrived back at their father's home.

When their stepmother saw them, she said, "You horrid creatures! We thought you were never coming back!"

Their father cried with joy to see them.

The stepmother was so angry about their return that she plotted their demise once again. One evening, Hansel and Gretel heard their stepmother order their father to leave the children in the forest. That evening, Hansel crept downstairs to collect more pebbles, but found that his stepmother had locked the door to the house. Hansel was resourceful and came up with another plan.

When morning arrived, the wicked stepmother woke the children and gave them each a meager piece of dry toast for dinner. They went with their father into the forest. Along the way, Hansel broke off pieces of bread and dropped the crumbs on the ground to make a trail leading back to their home. Once again, the father kissed the children and said good-bye.

That night, Hansel took his little sister by the hand, and they looked for the white bread crumbs that he had dropped. But they found no bread crumbs, because the creatures of the forest had eaten them all. Hansel, though, felt confident he could find his way out of the forest, even without the bread crumbs to guide their way.

Instead of leading his sister out of the woods, though, Hansel mistakenly led her deeper into the forest. They were very lost and extremely hungry and about to give up all hope, when just ahead in a clearing they saw the strangest little house. It had walls of sweet gingerbread, and a roof of frosted cake. The windows were made of clear sugar and the sidewalk of chocolate.

"I'm going to eat it all!" Hansel said. "I'm going to eat it all!" They both ran to the house and began breaking off pieces, for by now they were very, very hungry.

Then, a soft voice from inside said, "Nibble, nibble, those who roam, who is nibbling on my home?" The children answered, "Only the air, only the air. Blowing here and blowing there."

And they went on eating.

Suddenly, the door opened, and a woman as old as any they'd ever seen hobbled out. Hansel and Gretel were terribly frightened, but the old woman smiled and said sweetly, "Do come in and stay with me."

She led them inside and fed them pancakes and apples and sugar and nuts and cookies and cakes and puddings. Afterward, she tucked them into beds.

The old woman, who was really a wicked witch, had only pretended to be kind and sweet. While they were sleeping, she seized Hansel and locked him in a little closet behind a grated door. Then she shook Gretel and told her to fetch water and cook something good for Hansel.

"When he is fat," the witch said with glee, "I will eat him!"

Gretel cried, but she was forced to do what the wicked witch commanded. She cooked all the best food in the house for poor Hansel, but she was given nothing to eat but dry bread crusts.

Every morning, the old woman crept to the little closet and told Hansel to stretch out his finger to see if he would soon be fat enough to make a tasty meal. Hansel, however, was very smart. He stretched out a little chicken bone to her. The old woman, who had failing eyesight, thought it was his finger. Week after week went by, and she was astonished that he ate and ate without gaining a single pound.

When a month had passed, the witch told Gretel she could not wait any longer. "Whether Hansel is fat or thin, tomorrow I will kill him and cook him and eat him!" the witch laughed.

The next morning, the witch woke Gretel and told her that it was time to bake some bread to eat with her meal of Hansel. "The oven is warming and the dough is rising," the witch said. "Creep inside the oven and see if it is hot enough to put the bread in."

Gretel was smart, too, and she knew that the witch intended to lock her up in the oven, bake her, and eat her, too. "I don't understand," Gretel said, "How can I get in?"

"Silly," said the old woman, "that door is big enough. Look, I can fit in myself." The old witch crept up and thrust her head into the oven.

Then clever Gretel gave her a big push and shoved her all the way in. She shut the iron door and fastened the bolt. The witch began to howl and scream, but Gretel would not let her out.

Gretel ran like lightning to Hansel, set him free, and cried, "Hansel, we are saved! The old witch is dead."

They hugged and danced with joy. In the witch's house, they found chests filled with pearls and jewels. They filled their pockets with the treasures.

"But how will we get home?" Gretel asked.

"Don't worry," Hansel said, "I will find a way."

Fortunately for the children, the witch's house was not far from the wood-cutter's cabin, and soon they were home. They rushed into the parlor and threw their arms around their father's neck. He had not known one happy hour since he had left his children in the forest. And their stepmother was dead, poisoned by her own cruel spirit. Hansel and Gretel showed their father the pearls and precious stones, and they all lived happily ever after.

⮞ The End ⮜

Lazy Jack

Once upon a time there was a boy whose name was Jack, and he lived with his mother on a **common**. They were very poor, and the old woman made money by spinning. But Jack was so lazy that he would do nothing but relax in the sun in the summer and sit by the fire in the winter. His mother could not get him to do anything for her and at last told him that if he did not begin to work for his porridge, she would kick him out of the house.

This motivated Jack. He went out and hired himself for the next day to a neighboring farmer for a penny, but as he was coming home he lost the penny as he passed over a stream.

"You stupid boy," said his mother, "you should have put it in your pocket."

The next day, Jack went out again and hired himself to a dairy farmer, who gave him a gallon of milk for his day's work. Jack took the jug and put it into the large pocket of his jacket, spilling it all long before he got home.

"Oh, Jack!" said the old woman. "You should have carried it on your head."

So the following day, Jack hired himself again to a farmer, who agreed to give him a wheel of cheese for his services. In the evening Jack took the cheese and carried it home on his head. By the time he got home the cheese was ruined; part of it melted, and the rest was matted into his hair.

"You stupid **lout**," said his mother, "you should have carried it very carefully in your hands."

The next day, Lazy Jack went out and hired himself to a baker, who gave him nothing for his work but a large tomcat. Jack took the cat, and began carrying it very carefully in his hands; but in a short time, the cat scratched him so much that he was forced to let it go.

When he got home, his mother said to him, "You should have tied it with a string and dragged it along after you."

On the following day, Jack hired himself to a butcher, who rewarded him with a lamb shoulder. Jack took the meat, tied it to a string, and trailed it along after him in the dirt. By the time he got home, the meat was completely ruined. His mother was this time quite out of patience with him, for the next day was Sunday, and they only had cabbage for dinner.

"You should have carried the meat on your shoulder," she said to her son

On Monday, Lazy Jack went once more and hired himself to a dairy farmer, who gave him a donkey for his trouble. Now, though Jack was strong, he found it hard to hoist the donkey onto his shoulders, but at last he did it and began walking slowly home with his prize.

It so happened that in the course of his journey, he passed a house where a rich man lived with his only daughter, a beautiful girl who was deaf and dumb and had never laughed in her life. The doctors said she would never speak until somebody made her laugh. So her father had said that any man who made her laugh could marry her. Now this young lady happened to be looking out of the window when Jack passed by with the donkey on his shoulders. The poor beast, with its legs sticking up in the air, was kicking violently and *hee-hawing* mightily. The sight was so silly that the girl burst into laughter, and immediately recovered her speech and hearing.

Her father was overjoyed and kept his promise by marrying her to Lazy Jack, who then became a rich gentleman. They lived in a mansion, and Jack's mother lived with them in great happiness for many years.

⧼ The End ⧽

Little Red Riding Hood

Once upon a time there lived a little girl who was loved by all for her kind heart. Her grandmother especially loved her and had made her a cape of red wool. The little girl wore the cape all the time, which is why she became known as Red Riding Hood.

One day, her mother asked her to take some chocolate-chip cookies to her ill grandmother who lived across the woods in another village. Off Red Riding Hood went, but it wasn't long before she ran into Mr. Wolf. Being a cruel creature, he had a mind to eat her up. There were men working in the woods, though, and he didn't want to get caught eating the beloved girl, so he came up with another plan.

"Where are you going, my little pretty?" asked the sly wolf.

"I'm going to my grandmother, because she is sick. And I am taking her a basket of chocolate-chip cookies, because she loves them!"

"I see," said the wolf. "Well, I hope your grandmother gets well soon." With that, the wolf ran as fast as he could to the grandmother's house.

When he got there, he knocked at the door. *Toc, toc, toc!*

"Who is there?" asked Grandma.

"Your granddaughter," lied the wolf, imitating Red Riding Hood's voice. "I have brought you some chocolate-chip cookies."

The grandmother invited him in and, before you could say Jack Sprat, he ate the grandmother with his sharp teeth. After he had finished, he climbed into Grandmother's bed and waited for Red Riding Hood.

It wasn't long before she knocked at the door. *Toc, toc, toc!*

"Who is there?" asked the deceitful wolf.

Red Riding Hood, hearing so gruff a voice, was afraid at first. She decided, though, that her grandmother must have a very bad cold indeed to sound so hoarse. So she said, "It is your granddaughter, and I have brought you some chocolate-chip cookies."

The wolf answered her in as soft a voice as he could, "Come on in, sweetie." And so she did.

Once inside, the wolf, who was hidden under the covers, said, "Please crawl in with me. I'm very cold."

Sweet little Red Riding Hood agreed and got into bed, but she was frightened by her grandmother's long ears, which were sticking out of her nightcap, and by her very long arms, which stuck out the sleeves of her nightie.

So she said, "My, my, what great arms you have got!"

"All the better to hug you, my pretty child."

"What long and great ears you have got!"

"All the better to hear you, my child."

"What great eyes and long teeth you have got!"

"All the better to see you, and to eat you up!"

And as soon as he had said these words, this wicked wolf flew upon poor little Red Riding Hood and ate her up.

A woodcutter happened by and witnessed the wicked deed. The man sprung into action. He seized the wolf and opened him up. Both Little Red Riding Hood and her grandmother jumped out, a bit frightened but otherwise unharmed.

⁀ The End ⁀

Master of All Masters

Once upon a time, a peasant girl decided to earn some money by becoming a servant. It took her some time to find a job, but at last a funny-looking old fellow hired her.

When she first arrived at his house, he told her that he had many things to teach her because in his house he had his own names for things.

He asked her, "What will you call me?"

"Whatever you like, sir," she answered politely.

He said, "You must call me 'Master of All Masters.' And what would you call this?" he asked pointing to his bed.

"I'd call it a bed," she answered.

"No, that's my 'barnacle.' And what do you call these?" he asked, pointing to his pants.

"Pants or trousers, or whatever you like."

"You must call them 'squibs and crackers.' And what would you call her?" he asked, pointing to his calico cat.

"Cat or kitten, or whatever you like."

"You must call her 'white-faced simminy.' And what would you call this?" he asked pointing at the fire.

"Fire or flame, or whatever you like."

"You must call it 'hot cockadoodle.' And what is this?" he went on, pointing to the water.

"Water or wet, or whatever you like."

"No, 'like-a-pondum' is its name. And what do you call all this?" he asked as he pointed to his home.

"House or cottage, or whatever you like."

"You must call it 'high topper mountain.'"

That very night the servant woke her master up in a fright and said, "Master of All Masters, get out of your barnacle and put on your squibs and crackers, for white-faced simminy has got a spark of hot cockadoodle on its tail, and unless you get some like-a-pondum, high topper mountain will be all on hot cockadoodle."

As you can see, the servant girl was a quick learner. They quickly put out the hot cockadoodle and lived happily ever after.

⌒ The End ⌒

You can be like the Master of All Masters and make up your own language, too. The sentence "Do you have a finger-tickler on your smellephant?" translates into "Do you have an itch on your nose?" when you change "finger-tickler" to "itch" and "smellephant" to "nose." Try making up your own language. Be creative. Maybe a flower should be called a "petal-popper" or a car a "wheel-a-turning." You can have lots of fun creating your own language. Then you can tsry using your new language with a brother, sister, or friend. Or, write your own fairy tale or story using your own one-of-a-kind language!

Mr. Miacca

Once upon a time there was a boy named Tommy Grimes. His mother used to say to him, "Tommy, be a good boy, and don't go out beyond our street, or else Mr. Miacca will get you."

And, sure enough, one day when Tommy was being bad, Mr. Miacca did catch him, threw him into a bag, and took him off to his house.

When Mr. Miacca got Tommy inside, he pulled him out of the bag and sat him down, and felt his arms and legs.

"I don't think you'll be very tender," he said disappointedly, "but you're all I've got for supper. Maybe you'll soften up a bit if I boil you. Oh no, I can't find the herbs. I have to have some herbs in order to prepare you properly! Wife, come here," he called Mrs. Miacca.

Mrs. Miacca came out of another room and said. "What is it, dear?"

"Watch this boy while I go out and fetch some herbs."

"All right, dear," said Mrs. Miacca, and off he went.

Tommy then asked Mrs. Miacca, "Does Mr. Miacca always have little boys for supper?"

"Usually, " said Mrs. Miacca, "if little boys are bad enough, and get in his way."

"And don't you have anything else but boy-meat? No dessert?" asked Tommy.

"Oh, I love dessert, especially a bit of pudding," said Mrs. Miacca. "But it's not often that I get dessert."

"Why, my mother is making a pudding today," said Tommy, "and I am sure she'd give you some, if I ask her. Shall I run and get some?"

"Oh, you're a thoughtful boy," said Mrs. Miacca, "just make sure you get back in time for supper."

So off Tommy ran, relieved to have escaped being made into boiled boy-meat. He was good for some time, until one day he wandered too far from home. As bad luck would have it, Mr. Miacca grabbed him again!

When he brought him home, Mr. Miacca dropped him out of the bag. When he saw who it was, Mr. Miacca said, "Oh, you're the fellow who tricked me, leaving us without any supper. Well, you won't do it again. I'll watch over you myself. Here, get under the sofa, and I'll sit on it and watch the pot boil for you."

Poor Tommy had to creep under the sofa, and Mr. Miacca sat on it and waited for the pot to boil. They waited and they waited, but still the pot didn't boil. At last Mr. Miacca got tired of waiting, and he said, "I'm not going to wait any longer. Put out your leg and I'll make an appetizer of that."

So Tommy put out a leg. Mr. Miacca got a chopper, and chopped it off, and popped it into the pot.

Suddenly he called, "Wife, my dear!" but nobody answered. He went into the next room to look for Mrs. Miacca. While he was there, Tommy crept out from under the sofa and ran out of the door, for it was a leg of the sofa that he had handed Mr. Miacca.

Tommy ran home, and from that day on he never misbehaved again. And Mr. Miacca still can't believe he let Tommy get away twice!

 *The End*

Mr. Vinegar

Once upon a time there was a tiny couple named Mr. and Mrs. Vinegar. This little pair lived in a vinegar bottle. Now, one day when Mr. Vinegar was away from home, Mrs. Vinegar was busily sweeping her house, for she was very careful to keep the bottle nice and neat. Suddenly, an unlucky thump of the broom brought the whole house crashing down around her ears. The bottle was in shards. Anxiously, she hurried to meet her husband who was just then coming home.

"Oh, Mr. Vinegar," she sobbed. "We are ruined. I have cleaned with such determination that I've knocked the house down."

"Let us see what can be done," reassured Mr. Vinegar. "Here is the door that has fallen off. I will take it on my back, and we will go together to see what we can do with this door."

They walked and walked all that day (truthfully, Mr. Vinegar was becoming quite tired from carrying the heavy door on his back) and at night entered a thick forest. They were both exhausted.

Mr. Vinegar climbed up a tree, dragging the door behind him. Mrs. Vinegar followed, and they stretched out for some sleep, covering themselves with some tender leaves.

In the middle of the night, Mr. Vinegar was disturbed by voices below and found that the voices belonged to a group of thieves sorting their loot. Mr. Vinegar was so scared that he trembled and trembled until he shook the door down upon the group of thieves.

The falling door frightened the thieves and they hurried away. When Mr. Vinegar climbed down the tree in the morning (for he was too afraid to leave the tree during the night), he lifted the door and found several gold coins beneath it. When Mrs. Vinegar climbed down the tree and saw the coins, she jumped for joy.

"Now, Mr. Vinegar," she said to her husband, "you take these coins and buy a cow. We can make butter and cheese and sell them at the market and then we can live happily."

Mr. Vinegar agreed and set off to buy the cow. When he arrived at the next town, he found a red cow, perfect in every way. So, Mr. Vinegar offered the cow's owner all of his gold pieces. The owner agreed, so the deal was made, and Mr. Vinegar began to make his way back to his wife.

Along the way, he saw a man playing the bagpipe. Children followed him about, and he appeared to be pocketing money on all sides.

"Well," thought Mr. Vinegar, "if I had that lovely instrument, I should be the happiest man alive, and rich too." He so wanted the bagpipe that he traded his red cow for the instrument. He walked up and down with his bagpipe, but he was unable to play a song and instead of pocketing money, the kids followed him, laughing and throwing pebbles.

Poor Mr. Vinegar's fingers began to grow very cold as he continued his way back to his wife. He soon met a man wearing a fine, thick pair of fur gloves. "Oh, my fingers are so very cold," said Mr. Vinegar to himself. "Now, if I had those beautiful gloves, I should be the happiest man alive."

Mr. Vinegar proposed a trade to the man wearing the gloves, offering his bagpipe for the fine gloves. The man readily agreed and Mr. Vinegar went on his way, enjoying the warmth of his new gloves.

Before long, though, his feet began to ache from his long journey. Soon he saw a man using a branch as a walking stick. "Oh," Mr. Vinegar thought to himself, "I'd do anything to have such a walking stick, my feet ache so."

Mr. Vinegar called to the man with the walking stick and they arranged a trade. Mr. Vinegar gave him his fur gloves in exchange for the twig walking stick.

And so Mr. Vinegar made his way back to Mrs. Vinegar, enjoying his firm new walking stick. When he arrived, he told Mrs. Vinegar about his day's work, feeling rather proud of the results.

Mrs. Vinegar was not so pleased to see the golden treasure left by the robbers traded for a mere twig walking stick. Some say, she has remained displeased with Mr. Vinegar to this day.

⌒ The End ⌒

The Nail

Once upon a time, a merchant had done very good business at the fair. He had sold all of his merchandise and filled his moneybags with gold, silver, and jewels. He wanted to travel back home and sleep in his own bed. So he packed his riches in his trunk and put it on his horse and rode away.

At noon he rested in a town. When he wanted to move on, a stableboy brought out his horse and said, "A nail is missing, sir, in the shoe of its near hind foot."

"Oh don't bother me with these little things," answered the merchant impatiently. "The shoe will certainly stay on for the six miles I have still to go. I am in a hurry!"

In the afternoon, when he once more climbed on his horse and had the animal fed, another stableboy went to him and said, "Sir, a shoe is missing from your horse's near hind foot. Shall I take him to the blacksmith?"

"No," answered the man. "The horse can very well hold out for the couple of miles that remain. I am in a big hurry."

So, he continued on, but before long the horse began to limp. It had not limped long before it began to stumble, and it had not stumbled long before it fell down and broke its leg.

The merchant was forced to leave the horse where it was, unbuckle the trunk, take it on his back, and go home on foot.

He didn't arrive there until quite late at night.

≈ *The End* ≈

Narcissus

The Roman poet Ovid wrote the best-known version of the Narcissus tale. Ovid lived in Italy from 43 B.C. to about A.D. 17, and is known for his witty love poems.

Once upon a time in Greece, there lived a young man called Narcissus. He lived in a tiny village on the sea and was greatly admired throughout the land because he was exceedingly handsome.

In fact, from the time he was born, everyone in Narcissus's coastal village exclaimed over his unusual beauty.

"My, what a handsome son you have," said one neighbor to Narcissus's parents when the boy was but a few days old.

"This must be a blessing from the gods," pronounced another neighbor, as he looked at the sleeping Narcissus in his little basket. "Who but the gods could have created such a beautiful creature?"

Villagers would turn on the streets to stare at the beautiful child. He had golden locks as fine as spun silk and skin as smooth as cream. He would toddle up and down the sidewalk outside his house, smiling at all who passed by.

As he grew, so too did his beauty. By the time he went to school, he was known not only in his village but in the surrounding countryside for his astonishing good looks.

Friends at school would compliment Narcissus on his handsome face and agile body.

And so it went. Villagers thought that Narcissus could not be any more handsome than he already was. But as the years passed and Narcissus became a teenager, his beauty grew and became so great that he was known throughout the entire country of Greece.

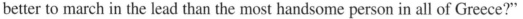

As he grew, Narcissus overheard these discussions of his beauty. And, in fact, he was very proud of his perfect face and graceful body. He loved to look at himself and admire his beauty. Perhaps he grew a bit too aware of his handsome countenance.

When it came time for the annual celebration of the gods in his small village, Narcissus expected to be selected to lead the parade through the village. "After all," he thought, "who better to march in the lead than the most handsome person in all of Greece?"

When the town council met to select a parade leader, they chose a kind-hearted and helpful boy named Ajax, who was honored to have been the one chosen.

Narcissus couldn't understand why he hadn't been chosen. "Why would they not select the most handsome person in all of Greece?" he asked himself.

Narcissus never lost an opportunity to catch a quick glimpse of his reflection. On passing the window of the bakery in his small village, Narcissus thought to himself, "Why, even I can't believe how handsome I've become!" Passing a mirror, he always paused quickly to admire himself. And, whenever he chanced upon a pool of still water, he would take the opportunity to enjoy his reflection. At these tranquil pools, he would lie for hours at the edge of the water, admiring his gleaming, dark eyes, his aquiline nose, and the mop of curly golden hair that crowned the perfect oval of his face.

Several years went on in this manner, with Narcissus growing ever more beautiful and ever more obsessed with his own beauty. It got to the point where Narcissus would linger before any reflection of himself.

The villagers began to discuss this selfish behavior.

"I don't know what has come over Narcissus," the baker told the butcher one summer day. "He was such a gentle and nice child, always willing to help others. But now, he's only interested in his own image and in talking about his own good looks!"

"I know," answered the butcher. "I saw him outside my shop the other day, combing his hair in the reflection of my front window. It is sad, for I know the gods will not like this behavior. They don't want any human to admire himself so much. It's not right."

"Perhaps someone in the village should warn him that he risks angering the gods by his behavior," said the baker.

"I will speak to his parents about this matter," agreed the butcher.

And so, the butcher went to the parents who were saddened by the changes in Narcissus. They agreed that he was risking his well-being with his indulgent behavior and agreed to speak with him about it. That night, when Narcissus returned from a day spent admiring himself in the reflection of a wishing well, his mother quietly approached him.

"Narcissus," she said, "the villagers and your father and I are worried about you. We're afraid that you have listened too much to the talk about your beauty. Yes, it is true that you are handsome to behold, but it is not right to spend your days admiring yourself. The gods will be disappointed in you and may punish you for this behavior. Please think about this, dear."

"Oh, Mother," answered Narcissus, "please do not worry. The gods gave me my beauty. Surely, they will not mind that I admire it."

His father, too, tried to reason with him, but Narcissus wouldn't listen, insisting that a beauty such as his should be admired by all—including himself.

Not long after this conversation, Narcissus found himself walking close to the edge of a cliff near his little village. He looked over the edge and saw that the clear waters of a cold mountain pool perfectly mirrored his beautiful face. He paused to look at himself.

"Oh! You are so handsome, Narcissus!" he told himself as he bent down to admire his reflection more closely. "There's nobody more handsome in the whole world! I'd love to kiss you. And that's just what I'll do!"

He leaned closer to the water. Suddenly, though, he lost his balance and toppled into the pool.

Narcissus struggled to reach the edge of the pool, but he could not swim (he had been too busy admiring himself to take swimming lessons!) and so he drowned.

When the gods discovered that the most beautiful being on earth had died, they decided that such beauty could not be forgotten. Although they were upset that Narcissus had spent so much time admiring himself, they could not forget his incredible beauty.

So the gods turned Narcissus into a scented flower, which, to this day, blossoms in the mountains in spring and inside homes during the holidays. And this beautiful, scented flower is still called Narcissus.

≈ *The End* ≈

The Pied Piper of Hamelin

Once upon a time on the banks of a great river in northern Germany there was a town called Hamelin. The citizens of Hamelin were honest and content. Many peaceful, prosperous years passed until one day, an extraordinary thing happened to disturb the peace.

Hamelin had always had many rats, but they had never been a danger, because the cats had always kept their numbers down. Suddenly, however, the rats began to multiply. Soon a black sea of rats swarmed over the whole town. First, they attacked the barns and warehouses; then, they gnawed the wood, cloth, and everything else within their reach. The only thing they didn't eat was metal.

The terrified citizens begged the town councilors to free them from the plague of rats. But the council had, for a long time, been trying to think of a plan. "What we need is an army of cats!" But all of the cats were dead. They had all died from a strange illness the year before. "We'll put down poisoned food then." But most of the food was already gone, and even poison did not stop the rats. The meeting was interrupted by a loud knock at the door.

They opened the door and there stood a tall thin man dressed in brightly colored clothes, with a long plume in his hat. He was waving a golden pipe at them.

"I've freed other towns of beetles, bats, and rats," the stranger proclaimed, "and for a thousand florins, I'll get rid of your rats!"

"A thousand florins!" exclaimed the mayor. "We'll give you one hundred thousand if you succeed!"

At once the stranger hurried away, saying, "It's late now, but at dawn tomorrow, there won't be a rat left in Hamelin!" The sun was still below the horizon when the melodic sound of a pipe wafted through the streets of

Hamelin. The **pied piper** slowly made his way through the houses, and behind him flocked the rats. Out they scampered from doors, windows, and gutters, rats of every size, all after the piper. As he played, he marched down to the river and straight into the water, up to his waist. Behind him swarmed the rats, and every one was drowned and swept away by the current. By the time the sun was high in the sky, there was not a single rat in the town.

There was great delight at the town hall, until the piper tried to claim his payment.

"One hundred thousand florins?" exclaimed the councilors, "Never!"

"A thousand florins at least!" cried the pied piper angrily.

But the mayor broke in. "The rats are all dead now and they can never come back. So be grateful for fifty florins, or you'll not get even that."

His eyes flashing with rage, the pied piper waved a threatening finger at the mayor. "You'll bitterly regret ever breaking your promise," he said, and vanished.

A shiver of fear ran through the councilors, but the mayor shrugged and said excitedly, "We've saved nine hundred and fifty florins!"

That night, freed from the nightmare of the rats, the citizens of Hamelin slept more soundly than ever. And when the strange sound of piping wafted through the streets at dawn, only the children heard it. Drawn as if by magic, they hurried out of their homes. Again, the pied piper paced through the town, and this time, it was children of all shapes and sizes who flocked at his heels to the sound of his strange piping. The long procession soon left the town and made its way through the wood and across the forest, until it reached the foot of a huge mountain. When the piper came to the dark rock, he played his pipe louder still, and a giant door opened. Beyond it was a cave. In went the children behind the pied piper, and when the last child had gone into the darkness, the door slowly shut.

A great landslide came down the mountain blocking the entrance to the cave forever. Only one little lame boy escaped this **fate**, and he told the anxious citizens of Hamelin who were searching for their children what had happened.

No matter what the people did, the mountain never gave up its victims. Many years were to pass before the merry voices of other children would ring through the streets of Hamelin, but the memory of the harsh lesson remained etched in everyone's heart and was passed down through the generations.

⌒ The End ⌒

The Rose Tree

There once was a good man who had two children: a girl by a first wife, and a boy by the second. The girl was beautiful and beloved by her brother. Her wicked stepmother, though, hated her.

"Child," ordered the stepmother one day, "go to the market and buy some candles."

She gave her the money, and the little girl went, bought the candles, and started home. There was a **stile** to cross, so she put down the candles so she could get over it. Just then, a dog came up and ran off with the candles.

The girl went back to the grocer's and got a second bunch. She came to the stile, set down the candles, and proceeded to climb over. Up came the dog and ran off with the candles.

She went again to the grocer's and she got a third bunch of candles, but the same thing happened. Although she was frightened to go home, the little girl felt she had no choice, so she went to her stepmother, crying, and told her what had happened.

The stepmother was not as angry as the girl expected. She said to the child, "Come, lay your head on my lap, so I can comb the tangles from your hair."

The little one laid her head on the woman's lap, and she proceeded to comb the yellow silken hair. As the stepmother combed, the hair fell over her knees and rolled right down to the ground.

And the stepmother hated the child even more because of the beauty of her hair. So she said to her, "I cannot part your hair on my knee. Go fetch a **billet** of wood." The girl fetched it, and the stepmother said, "I cannot part your hair with a comb, fetch me an ax." So the girl fetched it.

"Now," said the wicked woman, "lay your head down on the billet while I part your hair."

She was a trusting girl, so she laid down her little golden head without fear. Bang! Down came the ax and her head was off. The stepmother quickly buried the girl under a rose tree in the garden. When her father and brother woke up the next day, the wicked woman told them that surely the girl had become lost while fetching candles.

One day the rose tree flowered. It was spring, and there among the flowers was a beautiful white bird that sang, and sang, and sang like an angel out of heaven. Away she flew, and she went to a cobbler's shop and perched on a tree there. She chirped away in a sweet voice, *"My wicked mother killed me; my wicked mother killed me."*

"Sing that beautiful song again," said the shoemaker.

"I will if you'll first give me those little red shoes you are making." The cobbler gave her the shoes, and the bird sang the song. Then she flew to a tree in front of the watchmaker's and sang, *"My wicked mother killed me; my wicked mother killed me."*

"Oh, what a beautiful song! Sing it again, sweet bird," said the watchmaker.

"If you will give me that gold watch and chain in your hand, then I'll sing it."

The watchmaker gave the bird the watch and chain. The bird took it in one foot, the shoes in the other, and, after having repeated the song, flew away to where three **millers** were working. She perched on a tree and sang, *"My wicked mother killed me; my wicked mother killed me."*

"Oh, what a beautiful song! Sing it again, sweet bird," the three men said in unison.

"If you will put the **millstone** round my neck," said the bird. The men did what the bird wanted and away it flew with the millstone round its neck, the red shoes in one foot, and the gold watch and chain in the other. It sang the song and then flew home.

It rattled the millstone against the eaves of the house, and the stepmother said, "It's thundering outside."

Then the little boy ran out to see the thunder and down dropped the red shoes at his feet. It rattled the millstone against the eaves of the house once more, and the stepmother said again, "It's thundering out."

Then the father ran out and down fell the chain about his neck.

In ran father and son, laughing and saying, "See, what fine things the thunder has brought us!"

Then the bird rattled the millstone against the eaves of the house a third time, and the stepmother said, "It thunders again. Perhaps the thunder has brought something for me," and she ran out. The moment she stepped outside the door, down fell the millstone on her head. She died instantly, and nobody was terribly sad that she was gone.

 The End

Salem and the Nail

Once upon a time in a small but prosperous village, there lived a very successful businessman named Salem. Salem made his money selling carpets. He was known for his impressive inventory, with rugs from all corners of the world. There were magnificent wool rugs from Belgium, there were intricate silk rugs brought from distant China, and there were brilliantly colored cotton rugs imported from India.

Salem was a good merchant. Although he drove a hard bargain, he never cheated any of his customers. Though a customer might wander in, requesting a small rug, by the time Salem was finished, the customer might leave the shop with half a dozen large rugs. But Salem was never dishonest, just clever—and convincing.

All went along in this manner for many, many years. Salem prospered and became famous, both for his rug selection and for his sales technique. Then, tough times came to Salem and his business.

One night, as he lay sleeping, tucked in under one of his softest carpets, he heard an urgent knock at the door.

"Who is there?" cried Salem in alarm.

"Come quickly," said one of the villagers. "Your shop is on fire."

Salem jumped out of bed, racing to the shop in his slippers and pajamas. It was of no use, though; by the time he arrived at his rug shop, it had burned to the ground.

A dejected Salem surveyed the damage and then slowly walked home, trying to decide what to do with his now dismal-looking future. But by the time he returned to his snug bed with its special blanket, that clever Salem had come up with a plan for his future. "Tomorrow," he thought as he drifted off to sleep, "I shall put this plan into action."

The next day, he went from merchant to merchant in the village and announced that he would be selling his house, since it was all he had left in the world and he needed to raise some money.

Salem did not ask a high price for his house, though. The merchants all wondered why he wasn't asking for more. However, Salem made a most unusual request of all the prospective buyers. "I'll sell you this fine house, including all of its extremely fine furniture and exceptional carpets. I'll sell everything in the house, except for that nail in the wall. That remains mine!"

Each prospective buyer walked off, shaking his or her head, muttering and puzzling over what the savvy Salem meant by this strange request.

Finally, after interviewing many would-be buyers, Salem believed he had found a buyer for his house. Abraham, this would-be buyer, was a rather stingy fellow, so he was pleased with the low price Salem was asking. But, even though he thought the price for the house was quite fair, he bargained ardently for an even lower price. Salem played along with him, haggling and arguing until finally they agreed on a price. Abraham was pleased, feeling that he had bested the famous merchant at his own bargaining game.

So the new owner took over the whole house, except for the nail. Although Abraham was puzzled by this provision, he decided not to worry about any possible complications caused by it.

He spent the first week in the house, enjoying all of the beautiful furnishings and feeling quite gleeful about his new surroundings.

His glee was short-lived, however. After just one week, the wily Salem knocked at Abraham's door. "I've come to hang something on my nail. I know you won't mind, since, after all, it's my nail," he said.

Abraham chuckled as he let him in. He thought Salem must feel rather wistful, walking into a house that he no longer owned. Salem, though, didn't seem to notice Abraham's manner. He hung a large empty bag on his nail and said a chipper good-bye. Then he left.

Abraham was a bit puzzled by this behavior and, truth be told, started to feel a bit uneasy about just what Salem had in mind. But Abraham decided he wouldn't worry about this odd nail situation. "After all," he thought, "what possible harm could come of Salem owning a single, simple nail?"

So, Abraham continued to enjoy the beautiful home, luxuriating in his beautiful surroundings and raiding the abundant pantries and wine cellar of what had once been Salem's home.

A few days later, Salem reappeared at Abraham's door.

"What are you here for?" asked Abraham.

"Oh, no big deal, really," said Salem. Then, he walked through the door and hung a tattered, rather unsightly old coat on the nail.

"Well," said Salem, "I'll be seeing you." And, off he went.

Now, Abraham really was starting to get nervous about the meaning of this nail. But try as he might, he couldn't conceive of any possible plan Salem might have devised. So Abraham tried to relax and enjoy the spoils of what was left of the pantry.

A day or two later, though, Salem reappeared, this time with a pair of old boots to hang on the nail. These really were rather nasty boots that were filled with holes and had a bit of an odor.

And, from then on, so it went. Salem's visits became regular. Just when Abraham thought that he'd seen the last of

Salem for the day, Salem was back, rapping at his door. In fact, Salem was for-ever coming and going, taking things off the nail or hanging other things up in their place.

This went on for several weeks, annoying Abraham to no end but causing him little other discomfort.

This all ended one evening when, much to the astonishment and shock of Abraham and his family, Salem arrived dragging a dead donkey.

"What are you doing, Salem?" asked Abraham.

Salem didn't answer. Instead, he dragged the donkey through the door, and with a struggle, he hoisted it up and roped it securely to the nail.

Abraham and his family complained about the terrible smell and the dreadful sight of the dead animal, but that clever Salem calmly stated, "It is my nail and I can hang anything I like on it!"

Abraham and his family, naturally, could no longer live in the house under such conditions. The smell was overwhelming. In fact, even the neighbors began to complain as the smell wafted out the windows to their homes.

But Salem refused to remove the donkey. "If you don't like it," he said, "you can get out of my house, but I'll not pay you back a penny!"

Abraham did his best to persuade Salem to take the donkey down, for it smelled so terrible that it was making him and his family ill. But Salem refused to budge, saying he was acting in a fair manner.

In the end, Abraham and his family were forced to leave, because they couldn't stand the sight and smell of the dead animal. And Salem, the savvy salesman, got his house back without paying a penny for it!

⇒ The End ⇐

A Shrewd Farmer's Story

Once upon a time there lived a farmer who worked far from his home in the fields of a rich **baron**. In the past, gangs of robbers had terrorized the region, but the emperor had sent his soldiers to drive out the thieves and now the area was peaceful and safe. Every once in a while, though, old weapons from the past battles of the robbers and soldiers were found in the fields.

While he was chopping down a tree one day, the farmer found a bag full of gold. The farmer had only ever seen silver coins, and he could hardly contain his surprise when he found the gold.

On his way home, the farmer thought about the problems that this sudden wealth could cause him. First of all, everything found on the baron's territory belonged to the baron. By law, the farmer had to hand the gold over to him. The farmer decided that it was much fairer for him to keep the treasure because he was very poor, rather than give it to the baron who already had a lot of money. He realized the risk he would run if anyone found out about his luck. He would never tell anyone, of course. But his wife had a reputation for talking too much, and she would never keep a secret. Sooner or later he felt sure that he would end up in jail. He thought the problem over and over until he found a solution.

Before arriving at his home, he left the bag full of gold in a bush next to some pine trees. The day after, instead of going to work, he went by the village to buy some fish, some pastries, and a rabbit. In the afternoon he went home and said to his wife, "Get your basket and come with me. Yesterday it rained and the wood is full of mushrooms. We must get to them before someone else does!"

The wife, who loved mushrooms, picked up her basket and followed her husband. When they got to the woods, the farmer ran to his wife, shouting,

"Look! Look! We have found a pastry tree!" and he showed her the branches he had decorated with pastries. His wife was astonished, but she was even more perplexed when, instead of mushrooms, she found trout in the grass.

The farmer laughed happily. "Today is our lucky day! My uncle Ichabod said that everyone has one lucky day. We might even find a treasure!" In addition to being a gossip, the farmer's wife was also a bit of a fool. So she believed her husband and chanted, while looking around, "This is our lucky day; this is our lucky day."

The woman's basket was full of fish by now. When she and her husband reached the banks of the river, the farmer ran ahead of her, looked into the thicket, and said: "Yesterday I laid out my nets, and I want to check whether I've caught anything."

A few minutes later the wife heard the husband shout, "Look at what I've caught! What an amazing thing! I've caught a rabbit!"

They were walking back home, and the wife kept talking excitedly about the great dinner with the pastries, the fish, and the rabbit. The husband said, "Let's go by the wood again. We could find other pastries!"

They went to the spot where the farmer had hidden his gold coins. The farmer pretended to find something. "Look over here! There's a strange bag, and it's full of gold! This is a magical forest. We found the pastries on the branches of the trees, then we found the trout in the grass, and now gold."

His wife was so overcome that tears filled her eyes. She was speechless with disbelief, and she gulped as she touched the shiny gold coins.

At home, after dinner, neither of the two could fall asleep. The farmer and his wife kept getting up to look over the treasure they had hidden in an old, worn-out shoe. The next day the farmer went back to work, but first said to his wife, "Don't tell anybody about what happened yesterday." And he repeated the same thing every day after that.

Pretty soon, however, the entire village had heard about the treasure. The baron soon asked the farmer and his wife to come to his home. When they went to see the baron, the farmer tried to stand behind his wife. At the request of the baron, she spoke first of the pastries, then of the trout on the grass, and finally of the rabbit in the river.

Meanwhile, behind her, the husband kept tapping his forehead with his finger and gesturing to the baron. The baron began looking at the woman with pity. "And then I bet you found a treasure, too."

"That's right, sir!" the woman said.

The baron turned to the farmer and, tapping his finger on his forehead, said sympathetically, "I see what you mean. Unfortunately, I have the same problem with my wife."

Then, the baron took the farmer aside and said, "Let's pretend we believe your wife's story. You may keep the gold. I know from experience with my own wife that once she's convinced of something, it's hard to change her mind!"

And so the farmer and his wife were sent home and the **shrewd** farmer spent his money wisely.

⇒ The End ⇒

The Snow

*This tale was originally written by Leonardo da Vinci. He was born in
1452 in Italy and died in 1519. Today, he is better known as an artist
than a writer. You have probably seen pictures of his famous portrait of
the Mona Lisa.*

Once upon a time at the top of a very high mountain there was a massive rock. And on the tip of the rock there was a tiny flake of snow.

The snowflake began examining the surrounding universe. Nearby, he saw a sparkling icicle.

"Wow," thought the small flake, "it must be quite amazing to be a giant icicle." Of course, to the tiny snowflake, the icicle did appear to be amazingly immense. "It must surely give the icicle tremendous confidence to be such a dazzling, substantive creature that glitters in the sun's rays and is almost iridescent."

The snowflake continued casting his eyes about, looking to see what surrounded him.

He next caught sight of a snowman built on a ledge some distance down the mountain.

"Oh, my," thought the little flake. "I wonder what it feels like to be such a creature as a snowman? This one has a lovely nose and dark eyes, a colorful scarf—he even carries a broom."

The snowflake continued to look around him, perched high atop the mountain. After all, the little white speck had little else to occupy his time.

Soon, he spied a frozen spring, emerging from one of the mountain's rugged sides.

"Now, certainly, it must be very grand to be as important as a spring must be. Why, a spring is a very important thing, indeed," decided the snowflake.

All of this observing had left the snowflake a bit confused, for he had always held a rather lofty opinion of himself. But now that he'd spent some time observing his world, he wondered if perhaps he was no more than an insignificant speck in this snowy, mountainous landscape.

The more the snowflake pondered his role in the world, the more discouraged he became. "People will say I am vain and presumptuous, and it is true! I really have been vain, thinking I'm so grand. What am I next to, say, a frozen mountain spring, a snowman, or even an icicle? When others find out what I've been thinking about myself, they'll think that I think too much of myself. And, I'll have to admit that they are probably right. How can a little bit of snow, a mere snowflake like me, so small as to be practically invisible, possibly stay up here without shame among all of these other more grand and important creations?"

The snowflake thought some more about his circumstances but could find no happy note in his pondering. "Anyone looking up at this mountain can see all the rest of the magnificent creatures that live here. They can see the sparkling icicles, the playful snowman, and the glittering frozen springs from a great distance. But they won't be able to see me from down the mountain. And here I am, perched in such a magnificent spot, with a view that reaches for miles. It really isn't right. Such an insignificant scrap of snow as I am has no right to such dizzy, glorious heights. Why, it would be no more than I deserve if the sun treated me as he did all my snowflake friends yesterday and melted me with a single flare of his golden rays. Who am I to think I am above this? First, though, I'll escape the sun's anger by going down to a level more fitting for something as small and inconsequential as I am."

Having said all of this, the little flake of snow, hard and stiff with cold and discouraged by his its day's disturbing thoughts, tried to throw himself from the massive rock. At first, the snowflake was unable to budge, and he thought, "All the greater the humiliation. I can't even move myself down the mountain. I really am not good for much."

But, the snowflake was a determined thing, so he pushed and pulled and with a great effort rolled down from the mountain peak. Then, an interesting thing began to happen to this tiny snowflake. The farther he rolled, the bigger he became. On and on the little snowflake rolled, and soon he wasn't so small anymore. If fact, he had become a great snowball. And, yet, he continued to roll, turning into a huge, heaving, thundering avalanche.

Finally, the snowflake came to rest on a hill, and the avalanche was at least as vast—if not more so—as the hill beneath it. And so in the summer this tiny flake was the last of the snows, rather than the first, to melt in the sun.

In life, one never knows how things will turn out. Even a seemingly inconsequential snowflake may be destined for great things, as this little one was.

⌒ The End ⌒

A Story of a Darning Needle

There was once a regular darning needle that thought she was so superior that she believed she was an embroidery needle. She didn't want to be used for regular, tedious mending and repair jobs.

One day the fingers used the needle on Cook's shoe because the leather had come unstitched.

"Oh, no!" cried the needle. "I shall never get through it. I am breaking! I am breaking!" And she did break. "Didn't I tell you!" said the darning needle. "I am too good to be used for common, dirty work."

"Now you're good for nothing!" said the fingers. The cook put some sealing wax on the needle and stuck it to the front of her dress.

"Now I am a **brooch**!" said the darning needle. "I always knew I was meant for great things!" And she laughed to herself. Then she sat up, proud as could be and looked all round her.

"May I ask if you are gold?" she said to her neighbor, the pin. "You have a very nice appearance, but your head is too small! You must try to make it grow, for it is not everyone who has a head of sealing wax as I do."

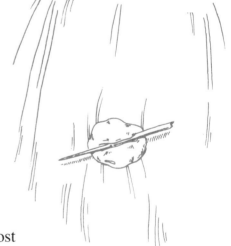

And with these words the darning needle raised herself up so proudly that she fell out of the dress and right into the sink, which the cook was rinsing out.

"Now I am off on my travels!" said the darning needle. "I hope I don't get lost!" She did indeed get lost and found herself washed into a gutter.

But the darning needle remembered her elevated origins and did not lose her good temper. All kinds of things swam over her—shavings, bits of straw, scraps of old newspapers, and pieces of glass.

"Just look how they sail along!" said the darning needle. "They have no idea that someone as important as I am is right beneath them. There goes a scrap thinking of nothing in the world but itself, a mere scrap! There goes a straw, a lowly straw. There goes a bit of paper. What is written on it is long ago forgotten. I am sitting patiently and quietly. I know who I am, and that is enough for me!"

One day something lay near her that glittered so brightly that the darning needle thought it must be a diamond. It was only a bit of glass, but because it sparkled, the darning needle spoke to it, telling the glass she was a brooch.

"You must be a diamond," the darning needle said.

"Yes, something like that," the glass replied, and each believed that the other was something very important and expensive. They both said how very proud the world must be of them.

"I have come from a lady's sewing box," said the darning needle, "and this lady was a cook. She had five fingers on each hand; she was proud of those fingers! And yet they were only there to take me out of the sewing box and to put me back again!"

"Were they royal fingers, then?" asked the glass.

"Oh no, but they were proud," said the darning needle. "They were five brothers, all called 'fingers.' They held themselves proudly one against the other, although they were of different sizes. The outside one, the Thumb, was short and fat. He had only one bend in his back and could make only one bow; but he said that if he were cut off from a man, then that man was no longer any use as a soldier. Dipper, the second finger, dipped into all things, pointed to the sun and the moon and the stars, and guided the pen when they wrote.

Longman, the third finger, looked at the others over his shoulder. Ringer, the fourth, had a stiff gold belt round his waist. Little Pinkie did nothing at all, and was proud of it! They thought too much of themselves, so I ran away!"

At that moment more water came into the gutter and washed the bottle-glass shard away.

"Oh, now he has been promoted!" said the darning needle. "I remain here." And she sat there very proudly, thinking lofty thoughts.

One day two kids were playing and wading in the gutter, picking up old nails, pennies, and such. It was rather dirty work, but fun to them.

"Oh, look!" cried out one, as he pricked himself with the darning needle. "He is a fine fellow, isn't he?"

"I am not a fellow! I am a young lady!" said the darning needle; but no one heard. The sealing wax had fallen off, and she had become quite black. But black makes one look very slim, and so she thought she was looking even finer and more fashionable than before.

"Here comes an eggshell sailing along!" said the boys, and they stuck the darning needle into the eggshell.

"The walls are white and I am black—what a great contrast!" said the darning needle. "Now I can be seen at my most flattering."

Just then the eggshell went "crack" as a horse's hoof crushed it.

"Oh! How it hurts!" said the darning needle. "I am breaking!"

But she did not break. After the horse passed, she lay there at full length. And, I hear, she rests there still, feeling quite proud of herself.

 The End

Three Sillies

Once upon a time there was a farmer and his wife who had one daughter, and a gentleman courted her. Every evening he came to see her and ate supper at the farmhouse. Every night the daughter was sent down into the basement to get beer from a barrel for supper.

One evening when she went to get the beer, she happened to look up at the ceiling and saw a mallet stuck in one of the beams. It must have been there a long, long time, but somehow or other she had never noticed it before.

She began thinking, "It's very dangerous to have that mallet there. Suppose the gentleman and I are married, and we had a son, and he was to grow up to be a man. And then, he came down into the cellar to draw the beer, just as I'm doing now. And what if the mallet were to fall on his head and kill him? Oh, how awful!" And she put down the candle and the jug, and sat down and started to cry.

Upstairs, they began to wonder what was taking the daughter so long. So her mother went down to see after her, and she found her daughter crying and beer running all over the floor.

"Why, what's the matter?" said her mother.

"Oh, Mother!" she said. "Look at that horrid mallet! Suppose my beau and I were to be married and have a son, who grew up, and came down to the cellar to draw the beer, and the mallet fell on his head and killed him. What a dreadful thing it would be!"

"Dear, dear! That's terrible!" said the mother, and she sat down by her daughter and started crying too.

Then after a bit the father began to wonder why they hadn't come back. So he went down into the cellar to check, and there they sat, crying, while the beer was running all over the floor.

"What's the matter?" he asked.

"Why," said the mother, "look at that horrid mallet. Just suppose, if our daughter and her sweetheart were to be married and have a son, and he grew up and came down into the cellar to draw the beer, and the mallet fell on his head and killed him. What a dreadful thing it would be!"

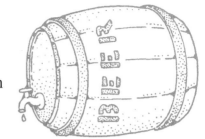

"Dear, dear, dear! That's the worst thing I've ever heard!" said the father, and he sat down and started crying.

The gentleman got tired of waiting by himself. So at last he went down into the cellar, too, to see what had happened. There they were, crying, and the beer was running all over the floor. And he ran straight and turned off the tap. Then he said, "Whatever are you three doing, sitting there crying, and letting the beer run all over the floor?"

"Oh!" said the father, "look at that horrid mallet! Suppose you and our daughter were to be married and have a son, and he grew up and came down into the cellar to draw the beer, and the mallet fell on his head and killed him!"

And then they all started crying more than before. But the gentleman burst out laughing, and reached up and pulled out the mallet. Then he said: "I've traveled many miles, and I've never met three such big sillies before. Now I shall start out on my travels again, and when I find three bigger sillies than you, then I'll come back and marry your daughter."

He said good-bye and set off and left them all crying because the girl had lost her sweetheart. Now they felt really silly!

The gentleman traveled a long way. At last he came to a woman's cottage that had some grass growing on the roof. And the woman was trying to get her cow to go up a ladder to the grass, but the poor thing wouldn't go. So the gentleman asked the woman what she was doing.

"Why, look at it," she said, "look at all that beautiful grass. I'm going to get the cow onto the roof to eat it. She'll be quite safe, for I shall tie a rope round her neck and pass it down the chimney. I'll tie it to my waist as I go about the house, so she can't fall off without my knowing it."

"Oh, you poor silly!" said the gentleman. "You should cut the grass and throw it down to the cow!" But the woman thought it was easier to get the cow up the ladder than to get the grass down, so she pushed her and coaxed her and got the cow up on the roof. Then she tied a rope around the cow's neck, passed it down the chimney, and fastened it to her own waist. And the gentleman went on his way, but he hadn't gone far when the cow tumbled off the roof. She hung by the rope tied around her neck and was strangled. The weight of the cow tied to the woman's waist pulled her up the chimney, and she stuck fast halfway up for more than two days before a neighbor found her!

That was one big silly.

The gentleman went on until he came to an inn to spend the night. The inn was so full that he had to share a room with another traveler. The other man was a very pleasant fellow. But in the morning, when they were both getting up, the gentleman was surprised to see the man hang his pants on the knobs of the chest of drawers and run across the room and try to jump into them. He tried over and over again and couldn't manage it. The gentleman wondered what he was doing.

At last he stopped and wiped the sweat off of his face with his handkerchief. "Oh dear," he said, "I do think trousers are the most awkward type of clothes that ever were. I can't think who could have invented such things. It takes me almost an hour to get into mine every morning, and I get so hot! How do you manage yours?"

So the gentleman burst out laughing and showed him how to put the trousers on.

That was another big silly.

Then the gentleman went on his way again. He came to a village. Outside the village there was a pond, and round the pond was a crowd of people. They had rakes and brooms and pitchforks, and were reaching into the pond. The gentleman asked what was the matter.

"Oh, it's a disaster," they said, "The moon's tumbled into the pond, and we can't rake her out!"

The gentleman burst out laughing and told them to look up into the sky, and that it was only the moon's reflection in the water. But they wouldn't listen to him!

So, he found, there were a whole lot of sillies bigger than the three sillies at home. The gentleman turned back and married the farmer's daughter. I hear she's still silly, but the gentleman loves her anyway!

⌒ The End ⌒

Toads and Diamonds

Once upon a time there was a widow who had two daughters. The elder daughter was just like the mother, both in how she looked and how she behaved. And, truth be told, both were quite unpleasant. The younger daughter was sweet and courteous and one of the most beautiful girls ever seen. The mother, though, doted on her elder daughter and disliked her younger daughter. She made her eat in the kitchen and work constantly.

Among other things, twice a day, the poor child was forced to draw a pitcher full of water from a well more than a mile and a half from the house, and bring home a full pitcher. One day, as she was at the well, a poor woman came to her and begged for a drink.

"Of course," said the pretty little girl. She gave the woman the pitcher and let her drink as much as she liked.

After quenching her thirst, the woman said, "You are so very pretty, my dear, so good and so kind, that I cannot help giving you a gift." For she was actually a fairy who had taken the form of a poor countrywoman, to see how polite this pretty girl would be.

"Every time you speak," continued the fairy, "a flower or a precious jewel will come out of your mouth."

When the girl got home from the well, her mother scolded her for taking such a long time.

"I'm sorry," said the poor girl, "for not being faster."

And in speaking these words, two roses, two pearls, and two diamonds came out of her mouth.

"What is it I see there?" said the mother, quite astonished. "I think I see pearls and diamonds coming out of the girl's mouth! How did that happen, child?"

This was the first time she had ever called her "child."

So the daughter told her mother what had happened.

"Oh my," cried the mother, "I must send my other daughter. Come here, Fanny. Look what comes out of your sister's mouth when she speaks. Go to the well, Fanny, and see if the same thing happens to you."

"I don't want to go get water," said this ill-bred girl.

"You shall go this minute!" said the mother, who wanted more diamonds from her elder daughter.

So away she went, grumbling all the way, taking with her the best silver **tankard** in the house.

No sooner did she arrive at the well than she saw a lady in fancy clothing coming out of the wood. She came up to the girl and asked for a drink. This was, you must know, the very fairy who had appeared to her sister, but now had transformed herself into a princess to see how far this girl's rudeness would go.

"You think I brought this fancy tankard just for you, don't you? Well, go ahead, drink out of it if you like, but you'll have to draw your own water from the well," said the nasty daughter.

"You are not very polite," answered the fairy. "For a gift, at every word you speak, there will come out of your mouth a snake or a toad."

So soon as her mother saw her coming, she cried out, "Well, daughter?"

"Well, mother?" answered the obnoxious daughter, throwing out of her mouth a rattlesnake and a toad.

"Oh no," cried the mother. "What is this? Your sister will pay for this!" Immediately she ran to scold her. The poor child fled and went to hide herself in the forest, not far away.

The king's son, just returning from a hunting excursion, met her, and was astonished at her beauty. He asked her why she was crying so.

"My mother has kicked me out of the house."

The king's son, who saw five or six pearls and two or three diamonds come out of her mouth, asked her to tell the whole story. As she spoke, the king's son fell in love with her. Soon, they were married.

Her mother and sister lived out their wretched lives together, despised by almost everyone.

⌐ The End ⌐

The Walnut and the Bell Tower

Once upon a time, a hungry black crow picked up a walnut he saw amidst some leaves on the ground. The big bird carried it in his beak up to the top of a high bell tower. This bell tower was at the top of a magnificent church, one famed throughout all of Italy for its beauty and design.

Once the bird had perched himself on the bell tower, he took hold of the nut between his claws and then began to peck at it with his beak to open it and get at the meat. He worked at this for some time, but he was having no success in getting the walnut open because the shell was especially hard.

Suddenly, to the crow's immense frustration, the nut slipped out of his claws, rolled down, and disappeared into a crack in the church wall.

The crow flew down to the crack in the wall and poked his beak in, trying to reach the walnut. But it was wedged in just out of his reach.

"This is such a disappointment," thought the crow. He had been looking forward to a lunch of walnut meat. "Oh, well. I'll simply have to find another." And, off he flew in search of something else to eat.

This left the walnut in a rather difficult position. Now that he realized he had been freed from the crow's fearful beak, he did not want the wall to squeeze him out from the crevice in which he'd landed. He was afraid that if he were expelled from his hiding place, the crow or another bird might once again try to eat him.

So the walnut asked the wall to help him out.

"Wall, fair Wall," begged the walnut, "in the name of God, who has been so good to you, making you tall and strong, graceful and beautiful, and giving you all of these fine bells that sound so beautiful, please save me. All of my life, I felt that I was destined to fall beneath my old father's branches and to rest in the rich earth covered with yellow leaves. Once there, I'd hoped to grow by my father's side and become a beautiful tree that could cast shade on a hot day, offer shelter from a rainstorm, and beauty to the landscape. Oh, fair Wall, don't abandon me, please. When I was in the terrible, frightening beak of that fierce crow I made a promise. 'If I ever escape,' I said to myself, 'I promise to finish my days in a little hole, causing problems for no one.' "

The bells in the tower, with a gentle, jingling murmur, warned the bell tower to be careful. The bells felt that the walnut might be dangerous and could cause problems for the wall. "How could the wall be sure about the walnut's character?" they asked with their gentle chimes.

But the wall, being a rather kindhearted sort of fellow and feeling sorry for the walnut, decided to shelter it. It allowed the walnut to stay where it had fallen from the crow's beak. For a time, things went well. The walnut stayed nestled in its snug hiding place, and the wall continued to support its part of the bell tower.

But eventually, the walnut began to regret its promise to live in the little hole. It longed to reach out and grow. So one day the walnut opened up and put its roots through some cracks in the stone wall. Then the roots started to do damage, forcing their way between the blocks of stone until finally little branches began to peep out of the hole in the wall. As the years passed, the branches grew thicker and became stronger and stretched up above the top of the bell tower. And the roots, by now massive and twisted, began to make more holes in the walls, pushing out all of the old stones.

The wall realized too late that the walnut's humility and its vow to stay hidden in the hole were not sincere. The walnut said what it had to say in order to convince the wall to keep it safe. The wall now regretted not having listened to the savvy words of the wise bells.

By now, though, the wall had no recourse and could do nothing to stop the damage of the walnut tree. In fact, the walnut tree went on growing and the poor, unhappy, deceived wall crumbled and fell.

If you care to visit, the walnut tree is growing there still. And surrounding it, is a heap of stones that once made up the gentle wall of the bell tower.

⌒ The End ⌒

What Other People Think

*O*nce upon a time a farmer and his son went to market to sell a donkey. These were goodhearted people who worked hard, growing crops and tending their livestock. It's true that sometimes they weren't as clever as most folk, but their hard work and winning ways made up for any other deficiencies.

It had been a trying year for their farm. Spring had come late and winter early, so the growing season was short and not very substantial. They hadn't made much money when they sold their few crops, and they worried about how they'd find money to buy next year's seeds and supplies.

The father and son sat down at the kitchen table together to discuss their options.

"I know," said the son. "We could sell all of the vegetables in our cellar. Then, we could spend the money on seed and other supplies for next year, so we'll have more seeds than usual and produce a bigger crop."

At first, the father thought this sounded like a wonderful idea, helping to ensure a better time of it next year. But after an awful lot of head scratching and brow mopping (remember, being clever is not the strength of these two!), he said, "Say there, Son. I've just realized that we can't sell the vegetables in our root cellar. If we did that, we would have nothing to eat and we might starve during the winter. No, I like the idea of buying seed and supplies for next year, but somehow we'll have to do it without selling all of our stored food."

So, they put their heads together and thought some more. It actually took several days of thought, but finally they had an idea they both felt was a winning one.

"Son, why don't we sell Edgar, the donkey?" asked the father enthusiastically. "After all, we have two other donkeys, and they eat an awful lot. Perhaps we could sell Edgar and use the money from his sale to buy seeds for next year and food for this winter, if we need more than we have stored."

"What a great idea, Father," agreed the son. And although they were a bit sad because they were fond of old Edgar, they decided that the animal would be sold at market the very next day.

In the morning, they loaded the donkey—with quite a lot of effort—into their big red wheelbarrow, so that he would not be worn out when they reached the market. After all, they were fond of Edgar and wanted him to have a comfortable time of it. They pushed the wheelbarrow along the road in this fashion, pausing frequently to catch their breath. Edgar was a heavy donkey.

When people along the roadside saw such an odd sight, they said: "Those two men are crazy! Whoever saw a donkey being taken to market in a wheelbarrow! I've never seen such a thing!"

Although the farmer and his boy felt they were doing the best possible thing for Edgar, they overheard the roadside chatter and became more and more confused. The farther they went, the louder the comments became, and the more people gossiped about the donkey in the wheelbarrow.

Finally, the farmer stopped, frustrated by all that he had heard. He and his son heaved the animal out of the wheelbarrow. Then, the farmer climbed onto Edgar's back, while his son walked behind them. This didn't help, though. In fact, this arrangement seemed to make matters even worse. All along the roadside, people continued to point fingers and complain.

A group of women going home from market with their baskets ridiculed him, saying, "You are a cruel and thoughtless man! And besides that, you're a big oaf, riding the donkey while your poor little boy runs along behind you! You ought to be ashamed of yourself!"

What was the poor farmer to do? He really was very confused. Finally, after listening to more gossips along the side of the road, he slid off the donkey. Now, though, he had no idea what to do next. He took off his cap and mopped his sweaty brow. Then he sat down on a stone, put his head in his hands, and tried to make some sense of the situation.

"Oh my," he exclaimed to his son, "I never imagined it could be so difficult to take a donkey to market. First, we tried taking Edgar in the wheelbarrow and people complained about that. Then, I tried riding him, hoping that would please people, but clearly it didn't. What shall we do?" Finally, after a lot more thought, he hoisted his little boy onto the donkey and walked along behind them. Maybe this scenario would be more pleasing, he hoped.

This time, a cluster of men on their way back from fishing began to protest. "Look at that! I can't believe my eyes. There is a lazy boy sitting on top of a donkey, while his weary old father has to go on foot! What a selfish, thought-less child! There you go, that's how children behave these days!"

This really was most frustrating to the father and son. Once again, the two of them came to a halt. How could they stop people from criticizing everything they did? It certainly was a troubling trip to the marketplace.

This time, they both sat on a rock, placing their heads in their hands, deter-mined to come up with a solution that would be pleasing to all of those they passed on their way to the market. They sat there for some time. In fact, hours passed as they tried to come up with an idea that might work. Finally, they agreed on a plan: They both climbed on the back of the poor donkey.

And, what do you supposed happened then? Did the groups along the roadside stop complaining? Not at all!

"What heartless folk!" exclaimed everyone watching the father and son ride by. "Two riders on one little donkey! These really are cruel people, burdening a poor animal like that."

This really was more than the poor farmer could stand. Now, the bewildered man had completely lost his patience. He gave poor Edgar a terrible kick, saying, "Giddy up! From now on, I'll do things my way, and pay no attention to what other people think!"

⮞ The End ⮜

This story is a parable, a tale from which a moral or other lesson can be learned. What did you learn from this story? One lesson: Don't always feel as though you have to react to what others say. Although the farmer and his son are a bit silly (after all, who puts a donkey in a wheelbarrow!), they aren't harming anyone as they set off for market. Influenced by their side-of-the-road critics, though, they decide that they both should ride on the overburdened donkey. By listening to others, they make bad decisions. With both of them on the donkey, the beast is sure to arrive at market exhausted and will end up being worth less. So much for what other people think!

Whittington and His Cat

During the reign of the famous King Edward III, there was a little boy called Dick Whittington whose father and mother had died when he was very young. Dick was very poor and rarely had enough to eat.

Dick had heard many strange things about a big city called London. For one thing, he had heard that the streets there were all paved with gold.

One day a large wagon and eight horses drove through the village. Dick thought that this wagon must have been going to the fine town of London, so he asked the driver to let him walk by the side of the wagon. The driver agreed to this.

When Dick got to London, he was in such a hurry to see the fine streets paved with gold that he did not even stay to thank the wagon driver. He ran off as fast as his legs would carry him, through many of the streets, thinking at every turn he would come to those that were paved with gold. It grew dark and still Dick hadn't found a street of gold.

Little Dick slept in a doorway that night and awoke feeling faint with hunger. He began begging for a penny to buy some food. For a long while, no one spoke to Dick, but finally a handsome gentleman saw how hungry he looked. "Why don't you go to work, my lad?" he asked Dick.

"I would, but I do not know how to get a job," answered Dick.

"You can work for me, if you like," said the man, who made his living as a farmer. Dick agreed and went to work with him. He stayed until the harvesting was done, but then he was without work again.

After this he found himself almost as badly off as before. He started to sleep on the streets again, where he stayed until a rich merchant named Mr. Fitzpatrick stumbled upon him. After Dick asked for a job and promised to work very hard, Mr. Fitzpatrick agreed to hire him and provide him with a place to live.

At Mr. Fitzpatrick's house, Dick was given a room in the garret. Although Dick was very happy to have a roof over his head, the garret was full of rats and mice that tormented him. Dick decided to buy a cat and bring it to the garret to live with him. The next day he bought one from a girl for a penny. Dick hid his cat in the garret and always took care to save part of his dinner for her. In a short time, he had no more trouble with the rats and mice. From then on, he slept well every night.

Soon after this, his master made preparations to send his ship on a long journey. As was the custom, he asked the servants what they would like to send on board the ship. By sending something, the servants had a chance at good fortune.

Poor Dick had only his cat. Reluctantly, he parted with her, knowing that now he would be tormented again by the mice and rats.

The master's daughter, Alice, felt sorry for Dick, so she gave him a penny to buy another cat. This made the other servants so jealous that they scolded Dick cruelly. The cook even beat him with her wooden spoon.

Finally, Dick decided to run away, so he packed up his few things and started very early in the morning. He walked as far as Holloway and there sat down on a stone, which to this day is called "Whittington's Stone," and began to think about which road to take. After lots of thought, he decided, with some regrets, that he was

probably better off in his garret, even if the servants were cruel, especially the cook who misused her wooden spoon.

So Dick went back. He was lucky enough to get into the house and back to his work before the old cook came downstairs.

But what had happened to Dick's cat, the one that was sent on the ship?

The ship with the cat on board was a long time at sea and was at last driven by the winds to the coast of Barbary. The captain sent some of his best cargo to the king, who was so pleased that he sent for the captain to come to the palace. They all sat down to dinner when a vast number of rats and mice rushed in and devoured all the meat in an instant. The captain asked if the vermin were a major problem.

"Oh, yes," the people said, "they are very offensive. The king would give half his treasure to be rid of them. Not only do they eat his dinner but they bother him while he sleeps."

The captain jumped for joy, remembering the cat, and told the king he had a creature on board the ship that would do away with these vermin immediately. The king jumped so high with happiness that his turban fell off his head.

"If this cat drives away the vermin, I will load your boat with gold and jewels," the king promised.

So the captain fetched the cat, and when he returned another dinner was ready. When the cat saw the table full of rats, she killed most of them in a flash. The rest of them scampered away to their holes.

The king bought the cat from the captain for a vast quantity of gold.

The captain then returned to London, his ship filled with treasures and gold that had been given in exchange for Dick Whittington's cat.

Mr. Fitzpatrick now proved himself to be an honest man, for he planned to give Dick all of the gold and treasure, keeping none for himself. After meeting with the captain, he sent for Dick.

"Mr. Whittington," said the merchant, "Your cat has been sold to the king of Barbary, for more riches than I possess in the whole world. I wish you may always enjoy them!"

Mr. Fitzpatrick then told the men to open the great treasure. Poor Dick hardly knew how to behave because he was so happy. He begged his master to take part of it because of the kindness he'd shown Dick.

"No, no," answered Mr. Fitzpatrick, "this is all for you and I have no doubt but you will use it well."

Dick gave some of the treasure to the servants and to the ship's mates. He even gave some to the surly cook! He bought some new clothes and scrubbed himself. Then he was as handsome as any young man who had ever visited at Mr. Fitzpatrick's. Miss Alice became his sweetheart. Mr. Fitzpatrick soon saw their love for each other and proposed they get married. A day for the wedding was set and they were soon married in very grand fashion. They lived happily ever after.

The End

Why the Sea Is Salty

Once upon a time there were two brothers, one rich and one poor. On one Christmas Eve, the poor brother had nothing to eat, so he went to his brother and begged him to give him something for Christmas Day. It was not the first time that the poor brother had asked his brother for a favor. The rich brother was tired of being asked to help out, so he devised a plan.

"If you will do as I ask, you shall have a whole ham. You must spend a night in the Haunted Cave," he told his poor brother. The poor one thanked him and agreed, since he had no other options.

"Well, I will do what I have promised," said the poor brother, and he took the ham and set off. He went on and on all day, and at nighttime he came to a place where there was a bright light.

"This must be the place," he thought.

An old man with a long white beard was outside chopping Yule logs.

"Good evening," said the man with the ham.

"Good evening to you. Where are you going at this late hour?" asked the man.

"I am going to the Haunted Cave. Am I headed in the right direction?"

"Oh! Yes, you are already there," said the old man. "When you get inside, they will all want to buy your ham, for they don't get much meat to eat there. But you must not sell it unless you can get the **hand-mill**, which stands behind the door. When you come out again, I will teach you how to properly use the hand-mill; it is useful for almost everything."

So the poor man thanked the old man for his good advice and knocked at the door. When he got in, everything happened just as predicted. People came around him like ants on an anthill and tried to outbid each other for the ham.

"I really shouldn't sell it," said the man. "But, if I do decide to sell it, I would like to have the hand-mill that is standing there behind the door."

At first they said no, but eventually they gave in and traded the hand-mill for the ham.

When the man came out again into the yard, he asked the old woodcutter how to use the hand-mill, and when he had learned how he headed home. He got there just as Christmas Day arrived.

"Where in the world have you been?" asked his wife. "I have no firewood and nothing to eat."

"Oh! Wait until you see!" said the man. Then he set the hand-mill on the table and told it to grind firewood, then a tablecloth, some meat, and something to drink, and everything else that was good for a Christmas dinner. The mill ground all that he ordered.

"Amazing!" said his wife as one thing after another appeared. She wanted to know where her husband got the mill, but he would not tell her.

"Never mind where I got it. You can see that it is a good one," said the man. So they had meat, drink, and all kinds of tasty things to last all Christmas season. On the third day the man invited all his friends to come to a feast.

When the rich brother saw all that there was at the banquet and in the house, he was quite put out about his brother's new wealth.

"Tell me where you got your riches," he said to his brother.

"From behind the door," he said, but he did not say which door. Later in the evening, though, he was so excited about his new hand-mill that he told his brother where he had found it. "Look at what has brought me all my wealth," he said, and brought out the mill, and made it grind first one thing and then another. When the brother saw that, he insisted on having the mill. After a great deal of arguing, he got it. First though, he had to pay three hundred gold pieces, and the poor brother was to keep it 'till the fall harvesting was over, for he thought, "If I keep it as long as that, I can make it grind meat and drink that will last many years."

During that time, the hand-mill was used a great deal. When it came time for the rich brother to get it, the other brother did not teach him how to stop it.

It was evening when the rich man brought the mill home, and in the morning he told his wife to go out and run errands, and that he would clean the house himself that day.

When dinnertime drew near, he set the mill on the kitchen table, and said, "Hand-mill, grind herrings and milk **pottage**, and do it both quickly and well."

So the mill began to grind herrings and milk pottage. First, all the dishes, pots, and pans were filled, and then it flowed out all over the kitchen floor. The man twisted and turned the hand-mill and did all he could to make it stop. No matter what he did, the mill went on grinding; and in a short time the pottage rose so high that the man was afraid he'd drown in it.

So he threw open the parlor door, but it was not long before the mill had ground the parlor full too, and it was with difficulty and danger that the man got through the stream of pottage and got hold of the doorknob. When he wrenched the door open, he did not stay there long but ran out, and the herrings and pottage came after him and streamed out over everything.

Now his wife, who was just returning home, began to get hungry. She'd just started up the hill by her home when she ran into the herrings and pottage, pouring in rivers out of the house, and her husband running in front of the flood.

"Take care that you are not drowned in the pottage!" he cried.

The rich brother ran to where his brother lived. Then he begged him to take the mill back again. But the brother would not take it until the other paid him another three hundred gold pieces, which he agreed to do.

Now the poor brother had both the money and the mill again. So it was not long before he had a farmhouse much finer than his brother's. The mill ground him so much wealth that he covered his home with siding made of gold. The house was by the seashore, so it glittered far out to sea.

After many years, a skipper came by and asked to see the mill. He asked if it could make salt.

"Yes, it can make salt," said the mill's owner. When the skipper heard that, he wished with all his might to have the mill because he was in the business of buying and selling salt. The skipper offered the man bags of gold and riches, even a stake in his trading business, but the man flatly refused.

That same night, the skipper snuck into the man's house to steal the mill. The skipper tucked the hand-mill under his arm and quickly left. Once on board his ship, he took the mill out. "Grind salt, and grind both quickly and well," said the skipper.

So the mill began to grind salt, until it spouted out like water. When the skipper had filled the ship, he wanted to stop the mill, but no matter what he did, it went on grinding. The heap of salt grew higher and higher, until at last the ship sank like a stone to the bottom of the ocean.

And to this day, the mill remains at the bottom of the sea and grinds on. If anyone ever asks, that is why the sea is salty!

The End

Glossary

Alchemists: People who studied alchemy, the practice of trying to transform common materials into gold.

Balalaika: A triangle-shaped musical instrument with three strings that produces sounds similar to those of a mandolin.

Baron: A European nobleman; someone with wealth and power.

Billet: A short, thick piece of firewood. The little girl in "The Rose Tree" put her head on a billet.

Billy goats: Male goats. A female goat is known as a nanny goat.

Brahman: Someone of a high social class in India.

Brewery: A place for making ale, a drink similar to beer.

Brooch: A type of jewelry; an ornamental pin.

Carding comb: A tool used to brush wool. It is used during the process of spinning wool.

Chamberlain: A member of an emperor's court who advises him on a variety of matters. In the case of "The Emperor's New Clothes," a key duty for the chamberlain was to help the emperor with his daily wardrobe changes and ensure that his wardrobe was kept up to date.

Cockerel: A young rooster, usually less than a year old.

Coffer: A small chest for holding valuables, such as gold and jewels, often elaborately decorated with paint and precious stones.

Common: Public land, like a park. In the story "Lazy Jack," Jack and his mother lived on a common.

Courting: These days, we don't use the word *courting* very often; but at one time, it was commonly heard. In "The Three Sillies," the gentleman comes to court the daughter, arriving each evening for dinner. He is wooing her and trying to gain her affections, so she will someday marry him.

Damask: A type of luxurious, fairly firm fabric used for everything from royal robes to regal curtains in the sultan's palace.

Dowry: The property a woman, or her family, gives a man when they are married. It might be land, money, treasures, or other valuables.

Dragoon: An adept soldier who has been trained to fight on horseback and on foot.

Fakir: A poor man who usually makes his money by begging. Fakirs often claim to be able to work miracles, which they will offer in exchange for something.

Fate: A force or power that predetermines events.

Fen: A marshy land, like a swamp.

Flax: A type of plant. Fibers from the stem are spun into linen thread.

Florin: A kind of coin used in Europe a long time ago.

Garret: This is the space just under the roof of a house. It is also called the attic.

Genie: A supernatural, magical being that can take human or animal form. They often have strong powers and are able to affect other humans and even the course of nature.

Grand vizier: A very important person in the royal family's government. He takes on many of the royal family's duties—including, in "The Princess and the Mouse," meeting with the evil magician to find a solution to the mystery of the missing royalty. He is also responsible for managing other servants, meeting with visitors to the castle, and helping the royal family arrange their schedules.

Hand-mill: A machine used to grind things; for instance, a coffee mill is used to grind coffee beans. The hand-mill in "Why the Sea Is Salty" is a magic one that not only grinds but also seemingly creates food and drink out of thin air.

Hovel: A small hut, usually made of dried mud, and not really fit to live in.

Kettledrum: A special type of drum made of copper or brass with a parchment top. As the top is tightened or loosened, the sound of the drum changes.

Leper: Someone who has Hansen's disease, also known as leprosy. The king in "The Story of the Greek King and the Physician Douban" had leprosy. It is a very serious infectious disease that attacks the skin and muscles.

Lout: A clumsy, stupid person.

Lute: A stringed instrument, similar to a guitar. Its body is shaped like one half of a pear, and it has from six to thirteen strings (a guitar usually has just six strings).

Magpie: A member of the crow family, this bird is known for its noisy chattering. As a result, people who talk a lot are sometimes called magpies!

Marquis: Pronounced *mar-key,* he is a nobleman in a European country. He ranks just below a duke; a duke ranks just below a prince.

Marsh: Swampy, soft land.

Mermaid: An imaginary sea creature. A mermaid has the head and upper body of a person and the tail of a fish. Mermaids have appeared in many stories. Even William Shakespeare used a vision of a mermaid in his play *A Midsummer Night's Dream.*

Miller: A person who runs a mill. A mill is a building with machinery for crushing grain into flour or meal. The flour would be used to make breads and other baked goods.

Millstone: Large, usually round stones that are used to grind grain.

Miser: A person who is greedy and stingy and hoards money.

Mortar: A bowl for grinding things. For instance, nuts or seeds can be ground or pounded in a mortar. The mortar in "The Monkey–Crab War" is cut from the stump of a tree. It was made from a knot in the tree, which was then hollowed out to form a bowl.

Mosque: A house of worship used by Muslims.

Musketeer: A soldier who uses a musket. A musket is a gun commonly used before the invention of the rifle.

Nightingale: A type of thrush; thrushes are songbirds, usually with plain plumage. Nightingales are found in Europe, Asia, and North Africa. They are a medium brown color with a paler chest. They are famous and beloved for their beautiful song, which they usually sing at night.

Northern Lights: Also called *aurora borealis*, these lights are probably caused by electrical charges in the air. The Northern Lights look almost like colorful glittering streamers pouring down from the sky.

Persia: A big chunk of ancient Persia is now known as Iran, a country in the southwest area of Asia. However, ancient Persia was at times a very large and grand empire.

Persimmon: A type of fruit that grows on an ebony tree. The fruit, when ripe, is very sweet.

Pied piper: If a pied piper appeared at your door, you'd be looking at a person wearing patchwork clothes made from pieces of other clothing. And this patchworked person would be carrying a musical instrument called a pipe. A pipe is similar to a recorder or a clarinet in how it is held and played.

Polo: A game played on horseback by two teams, each made up of four players. The goal is to drive a ball through a goal, using a long-handled mallet.

Pottage: A type of thick soup or stew made with meat and vegetables.

Rushes: A type of plant that thrives in a wet environment, like a fen. The stems are very flexible, so they are used to make baskets and mats, or, as in the tale "Cap o' Rushes," a concealing cloak.

Scepter: A highly decorated stick or rod that rulers carry, often at ceremonies.

Shah: Someone like a king.

Sheik: A Moslem religious leader or a leader of an Arab family or village.

Shrewd: Someone who is cunning and wily, or just plain smart!

Shrine: A place of worship, often holding a special object. In the story "The Book of Spells," the special object is the angel.

Skein: A coil of thread or yarn.

Sprite: A type of fairy, goblin, elf, or pixie. Sprites can be good or bad.

Stile: Steps or rungs leading over a fence. While helpful to humans, stiles are supposed to remain a barrier to animals.

Sultan: Similar to a king, a sultan is the ruler of an Arabic kingdom.

Tablet: A flat, thin piece of stone with words carved into it.

Tankard: A large drinking cup with a handle. It often has a hinged lid as well.

Threshing floor: A floor or other area where grain is beaten out of its husk.

Trod: Walked on or crushed.

Troll: Trolls first appeared in Scandinavian folk stories. They are rather nasty creatures, prone to being ugly and cross-tempered. To complement these disagreeable features, trolls like to live in damp, slimy underground places!

Tundra: A flat, treeless plain in arctic regions—an ideal home for an evil Snow Queen who thrives in chilly climates!

Vermin: These are small animals, often thought to carry disease and to be a nuisance. There were vermin—rats and mice—in the garret in "Whittington and His Cat."

Wanderlust: An irrisitable urge or desire to travel about the world.

Wicket: A small door set within a larger door.

THE EVERYTHING SERIES!

BUSINESS

Everything® Business Planning Book
Everything® Coaching and Mentoring Book
Everything® Fundraising Book
Everything® Home-Based Business Book
Everything® Landlording Book
Everything® Leadership Book
Everything® Managing People Book
Everything® Negotiating Book
Everything® Online Business Book
Everything® Project Management Book
Everything® Robert's Rules Book, $7.95
Everything® Selling Book
Everything® Start Your Own Business Book
Everything® Time Management Book

COMPUTERS

Everything® Computer Book

COOKBOOKS

Everything® Barbecue Cookbook
Everything® Bartender's Book, $9.95
Everything® Chinese Cookbook
Everything® Chocolate Cookbook
Everything® Cookbook
Everything® Dessert Cookbook
Everything® Diabetes Cookbook
Everything® Fondue Cookbook
Everything® Grilling Cookbook
Everything® Holiday Cookbook
Everything® Indian Cookbook
Everything® Low-Carb Cookbook
Everything® Low-Fat High-Flavor Cookbook
Everything® Low-Salt Cookbook
Everything® Mediterranean Cookbook
Everything® Mexican Cookbook
Everything® One-Pot Cookbook
Everything® Pasta Cookbook
Everything® Quick Meals Cookbook
Everything® Slow Cooker Cookbook
Everything® Soup Cookbook

Everything® Thai Cookbook
Everything® Vegetarian Cookbook
Everything® Wine Book

HEALTH

Everything® Alzheimer's Book
Everything® Anti-Aging Book
Everything® Diabetes Book
Everything® Dieting Book
Everything® Hypnosis Book
Everything® Low Cholesterol Book
Everything® Massage Book
Everything® Menopause Book
Everything® Nutrition Book
Everything® Reflexology Book
Everything® Reiki Book
Everything® Stress Management Book
Everything® Vitamins, Minerals, and
    Nutritional Supplements Book

HISTORY

Everything® American Government Book
Everything® American History Book
Everything® Civil War Book
Everything® Irish History & Heritage Book
Everything® Mafia Book
Everything® Middle East Book

HOBBIES & GAMES

Everything® Bridge Book
Everything® Candlemaking Book
Everything® Card Games Book
Everything® Cartooning Book
Everything® Casino Gambling Book, 2nd Ed.
Everything® Chess Basics Book
Everything® Crossword and Puzzle Book
Everything® Crossword Challenge Book
Everything® Drawing Book
Everything® Digital Photography Book
Everything® Easy Crosswords Book
Everything® Family Tree Book

Everything® Games Book
Everything® Knitting Book
Everything® Magic Book
Everything® Motorcycle Book
Everything® Online Genealogy Book
Everything® Photography Book
Everything® Poker Strategy Book
Everything® Pool & Billiards Book
Everything® Quilting Book
Everything® Scrapbooking Book
Everything® Sewing Book
Everything® Soapmaking Book

HOME IMPROVEMENT

Everything® Feng Shui Book
Everything® Feng Shui Decluttering Book, $9.95
Everything® Fix-It Book
Everything® Homebuilding Book
Everything® Home Decorating Book
Everything® Landscaping Book
Everything® Lawn Care Book
Everything® Organize Your Home Book

EVERYTHING® KIDS' BOOKS

All titles are $6.95

Everything® Kids' Baseball Book, 3rd Ed.
Everything® Kids' Bible Trivia Book
Everything® Kids' Bugs Book
Everything® Kids' Christmas Puzzle
    & Activity Book
Everything® Kids' Cookbook
Everything® Kids' Halloween Puzzle
    & Activity Book
Everything® Kids' Hidden Pictures Book
    Everything® Kids' Joke Book
Everything® Kids' Knock Knock Book
Everything® Kids' Math Puzzles Book
Everything® Kids' Mazes Book
Everything® Kids' Money Book

All Everything® books are priced at $12.95 or $14.95, unless otherwise stated. Prices subject to change without notice.

Everything® Kids' Monsters Book
Everything® Kids' Nature Book
Everything® Kids' Puzzle Book
Everything® Kids' Riddles & Brain Teasers Book
Everything® Kids' Science Experiments Book
Everything® Kids' Soccer Book
Everything® Kids' Travel Activity Book

KIDS' STORY BOOKS

Everything® Bedtime Story Book
Everything® Bible Stories Book
Everything® Fairy Tales Book

LANGUAGE

Everything® Conversational Japanese Book
(with CD), $19.95
Everything® Inglés Book
Everything® French Phrase Book, $9.95
Everything® Learning French Book
Everything® Learning German Book
Everything® Learning Italian Book
Everything® Learning Latin Book
Everything® Learning Spanish Book
Everything® Sign Language Book
Everything® Spanish Phrase Book, $9.95
Everything® Spanish Verb Book, $9.95

MUSIC

Everything® Drums Book (with CD), $19.95
Everything® Guitar Book
Everything® Home Recording Book
Everything® Playing Piano and Keyboards Book
Everything® Rock & Blues Guitar Book
(with CD), $19.95
Everything® Songwriting Book

NEW AGE

Everything® Astrology Book
Everything® Dreams Book
Everything® Ghost Book
Everything® Love Signs Book, $9.95
Everything® Meditation Book
Everything® Numerology Book
Everything® Paganism Book
Everything® Palmistry Book
Everything® Psychic Book
Everything® Spells & Charms Book
Everything® Tarot Book
Everything® Wicca and Witchcraft Book

PARENTING

Everything® Baby Names Book
Everything® Baby Shower Book
Everything® Baby's First Food Book
Everything® Baby's First Year Book
Everything® Birthing Book
Everything® Breastfeeding Book
Everything® Father-to-Be Book
Everything® Get Ready for Baby Book
Everything® Getting Pregnant Book
Everything® Homeschooling Book
Everything® Parent's Guide to Children
with Asperger's Syndrome
Everything® Parent's Guide to Children
with Autism
Everything® Parent's Guide to Children
with Dyslexia
Everything® Parent's Guide to Positive Discipline
Everything® Parent's Guide to Raising a
Successful Child
Everything® Parenting a Teenager Book
Everything® Potty Training Book, $9.95
Everything® Pregnancy Book, 2nd Ed.
Everything® Pregnancy Fitness Book
Everything® Pregnancy Nutrition Book
Everything® Pregnancy Organizer, $15.00
Everything® Toddler Book
Everything® Tween Book

PERSONAL FINANCE

Everything® Budgeting Book
Everything® Get Out of Debt Book
Everything® Homebuying Book, 2nd Ed.
Everything® Homeselling Book
Everything® Investing Book
Everything® Online Business Book
Everything® Personal Finance Book
Everything® Personal Finance in Your
20s & 30s Book
Everything® Real Estate Investing Book
Everything® Wills & Estate Planning Book

PETS

Everything® Cat Book
Everything® Dog Book
Everything® Dog Training and Tricks Book
Everything® Golden Retriever Book
Everything® Horse Book
Everything® Labrador Retriever Book
Everything® Poodle Book

Everything® Puppy Book
Everything® Rottweiler Book
Everything® Tropical Fish Book

REFERENCE

Everything® Car Care Book
Everything® Classical Mythology Book
Everything® Einstein Book
Everything® Etiquette Book
Everything® Great Thinkers Book
Everything® Philosophy Book
Everything® Psychology Book
Everything® Shakespeare Book
Everything® Toasts Book

RELIGION

Everything® Angels Book
Everything® Bible Book
Everything® Buddhism Book
Everything® Catholicism Book
Everything® Christianity Book
Everything® Jewish History & Heritage Book
Everything® Judaism Book
Everything® Koran Book
Everything® Prayer Book
Everything® Saints Book
Everything® Understanding Islam Book
Everything® World's Religions Book
Everything® Zen Book

SCHOOL & CAREERS

Everything® After College Book
Everything® Alternative Careers Book
Everything® College Survival Book
Everything® Cover Letter Book
Everything® Get-a-Job Book
Everything® Job Interview Book
Everything® New Teacher Book
Everything® Online Job Search Book
Everything® Personal Finance Book
Everything® Practice Interview Book
Everything® Resume Book, 2nd Ed.
Everything® Study Book

SELF-HELP/ RELATIONSHIPS

Everything® Dating Book
Everything® Divorce Book
Everything® Great Sex Book

All Everything® books are priced at $12.95 or $14.95, unless otherwise stated. Prices subject to change without notice.

Everything® Kama Sutra Book
Everything® Self-Esteem Book

SPORTS & FITNESS

Everything® Body Shaping Book
Everything® Fishing Book
Everything® Fly-Fishing Book
Everything® Golf Book
Everything® Golf Instruction Book
Everything® Knots Book
Everything® Pilates Book
Everything® Running Book
Everything® T'ai Chi and QiGong Book
Everything® Total Fitness Book
Everything® Weight Training Book
Everything® Yoga Book

TRAVEL

Everything® Family Guide to Hawaii
Everything® Family Guide to New York City, 2nd Ed.

Everything® Family Guide to Washington D.C., 2nd Ed.
Everything® Family Guide to the Walt Disney World Resort®, Universal Studios®, and Greater Orlando, 4th Ed.
Everything® Guide to Las Vegas
Everything® Guide to New England
Everything® Travel Guide to the Disneyland Resort®, California Adventure®, Universal Studios®, and the Anaheim Area

WEDDINGS

Everything® Bachelorette Party Book, $9.95
Everything® Bridesmaid Book, $9.95
Everything® Creative Wedding Ideas Book
Everything® Elopement Book, $9.95
Everything® Father of the Bride Book, $9.95
Everything® Groom Book, $9.95
Everything® Jewish Wedding Book
Everything® Mother of the Bride Book, $9.95
Everything® Wedding Book, 3rd Ed.

Everything® Wedding Checklist, $7.95
Everything® Wedding Etiquette Book, $7.95
Everything® Wedding Organizer, $15.00
Everything® Wedding Shower Book, $7.95
Everything® Wedding Vows Book, $7.95
Everything® Weddings on a Budget Book, $9.95

WRITING

Everything® Creative Writing Book
Everything® Get Published Book
Everything® Grammar and Style Book
Everything® Grant Writing Book
Everything® Guide to Writing a Novel
Everything® Guide to Writing Children's Books
Everything® Screenwriting Book
Everything® Writing Well Book